MURDER GIRLS

CHRISTINE MORGAN

DEADITE PRESS

PORTLAND, OREGON

deadite press

DEADITE PRESS
833 SE Main Street #342
Portland, OR 97214
www.DEADITEPRESS.com

AN ERASERHEAD PRESS COMPANY
www.ERASERHEADPRESS.com

ISBN: 978-1-62105-329-3

Printed in the USA.

MURDER GIRLS

CHAPTER ONE

"I bet we could get away with it."

What Rachel had said. Eight little words. Thrown out as an offhanded remark while she was watching television and the rest of them were engaged in their own pursuits.

"I bet we could get away with it."

Eight little words.

And now here they were.

Standing around a body.

A bloody, muddy, crumpled, battered body.

The rain came down. Splish-splash-splatter-splat. In the puddles. On the grass. Dripping from the leaves and eaves. Soaking their hair, their clothes. Glimmering in the rectangles of light that spilled from the downstairs window and the wide-open back door.

Splish-splash-splatter-splat.

For a long moment, the only other sounds were wind-stirred branches, distant traffic, a sitcom laugh track from inside the house, and their own ragged breathing.

Gwen's throat worked, making little clicking-gulping noises. Annamaria stood motionless, her eyes huge pools in the dark, a fist pressed to her mouth. Darlene gagged, spun, and took two clumsy, stumbling steps away into the yard. She bent and puked in the bushes.

"Shit, Rache," Jessie said. Her voice was low, almost stunned. She let go of the old bowling pin, which struck the body with a meaty thump. "You were right. We did it. We actually did it. You were right."

Rachel passed a hand over her face in a slow, dreamlike swipe, smearing blood-spatter and rain into watery red streaks. "What?"

"Just like you said."

"Nuh-unh."

"Yeah-huh."

"That's not what I said."

Darlene straightened and turned toward them. Annamaria touched the crucifix she wore on a fine gold chain and murmured a prayer. Gwen crouched and reached trembling fingertips toward the body, but stopped several inches shy of contact.

"You did so," Jessie said. "You said you bet we could kill someone, and look. We just killed someone."

"I did not!"

"Both of you stop it!" Annamaria stepped between them. "Just stop."

"But she—"

"But I didn't—"

"Stop!"

They stopped. No one spoke. The rain fell. Splish-splash-splatter-splat. The body lay there. The old bowling pin, which was normally left on the back porch in case they needed a doorstop, lay beside it in the mud. Once white, age-yellowed like bone. With stripes like the fingermarks in blood across Rachel's cheeks.

Made quite a weapon. Jessie had been able to get some serious swing.

Did a hell of a number on a human head.

A baseball bat might have done no better.

Gwen reached out again, and this time gave the body's shoulder a slight nudging push. Darlene groaned.

"Rachel," Annamaria said. She'd been wet to begin with, straight out of the shower with no time to dry off, a hastily-donned robe now pasted to her like a coat of paint. Her hair hung long, black and sodden over her shoulders. "Rachel, isn't that what you said?"

"We all heard it." Jessie glanced to Gwen and Darlene for support. "Didn't we?"

"Yeah," Darlene said. "She said she bet we could kill someone."

"Well, that isn't exactly what she said, though." Gwen's words, soft and almost diffident, were barely audible over the rain.

"All right… then what *did* you say?" Annamaria asked Rachel.

"I bet we could get away with it," Rachel repeated.

Those eight little words again.

And now here they were, with a body at their feet.

The house they shared was shabby, drafty and a dump. It had mediocre wiring and sluggish plumbing. The water heater could handle maybe a shower and a half before going cold. The kitchen was done in vintage 1970s style. The living room's matted-down shag carpet was burnt-orange.

But it was close to campus, closer to the bus line, and cheap—even cheaper, with the rent split five ways. None of them could afford to be very picky.

The upstairs consisted of four bedrooms, arranged two-and-two with a bathroom in between each pair and a claustrophobic hallway running down the middle. Tiny bedrooms. Space enough for a twin bed and not much else. Wallpaper so ugly that posters were less about décor and more about self-defense. More matted-down shag carpet, forest-green.

Each of the bathrooms had a toilet, pedestal sink, and stall shower about as roomy as a phone booth. Faded linoleum. Chipped porcelain. Missing tiles. Rusty fixtures. Ceiling lights that shed an unreliable, jaundiced glow, making it a crapshoot to apply make-up.

Annamaria, who'd been there the longest, paid an extra twenty bucks a month for the sole downstairs bedroom. It was somewhat larger, and it connected to the downstairs bath, which was the only one with a tub.

When not sleeping, in class or at their various jobs, they spent most of their time in the living room anyway. Yes, it had that awful burnt-orange shag carpet… and warped wood paneling dotted with nail-holes and dart-holes, with a round, untouched space where a dartboard must once have hung. Yes, it had lumpy couches upholstered in coarse and hideous plaid, and mismatched furniture that Goodwill would snub.

But that was where the television was, and the cable box. That was where Darlene and Rachel had arranged a couple of computer desks with printers and internet access. That was where Jessie could set up her yoga mat and assorted exercise equipment, or where Gwen could cover a whole table with her jigsaw puzzles and craft projects.

That was where they'd all been when Rachel said those eight little words.

Given their schedules, Sunday evenings were about the only time all five of them were there and awake at once. This particular rainy Sunday was no exception. They'd worked out a rotating arrangement of each taking weekly turns to provide Sunday dinner for the house, which ranged from bringing in takeout to a full meal.

This week was Annamaria's turn, and Annamaria loved to cook.

Gwen curled in the corner recliner, studying, feet tucked under her. Jessie in sports bra and bike shorts, on the floor, stretching. Darlene hunched at the computer, frowning, occasionally rattling out machine-gun bursts of typing. Annamaria going back and forth from the kitchen, where things steamed and simmered and gave off tantalizing smells.

And Rachel watching television.

Talking.

The way she did. Not talking to herself, exactly, but not directing her words at any of them in particular either.

"I bet we could get away with it," she said.

Nobody replied. It was just another Rachel-remark, tossed out there casually as anything while she sat in front of the television with a bag of microwave popcorn leaning open against her knee.

"No one would ever suspect a bunch of college girls."

Rachel-remarks and Rachel-chatter. Washing over the rest of them like a steady breeze. She never seemed to expect—or wait for—an answer. Half the time, it seemed as if she didn't realize she was talking out loud.

"We would be basically the exact opposite of the profile."

She'd confessed to them that her brain was always running so fast, she sometimes had to run her mouth too. In order to keep herself from exploding. To relieve the pressure.

"I mean, they wouldn't even consider the possibility."

After so many months as housemates, they all knew that this kind of ongoing idle commentary was pure Rachel. It was as much a part of her as the upturned little nose and chipmunk cheeks. Some people said she looked like a cartoon character. Like a grown-up version of Bubbles from *The Powerpuff Girls*. Wide blue eyes, short blonde hair, curvy little bod. She was cute, that's all there was to it. Cute in a perky, cartoon kind of way.

"As long as we did it right. As long as we were careful to only leave the right kind of clues. Because, really, they'd be looking for certain clues. Expecting them so much that they might overlook any that didn't fit the pattern. Once they've got a theory, they tend to zero in on evidence that supports it."

Annamaria said they'd either learn to live with it, or it would drive them nuts and they'd move out. She and Rachel had been housemates the longest, and had seen half a dozen come and go over the past couple of years. Not all of the turnaround could be laid at Rachel's feet, but not all of it couldn't, either.

The house was rented as 'partly furnished,' a phrase which really meant untold generations of previous tenants had left behind a hodgepodge of junk when they'd graduated and headed for greener pastures, or dropped out of college and vanished off the face of the earth.

"The hard part would be in making it not seem like some kind of cult or gang thing. Wouldn't want to get them thinking along those lines. It'd have to look genuine." Rachel paused long enough to cram a handful of popcorn into her mouth. She nodded, her alert blue gaze still fixed on the television, and made muffled, crunchy-sounding mumbles.

The television was one such relic of the past: a huge and heavy brute in an age of sleek plasma flat-screens. It loomed like a rhino or wildebeest at a watering hole. And the cable box on top was like one of those little birds that perched on the backs of such behemoths.

Rachel went *mumble-crunch-crunch-mumble*, swallowed, and added, "But the first one, you'd want it to be clumsy-looking. Rough and rushed and hesitant at the same time. Eventually, though, it'd have to look more skillful. More precise. You'd be getting practiced. Getting used to it. Getting confident."

The living room's bookshelves were crammed with secondhand paperbacks, old magazines, and outdated textbooks with highlighting and underlining done by several different students. The kitchen cupboards and drawers held a jumble of pots, pans, dishes and silverware.

"Arranging for them to be found might be tricky. Highest risk of someone seeing you. But they can't just disappear. That isn't the same. Being spotted doing the drop or the dump, though, that'd be bad. That could blow the whole deal right then and there."

But the rent was cheap. The location was convenient enough. It beat living in the dorms.

Their landlady, Lorna Hubert, was a stocky, hard-drinking old bitch who'd taken her big, bad-tempered hound dog and moved to a trailer park after the divorce. Not that anyone could have blamed Mr. Hubert for walking out. The wonder of it was that he'd stuck around as long as he had. Mrs. Hubert's legacy lingered in the décor, and Griz-the-dog's lingered in the scratched doors and walls, gnawed furniture, potholes dug in the yard, and landmines of ancient dogshit.

Griz's predecessors had left plenty of their own contributions over the years, and were memorialized now in a pet cemetery in one of the property's far corners. Woodburned names on plank markers: Bruno, Major, Rex.

"It'd have to get more flamboyant, too," Rachel said. "Making it a dare, a challenge. Throwing down the gauntlet. Catch me if you can!"

They even had access to their own washer and dryer, rather than having to take their laundry to a coin-op in town. Of course, the free ones were noisy and unreliable, and they were out in a shed attached to the garage, which meant that getting to them required a trudge out there, sometimes in inclement weather. There was a covered concrete breezeway between house and garage, but the sides were open to the elements and the roof leaked.

"But they'd never figure it out. They'd never guess it was us. I really do think we could do it. Get *away* with it, that's the big thing. I still bet we could, though. I bet we could get away with it."

And now here they were.

The body crumpled on the wet grass, crumpled in the mud. One arm outflung. Rainwater puddling in the cupped palm. A heavy ceramic coffee mug, astonishingly unbroken despite having been hurled full-force and connecting, rested nearby.

"Well," Jessie said, raking her fingers through her short hair and making it stand up in crazy spikes, "I got news for ya, Rache… we just did."

"We killed someone," Gwen moaned. She was still crouched, though she'd withdrawn her reaching hand.

"We're murderers." Darlene looked like she wanted to throw up again.

"Look," Rachel said, in a way that suggested she was trying very hard to be patient. "I wasn't talking about murder, okay? That isn't what I said. That isn't what I meant."

"Then what *did* you mean?" asked Annamaria.

"You guys never listen to me, do you? Weren't any of you watching that show? It was all about serial killers, okay? The way the FBI profiles them and everything. How it's almost always, when you've got a serial killer, it's almost always the same kind of person. White male, thirtyish, loner, history of cruelty to animals, starting fires, wetting the bed."

"Sure," Jessie said. "Like those guys in the news that have body parts in their fridges."

"Right!" Rachel's eyes gleamed. "Right, exactly. See, and that's just it. That's the profile."

"Wait… wait." Annamaria raised both hands, palms out. "Serial killers? They're monsters."

"Yeah! But, get it? The cops would never in a bazillion years suspect *us*. I mean come on! A group of five college girls? That's not the way serial killers operate. It's just so totally out there that they wouldn't ever believe it!"

Gwen rose slowly to her full height, which, tall as she was, took a while. "You think we're suh-suh-suh…" She shook her head, unable to say it.

Rachel rolled her eyes. "Well, no! Not hardly!"

"We're…" Darlene pointed down at the body. She swallowed thickly. "We're murderers."

"That's not the same. Besides, I said 'get away with it,' remember? There's a big difference between killing somebody and getting away with it." Rachel wiped more diluted blood from her face, looked at her hand, and showed it to them. "This is a mess, that's what this is."

"I'll say." Jessie picked up the bowling pin again, holding it gingerly by the end. She toed a saucepan, which had been pretty well dented even before Rachel landed a couple solid whacks with it. "What are we gonna do? We're fucked. We are just thoroughly fucked."

"Maybe we should call the police—" Gwen began, but bit off her words when she saw their expressions.

"If we do that," Rachel said, "then like Jessie said, we're absolutely effed."

"I don't want to go to jail," Darlene said, snuffling.

"Not to mention being expelled, evicted, and kissing your financial aid good-bye," Annamaria said.

"Then what *are* we going to do?" asked Gwen. "We have to do something. We can't… we can't just…"

"Say it was an accident?" Jessie grimaced. "Don't think anybody would buy it."

"What if we made something up?" Darlene gestured at Gwen. "You're good at that. Make up a story. Some… burglar or homeless guy or something."

"No good," Rachel said. "There'd be evidence. Prints, fibers. They'd question us. They'd find inconsistencies, contradictions. No matter how well we thought we'd prepared, some elements wouldn't add up."

"What, then?" Annamaria clutched her robe closer, though by the way the satin clung, it wasn't doing much for the sake of modesty. She was barefoot, bare-legged, mud-splashed, one knee seeping where she'd skinned it when she took a fall during the short, violent chase. But her dark eyes, fixed on Rachel, were calm and steady. "What should we do?"

"Hide the body," Rachel said. "Dispose of it, get rid of it. Make like it never happened. We don't know anything. We didn't see anything, hear anything. It'll seem like a disappearance then."

"You mean…" Darlene swallowed again and nodded toward the garage, where a collection of rusty old gardening tools hung on wall pegs. "You mean like get a shovel… dig a hole..?"

"Here on the property?" Gwen added. "Not out by the dog graveyard?"

"I know it's not ideal." Rachel sighed, started to bite her thumbnail–an *I'm thinking* habit of hers–but realized it was covered with blood and caught herself in time. "Moving it, though, that's risky too. How? Load it into the trunk of Jessie's car?"

"Fuck no, not *my* car, you don't!"

"Not mine, either!" Darlene said.

"Or mine," said Annamaria. "Not that it'd fit."

"See, if we do that," Rachel went on, "there's risk of leaving trace evidence. No matter how careful we are. And even assuming we didn't spill a single drop of blood inside, what then? Where do we take it?"

No one answered. The rain came down, splish-splash-splatter-splat.

Then, on the ground at their feet, the body gasped.

When it was Jessie's week to be in charge of the Sunday dinner, she usually opted for the self-serve route and provided sandwich fixings, a taco or baked potato bar, that kind of thing. Darlene tended to order pizza or Chinese or chicken-in-a-bucket. Gwen stuck to the basics: stews, casseroles, meatloaf. Rachel, when not watching true-crime shows, was a fan of the Food Network and might get experimental in the kitchen, with mixed results.

Annamaria, though… Annamaria had an impressive culinary repertoire. And she made it all look effortless. As if, ho-hum, she just wandered in there and decided on the spur of the moment to throw together a Thanksgiving feast.

"You ought to be fat," Darlene had once told her on a weeknight when each of the girls was fending for herself. "It's not fair you cook the way you do, eat the way you do, and *look* the way you do."

Darlene had, at that moment, been peeling the plastic cover-sheet off of a freezer-to-microwave meal that had some kind of limp vegetables, mixed rice, and unidentifiable meatlike substance. The cardboard packaging declared 'healthy!' and 'low-cal!' and 'weight-smart/heart-smart!'

Next to Annamaria's helping of homemade lasagna with golden-brown garlic bread…

But Darlene was the one who was broad-bottomed and dumpy, with stringy hair and bad skin. While Annamaria was, simply and no-denying-it, gorgeous.

Jessie had leaned over and inspected Darlene's dinner, then made a face. "Jeez, Dar. All that ell-eye-tee-ee 'lite' stuff is loaded with chemicals. It's twice as expensive, and not nearly as good for you as they want you to believe. Plus, it tastes like the plastic play-groceries that my niece got for her birthday."

"It's diet!"

"It's shit."

"What, now I'm supposed to learn to cook on top of everything else?"

"Hey," Jessie had said, "I can't cook worth a damn either, but you still don't see *me* choking down that imitation food."

"Yeah, well, we don't all have your metabolism." Darlene shot an envious look at Jessie's legs, tanned and toned and muscular, showed off by a pair of skimpy denim cutoffs.

"It isn't about metabolism. It's about making choices. Healthy lifestyle choices."

"Spare me the lecture. I know how I look. You don't have to rub it in."

"I'm just saying that if you're really serious about getting fit, there are better ways."

"Easy for you to say, Ms. Phys-Ed-major. You're not the one who's a big gross cow."

"No one's calling you a cow, Darlene," Gwen said, eating cold cereal, partly because of her budget and partly because she liked Crunchberries.

"They don't have to. Like you'd have any idea what it's like anyway, you people who never even have a pimple or a bad hair day in your whole entire fucking lives."

That had pretty much ended the conversation, each of them remembering an upcoming test, a paper due, an errand, a date, or any other spontaneous excuse they could come up with. By then, they'd known there were some arguments that just couldn't be won. Not with Darlene.

Gwen had tried once, tried pointing out that maybe she'd never been *fat*, okay, but she knew a little about what it was like to be teased for her looks. They used to call her "Stick-Bug." But Darlene had only given her a withering look and informed her that it wasn't the same thing. Not the same at *all*.

The Sunday of those eight little words, Annamaria had served chicken breasts baked in a sauce of mushrooms, cream and white wine. Over noodles. With baby carrots and rolls and green salad.

After the meal, Gwen and Rachel had insisted on doing dishes and clean-up, while Darlene hit the books and Jessie took a turn on the computer. Annamaria went to take a shower.

She'd come bursting out of the downstairs bathroom ten minutes later, struggling into her robe, suds still trickling down the side of her neck. Shouting. Swearing. Startling them all.

"That filthy little *fuck*!" Annamaria crossed the kitchen at a run, bashed open the back door, and plunged through it.

Here they were, and by the wheezing gasps that came up from the sluggishly-stirring shape on the ground, not murderers after all.

"Holy fucking hell," Jessie said, sounding almost impressed. "Still alive and kicking!"

"Oh, my God." Gwen swayed on her feet.

"Maybe we better call 911," Darlene said.

The body heaved and coughed. Ropy strands of spit and blood dribbled from the ruined wreck of a mouth. Something that looked like a tooth fell out. It clinked off the coffee mug and bounced away into the grass.

"Huh," said Rachel. Her expression was one of mild scientific interest, as if observing an unexpected chemical reaction. "Tougher than he looked."

"You bishesh, you crayshee bishesh!"

"Caught you this time, Donnie," Annamaria said. "Caught you at last, you pervert bastard asshole!"

Donnie Hubert, their landlady's nephew-by-marriage, rolled over and started pushing himself up. He groaned. The rain wasn't coming down hard enough or fast enough to wash away the thick crimson rivulets running down his face, which was already puffing with what promised to become spectacular bruises.

Not that it had been much of a face to start with. A few blows from a saucepan and a bowling pin couldn't do much to damage a walking train wreck. He had shoulder-length straggles of hair that managed to look greasy even when soaking wet and caked with blood. Stubble. Zits and pockmarks. Weak chin, sunken eyes. An amateurish neck tattoo of a pentagram, probably one he'd done himself.

"Bishesh bushted me up," he said. "Buncha cuntsh."

"Hey!" Jessie jabbed a finger at him. It wasn't her index finger. "We warned you. We warned you that if we ever caught you looking in the damn windows again, we'd kick your ass."

"He's really hurt," Gwen said.

"He deserved it." Annamaria eyed Donnie like he was the most loathsome creature she'd ever seen.

"Voyeurism is a gateway crime," Rachel said.

Darlene frowned. "You mean like pot is a gateway drug?"

"They start off peeping in windows." Her nose wrinkled. "You know, masturbating and stuff."

Annamaria and Gwen made revolted noises.

Jessie sneered down at Donnie. "That what you're doing, Don-O? Jackin' it while you watched Anna in the shower?"

He was more or less sitting up, now, cradling his head in both hands. A flinch was the only answer he gave.

"And I bet he stole all those panties," Rachel went on.

"Say what?" Darlene asked.

"We've had some of our underwear disappearing from the laundry."

"I thought at first it was the machines," Annamaria said. "The dryer we had at home was always eating socks. But then I mentioned it to Jessie and she said was missing a pair."

"Rache overheard," Jessie said, "and told us that what do you know, so was she!"

"Um…" Gwen said, unable to meet any of their gazes. The darkness made it hard to tell how badly she was blushing. "Um… yeah… same here."

Donnie hunched into an abject, cringing ball. "Shorry, okay, Jeeshush, you din't have to *hit* me!"

"So first the voyeurism," Rachel said, "and then stealing our underwear. Probably he's been taking pictures, too."

"Pictures?" Gwen yelped.

"Is she right, Don-O?" Jessie thwacked the bowling pin into her palm. It made a loud, satisfying sound. "Taking pictures of us? You keep them for yourself or post them on the internet for all the other sleazeballs who can't get laid?"

"Oh, you *better* not!" Annamaria's hands flexed like she wanted to go for his throat, or maybe hook her fingernails into his eyeballs.

Rachel ignored their outbursts and continued in lecture-mode. "Eventually, though, it wouldn't be enough and he'd have gotten bolder. A lot of sex offenders start out just that way."

"Rapists, you mean," Darlene said, and gave Donnie the blackest of scowls.

Between his mangled mouth and the way he was still hunched, his protesting wails were indistinct. Something about how they weren't being fair, he hadn't hurt anybody, he wouldn't hurt anybody, all he'd done was look, they didn't have to beat the shit out of him, he was no rapist.

"Not yet, maybe," Rachel said. "That's what I'm saying. This is how it sometimes starts."

"I say we kill him," Jessie said.

"What?" Gwen stared at her.

"If we—" began Rachel.

"Yeah!" said Darlene in a near-growl. "We thought we already did, so why not? Let's kill the asshole! Let's stomp his fucking brains in."

"*What* fucking brains?" Annamaria tossed her head, sodden hair flinging like dark snakes around a face that was suddenly imperial and cold. "Jessie's right. Let's kill him."

They had gone charging out the back door after her, voices a clamor of questions and shouts. Gwen and Rachel, having been at the sink, were closest behind Annamaria, and in their rush they hadn't stopped to set down what they were holding: Gwen a soapy sponge and a coffee mug, Rachel a dishtowel and saucepan.

Jessie, who ran track, played soccer, biked to campus, hiked on summer weekends and skied on winter ones, overtook them like a cheetah. She hadn't even missed a stride as she'd bent and snatched up the bowling pin where it sat on the back porch, beside the crappy charcoal grill and a pile of other junk.

Darlene lumbered out last, but in time to see Annamaria slip, screaming obscenities and waving her fists at the fleeing Donnie… in time to see Gwen hurl the coffee mug with an accuracy and aim she never would have attained if she'd stopped to think about it… in time to see the mug carom off the side of Donnie's head.

He had stumbled, sprawling in the slick grass, and Rachel uttered a shrill war-whoop entirely at odds with her Bubbles-the-Powerpuff-Girl appearance. She and Jessie rushed him, with the others not far behind.

As Donnie had shoved himself up on hands and knees, Rachel brought the dented old saucepan down square in the small of his back. He'd yelled and belly-flopped flat again, whereupon Jessie drove the toe of her athletic shoe into his thigh, telling him to get up and fight like a man.

Donnie, far more interested in escape, had gone scrambling sideways like a crippled crab, with Jessie still kicking and challenging, Rachel whaling away with the saucepan,

Annamaria hammering her fists at whatever she could reach, and Gwen slapping wildly with the soapy sponge. Darlene arrived and clawed her stubby fingers into the back of his collar, yanking him so he reared back on his haunches.

That was when he'd lashed out, in blind panic as much as anything. His flailing knuckles had grazed Jessie's boob and she'd let him have it with the bowling pin. Top of the skull, sweet spot, an authoritative *crack!* like the sound of a league champion scoring a game-winning strike.

His scalp had split with a vigorous spraying of blood, Rachel getting the brunt of it: a hot, sticky, red, money-shot faceful.

Rather than lay him out, the blow had brought Donnie lunging to his feet. He punched Jessie in the stomach, knocked Gwen into Annamaria so that both of them nearly went over, and would have made a break for it, but Darlene still had him by the shirt, and damn near strangled him on his own collar.

They'd surrounded him again, and at last Donnie fell, a body crumpled at their feet. Battered and bloody in the mud and the rain.

"Pleashe," he said now, making a plaintive palms-up gesture. "C'mon. Pleashe. I shaid I wazsh shorry."

Tears ran from his eyes, snot ran from his nose, slobbery spit ran from his mouth, and blood ran from everywhere.

And the rain came down. Splish-splash-splatter-splat.

No neighbors ventured out to investigate. The house was on a large chunk of land, once a farm but with its back acreage now devolved into a tangle of weeds, blackberries, spindly second-growth trees and waist-high scrub.

There *was* the one-room apartment over the garage, but that was where Mrs. Hubert let her nephew live rent-free in exchange for doing repairs, yard work and other odd jobs. Where he had easy access to the washer and dryer. And an unobstructed view of the upstairs bedroom windows on the west side of the house, which was why Gwen and Rachel always kept their curtains closed.

The property to the east was owned by a sweet elderly couple who raised alpacas as a way of keeping busy in their retirement. They both wore hearing aids and took them out at night. Not even the loudest party disturbed them. The hired man who helped out around the place was only there during daylight hours.

The property to the west might have posed a problem, but the condo complex being built there was still in the most basic stages of construction, all rearranged dirt, heavy machinery, skeletal framework, and pipes sticking up from the bare earth.

To the north was the road, curving around what was either a mosquito-infested swamp or a natural wetland habitat, depending on which side of the debate was talking. The plans to fill it in, pave it over and turn it into a shopping center had been in the works and hotly contested for as long as Annamaria had been renting from Mrs. Hubert.

To the south was a mile or so of nothing-much fields with creeks running through and occasional grazing cattle, horses or goats. Beyond that was the high-walled back side of a planned and gated community.

So, isolation and remoteness and quiet. Nobody to hear the angry shouts or the pained screams. Nobody to hear Donnie's pleading howls.

"I shaid I wazsh shorry! I'll never do it again, I promishe!"

"We'll get in trouble," Gwen said. "Maybe we should let him go."

"Fuck that, we'll get in trouble anyway," said Jessie. "He'll go to the cops."

"I won't! I shwear!"

"He'll tell his aunt," Annamaria said.

"He called us cunts," Darlene said. "And bitches, he called us bitches."

"I'm *shorry!*" he wailed.

"But we can't just—" Gwen danced backward as Donnie clutched imploringly in her direction. "Gross-don't-touch-me!"

"Don't touch her!" Jessie brought the bowling pin down on his hand.

Crunched it like someone stepping on a bag of pretzels.

Donnie shrieked.

"Nice one, Jess," Darlene applauded.

He looked at the jutting cluster of broken fingers and shrieked again.

And shrieked. And shrieked.

"God, make him stop!" Gwen bent double, eyes squeezed shut, hands over her ears. "I can't take it, I can't stand it, make him stop!"

"Shut *up!*" Rachel stepped forward and slapped him across the face.

His head snapped sideways. More blood flew from his ruined mouth. "You fuhkink cunt!"

"He said it again," said Darlene, and kicked at his crotch. Missed. Skidded in the mud. Almost fell on her ass. "Damn it!"

Donnie went for Rachel. It was with his off-hand, his left, the right being the cluster of broken pretzel sticks he held stiffly out away from him, the fingers poking in directions and at angles nature had never really intended.

Off-hand or not, he still got her by a fistful of hair.

"Ow!"

"Get your fucking hand off her!" Annamaria grabbed his arm and sank her teeth into the fleshy part just below the elbow.

He shrieked yet again, yanking away, deep bleeding crescents of bite marks in his forearm and strands of Rachel's short blonde hair snarled around his fingers.

Darlene tried for another groin kick, putting all of her considerable weight behind it, and connected.

Donnie didn't shriek. Donnie screeched like a power drill hitting sheet metal. He fell spraddle-legged, head back, screeching at the sky until it seemed miraculous that every window in the house didn't shatter.

Then Jessie swung the bowling pin again. It struck him in the exposed arch of his throat and crushed it the way she might have crushed a Styrofoam cup under her heel.

The screech instantly became a clotted, strange gurgle. Donnie fell on his back in the wet grass. The fingers of his undamaged hand clawed at his neck. His face—what they could see of it through the blood and mud and shadows—turned bluish. Thin jets of fluid—saliva, bile, vomit?—shot from his mouth. His whole body bucked and wallowed.

"He's asphyxiating," Rachel said. Sounding calm. Even clinical.

"Good," Annamaria said, wiping Donnie's blood from her lips.

"He can't breathe?" asked Gwen. She was paler than milk, ghostly in the gloom.

"Not without a tracheotomy." Rachel tapped the hollow of her own throat. "You know, where they cut and insert a tube to open the airway. I hear you can do it with a pen, or a knife and a straw."

"If we wanted to," Jessie said.

"Yeah, screw that, I say we let the bastard strangle," Darlene said.

So they stood around Donnie as he thrashed and foamed and gurgled and pissed his pants. They stood around him as his struggles weakened into a feeble twitching. They stood around him and watched without another word until he shuddered and went limp.

Finally, Annamaria turned to Rachel. "All right," she said. "Now what?"

CHAPTER TWO

The rain fell harder than before. No more splishing and splashing. The drops were small and fast, a torrent of them, cold wet birdshot from the sky.

Rachel lifted her face, eyes shut, trying not to wince as the water pelted and stung, letting it sluice Donnie's blood from her skin. "Okay," she said. "First thing is, nobody freak out."

Gwen's laugh was a frail cackle. "Easier said than done."

"Yeah." Darlene made an urping noise, as if on the verge of puking again.

"Chill already," said Jessie.

"Everyone calm down," Annamaria said.

"But we killed him," Gwen said. "We killed Donnie."

"Omigod, they killed Donnie, you bastards," Jessie said in a high, mimicking cartoon way.

"This isn't a joke!" Gwen's voice splintered.

Interesting. Rachel hadn't known voices could actually do that. Could splinter. Like wood. Poor Gwen.

"He deserved it," said Darlene. Sounding queasy, but also indignant. "The fucking lowlife deserved every bit of it."

"Look, you guys," Rachel said. "We have to be smart about this."

"Can we be smart about it inside?" asked Annamaria, hugging herself. "I'm soaked, and I'm freezing."

Jessie wasn't much better off, in bike shorts and sports bra, but then Jessie never let anything as minor as bad weather stop her. "What about *him*, though? Do we just leave him lying there?"

"You think he's gonna get up and walk away?" Darlene prodded Donnie's side with her foot. "He's dead. He's total roadkill."

"Don't do that," said Gwen.

"He's *dead!*" She joggled him more vigorously, and he wobbled, loose and boneless. Deadweight.

All five of them stared down at Donnie for most of a minute. Nothing. Rachel, for one, had no doubts.

"Maybe we should make sure," Jessie said.

That frail cackle of a laugh came from Gwen again. "How? You want to cut off his head or something?"

"I was gonna say take his pulse, but whatever works for you, Guinevere."

"Hey, can we be serious here?" Rachel asked.

"Yeah, enough," Annamaria said. "Your call, Rachel."

"We can go in, sure. He's not going anywhere. I mean, we can't *leave-him-there* leave him there, not indefinitely, but for now it's okay."

"What if someone sees him?" Jessie asked.

"Who?" Darlene pointed around the dark, rainswept yard. "It isn't like anybody's going to stroll on by."

"What about..." Gwen paused, took a fortifying breath, and continued. "What about... animals?"

"Animals?" Jessie gestured around. "Vultures, hyenas, that kind of animals?"

"Rats, maybe," Gwen said. "Or a stray dog."

"We're going to deal with it," Rachel said. "Honest. Right now, let's just go in, dry off, and figure out the next step."

"Good plan." Annamaria headed for the door leading to the kitchen.

Jessie hesitated. "Should we cover him up? What if Gwen's got something there, you know, about the rats?"

"Later." Rachel herded them after Annamaria.

This was going to be a tricky one. This wasn't what she'd had in mind at all. Beating a guy to death with a saucepan and a bowling pin... a guy they *knew*, a guy it was obvious they each had reasons to dislike... dumb. Dumb, dumb, dumb. Stupid, spur-of-the-moment impulse. Unsophisticated, crude, violent, brutish.

Sloppy.

Jeepers creepers, was it ever sloppy!

She'd have to think fast.

Inside, they split up to dry off and change clothes.

"Whatever else you put on is also going to get wet and messy," Rachel called after them. "We aren't done yet. Bring down all your wet stuff, though, and the towels. We'll have to run a couple loads of laundry."

"There's blood on my shirt," Gwen moaned from her room.

"Remember, don't freak out," Rachel said. She dragged her laundry basket out of the closet and, as she undressed, piled the soggy garments directly into it.

After—by automatic instinct—checking to be sure the curtains were closed.

Not that there was any risk of Donnie Hubert spying on her with binoculars from his above-garage apartment. Not now. Not anymore.

She checked anyway. The curtains were closed.

In here, in Rachel-space, the posters on the walls were of the solar system, the periodic table of elements, montages of scientists and inventors and historians, a world map, Roman ruins, a shuttle poised for liftoff, a thermonuclear explosion in the desert, a timeline of civilization.

The top of her dresser held a globe, an old-fashioned microscope with collection of slides, a model dinosaur, a 1/10-scale replica of a human skeleton, a radio built from a kit, and one of those ant farms where the ants burrowed through translucent blue jelly.

Her bookshelves were full of college texts, reference books, binders, document boxes with dates neatly labeled on the end-tabs, works of non-fiction such as *The World Without Us* and *The Hot Zone*, and a little bit of hard sci-fi more sci than fi.

She got into grubby painting-pants, and a navy blue tee shirt with a cartoon depicting "the evolution of Man" from ape to upright to bent-over-a-computer printed on it in white. She put on fresh socks.

Hmm.

Shoes.

Shoes might be a problem.

Rachel sat on the bed, which was an afterthought crammed

in the corner, indifferently heaped with quilts and afghans. She turned a shoe over and over in her hands, thinking.

The shelf above the bed held her rock-and-mineral collection in its compartmentalized clear plastic box, her laptop, her alarm clock, and her most prized possession from junior high: an autographed photo of *Jeopardy* whiz Ken Jennings.

Rachel-space. She knew the other girls griped about the rooms being so tiny, but as far as she was concerned, this was perfect. Her own room. Bigger than the one she'd shared with her younger sisters, and all hers. She could leave stuff out instead of having to lock it all up in her single private cabinet, never having to worry that she'd come home from school and find that the twins had gotten into and/or destroyed something.

Her own room, her own money, her own freedom, her own life.

Way overdue, and way, *way* welcome.

But first… what about the shoes?

Footprints. Tread patterns. Impressions and molds.

Have to consider that.

She put them on, tied them snug, combed her fingers with her hair, and went into the bathroom she shared with Gwen to inspect herself for blood.

There. And there, too.

And a big smear of it below and slightly behind her right ear.

It had really sprayed. When Jessie split his scalp, it had been like ripping the peel off a ripe orange, or sticking a spoon into a grapefruit-half. Pssssht and out it came.

Just her luck to be short enough that she'd got it right in the face.

Oh, well.

It was only blood. It washed off.

That, Rachel knew, wasn't technically the case. They had ways of detecting blood even when it was no longer visible to the naked eye. Sure, you could clean it with bleach… but, ha-ha, they also had ways of detecting bleach.

She washed anyway. Scrubbed face, neck, upper chest, hands, arms most of the way to the shoulder.

Silly. She'd just have to do it all over again later. They weren't done. They had to take care of Donnie's body. Clean up, cover up, conceal.

First, though, she had to explain the plan to her housemates… and that'd be hard enough already. No sense making it worse than it had to be.

"Gwen?" She tapped on the connecting door. "You ready?"

A sort of sighing whimper was the only answer.

Rachel tapped again. "Gwen?"

"I'm… I'm okay…"

"Can I come in?"

"I guess so."

Gwen's room was the polar opposite of Rachel's own. The posters on the walls were of dragons, unicorns, flying castles, knights and ladies. And the movie posters. *The Lord of the Rings*. *Harry Potter*. The *Chronicles of Narnia*. A life-sized cardboard stand-up of Cameron Mack in his Robin Hood outfit wedged behind the door. An Orlando Bloom calendar.

Paperback fantasy novels. Stuffed animals, mostly more dragons and unicorns, with a few kitty cats and teddy bears thrown in. A hanging mobile of stained-glass fairies. Boxes of jigsaw puzzles, their colorful covers depicting wizards, or mermaids, or gnomes with cottages made out of mushrooms.

Well, some people were into all that.

And Gwen was one of them.

No wonder she sometimes got teased, got called Guinevere or Galadriel or The Queen of Elfland.

Didn't hurt that she looked the part, too. Tall, slim, pale, graceful, silky-fine hair, big grey-green eyes. Not just 'tall' as in 'tall compared to Rachel,' because 'tall compared to Rachel' was pretty much everyone else on the planet above the age of twelve.

All Gwen needed was a flowing gown and a balcony.

Right now, though, she had neither. She'd put on faded jeans, fuzzy pink slippers, and a men's checkered flannel shirt several sizes too big. Her damp hair hung down her back in a ponytail. She sat on the floor by the foot of her bed, knees drawn up, arms around them.

Her eyes were very red, and her chin quivered.

"Are you crying?" Rachel asked.

Gwen pressed her lips together, making a thin white line, and nodded.

"Because of *Donnie?*"

"We killed him, Rachel. We killed him and he's out there in the backyard, out there in the mud, dead. And it's all our fault."

"He shouldn't have been spying on Annamaria. He shouldn't have stolen our underwear."

"That doesn't mean we had to *kill* him."

Rachel patted her shoulder. "But we did."

"We'll go to jail."

"Not necessarily."

"We will. We'll go to jail and it'll be horrible." Gwen buried her face against her raised knees. Beneath Rachel's hand, her shoulder shook. "What if they give us the death penalty?"

"Gwen, stop. Listen to me, okay? We're not going to jail."

"But we killed him."

"I know."

"We're murderers."

"Only if anybody finds out. We just can't let that happen. Come on downstairs. We have to talk this out, the five of us. But you have to believe me… if we stick together, we won't have to go to jail. We won't get caught."

"You don't know that." But Gwen looked up, eyes wet, tentatively less dismal.

"Sure I do." Rachel smiled. "It's about outthinking them, right? I can do that. No problem. Trust me, okay? We *can* do this."

"O-ok-kay."

Rachel helped her up, and grabbed a pair of ratty old sneakers from Gwen's open closet. "You won't want to wreck your favorite slippers."

In the living room, the television was off. The computer was in screensaver mode. Except for the pellets of rain on the windows, the room was thick with a heavy, ominous quiet.

Jessie wore grey sweats with the university athletic department logo stenciled on the chest. It almost looked, Rachel thought, like a prison uniform. She mentally winced and hoped Gwen didn't notice. Darlene had on a pair of frumpy brown cords—pants she said she hated because of the noise the textured fabric made when her thighs rubbed together—and a Garfield tee shirt that proclaimed, "I hate Mondays."

"Where's Annamaria?" Rachel asked, as Gwen sank into her favorite chair and tucked her long legs up.

"Here." Annamaria came in from the kitchen, carrying a plate and wearing khaki shorts over a bathing suit. It was just a plain navy blue one-piece, drab and unflattering, but this being Annamaria, she still could have posed for the *Sports Illustrated* swimsuit issue.

"Uh, what's with the outfit?" Jessie asked, eyebrow hoisted.

"And what's with the cookies?" Darlene added.

"Well, since we didn't have a chance earlier, we can have dessert while we talk."

Annamaria set the plate on the coffee table, which was scarred wood with a design of condensed-moisture rings and cigarette burns, and had one uneven leg. At some point in the house's past, a previous tenant had wedged a folded *Cliff's Notes* under there.

"So we'll sit here eating cookies and deciding what to do with the guy we snuffed?" Jessie picked up a cookie, regarded it, took a bite. "Any milk?"

"Get it yourself, I'm not your waitress."

"Attitude like that is why you don't get good tips."

"I get good tips," Annamaria said. "But I'm not at work right now, am I?"

"I can't believe this," Gwen said. "Have you forgotten what happened out there? Have you forgotten what we *did*?"

"Hey," Jessie said, indignant. "Didn't I just say—?"

"Guys!" Rachel stayed standing, and for once she had the advantage of elevation on the rest of them. Little Rachel, cute-blonde-perky little Rachel. Strafing them with an impatient glare. "Gwen's right. We need to focus here, okay? We don't want to get in trouble. Do we?"

Heads shook and negatives were mumbled around mouthfuls of cookie. Darlene shot a longing look at the plate, a reproachful one at Annamaria, then another longing one at the plate. Then she grabbed a cookie.

Annamaria felt a twinge of guilt. Was it mean of her to make cookies for her friends? Should she *not* do it, solely because Darlene was weak when it came to resisting temptation?

"Lay it out for us, Rache," Jessie said. "What's the game-plan?"

"As I see it," Rachel said, "the main issue is the body. It's got to be disposed of, in a way that means it won't be found… or if it *is* found, in a way that means it can't be traced back to us. Which *also* means we have to get rid of any evidence around here. On our clothes, in the yard, whatever."

"So what do we do with him?" Darlene asked, crumbs on her lip and chin. "Bury him like we said earlier? Or take him somewhere and dump him?"

Jessie grinned. "You know what would be awesome? Have you ever seen those anti-smoking ads, the ones where they go around yelling about the dangers of tobacco and everything? There's this one where they put a bunch of fake body parts sticking out of trashcans all over the city, with these signs about how smoking kills. And everybody who sees it, they know it's this public service performance art thing, yeah? We could do something like that!"

"You've got to be kidding," Annamaria said.

"Think about it! People would be all *oh, this is one of those things again…* and it'd never fucking even occur to them that they were real body parts!"

"Excuse me." Darlene raised her hand like she was in class. "I am not cutting anybody into bits. Not even Donnie. That's disgusting. And messy. And a lot of goddamn work, too."

"No more work than digging a hole in the backyard," Jessie said. "No more messy and disgusting than dressing out a deer, and I've done that before."

"You killed a deer?" Gwen piped up, horrified.

"Nah, one of my brothers did, but they let me help dress it out."

"It's a neat idea, Jessie," Rachel said. "It really is. But it's too… too public. Sooner or later, someone *would* realize they weren't fake body parts."

"Yeah," said Darlene. "They'd start to stink. There'd be flies." A greenish look crossed her face and she set down her second cookie without biting into it. "Wish I hadn't said that."

"Yeah, but," said Jessie, "they'd stink, sure, and there'd be flies, and that's why you put them in a garbage can anyway! Of *course* there's gonna be stink and flies!"

"Too public," Rachel repeated. "Too sensational, too much like a big shout for attention. Too risky."

"Hey, I'll do it myself if the rest of you are too chicken. I'm not afraid of a little risk, a little mess." Jessie bridled, a swagger to the set of her shoulders.

Annamaria stifled a sigh. "No one said you were, Jessie."

"Yeah, it isn't that," Rachel said. "The police would be brought into it. They'd identify the body, come around here, talk to us. They'd maybe find witnesses who saw something. No matter how careful we were, placing the… parts… someone might see. All it would take was one smart cop putting two and two together. The best way—"

"I can do it! I wouldn't let anybody see me. I'm not a moron."

"Jessie, shut up and let her finish," Annamaria said.

Rachel nodded thanks at her. "The best way is to make it seem like Donnie took off. He was always complaining, right? Hated it here, hated his aunt, couldn't wait to get out. Right?"

Darlene, still greenish, toyed with the cookie. "Wasn't he bragging about how he was gonna buy a motorcycle, go to Mexico?"

"I remember that," Gwen said. She glanced at Jessie. "He was telling Etch about it, I think. That time you were going camping at the lake, and Etch showed up before you got home from class?"

"Right," Jessie said. "Etch thought it was lame and pathetic, what a loser, trying to impress him. He laughed his ass off."

Craig "Etch" Etchler was Jessie's boyfriend, though it had always seemed to Annamaria their relationship was based more on the spirit of competition than on romance.

Etch and his crowd were jocks and frat boys, all with short, snappy, macho nicknames: Chet, Skip, Chip, Etch, Chad, Butch. They were into snowboarding and surfing and extreme mountain biking and paintball. The first time Jessie had come back from a full Saturday out with them, she'd been dirty, scratched, bruised and looking like the aftermath of a drunken gangbang.

"Which means," Rachel said, bringing Annamaria's attention back to the matter at hand, "that what we have to do is make him disappear. Dispose of the body somewhere it won't be found for a long time, if ever."

"But Mrs. Hubert would report him missing," Gwen said. "He *is* her nephew."

"Her ex-husband's nephew," Darlene said. "I don't think she gives a rat's ass about him, either, except that she gets free work out of him in exchange for that shitty apartment."

"Never mind that," Annamaria said. "Rachel? You were saying?"

"I was saying that okay, he gets reported missing. Okay, the police ask around, and what do they hear? They hear how Donnie wanted to get a motorcycle and head for Mexico. If there's no signs of foul play—"

"Jesus, foul play, I can't believe you really said that," said Jessie.

"—and there's no body," Rachel continued, "they wouldn't bother looking for him for long, would they? He's an adult, right?"

"Barely," Darlene said.

"But he is. The police have more important things to do than worry about a grown man who took off. They'll file a report and that's it, until the body does get found. *If* it does. And by then…" Rachel spread her cunning little hands as if to mime releasing a bird.

Annamaria glanced at the others.

Gwen alone among them looked troubled, pensive. But even someone who had her head in a fantasy world most of the time had to know that they didn't have a whole lot of choice. She couldn't face being arrested or expelled. She couldn't face having her friends mad at her. She'd go along.

They all would go along.

"First, we have to take care of the body," Rachel said. "That'll be your job, Jessie, Darlene."

Brisk and businesslike. Scary-smart. Jessie made a mental note: never get Rachel pissed at you. Her revenge wouldn't be a blind rage. It'd be calculated and lethal.

And most people would never see it coming, because they'd think that this was only Rachel, five-foot-nothing and cuter than Tinker Bell. Their last words, if they had time for last words, would be along the lines of, "Wait, what?"

"Oh shit, why me?" Darlene asked in a sickened whine. "I don't want to touch him. Why can't I do the apartment?"

Rachel's mouth tucked down at the corners. "We can't have Gwen do this."

"Well, what about Annamaria? She's the one he was peeping at. She's the reason he's dead. *She* should have to move his dead, ugly ass."

"For fuck's sake, Dar," Jessie said. "We can handle this. No big deal."

"I'll puke again. Swear to God. I'll puke right on him."

"So you'll puke. You've had like one cookie."

"Annamaria wants to talk to Gwen," Rachel said patiently. "Alone. She knows Gwen's having a hard time."

"And I'm not?"

Jessie snickered. "Look at it this way... you puke, hey, it's like temporary bulimia. Plus you'll get some exercise. It's the dead-guy fitness plan."

Normally, Darlene kind of looked like a frog. Bulgy eyes, wide mouth, fleshy lips, a double chin and a fat neck. When she glowered the way she was doing now, she looked more like a gargoyle or something. Jessie wouldn't have been surprised to see her eyes glow. Maybe shoot beams of fire.

"Would you both just quit it? Jessie, leave her alone. Darlene, enough with the complaining. We all gotta work together on this or we're sunk. Okay?"

"Okay," grumbled Darlene. Still with the eye-beams aimed at Jessie.

"Okay, okay, jeez. Excuse the shit out of me for trying to lighten things up," Jessie said. "What do you want us to do with him?"

"Strip him."

"Say what?" Darlene recoiled. "Donnie Hubert, naked? No thanks!"

"We've been over this," Rachel said. "They can get evidence off the clothes. Fibers and stuff. We have to get rid of all that separately. Burn it, I think. Along with the bowling pin."

"Aw, I *like* that bowling pin," Jessie said. "It's my lucky creep-whackin' club. Can't burn my lucky creep-whackin' club!"

"Jessie, we can't *keep* it. It's the murder weapon. It's bloody."

"So I'll wash it."

"They could match it to the wounds."

"Only if they find him, and according to you, Ms. Genius, they won't. And anyway, that bowling pin's been on the back porch forever. Wouldn't it look weird if it was just suddenly gone? Wouldn't Mrs. H. wonder what had happened to it?"

"All right, fine," Rachel said. "But wash it really good to get all the blood off, and then maybe roll it in the dirt so it looks the same way it used to. Because it'd also be weird if Mrs. Hubert noticed that it was clean for a change."

"I still don't see why we have to take off all his clothes," Darlene said, grimacing. "Who wants to see Donnie Junior? Eeeuugh!"

"What, never seen a dick before?" Jessie asked.

She flushed a mottled plum color. "I've seen them!"

"So it's no big deal," Rachel said.

"No big deal… heh… explains why he had to get his jollies window-peeping and panty-raiding," Jessie said.

"You know, Jessie, the smartass remarks are getting pretty old," Rachel said. "I'd like to get this done before midnight, if it's all the same to you."

Darlene started to say something, then stared past Rachel and burst out in snorting, whoofing laughs.

Jessie turned, gaped, then hooted. "Oh, shit, you guys! That's great! What're you supposed to be? Bag ladies?"

Annamaria cast her eyes heavenward and shook her head. Gwen only shuffled awkwardly along beside her, unsure as a new colt. They were backlit by the porch bulb, which Rachel had turned on after deciding it was more important for them to be able to see what they were doing than it was to worry about someone passing by.

A slick, brownish-black trash bag, the big lawn-and-leaf kind, covered each girl to mid-thigh, with holes slit for the head and arms. More trash bags made makeshift boots, cinched at with strapping tape. Their hands were hidden by big green rubber dishgloves reaching almost to their elbows. They had flowered old-lady-style shower caps on, their hair tucked up beneath them.

"It's for when they go into his apartment," Rachel explained. "To keep them from leaving any trace evidence. None of us have ever been in there before. If the police decide to search the place, we don't want to give them any reason to think we were."

"No hazmat jumpsuits?" Darlene asked, amid snorts. "No beekeeper outfits? No spacesuits?"

"How about scuba gear?" Jessie chimed in. "I bet Etch and his buddies would lend you some scuba gear."

"Ha, ha," Annamaria said, and tossed a rectangular box of garbage bags onto the lawn. "Here you go."

"It's brand new," Rachel said. "Those are the first bags off the roll. As long as we don't do something stupid like save the rest, put them back under the kitchen sink or something, they won't be able to make a match."

"You're not seriously saying you expect *us* to put on Hefty bag smocks," Darlene said. "*We're* not going in his dumb apartment."

"But you'll be handling the body," Rachel said. She pulled a wad of exam gloves from a carton Gwen gave her. "Glove up, too. Don't leave any fingerprints on his skin."

"Eeeuugh." Darlene plucked up one of the gloves and held it, dangling in the rain, before her eyes. "If we really gotta touch a naked Donnie Hubert, I want more than this flimsy little hand-condom."

"Yeah," said Jessie. "Welding gloves at least. Or those chainmail things they wear when they're gutting fish."

"To undress him, you'll need the flexibility. Even dish gloves would be too clumsy." Rachel passed each of them a pair, then produced the strapping tape from the carton. "This is brand-new, too. Take no chances, right?"

"Go on," Annamaria said. "We'll come back to help you with the actual moving of it, once we make sure there's nothing incriminating in his apartment."

She and Gwen headed for the garage, taking steps of exaggerated care because the grass was slippery and so were their garbage-bag boots. The rain made funny little plip-plip-plip noises when it hit them, and ran in silvery runnels over the dark, oily surfaces.

Muttering, Jessie and Darlene got into their own protective outfits. Rachel taped the bags around their legs, gave them shower caps—

"Where the fuck did these come from, anyway?" Jessie demanded, pulling hers over her hair. The tousled sticky-uppy tomboyish spikes went flat against her skull like a wet rag.

"The top cabinet in our bathroom," Rachel said. "I found them up there when Gwen and I did the big clean last spring. Didn't see any use for them, but I couldn't just throw them away, either. Good thing, now."

—and they gloved up.

"This is crazy," Darlene said. Her shower cap was clear, and with her chunky figure encased in the wrinkly brownish-black plastic, she looked like a giant raisin. "We're never gonna tell anybody about this, right?"

"That's sort of the point," Jessie said. "Seeing as how we *killed* a dude."

They approached Donnie. He wasn't gone, hadn't done a mysterious disappearing act the way so-called corpses often did in the movies. He wasn't shamming, either. No abrupt lunge as they got close, nothing. His eyes were still wide open to the stinging rainfall. He didn't move when Jessie kicked his foot.

"Won't he already have fingerprints on him?" Darlene asked. "You know, from the fight?"

"Hell, forget the fingerprints," Jessie said. She lifted Donnie's limp arm and rotated it. "Anna left fucking *bite* marks."

The crescent-shaped gouges in his flesh were no longer bleeding, and the rain had rinsed them clean enough to show the raw meat in gory detail by the porch light's pallid shine.

"This should hopefully take care of the fingerprints," Rachel said, reaching into the carton again. She held up a spray bottle and a rag, and gave a spritz that released a citrusy-smelling mist.

"That's Oxy-Orange," Darlene said.

"Right… it'll dissolve the oils on his skin. We wipe him down wherever we—"

"Hold the phone, hold the fucking phone!" Darlene spoke loud enough to make Rachel flinch. "Not only to we have to *strip* him, now you want us to give him a rubdown? What next?

A goddamn happy ending?"

"One-two-three-not-it," Jessie said in a rapid chant.

"Only his arms, his face, maybe his neck," Rachel said. "Wherever we might have touched him during the struggle. That's all. I mean, okay, we could douse the whole body in bleach, but…"

"Bleach," Darlene said. "Why not drain cleaner? Why don't we dissolve the son of a bitch? Then we could flush him down the toilet."

"Not our toilets," Jessie said. "They clog on a fucking Q-Tip. Anyway, fine, give me the orange stuff."

Rachel opened yet another big plastic trash bag. "Put all of his clothes in here," she said. "The rag, too, when you're done."

"But what about the bite marks?" Jessie asked. "Can't they do dental records or whatever, find out whose teeth did the biting?"

"Yeah." Rachel removed something else from her carton of supplies. "So we have to disguise the marks."

"Fuck, no, no, fuck," Darlene said. "Rachel, no, that's fucking gruesome."

"We have to," she said, kneeling beside the body and raising Donnie's arm, gripping his wrist in one gloved hand. The other held a paring knife. Small, but wickedly sharp.

Just like Rachel herself, Jessie thought.

"Uh… if you want to cut off his arm, Rache… you might maybe want something, you know, bigger. Like a meat cleaver. Or an axe. Hell, a chainsaw, go nuts. But that little knife, you'll be here all night. If it doesn't break on you. It's a cheapie. Didn't we get those like five-for-a-dollar at the discount store?"

"I'm not cutting off his arm. And since this is a cheapie, it's untraceable, we can get rid of it, no one will miss it. Now, shush."

"Did she really just 'shush' us?" Jessie asked Darlene.

Darlene didn't answer. Darlene got one eyeful of what Rachel was doing with the teensy little paring knife, and it was so long to that cookie.

"Rache? Anyone ever tell you that you're a psycho?"

"I'm not doing this because I enjoy it," Rachel said, as she sliced and gashed and cut. "If I was a psycho, if I was enjoying this, I'd be doing it while he was still alive. This is purely for practical purposes. There. See? I obliterated the bite marks. There's no way they could get a reliable dental impression from it now."

"Because now it looks like he stuck his arm in a lawnmower."

"But it doesn't look like he was bitten." She inspected his fingers, found a couple strands caught from when he'd grabbed her by the hair, and removed them. The strands, not the fingers. "Okay, you can start."

"C'mon, Dar," Jessie said. "If she can do that, we can cope with this."

"Speak for yourself."

"Don't be a wussie."

"Fuck you."

"Whatever. Get over here and help me with his clothes."

"Why can't Rachel do it?" Darlene pointed accusingly at Rachel, now on her hands and knees in the grass. "What's *she* doing?"

"I'm looking for his tooth," Rachel said. "Remember, he spit out a tooth? Need to find it."

Darlene shuddered, shedding raindrops from the folds of her garbage-bag smock. She didn't bother with any more protests, objections or complaints, just came over and started helping Jessie with Donnie Hubert's shoes.

Having to handle the body–

Donnie Hubert, that was Donnie, he had a name, he was a person, not just some meaningless thing, a person, no matter how nasty!

—would have been bad.

Going in his apartment, though, that wasn't exactly a treat either.

Gwen found herself wishing that in addition to the trash bags, gloves and shower caps, Rachel had been able to come up with masks. The stiff kind that painters wore, or even the simple cloth kind that they used in hospitals.

She settled for trying not to breathe deeply. Shallow sips of air. She wasn't sure whether it'd be better to breathe through her mouth to avoid having to smell it, or through her nose in hopes that the linings of her nasal passages did what they were supposed to do and filter out anything too unhealthy.

Annamaria led the way, and Gwen was glad. She could never do this on her own. Of course, on her own she wouldn't have ended up in this situation in the first place... but that didn't matter, did it?

Poor Darlene and Jessie. They had to *touch* it.

Him. Donnie. Donnie Hubert.

Would he be cold yet?

The night had been warmish before the rain started, but the rain itself would have hurried along the cooling process. So would being on the ground, on the wet grass and mud.

Yes, most likely, he was cold. Or at least... room temperature, if that phrase was applicable to the outside.

Not stiff yet with rigor mortis. Not rotting yet. Not seething with maggots.

"Ohhh," Gwen said, and had to stop and lean against the wall.

"Are you all right?" Annamaria asked.

"Give me... give me a minute?"

"Sure. I'm going to start with that nightstand. When you're ready, could you manage the closet?"

"I think so."

The apartment was a single room, with a kitchenette along one side and a bathroom in the back corner. In lieu of curtains or shutters, threadbare old blankets were thumbtacked above the windows. The floor was carpeted with more of the ever-popular shag from the 1970s—not burnt-orange or forest-green like in the main house, but a sort of black-umber-rust-tan that made Gwen think of the tortoiseshell cat her grandmother used to have.

Unless maybe the carpet wasn't really that color. Unless those were years' worth of accumulated stains. It wouldn't have surprised her.

Yuck.

Squalor.

Donnie Hubert had lived in squalor. The air stank of stale beer, staler pizza, foot fungus, body odor, farts, and worse.

He didn't even have a bed. There was a fold-out couch that probably hadn't been folded-in since Gwen's high school graduation. No sheets. An unzipped-all-the-way olive green sleeping bag, a pillow with no pillowcase, a lumpy, discolored mattress.

"Holy Mary Mother of God," Annamaria said.

The nightstand wedged between the couch and the wall had a gooseneck lamp and a clock radio on top, a bunch more magazines—

Girlie magazines, porn, like the ones on the floor… the models looking bored and/or stoned, hard-faced, empty-eyed… gigantic implants… tattoos… and why would someone do that to their pubic hair anyway? Did men actually think that was sexy? Or the piercings? How could anybody think that was sexy?

—untidily jammed in the open compartment below, and a bottom drawer, which Annamaria had just opened.

The first item she tossed onto the mattress was a blocky black gadget that Gwen couldn't immediately identify. Then she realized it was an archaic Polaroid camera, the kind that not only used film, but special film so that it could spit out the picture then and there.

Then Annamaria fanned out a stack of Polaroid photos. "Rachel was right."

"Are those of… of you? In the shower?"

"Not just me." She flipped one across the room.

Gwen missed the catch and the square landed facedown at her feet. She fumbled to pick it up, the thick dish gloves making her feel like she was all thumbs. At last she got it, turned it over, and her jaw dropped in hurt shock. "This is *me*!"

"He must've used a ladder," Annamaria said.

The house's bathroom window was pebbled glass, but in the summers they had to open the bottom pane or else the walls would mildew. The window screen made a blurry grid across the photograph, and the shower stall's glass door was further clouded with steam, so the effect was beyond soft focus. The figure in the shower was a barely-distinct smudge from the collarbones down.

But from the collarbones up… it was Gwen, all right. Head tipped far back, which she had to do because the showerhead was situated lower on the wall than she was tall. Rinsing lather from her long, strawberry-blonde hair.

"Here's me," Annamaria said, sifting through the Polaroids. "Here's Jessie washing her car... here's a bunch from the day we had the barbecue party... here's me again... here's Rachel in the kitchen in her pajamas... here's Jessie's ass while she's bent over stretching... here's me *again*, that bastard..."

"He took pictures of us," Gwen said. "He really did."

"Oh, and would you look at this?" Annamaria delved into the drawer again. "Donnie's underwear collection. These ones are mine. Those have got to be Jessie's. Are these yours? And I wonder whose bra this is?"

"This is horrible," Gwen said, almost in tears. "How could he *do* things like that?"

"Men are scum."

"Not all of them."

"Name one."

"Um..."

"And don't," added Annamaria with a half-smile, "say Cameron Mack."

"But he's not scum! He's nice!"

"He's a movie star. He only pretends to be nice."

"I don't believe that for a second." Gwen drew her chin up. "I can tell."

And she was right. She'd never met him, but she didn't have to meet him to know that he was special. Genuine. It didn't matter what Annamaria thought. Cameron Mack didn't pretend to be nice. He really was.

"Well, then, name another," Annamaria said.

"What about Etch?"

"Etch?" she echoed, and scoffed. "Etch is a dudebro asshole."

"He's Jessie's boyfriend."

"Jessie has bad judgment. Anyway, never mind. Let's finish this. I want to get out of here."

"Okay." Gwen steeled herself and slid back the closet door to reveal a mound of unwashed laundry on the floor, a bar where empty hangers hung, some musty old shoeboxes on the upper shelf, and a milk crate full of videocassettes with titles that left no doubt as to their contents.

She looked around for a VCR and saw none. Did they even sell those anymore? There was a television, old, but not as old as the Polaroid camera. No cable box. No digital whatchamacallit. But there was a DVD player, beside another milk crate, this one filled with DVD cases. More porn. And movies in which lots of people got tortured in lots of ways.

"I found his binoculars," Annamaria said from the window nearest the house. She held aside the blanket-curtain and raised the binoculars to her eyes. "As we figured... good thing you and Rachel kept your blinds drawn."

Gwen wanted to sit, but didn't want to sit on anything in Donnie's apartment. She wanted to cover her face with her hands, but her hands had touched stuff in here and she wasn't about to put those gloves anywhere near her face.

"It's so... so..." she said, and couldn't go on. Tears spilled over her lashes and tumbled, unchecked, down her cheeks.

"I know." Annamaria dropped the binoculars on the tortoiseshell carpet and came to Gwen. "And I know this is really rough on you. It's rough on all of us, of course... but roughest on you."

"I never thought I'd... I'd kill anybody."

Plastic crinkled as Annamaria gave her a hug. "Me either."

"How could we *do* that?"

"We didn't have time to think. We just... reacted. It's probably a good thing we did, though. Rachel knows what she's talking about. It started with watching us, then the pictures, then our underwear... what would he have done next?"

"We should have just called the police."

"We should have," Annamaria said, patting Gwen's back through the garbage bag smock. "But we didn't, and now we have to deal with it. None of us want to get in trouble. None of us want to go to jail. We've got to look out for each other, Gwen. We're friends, aren't we?"

"Friends," she said.

"And we're all in this together now."

"I... I guess so," Gwen said, and managed a smile through her tears. "Thank you, Annamaria. Thank you."

***

Donnie's body was wet.

Wet from the rain. Wet from the blood. Wet because he'd pissed himself.

He had also, Darlene and Jessie discovered when they peeled his sodden jeans down his legs, crapped himself.

"Gahhh," Darlene said.

It was only a little, but shit was shit, and he'd done it.

No underwear, either. And his jeans had been unbuttoned, half-zipped. As if he really had been about to whip it out and start wanking while he slobbered at the sight of Annamaria in the shower.

Bastard.

"Freeballin'," Jessie said. "Classy. Never knew Don-O was the commando type."

"This is disgusting."

"Yep."

"For real."

"Yep."

"I'm not wiping his ass."

Jessie shrugged. "Rock-paper-scissors?"

"Fuck that. I'm *not* wiping his ass. I wanted to spend my life wiping asses, I'd be in nursing school."

"Sissy."

"Up yours."

"I'll just get the hose. Bag his clothes, and we'll flip him over and give him the old pressure-washing treatment."

"And backsplash shit all over the place?"

"You got a better idea?"

Darlene twisted her lips at Jessie. "*You* could wipe him. You're the big brave hunter who can gut a deer. Donnie's fresh skidmarks should be no problem."

"I'll get the hose," Jessie said again.

She went to do so, and Darlene gingerly pinched up Donnie's jeans. They were soaked, heavy, and not easy to hold at arm's length. But no way in hell she was handling them any more than absolutely necessary.

Donnie Hubert, naked in the mud.

Not a pretty sight.

Of course, Donnie Hubert under any circumstances wasn't a pretty sight. He was a scrawny greaseball with bad teeth, and B.O. that could stop a truck. No real job, no real life. Just one more of the world's many socially-inept mouth-breathers and basement dwellers.

Bastard, bastard, bastard.

Looking in their windows. Watching them shower. Keeping tabs of when they did laundry so he could sneak in and swipe panties.

Him being dead, all bloody and bashed, that was gross. Gross enough that she'd puked until she thought her guts would turn inside-out. Just the memory of it made her stomach lurch with dry heaves.

Jessie was at the corner of the house, saying something to Rachel. Darlene couldn't make it out above the steady downpour. She was still alone with the corpse.

Never seen a dick before? Jessie's voice teased in her memory. She had!

Okay, so… it was in pictures and movies mostly. Hardly ever in person. And never up-close. So what? She'd still seen some!

If she'd said that, Jessie would have laughed her head off.

What if she'd mentioned that she'd seen *Etch's*?

Wouldn't have been a lie, either. She had. By accident, through the ajar doors connecting her bedroom and Jessie's by way of the bathroom. A flash of the full-frontal before he'd turned. Only a glimpse, but a quality glimpse. A hard-on glimpse. Big and stiff and ready, jutting out from a golden nest of wiry pubic hair.

Lots bigger than the stupid little curl of fleshnoodle dangling limp against Donnie's pasty, skinny thigh. His ball-sack looked wrinkled and grungy. His pubes were as bad as the stuff on his head and face: a nasty-greasy-matted tangle.

Figured. Just her luck. Typical. Totally typical. Darlene Dunfey finally has a naked guy at her feet, and not only is he *dead*, he's a scummy little pervo loser hung like a Chihuahua.

"Hey, guess what?" Jessie asked as she returned, hauling the green length of garden hose. "Rachel was taking a look over by Annamaria's bathroom window, you know, to see if he'd left footprints in the flowerbed underneath, and guess what she found?"

"A video camera?"

"Like Don-O could afford a video camera. No, she found jizz-spots on the wall."

"Ugh," Darlene said. "Even in the rain?"

"Windowsill protected from some of it."

"Fresh?" As soon as she said it, Darlene wished she hadn't.

"Dried on. But lots of it."

"God, that's so sick!"

"Yeah. She's gonna clean it so there's no proof that he was doing anything. Doesn't want to give the cops a reason to look twice at us. That's why she's got Gwen and Anna going through his stuff. Stand back, Dar."

Darlene backed up, being very careful how she placed her feet, because the slick garbage bags on the slick grass weren't much in the way of traction. She squinted as Jessie opened up with the spray-nozzle. Part of her mind fully expected the blast of cold water to revive Donnie, bring him spluttering to consciousness after all.

Then what would they do?

Then, she supposed, they'd get to kill him again.

The water hit him in the face, and Donnie didn't react at all. Hose water flooded his open mouth and overflowed, sluicing with blood from his split lips and broken teeth. It gushed up his nose and into his wide-open eyes.

Jessie directed the stream down his body. Like hosing off the driveway. Like rinsing a raw chicken before putting it in the roasting pan. The force of the water-jet made his limp fleshnoodle dick flop around like a tadpole, and Jessie laughed.

Darlene couldn't help laughing too.

"I bet he always wanted to take a shower with a couple girls," Jessie said, "but I bet he never expected it'd be like this!" She let go of the nozzle, stopping the flow. "Okay, grab his ankles, let's flip him and do the other side."

The thin gloves did nothing against the cold-meat-bony feel of Donnie's ankles in her grasp. Darlene held on grimly, while Jessie crouched and took his shoulders. She counted, and on three they both heaved, and rolled Donnie onto his front. His knobby spine poked against zit-studded, pallid skin. His skinny, shit-streaked ass was even worse.

"Jeez," Jessie said. "Could almost turn me off men for good, except Don-O here barely counts as human in the first place."

She blasted him again, head to toe, and extra in the crack.

"Ice water enema," Darlene heard herself say.

"No way I'm poking the hose *up* there."

Donnie was rinsed clean, or at least as clean as he could be while still lying in the mud, with loose blades of grass clinging to his wet body. Jessie tossed the hose aside and they flipped him back over. Then she picked up the Oxy-Orange and the unopened roll of paper towels. She tossed the towels to Darlene.

"Oh, hey, no—"

"I wash, you dry. Like doing dishes."

"I'll wash."

"I already hosed him." Jessie began spritzing, releasing puffs of citrusy vapor that were quickly lost against the rain.

Darlene clenched her jaw and hunkered down to scrub at him, concentrating on the hands and arms. Erasing any fingerprints that might have been left by the beating, or by Annamaria seizing his forearm to bite him when he had Rachel by the hair.

"Won't there be bruises?" she asked. "Ones that come up later? Even though he's dead?"

"Post-mortem, you mean?" Rachel had come up to them, towing something that rumbled along behind her. "It's a possibility. You see that in strangulation cases a lot. But bruise patterns are harder to match than fingerprints. And with the amount of bruises he's likely to have…"

"Well, and they're not going to find him anyway, right, Rache? That's why we're doing all this. You've got it worked out. You're the genius."

"Yeah, okay," Rachel said. "But this sure isn't what I had in mind!"

CHAPTER THREE

Annamaria and Gwen slip-shuffled back across the yard to rejoin the others around Donnie Hubert's body. Annamaria carried a white grocery bag, pendulous with the bulky, odd-shaped weight of the Polaroid camera. Gwen had a shoebox taken from Donnie's closet.

"He didn't have a lot of cash that we could find," Gwen told Rachel. She was still paler than usual, but her voice was steadier than it had been, and her grey-green eyes seemed resolute. "We got his wallet, his bus pass, and some other stuff that seemed like things he might want to take with him if he was leaving town but traveling light."

Rachel glanced to Annamaria and received a single nod by way of reply. She nodded back. "Okay, good. Great job, you guys. I know this is kind of crazy, not how any of us planned to be spending our evening. This part's almost done, though."

"Did he have pictures like we thought?" Jessie asked.

"A whole scrapbook's worth," Annamaria said.

"What else did you find?" Darlene asked, looking at the bag swinging at the end of Annamaria's arm. Blobs of color pressed against the thin plastic. Red, blue, black, leopard-print. "Those the missing undies?"

"Yes," Gwen said, the single word clipped and tight.

"Not just ours," Annamaria said. "Some in here, I don't know *whose* they are. This bra, for instance." She held it up by a strap. "Anyone recognize it?"

"Damn with a capital quadruple D!" Jessie said, goggling. "All of us together don't have tits enough to fill *that* baby."

"It might be Mrs. Hubert's," Rachel said.

"Sick!" yelped Darlene. "His *aunt*?"

"His uncle's wife, technically."

"Technically or not, it's still fucking sick!"

"But it looks like it could be hers. I mean…" Rachel cupped her hands well out from her own chest. She was buxom enough for her size; she just was of a small size. "Mrs. Hubert is a big lady."

"I agree with Dar," Jessie said. "Fucking sick."

"No one is arguing that point," Rachel said. She added the news about what she'd found on the wall beneath Annamaria's windowsill.

"If he wasn't already dead, I'd kill him," Annamaria said, with a venomous glare at Donnie's lifeless face as she stuffed the immense black-lace-and-red-velvet-rosettes underwire bra back into the bag.

"And it wouldn't surprise me at all if his apartment was full of pornography," Rachel went on.

"It was," Gwen said. She took a breath. "It was horrible."

"Any video of us?" Jessie asked.

"No, thank God." Annamaria hoisted the bag. "Just pictures and underwear. What should I do with these? Put them in with his clothes?"

"No," Rachel said. "We'll want to dispose of those separately."

Gwen raised a hand. "I vote burning."

"Yeah, no shit," Jessie said. "I know I sure as hell don't want *mine* back after what he was probably doing with them."

"You could wash them," Darlene said.

"Fuck that. I'd rather burn them and buy new ones."

"Me, too," said Annamaria.

"Later, okay, you guys?" Rachel waved to get their attention. "Still got a body laying here. Let's deal with that first. Now, Jessie and Darlene got him all undressed and cleaned off. I carved up the bite wound–Gwen, take it easy, I *had* to–and I found the tooth that got knocked out. There's still going to be blood and whatever in the grass. The rain should take care of a lot of that, and we can hose it down real good too. I think that takes care of the scene of the crime."

"What's with the trash can?" Darlene asked.

The object that Rachel had drag-rumbled over to them was the large yard-waste can, of sturdy rubberized plastic so deep a green it looked black in the darkness. It had a hinged lid, a handle, and widely-spaced wheels.

"You're going to put him in there?" Gwen gazed at the corpse, then the can. "Will he fit?"

"He'll fit," Jessie said, also scrutinizing both. "We might have to scrunch him some, but he'll fit."

"It's the best way to move him without being seen," Rachel said. "Sure, we could sling him on a blanket, but that'd be conspicuous."

"Isn't there a wheelbarrow in the garage?" asked Annamaria.

"Too tippy with just that one front wheel," Rachel said. "Also conspicuous. Even if we covered him, it'd still look like a body."

"You said no one would see," Gwen said, wringing her hands. The dish gloves squeaked against themselves in an almost nails-on-chalkboard noise.

"No one will. This is just in case. We put him in the can, and if anybody *does* drive past, they'll think we're hauling yard waste. Grass clippings, weeds, raked leaves. No big. They won't give it a second thought."

"So we scrunch him." Jessie opened the lid and looked in. "Yeah. It'll work."

"You're *sure* we can't just bury him?" Darlene asked.

"I told you, we can't bury him on the property," Rachel said. Impatience crept into her tone again. "The construction site over there, on the one hand that'd be good because once the foundations were poured and everything, he might never be found. But there's a lot of people around, workers and contractors, every day. All it'd take was for one person to notice something, and game over."

"This isn't a game," Annamaria said.

"Figure of speech already! Since we can't dump him on the side of the road either, and we can't transport him in any of our cars, it's got to be the marsh."

"Some people do go there," Gwen said. "Birdwatchers, environmentalists—"

"Swamp elves," Jessie said.

Gwen turned to her, frowning. "This is serious, I hope you know."

"I know, I know, but still, jeez."

"People *do*, okay, right," Rachel said. "But not a *lot* of people. It's a risk, sure. We'll have to weigh him down so he doesn't go floating to the surface."

"With what?" Darlene asked. "You mean like tie a cinderblock to his feet, bucket of cement, that kind of thing? Like in the gangster movies?"

"It's gas bubbles, isn't it?" asked Jessie. "Couldn't we just..." She made jabbing gestures. "You know, like when you put a baked potato in the microwave? You poke it a few times with a fork so it doesn't explode?"

"Perforate him?" Rachel asked. "Puncture his internal organs, his intestines, with a long knife?"

"One-two-three-*not* it!" Darlene snapped, directing a hard look at Jessie.

Gwen wobbled, and Annamaria had to put an arm around her.

"It *could* work," Rachel said after a thoughtful moment. "But it'd be messy, it'd leave more wounds. I'd rather take a chance on using a chain or a rock or something."

"Oh, good," Gwen said faintly.

"There's some old chains in the garage too, I think," Annamaria said. "Should I go get some?"

"I'll go," Rachel said. "Have to make sure it's not a part of something that can be traced back to here. You guys load up the body, okay? Get him in the can, and then we can push it across the street."

She trotted off, surprisingly sure-footed in the slick makeshift trash bag galoshes, and the other four stood in an unsure circle, nobody quite willing to meet anybody else's eyes. The body still sprawled at their feet in the wet grass, washed clean now, the skin on his fingers and toes beginning to go pruney.

Jessie let out a slow whistle of exhalation. "Okay, girls, arm and arm and leg and leg and upsy-daisy away we go."

"Do we... uh... do we want to put him in... head first, or

feet first?" Darlene asked.

"I don't think I can touch him," Gwen said.

"You can." Annamaria patted her shoulder. "I know you can. We need you."

"Yeah, all for one and whatever," Jessie said. "We're like *The Three Musketeers*, except there's five of us."

"And we're chicks," Darlene said.

"*That* doesn't matter," Jessie retorted. "Give me a sword and a hat with a big fancy feather and I could kick their butts."

"Come on." Annamaria bent and took hold of Donnie's ankle. "Feet first?"

"Head first," Jessie said. "That way, we can bend his legs down."

"But his ugly ass will be sticking up," Darlene said. "I don't want to look at that."

"Which is why we shut the lid, Dar. So none of us have to look at it."

"If we put him in feet first," Annamaria said, "won't his knees bend anyway?"

"Fine, jeez, feet first, let's just do this." Jessie got an arm. "Ready?"

"Fuck," Darlene muttered, and grabbed the other arm.

The three of them peered expectantly up at Gwen.

"We need you," Annamaria said again, her voice soft. "Please, Gwen."

A convulsive tremor wracked her slender frame, but Gwen sank her teeth into her lip and wrapped her hands around Donnie's calf and ankle.

"Lift with the legs, not the back," Jessie said.

"Yes, Coach," Darlene said.

"Shut up. On four… one… two… three… and four!"

They heaved, and although each girl but Jessie had a bad moment in which it seemed that her plastic-clad feet wanted to shoot sideways out from under her, no one fell. Donnie's deadweight came up easier than any of them had expected. Gwen and Annamaria maneuvered until they'd gotten his lower legs into the can.

"All right, there," Annamaria said.

"Tip him up and shove," grunted Jessie.

Donnie slid into the can. His feet hit bottom, jarring his

body, and there was a burbling biological noise from inside him that made them all prance back, cawing in disgust. He stayed upright for a moment. Then his knees buckled and his torso sank down. His back squeaked along the rubberized plastic. He stopped with his head and shoulders above the rim.

"He burped," Gwen said. Her eyes were huge deer-in-the-headlight eyes, twin pools of shock. "He burped, didn't you hear it?"

"Doesn't mean anything," Jessie said. "It's a... uh... reflex or something."

"A reflex?"

"Sure. Ask Rache. She'd tell you so."

"He doesn't fit," Darlene said. She lowered the lid until it struck the top of Donnie's head. There was a wedge-shaped gap about eight inches high at its widest. "Shit... now what?"

"Shake the can, he'll... wiggle," Jessie said.

"Contents may have settled during shipping," Gwen said, and laughed a high, shrill, tittering laugh that made the others look at her like she'd just lost her last marble.

Darlene shook the can. Donnie's flesh squeaked again. His head thumped forward until his chin was resting on his collarbones. A line of watery, blood-pinkish drool ran over his lower lip.

"Like Jessie said, scrunch him." Annamaria pressed on top of the lid, attempting to push it all the way closed.

"You want I should climb up there, jump up and down a few times?" Jessie asked. "Like when you pack your suitcase too full?"

"I've got it, I've got it." To prove she did, Annamaria leaned with her entire upper body weight. The lid went down another half-inch, and then there was a squelchy crunching sound and it dropped two more inches.

Gwen and Darlene screamed in unison, short screams that in Darlene's case were quickly cut off by more dry heaves, and in Gwen's case trailed into a long hollow moan.

Jessie peeked in. "Yup. That was his skull."

"Oooohhhh..." Gwen said. And flump, down she went, out cold.

"Damsel in distress fainted on us," Jessie said.

"She'll be fine, never mind her. His head, is it…" Annamaria couldn't find a good word.

"Did it burst?" Darlene asked, still looking green around the gills.

"Nah," Jessie said. "It's just flatter on top than it used to be. Might be some more stuff coming out. Looks like it went along the cracks we already made. Like, you know, fault lines."

"That is so fucking gross you have no idea," Darlene said.

"What part of this isn't?" Annamaria pointed out.

"True."

"Let's get the lid shut, okay? Reach in and push on his shoulders," Annamaria said.

"You guys hold the can so I don't dump it over." Jessie waited until Darlene and Annamaria were bracing the yard-waste container, then set the heels of her hands on Donnie's shoulders and pushed.

His skin made a few more stubborn, protesting squeaks, but she forced him down far enough for the lid to close. Not enough for it to *latch*, but they figured it was as good as they were going to get.

Rachel came back with something dark slung over her shoulder, staggering beneath its weight.

"The hell, Rache?" said Jessie.

As she got closer, they saw that it was yet another of the brownish-black garbage bags. "What happened to Gwen?" Rachel asked, alarmed.

"Fainted," Darlene said.

"We kind of gooshed Donnie's head," Jessie said. "What's with the bag? I thought you wanted a chain or a cinderblock or something. Weren't there any?"

"There were, but that's just it," Rachel said. "Anything from the garage, there's a possibility that Mrs. Hubert or someone might recognize it. For instance, there was a big old chain, that would have been perfect, but—"

"But that's what she used to use to chain up the dog," Annamaria finished.

"Exactly. So I took another of the trash bags and poured in the sand left over from when Donnie put in the flowerbeds out front. It should make an okay anchor, once we tie it around his middle."

"With what?" asked Annamaria. "Did you find some rope?"

"Tape it, I meant." She held up the roll of strapping tape. "We'll get rid of this afterward, so we might as well use as much of it as we can. Are you sure Gwen's okay?"

On the ground, Gwen moaned again and her eyelids fluttered. "What?"

"You fainted," Jessie told her.

"I did?" She peered up at them through the rain, raising a hand to keep it out of her eyes. "Thanks for catching me."

"Any of us look like your Prince Charming?" Darlene said snidely.

"Not really, no."

"Did you really goosh his head?" Rachel asked.

"It's not *totally* gooshed, not flat as a pancake or anything," Jessie said. "Maybe more like when you whack a soft-boiled egg with a spoon."

"Interesting," Rachel said. She took a peek. Her pert, upturned nose wrinkled a little. "Well, it's not as if it can hurt him any worse."

"Please can we get this over with?" Gwen got up, then bent to stand with her hands on her knees and her head down. "I don't feel so well."

"Almost done," Rachel told her. "Someone go out front and check to make sure there's no cars coming, nobody out for a walk."

"Who'd be out for a walk in this fucking weather?" Jessie shook rainwater from her shower cap and it sprayed in all directions.

"I'll go," Annamaria said.

"What if there *is* someone?" Darlene asked. "What if they see us?"

Jessie did the wild-maniac-grin. "Then we'll have to kill them, too!"

"I'm being serious here."

"We'll worry about that if and when," Rachel said. "Come on. It's heavy, and it won't want to push on the grass or the wet ground. We all need to help. Around the house, across the street."

"I don't think I can," Gwen said.

"How about the sandbag and the tape? Can you take those?"

"Tape it to him, you mean?"

"No, only carry them for now."

"All right." Not without reluctance, Gwen accepted the heavy bag and the roll of tape.

Rachel had double-bagged, squeezed the excess air out, and double-knotted. No trapped air pockets, no tell-tale trickle of sand like something out of the Hansel and Gretel story. Careful Rachel.

She, Jessie and Darlene positioned themselves behind and to the sides of the yard-waste container, grabbing the sturdy handle. They tugged in an effort to tip the can, needing to get the bottom leading edge of it off the ground so that its full weight would rest on the two wheels in the back. It resisted.

"Come on, you guys, pull," said Jessie through gritted teeth.

They pulled again. The can teetered. Then the deadweight inside it shifted. There was a fleshy smack and another crunch.

"Whoops," Darlene said. She levered up the lid, looked, grimaced. "Faceplanted into the wall. I bet his nose is busted."

"I bet it was already busted anyway," Jessie said. "Forget it. The sooner we get rid of him, the better."

The three of them fought to trundle the large dark-green container around the corner of the house. It rolled fine on the breezeway, but Rachel had been right about it bogging down in the grass and on the wet ground. She fretted about the tracks they might be leaving, but there was nothing to be done about that right then and there.

"We'll have to see how it looks in the morning," she said. "The grass is good and springy, so it might be no problem."

Annamaria was waiting for them in the front yard, which sloped toward the edge of the road. The yard was bordered with flowerbeds built up and contained by salvaged or scavenged railroad ties, tarred and black. Most of the plants in them were short evergreens and other low-maintenance shrubs. A sidewalk bisected the lawn and ended beside a barn-shaped mailbox on a post.

The road itself was plain two-lane blacktop with a broken

yellow line down the middle. No sidewalks flanked it, though nice new concrete ones were already going in over at the new housing development, and might extend this way in a few more years. There was just a bare dirt-and-gravel shoulder—*mud-and-gravel* now—and a wide space for extra parking when the breezeway was occupied. At the moment, only Jessie's Mustang sat there.

"Coast is clear," Annamaria said. "There's a light at the Gerrittsons', but it's just their porch light and they always leave it on. No cars have been by at all."

"Good," Rachel said. "You're the lookout, okay? Help us steer this thing, but keep your eyes open for trouble."

They got the yard-waste can to the road's edge with a minimum of grunting and swearing, and only pushed it over Darlene's foot once.

"Ahhh shit ow shit that hurt!"

"Nice move, twinkle-toes."

"Fuck you, Jessie!"

Still no gleam of approaching headlights, no insanely dedicated neighbors out for a late-night jog or dog-walk in the rain, no other signs of movement or life beyond the swaying of the windblown trees.

The can's wheels sounded horrifically loud on the asphalt, grinding and scraping, rumbling. All of the girls winced and hurried along, figuring that if there was no way to quiet the process, at least they could be faster about it.

Across the road. Up the gravel shoulder on the other side. Then up a weedy, earthen hump. That required the strength of all five, Gwen having to set down the bag of sand to help.

"A little more," Annamaria coached from the top. "A little... good... okay, more... there we go, that's got it. Nice job!"

Even Jessie was breathing hard. "Whew," she said. "We're going to be sore tomorrow."

"Now where?" asked Darlene. "We don't want to dump him right opposite the house, do we?"

"No," Rachel said. "There should be a trail at the bottom of this hill. We can go along it for a while, and it'll come to a sort of pond."

"How do you know?" Jessie asked. "Spend a lot of time hiking around the swamp, there, Rache?"

"When I took botany last semester."

"Oh."

"Careful!" Annamaria said, skipping out of the way. "It's steep."

They almost wiped out going down the far side of the rise between road and wetland. Rachel and Darlene both slipped, Rachel thudding down on her knees, Darlene landing flat on her ass. Jessie barely kept the can from hurtling down into Annamaria when Gwen lost her tenuous one-handed grip.

"Whee," Jessie said once she'd stabilized their load. "Everyone in one piece?"

"Barely," Darlene said.

"At least we're out of sight of the road now," Rachel said. "And the trail should be just up here."

"Why didn't we think to bring a flashlight?" asked Annamaria, eyeing the surrounding darkness. It was drippy, shadowy, and strange.

"Miner's headlamps," Jessie said. "Hands-free."

"Too suspicious." Rachel found the trail and guided them to it by the faint and distant yellowish illumination trickling in from streetlights along the sweeping curve of road.

Calling it a trail was exaggeration. It wasn't much more than a narrow walking-path winding between trees; mostly puddles oozing sticky mud, exposed and slick-glistening roots sticking up like disinterred bones, rocks, and fallen leaves decayed into squishy mulch.

The outside air had been humid enough already, what with the rain. In here, in the wetland-or-swamp, it was more than humid. It was moist, dank, fetid.

"Stinks," Darlene said.

"It's a green smell," said Gwen. "But not a good, clean green smell."

"Algae," said Rachel.

"Pond scum," said Jessie.

"I think those are the same," Annamaria said.

Frogs croaked somewhere off to their left. A bird voiced a weird hooting call. Unidentified things splashed and slithered.

"Are there alligators?" Gwen asked.

Jessie scoffed. "Where the fuck do you think we are, Florida?"

"I'm just saying…"

"No alligators," Rachel interrupted.

"Inbred hillbilly cannibal mutants?" asked Darlene.

"What I don't get," said Jessie, wrangling the yard-waste can over a particularly difficult cluster of roots, "is why anybody wants to preserve this place. Natural beauty, sure, that's just great for the glaciers, the old-growth forests, the mountains. But why a shithole swamp?"

Rachel began going on about the environment, ecosystems, habitats. Annamaria shot Jessie a you-asked-for-it look. Darlene complained that her foot was getting wet; she must have torn a hole in her protective covering when she fell. Jessie asked her if that was like when the condom ripped. Gwen huddled close to the others, gazing around as if not entirely reassured on the subject of alligators.

"What about snakes?" she asked.

"Oh, sure," Rachel said, and went from listing the varieties of birds found in wetlands like this to types of snakes, frogs, and other reptiles and amphibians. "There's fish, too. Tiny ones. I don't know what kind they are."

"Whoa," Jessie said. "Something that Rache doesn't know?"

"Big snakes?" Gwen's voice was high and thin, as if she'd been sucking on a helium balloon.

"Little snakes," Rachel said.

"Poisonous ones?"

"Probably not."

"Gwen," Annamaria said, "it's fine… snakes don't come out in the rain."

"Really?"

"Really. They're cold-blooded. They only come out when it's sunny."

Gwen's brows knit, but she didn't argue.

"Dunno how much further we can push this fucking thing, Rache," Jessie said. "Aren't we far enough? Be a good joke on us if we came right out the other side and all of a sudden there's a Wal-Mart."

"We haven't been going *that* long," Rachel said. "But yeah, this should be okay."

They'd gone well beyond any helpful trickle of light from the road, and now Rachel fumbled around inside her garbage-bag smock until she could dig into a pocket and bring out her keys. She had a squeeze penlight on her keychain. When she squeezed it, a fine blue-white beam lit a bright circle on the nearest tree trunk.

"You had a light all this time?" Annamaria asked, sounding less than happy.

"Couldn't have used it before now anyway." She shined it around.

"I almost think I liked it better dark," Gwen said, hugging herself.

They all looked at the dense, dripping, overhanging foliage. Pallid, whitish mushrooms rose in clusters from the mulchy earth. A snail the size of a walnut clung to the nearest rock, its slimy trail visible even on wet stone. The penlight's beam caught and glimmered on the raindrop-strewn strands of a spider web at least three feet across, and even Jessie gulped.

"This *better* be far enough," she said.

"Down there." Rachel trained the light beyond the so-called trail, where the ground dropped away to an expanse of murky water from which tall cattails and reeds grew. "We tape the sandbag anchor to him, and throw him in. He'll sink straight to the bottom."

"Let's do it," Annamaria said, taking the tape and sandbag from Gwen. "Get him out, I'll tape him up."

"Okay, here goes." Jessie nodded to Darlene and Rachel. "We lay it down on its side and then we can kind of pour him out, ready? You two get his arms and pull. Gwen and I'll pull the can off his legs. Then Anna tapes him, and we all five pick him up and give him the old heave-ho."

"Sounds good," Darlene said.

They tipped the can again, Jessie straining against it to make sure that it went over in a controlled fall. A good intention, but as Donnie's weight shifted again, smacking into the other side of the can's interior, she lost her grip. Tried to regain it. Only succeeded in slewing the can around. It crashed down on its rounded corner, rolled sideways, and overbalanced at the edge of the path.

"Shit!" Jessie cried. "Grab it!"

She caught hold of it again, but Gwen and Darlene had both instinctively leapt back. Rachel had as well, though she recovered fast and tried to help. Clumsy gloved hands. Clumsy feet in garbage bag boots. Rachel belly-flopped. Jessie's legs tangled in hers and she landed on Rachel's back.

"No!" Annamaria lunged, too late.

The can rocked-slid-tumbled. Down the slope it went, tearing through weeds, grinding over half-buried rocks, flattening reeds and cattails. The lid flapped like a stuttering mouth. One of Donnie Hubert's limp arms flailed out, bouncing along the ground.

Ker-splash, into the pond it went.

Tidal waves of ripples roiled the surface, lily pads riding the swells. A startled frog sprang away with an annoyed croak. A bird somewhere nearby took to the air in a sudden whirring of wings.

Mucky pond-water rushed in around Donnie. Large flatulent air bubbles blorped out. The can began to sink.

Still swearing, Jessie scrambled off Rachel and charged headlong after it. Darlene and Gwen yelled at her to stop. Rachel, who'd taken Jessie's knee in the back and had the wind knocked out of her, could only gasp. Annamaria flung down the sandbag and tape, following Jessie.

The pond undercut the land, making a kind of earthen shelf that had crumbled away where the can went over. Jessie realized that as soon as it started to give beneath her feet, and jumped before she could have the ground fall out from under her.

Not her best jump. Not a track-and-field long-jump. A crazy, arms-waving jump that made her look as if she'd been fired from a catapult. Her bag-wrapped feet hit the side of the can, indented it, and then skidded. Her butt hit next, indenting the can further. Her legs flew up. She did a backwards somersault off the half-submerged container and into the water. The garbage bags she wore billowed up in the same comical way that loose swim trunks did when air pockets got trapped in the fabric. They supported her like a child's inflatable water-wings.

Annamaria also jumped, aiming off to the right. She landed with a great geyser of muddy water, lower legs mired most of the way to the knee in slime and silt.

Jessie reared up, hacking and spitting. Her shower cap had come off. A stringy green weed lay over her shoulder. She floundered to her feet, fell over, floundered upright again.

"Oh, my God, are you okay?" Gwen asked from the relative dryness and safety of the trail, where she'd knelt to help Rachel into a sitting position.

Darlene had picked up the keychain, and aimed the penlight beam first at Jessie, then at Annamaria, then at the yard-waste can. Its bottom half protruded above the surface at an angle, another air pocket trapped, while the top was under.

Donnie's body had come halfway out, bobbing face-down, arms splayed and drifting, hair floating.

"We don't tell *anyone* about that," Jessie said, plucking the stringy weed and tossing it. "No one. Got it?"

"We aren't telling *anyone anything* about *any* of this," Annamaria said.

"Oh, yeah. Right." She rubbed her tailbone. "What a fucking blooper reel this turned out to be. *Now* what do we do?"

"The plan's unchanged," Rachel said, still a little breathless from having Jessie land on her. "Weigh him down. Darlene, give them the stuff."

"I'm not going in there," Darlene said. "What if there's leeches?"

"Thanks, Dar," Jessie said. "Thanks loads."

"*Are* there leeches?" Gwen asked Rachel, round-eyed.

"Just give them the stuff," she told Darlene, ignoring Gwen's question.

Annamaria and Jessie hauled Donnie the rest of the way from the can, finding it easier what with him and it both suspended in the pond. He spun there, a bizarre pale starfish. Jessie wrestled the can to the edge, where the others managed to drag it back to more-or-less dry land. Darlene extended the sandbag and tape to Annamaria, who waded over to Donnie.

"Hold him," she said to Jessie.

While Jessie supported the body, Annamaria placed the loose-heavy plastic sack on Donnie's chest, then circled it and his torso with several turns of strapping tape. He was face-up now, more of the stringy weeds on his face, his open eyes goggling vacantly at the rainy sky.

"What about the rest of the tape?" Jessie asked. "Do we have anything to cut it with? Because damned if I'm going to use my teeth, not in this shit-pit."

"Leave the roll," Rachel said. "We wouldn't have kept it anyway, and we all used gloves the whole time we were handling it. I even had gloves when I took it out of the package. No prints. Leave it."

"Here goes, then," Annamaria said.

They released him, wading backwards a pace or two, and all five watched with tense, silent expectation to see what would happen.

Slowly, but inexorably, he sank.

"Hey hey," said Jessie. "It's working!"

His arms and trailing hands with their pruney fingers vanished last. The water was deep enough, perhaps just barely but still deep enough, for them to go under. And as murky as it was, nearly an opaque green-brown even by brightest sunlight according to Rachel, there was little chance of him being seen.

"Is that good enough?" asked Annamaria.

"Kind of has to be," Rachel said. "Not ideal, but it'll have to do."

Annamaria nodded, waded to the edge, and clambered out. The garbage bags hung around her, water coursing down her legs. She was more bedraggled than a dog caught in a flood. And somehow, despite it all, still gorgeous.

"Great," Jessie said. "I'm dying for a shower and a beer. Not necessarily in that order. Maybe a beer in the shower."

"Jessie, your cap," Gwen said, pointing.

"Who gives a—"

"Get it," Rachel said. "We've made enough of a mess already. Don't leave a cap with your hair samples in it."

"Okay, okay, jeez." Jessie splashed across the pond and retrieved the cap, then mimicked Annamaria's example and clambered her way out.

Yard-waste can, check. Dented from where Jessie had bounced on it, filthy with mud and swamp-water, the wheels caked with mangled green plant-residue. But still, check. It was intact. They could pop out the dents in the rubberized plastic sides, they could hose it out until it was good as new.

Everything else they'd brought with them, check. Garbage bag smocks and leggings, gloves, shower caps. Rachel's keys and penlight. That was it, except for Donnie and the sandbag and the tape. All of which were now at the bottom of the pond.

They looked at each other. No one said anything.

Rain pattered and splashed. Frogs croaked. The bird gave its weird hooting cry again.

The trip home seemed hundreds of miles long. A trudging, plodding, miserable hundred miles to get back to the road. A bleak no-man's-land to cross the road. Another hundred or so miles to the house.

The going should have been easier, what with the yard-waste container empty. They didn't even have to roll it. Jessie could carry it all by herself, heaved onto her back like some native porter toting supplies through the deepest jungle.

Gwen led with Rachel's keychain-penlight, on full creepy-crawly alert for spiders, slugs, snails and anything else that might be lurking in the gloomy, dank shadows. Darlene complained the whole way about their trash-bag outfits.

"Can't we take off these damn things *yet?*" she asked in a peevish tone once they'd crossed the road. She reached for the shower cap, which had come askew so that straggles of her lank, brownish hair hung out on one side.

"Around back," Rachel said.

"I'm sweating to death!"

"We all are," Gwen said.

"Yeah but I'm sweating *more*."

"Pretend it's a sauna," Jessie said. "Some spas, they'd charge you eighty bucks to wrap you in plastic and steam off a few pounds."

"Yeah?" Darlene turned to scowl at her. "How much would they charge you for that mud-bath and slime facial *you* got?"

They reached the back yard, and under Rachel's direction,

stripped out of their garbage bag smocks and leggings, their shower caps, their gloves. Rachel collected every article, rolling them as tight as she could, mashing the plastic together, twisting it, forming it into a single compact log about the size of a weightlifter's arm.

Jessie threw herself on her back in the grass, well away from the trampled patch where Donnie's body had lain. "Check it out, I'm making a rain-angel."

Gwen and Annamaria didn't check it out. They just stood, heads tipped back, faces upturned, eyes shut, letting the droplets rinse them.

Darlene looked at the bag that held Donnie's clothes. Beside it were the saucepan, Jessie's lucky creep-whacker bowling pin, the coffee cup Gwen had chucked at Donnie's head, and the end of the hose. She picked up the hose and twisted the nozzle, biting back a bleat as the icy water cascaded over her.

"What are you doing?" Gwen asked, startled.

"Getting it over with," Darlene said. "No way there'll be enough in the water heater for us all to get a shower, and you beauty queens always make me wait until last."

"Don't be like that, Dar," Jessie said from the lawn.

"It *is* like that."

"The water heater *is* a piece of junk," Annamaria said. "But that's no—"

"We'll all use the hose," Rachel said. "Otherwise, we'll track muck into the house. First, though, somebody grab the barbecue."

"We having a weenie-roast?" Jessie sat up, eyebrow arched.

"We should burn this." She held up the log of compacted plastic.

"News flash, Rache, that's not gonna burn. That's gonna melt and shrivel and stink like crazy."

"So we melt and shrivel it," she said. "We have to get rid of it."

"Why didn't we sink it in the damn swamp, then?" grumbled Darlene.

"We have to burn his clothes, too," Rachel said.

"I'll get the barbecue," Annamaria said. "There's still half a bag of briquettes in the garage, and the lighter fluid and matches."

"I'll get those," Gwen said.

"Okay." Jessie flopped back down in her rain-angel position.

"Hose me, Dar. Lemme have it."

A grin that was close to cruel scrawled its way across Darlene's lips. She aimed the hose at Jessie, squeezed the nozzle, and blasted her with a hard jet of cold water.

"Mother *fuck*!" Jessie yelped, but she submitted to the pressure-wash, turning over and standing up and revolving in a full rotation with her arms out. "Okay, okay, that's good… give me the hose… payback time!"

Annamaria fetched the barbecue grill from beneath the porch overhang. It was a cheap, squat little thing with three short legs and a wide brazier painted a chipped and peeling Coleman-stove-green. She set it up on the breezeway while Jessie hosed down Darlene, then endured her turn under the icy spray.

Gwen brought the half-bag of charcoal briquettes, the lighter fluid, an old newspaper for kindling, and a box of wooden matches. The roof over the breezeway leaked, but she and Rachel were able to find a good spot and get a pyramid of coals burning, thanks to Jessie's experienced-camper advice.

"What if someone sees the fire?" Gwen asked.

"We'll tell them we were having a weenie roast, toasting marshmallows," Jessie said, poking the coals with a stick.

"Should I go in and get the marshmallows, just in case?"

"Oh for fuck's sake, Guinevere! You want to toast marshmallows over the fire that we're burning a dead guy's clothes on?"

"Jessie, leave her alone," Annamaria said. "Gwen, it's late, and we're between the house and the garage. No one will see from the road."

Rachel and Gwen got doused with the hose next. By then, all five of them were shivering, teeth chattering, lips turning blue. They huddled around the little barbecue.

"Uh…" Darlene said. "His clothes are wet. They're not gonna burn."

"They're not *that* wet." Rachel, the only one of them still wearing latex gloves, reached into the bag and pulled out Donnie's shirt. "Not, you know, soaked."

"Should we wait until they're dry?" Annamaria asked. "Or put them in the dryer? It wouldn't take long. Twenty minutes or so."

"Dunno about the rest of you," Jessie said, "but I just want this over with. Chuck 'em on the fire already. If they burn, great. If not, we'll think of something else."

The shirt hissed and steamed when put on the fire. For a while it looked like Darlene's prediction was going to be right, but then the cloth began to smolder. Then catch, and burn.

"Some pieces won't, though," Rachel said. "Anything metal, for instance. Zippers and stuff. This fire can't get that hot, not hot enough to melt metal. We'll have to bury the ashes."

"Murder's a lot of damn work," Jessie said, and they all gave her scolding looks. "What? It is!"

The jeans took even longer. The canvas sneakers went next, rubber soles bubbling and running, laces sizzling bright like fuses. His socks smelled bad even before Rachel dropped them in the fire.

Then the Polaroids, images distorting into grotesque blisters before flaring, curling, charring and vanishing.

"The camera won't burn," Annamaria said.

"We'll throw it in a Dumpster with his backpack and the other clothes you got from his apartment," Rachel said. "Now the underwear."

"You really are burning them?" Darlene asked.

"Who'd want to *keep* them?" Gwen twitched. "After… after *he* had them… after he did God-knows-what…"

"Well you could run them through the wash."

"I don't care. I'd never want to wear them again!"

"Yeah," Jessie said.

"Burn them all." Annamaria took the bundle from Rachel and flung it into the flames. Wispy nylon, cotton, silk and lace ignited like so much tissue paper.

Gwen grabbed the can of lighter fluid and gave it an extra squirt, and the pile of undergarments flared into a miniature inferno. The enormous bra was soon reduced to ashes and two lengths of curved wire that glowed dull amid the embers.

Last but not least, Rachel tossed in the arm-sized log of rolled-up and compacted trash bags, rubber gloves, shower caps and strapping tape. As Jessie had said, the materials didn't want to burn. They melted and shriveled. They blistered like the Polaroids had done, and bubbled like the soles of Donnie Hubert's sneakers.

And they stank, all right. The smoke that arose was the same blackish-brown as the bags themselves, molten plastic, unnatural, sickening. Cold though they were, it was enough to drive them away from the heat of the flames.

"Okay," Rachel finally said. "That's probably as good as we're going to get. We're done. We did it."

Then, with no warning whatsoever, Annamaria burst into tears.

CHAPTER FOUR

Rachel woke early Monday, before the others. Sleep hadn't been anyone's friend that night, and she'd lain awake until nearly 2:00 AM with her mind racing, racing, racing.

Once daylight turned the sky a thin, watery greyish-pink, she went out to scoop up the ashes. They were cool, and damp from the rain, making a sort of gritty, grey-black paste. She buried them under an evergreen bush in one of the flowerbeds.

Darlene, Gwen and Jessie wanted to stay around the house, but Rachel reminded them that doing anything that varied from their normal routine was a bad idea.

"You honestly expect," Gwen said as they were dashing around scarfing breakfast and getting their books together, "that we'll be able to spend the day at lectures and labs like ordinary?"

"We have to," Rachel said. "We all have to."

"What if we're not feeling well?" challenged Darlene.

"Yeah, puking our guts out," Jessie said. She chopsticked a huge wad of cold leftover pork lo mein directly from its takeout container, then smirked at Darlene with noodles and thin shreds of cabbage dangling from the corner of her mouth.

Darlene had taken three bites of bagel and one swig of a chocolate-flavored diet drink for breakfast, and then barfed it all right back up into the sink. She tried to give Jessie a withering look and failed utterly. "Har, har."

"Guys, look." Rachel tucked an energy bar into the side pocket of her backpack and popped the top on her second Mountain Dew of the day. "This is important. Now more than ever, we have to act like everything's normal. We can't make it look suspicious."

"But…" Gwen stirred her cereal. The milk had turned a pastel purple, the multicolored cereal bits bloated into soft mush. "But we—"

"We *have* to," Rachel repeated. "We have to be smart about this, you guys, right? If we're not smart, they'll figure it out. We can't give them *anything*."

"We understand, Rachel," said Annamaria, still in her nightgown with her hair uncombed, because she didn't have anything Mondays until the afternoon. Anybody else would have looked like a witch. She looked like a movie star. "We know. It'll be business as usual. Life like normal."

Her tears had shocked the hell out of the others.

None of them had seen Annamaria cry before.

Not once. Not ever.

Rachel had known her longest, for almost three years now. Three years that had included Annamaria receiving news of the deaths of two grandparents, and getting e-dumped by her hometown boyfriend. Even then, Rachel had never seen her cry.

Which was just as well, as far as Rachel was concerned. Being book-smart was one thing. A high IQ and a good memory did wonders when it came to the old G.P.A., had been a godsend for landing the sitting-pretty scholarships, but it meant squat when dealing with the personal, emotional stuff. She'd never been good at consoling people, never knew what to say, felt awkward and stupid whenever *anybody* cried.

That was one reason why she liked living with Annamaria. Annamaria glided through life like a shadow, dark and cool and aloof, passing over things without seeming to come into actual contact with any of them. She was above it all, removed from it all.

So, her tears had shocked Rachel the most.

The outburst had been brief but intense. A summer squall, blowing in out of nowhere, letting loose like doomsday, and then dissipating. By the time any of them, even sensitive and compassionate Gwen, could muster herself to move, Annamaria was back to her regular self.

Now she smiled around at the rest of them as she repeated her words. "Business as usual. Life like normal."

"I threw the camera away in one Dumpster," Jessie reported later that evening, feeling pleased and proud of herself. Mission-fucking-accomplished. "The one behind the hardware store. The backpack with some of his clothes and crap in it, I threw in another, a few blocks away."

"The wallet?" Rachel asked.

"Trash can in front of the Shop-N-Go."

"You wore gloves?"

Jessie waggled her fingers at Rachel. "Sure did."

"The saucepan and mug?"

"Donation box at the Goodwill."

"That was my favorite mug," Gwen said from the computer desk, where she'd been staring at the screen for over an hour.

"Yeah, but you were never going to drink out of it again," Darlene told her.

"That's for sure."

Rachel rapped her knuckles on the coffee table to get their attention. "The bowling pin?"

"Rinsed off and rolled in the mud like you wanted. Left it on the porch. Looks same as it ever did."

But it wasn't the same, was it?

God, the way it had felt in her hand... righteous and powerful. The way those first prehistoric apes must have felt when they figured out how to pick up a club and beat the shit out of each other.

Who's biggest? Who's baddest? Who's strongest? Who's toughest?

Survival of the fittest, that's what it was all about.

"Is the yard all right?" Annamaria asked, coming in dressed for her shift, hair smoothed back and held by a clip.

Rachel nodded. "The rain and the hose took care of it."

"*And* we hosed out the yard-waste container," Darlene said. "That's everything, right?"

"Everything we *can* do." Rachel shrugged, looking

dissatisfied. "The rest of it's beyond our control. Now, we have to wait and see."

So they'd waited.

Gone to class, gone to work, gone on dates.

Business as usual. Life like normal.

No Donnie Hubert in the apartment above the garage. No Donnie Hubert peeking in their windows.

They waited.

Nothing happened.

Tuesday was trash day, but with no Donnie around to haul the cans and recycling bins down to the edge of the road, it didn't get done.

"Oops," Rachel said when the big trucks rumbled by. "Forgot about that."

On Wednesday and Thursday, still, nothing happened.

Jessie was almost disappointed.

She went out with Etch and the guys for burgers and beer Thursday night and the whole macho bullshit bunch of them were bragging about kicking a rival frat house's collective ass in a football game.

Ooh, scary, she thought, and it took actual effort not to roll her eyes.

On Friday, which was the first of the month, Mrs. Hubert stopped by to collect the rent. Rumor had it that she went straight from the house to the bank, and straight from the bank to the Sky Eagle Casino. All-you-can-eat buffet, unlimited drinks, slots and blackjack until midnight or she was broke, whichever came first.

After she slipped the envelope–all cash, mostly small unmarked and non-sequential bills; Annamaria often said it was like they were paying ransom rather than rent–into her chunky imitation-leather purse, she asked if any of them had seen that no-good worthless piece of shit Donnie around.

"Not for a few days," Rachel said. Cautiously.

"Yeah, since last weekend, I guess," Jessie added. "Why?"

"I told him I wanted him to fix that damn mailbox," Lorna Hubert said, irritation creasing her forehead. She was a large woman, horse-faced and coarse-haired. "Seen the way that post leans? One of these times, mailman's going to clip it with his truck and knock it right over."

Rachel reiterated that they hadn't seen Donnie in a few days. Jessie mentioned that he hadn't taken care of the trash on Tuesday morning, either. Not exactly lies.

Both watched in breathless trepidation when, heaving a disgruntled sigh, Mrs. Hubert went outside and crossed the breezeway.

She didn't even glance at the crime-scene patch of ground. Walked right past the murder-weapon bowling pin. The yard-waste container didn't call out to her, draw her like some cursed, mysterious item in a Poe story.

"Think that really was *her* bra?" Jessie murmured to Rachel.

"Well… it'd be the right size…"

"Yeah, but still. That is not the kind of person who should be wearing sexy black bras."

Mrs. Hubert, puffing with exertion, lumbered up the exterior steps to the above-garage apartment. As she climbed, her ass looked like midget sumo-wrestlers squaring off inside a lime-colored polyester laundry bag. Her top was a tentlike, garish, floral-patterned thing. Her ankles were veined columns of fat that overflowed her shoes.

"Maybe she used to like to dress nice for her husband?" Rachel suggested.

"Didn't help. He still bailed on her, didn't he?"

At the top of the steps, Mrs. Hubert hammered on the door. "Donnie! Hey! Donnie! You better not be passed out drunk or stoned in there, you little son of a bitch!"

There was, of course, no answer.

She knocked again. Shouted again.

Dug into her purse.

Jessie looked at Rachel.

Rachel shrugged. "Here goes."

"Last warning, Donnie!" Mrs. Hubert jangled a keyring that had more souvenir casino key fobs on it than actual keys. "I'm opening the door now!"

There was, of course, still no answer.

She unlocked, opened, went in.

Silence.

A minute passed.

Two minutes.

Five.

Mrs. Hubert came back out. She shut the door behind her–*slammed* the door behind her–and waddled down the steps again.

"He's not home?" Jessie called.

"What," said Mrs. Hubert with scathing scorn, "was your first clue?"

"Hey, I—" Jessie began, bristling.

Rachel elbowed Jessie and gave her a significant look.

"I mean… I guess he must not be," Jessie finished.

"What?" asked Darlene from behind them, fresh from work in the campus clinic medical records office and grumpier than ever.

"Mrs. H. is here," Jessie said. "To pick up the rent."

"She's wondering if any of us have seen Donnie," Rachel said.

"Oh." Darlene dropped her bookbag on the couch.

"Well?" Mrs. Hubert asked as she came back into the house. "Have you?"

Darlene shook her head. "Not since last week. Why?"

"He was supposed to fix the damn mailbox, he should have mowed the damn lawn, and he hasn't tried to bum money off me in days. Figured the little shit was up there drunk, stoned, or dead."

Jessie saw Darlene flinch, and was too busy trying to keep her own poker face to do anything about it. Luckily, Rachel was on the ball and she stood up, the motion drawing Mrs. H.'s attention away from them.

"If we see him," Rachel said, "should we tell him to call you?"

"Gosh," Mrs. Hubert said, voice dripping sarcasm. "Would you? Would you really? That would be *very* nice of you."

"Sure, no problem." Rachel smiled. It was her best I'm-little-cute-and-harmless smile, which only worked because she was so little and so cute.

"He… um…" Darlene stammered. "He said… um…"

"Donnie? What? What did he say?"

"He said something about getting out of here," Darlene managed in a rush.

"Getting out of here," Mrs. Hubert said, marveling over the concept. "He took off? Is that what you're telling me?"

"Yeah... he said he was sick of this place, he was gonna go to Mexico or something. I wasn't really listening. I didn't think he meant it." Darlene looked as if she might throw up again, but Mrs. Hubert didn't notice.

"Mexico." She nodded, which did unpleasant things to her extra chins. "Doesn't that just figure? Doesn't that just goddamn figure? Him and that uncle of his, no-good deadbeats, running off to Mexico."

Rachel, Jessie and Darlene all stayed quiet. It seemed safest.

"Mexico," she said again. She bared her teeth, which were almost as bad as Donnie's. "Probably he'll catch the clap from some dollar whore, rot his brain on cheap tequila, get Montezuma's Revenge and shit himself to death in some Tijuana jail cell."

"Uh..." Jessie said, and threw a glance at Rachel.

"Gosh, that'd be too bad," Rachel said.

"Too bad?" Mrs. Hubert barked a laugh. "Serve him right, I say!"

And with that, she was off to the casino.

Saturday was sunny and mild.

Annamaria had taken an extra shift so one of her fellow waitresses could attend a birthday party. Jessie had a track meet, and plans to get together with Etch later. Rachel was at the campus library. Darlene was online, engrossed in a flame war when she was supposed to be working on a paper.

Gwen, who was also supposed to be working on a paper– the same one she'd been trying, and failing, to finish all week– went to the movies instead. The Orion had the recent film version of *Lord of the Flies*, starring Cameron Mack. Weekend matinee prices, two bucks.

The discount theater was old, and small, and musty. It had been an actual theater back in the forties and fifties, with a wooden stage, and an orchestra pit in front of the screen. The seats were upholstered in worn royal-blue faux velvet, and the walls were done in ornate molding that had once been painted gold but was now flaked and faded. There was an actual curtain that drew aside–grinding and rattling like a transmission about to die–when the lights dimmed. Everything smelled like overheated projectors, ancient popcorn, and dust.

She loved it. Far preferred it to the state-of-the-art multiplex at the mall, or the IMAX downtown. It seemed so much more personal, intimate, and real.

Plus, it was lots less expensive.

That was important to a girl who was getting by on grants, loans, and a pittance of a college fund left to her by her grandparents. Textbooks used, clothes from thrift shops, food and essentials at the grocery outlet, and her leisure reading came from Phoenix Pages, the biggest and best second-hand bookstore in the county.

And movies at the Orion. Two bucks to watch Cameron Mack in a loincloth on the big screen?

She couldn't pass that up.

Which wasn't to say she was here just to ogle his nearly-naked, tanned, toned body. She wasn't like those people who flew to New York or even London to gawk at Daniel Radcliffe in the buff in *Equus*.

Yes, Cameron Mack was handsome. It wasn't *only* that, though. It was that he was Cameron Michael Mack! Caring and thoughtful and sensitive. A special person, and Gwen had felt a special connection to him from the beginning. Even from way back when he'd been Little Mikey Mack, on TV shows and commercials.

Lord of the Flies had been his way of proving to the world that he was a real actor. Not just an adorable child star. Not just a wholesome teen heartthrob. A real actor. It had been daring, and bold.

She paid her two bucks, got a drink and a box of generic, candy-coated chocolate morsels for a dollar more, and sat in the musty, flickering darkness for the next couple of hours, gazing deep into Cameron Mack's soulful, expressive, beautiful blue eyes.

The only thing marring the experience was the homeless

man in the row behind her and a couple seats over. His breath whistled in and out of his nose. The smell of alcohol wafted around him like a miasma.

Gwen had seen him around the neighborhood before, one of the cardboard-sign-brigade who gravitated between the shelter and the liquor store.

He was tall, maybe thirtyish, skinny in a wiry-ropy-strong way. Coal-black rat's nests of hair and beard. Layers of ragged clothes, though not filthy.

His nose whistled, whistled.

Occasionally, she'd see him with a dog: a cheerful brown-and-white mutt with floppy ears, and a tail that never stopped wagging. It was the dog, she supposed, that mostly won over the charity of passersby.

On the screen, Cameron Mack grinned a glorious, savage grin as he streaked on warpaint and picked up a sharpened spear. "We'll hunt it," he said to the younger boys, all of whom regarded him with mingled awe and alarm. "We'll hunt it, and we will *kill* it!"

Behind her, the homeless man blew his nose. Then she heard a soft scraping and realized he had blown his nose into his hand, then wiped his hand on the seatback in front of him.

It made her very glad that she'd plaited her hair into a braid that morning, and the braid was lying over her shoulder and down into her lap.

Should she get up and move?

The audience was sparse. There were plenty of other seats.

But if she moved, the homeless man might think she'd moved because of him.

But if she moved, it *would* be because of him.

He'd be offended. His feelings would be hurt.

Though she'd lost her appetite for them, she stayed where she was, eating more of the candies and sipping at her drink. She tried to immerse herself in the movie again.

Cameron Mack on the hunt, lithe as a panther, lean muscles flexing as he prowled through the jungle. His blond hair glinting gold when rays of sunlight touched it. Sweat gleaming on his smooth, sculpted chest.

The homeless man inhaled with a mucusy, sinusy gurgle. *Huuaachhh.* Then spit. *Ptoo*! *Splat* on the floor. A movie theater floor. Already disgusting and gross. Already sticky with spilled soda and stepped-on candy. Already disgusting and gross.

Suppressing a shudder, she focused on Cameron Mack's dreamy azure eyes and did her best to ignore the icky creep behind her... but not ignore him *so* much that she wouldn't be aware of whatever else he might do... *without* letting on how nervous he made her...

It wasn't fair, it just wasn't fair, always having to be like this!

Darlene had the house to herself most of Saturday, and that was the way she liked it best.

None of the others around. Nobody making remarks when she went in the kitchen, or exchanging those smug-pitying looks that they thought she didn't see.

Life really wasn't fair.

Take the Autumn Epidemic, for instance.

Every year, it was the same thing. Classes started, the dorms filled, and all the students and faculty brought back whatever germs they'd picked up over the summer. The whole campus turned into one giant melting pot of colds, flu, strep throat, mono, the plague, whatever.

When most people got sick, they looked like crap. Reasonable enough.

Most people weren't Annamaria Voltaire.

At least when Gwen and Rachel came down with something, they had the decency to show it. Gwen, especially. She'd go all pale and haggard, nothing but skin and bones and hollow eyes, her hair like brittle straw.

Jessie was another matter because Jessie, the health-obsessed bitch, would start pounding the vitamin C and Echinacea and whatever-the-fuck-else at the first signs of a sore throat or stuffy nose. Then she'd strut around boasting about how she never got sick.

Annamaria, though...

Annamaria could sound like she should be hacking up blood and lung tissue any minute, but between coughing spasms, she'd recline all languid and sultry like Cleopatra on a barge. When she puked, it was almost glamorous.

She could make the damn Black Death look good.

It just wasn't fair.

On her worst day, her absolute *worst*, Annamaria looked a hundred times better than Darlene would ever would.

The most aggravating part? She acted like she didn't even know it.

Like she honestly had no idea how gorgeous she was.

The others were almost as bad. Rachel, perky-blonde and cute but dismissing it, as if looks didn't count as much as intelligence, wanting to be appreciated for her brains. Gwen, always so trying-to-sympathize by telling Darlene her own ugly duckling "oh I was so bony and skinny in high school and everybody made fun of me!" sob stories. Or Jessie, with her bullshit lectures about fitness and attitude.

As if any of that helped.

Easy for them to say. Easy for them to go on about how attractiveness didn't matter. Always real easy for the ones who *were* attractive. They didn't know. They could *have* dates if they wanted.

Dates… boyfriends… sex.

She thought about Jessie, who'd told them how she'd be meeting up with Etch later. That meant they'd do it. That always meant they'd do it.

Would they come back to the house this time?

Maybe.

There was the frat house, but on a Saturday night it'd be packed. Party night. Noisy. Rowdy. Keggers. Chug-a-lug and beer through a funnel. Frat boys and bimbos.

Or so she assumed, from what she'd seen in movies and on TV. It wasn't like she knew from personal experience.

So Jessie and Etch would probably come back here. A bed was better than the back seat of a car, or up against the wall outside a pool hall.

Again, so she assumed from movies and television.

They didn't always come back to the house. Etch hardly ever spent the night.

Too bad.

It was part of the agreement. If one of them wanted to have a regular overnighter or a live-in boyfriend, taking up space, using hot water and electricity, infringing on everyone else, then that person would have to kick in some extra money to cover the expenses and inconvenience.

Once in a while, though…

Like that one time… the time the doors hadn't been closed all the way, and she'd been able to see right into Jessie's room…

Her face felt hot, flushed.

She pushed away from the computer–the internet was full of losers, perverts and idiots anyway–and got a tub of ice cream from the freezer. Her name was on the label pasted to the lid.

That one time… whew.

Jessie must not have known anybody was home. It had been a middle-of-the-day thing, on a day when the rest of them should have been in their respective classes. Darlene's afternoon chemistry lab was canceled because some clown had set off a smoke bomb in the building, so she'd come home to take a nap.

Their voices woke her. Voices from the next room: laughing, suggestive. Groggy though she was, Darlene had known right away what she was hearing.

She'd also seen that the bathroom door was ajar.

So she'd tiptoed over and taken a look.

And gotten an eyeful, yes indeed.

Etch, naked and erect, in all his glory.

Then he'd moved out of her sight, and she'd only been able to hear the rest. But there was no mistaking *that*, either. Bedsprings creaking, the headboard whacking the wall, flesh against flesh. Etch saying, "Yeah… oh, yeah… yeah, that's good, you like that? Yeah!" and Jessie telling him to shut up and fuck her, fuck her harder.

Darlene remembered how tempted she'd been to creep into the bathroom and try to see the action. Her face flushed even hotter and she spooned as fast as she could, shoveling cold mint-chip into her mouth.

"Agh!" she said, pressing the heel of her hand to her forehead. "Agh, ow, shit!"

CHRISTINE MORGAN

Ice cream headache.

All because she'd wolfed it down too fast as some kind of half-assed attempt to quench one hunger with another.

If she couldn't get laid, she should at least be able to have a damn snack without feeling like a frozen spike had been driven into her brain.

That was no fair either.

And as if an ice cream headache wasn't punishment enough, all of a sudden she had to bolt for the bathroom to puke up a torrent of milky pale-green flecked with dark chocolate.

On Jessie's Sunday to do dinner, she hauled out the barbecue.

Annamaria thought that this was, all things considered, kind of tacky.

True, the weather had improved. No rain, nice warm sunlight slanting into the backyard, pleasant enough to wear shorts and sandals.

Still, kind of tacky.

Just a little.

Maybe a little more when Jessie broke out the foodstuffs. Packages of hot dogs and buns. A bag of marshmallows. She set them on the swaybacked old picnic table beyond the breezeway.

"You aren't serious," Gwen said. "Are you?"

"Weenie roast and marshmallow toast!" crowed Jessie. "And beer. Lots of beer. Somebody grab the cooler out of my car."

As the coals did their thing, she bounded back and forth to the kitchen, bringing assorted flavors of potato chips, relish, chopped onions, mayo-mustard-ketchup. Rachel and Darlene lugged the cooler, full of crushed ice and longneck bottles. Annamaria fetched paper plates, napkins, a box of plastic flatware.

"So… we're having a party," Darlene said.

"Dontcha think we could use one? I know I could." Jessie bounded up the steps and into the kitchen again.

"Are we going to… uh… talk about stuff?" Gwen ventured.

"Do we need to?" asked Rachel.

Jessie returned balancing a bowl of microwaved chili, a dish

80

of grated cheese, a deli container of macaroni salad, and serving spoons. "About last week, you mean?"

"*Don't* we need to?" Gwen's worried greyish-green gaze went from one of them to another, settling on Annamaria. "It's been all week."

"Yeah, and Rachel was right," Darlene said, helping herself to a beer.

"Fuck yeah, Rachel was right!" Jessie got a beer as well, and clinked bottlenecks with Darlene before taking a long swig. "We rock, we roll, we rule!"

"*Veni, vidi, vici,* that isn't," Annamaria said, and Rachel laughed.

"Same thing," said Jessie, hitching a shoulder in a half-shrug.

"But we—" Gwen stopped, glanced furtively around the yard, and dropped her voice to a whisper. "You know! Doesn't that... doesn't that *bother* you?"

Rachel quit laughing. "It was really wrong," she said.

Gwen sagged with relief. "Oh, good."

"We made a total mess," Rachel went on. "I mean, a total, *total* mess, right? It was clumsy, it was sloppy, it was spur-of-the-moment, not planned at all, complete improv. Botch City. Appalling. Horrible."

Darlene sulked. "It was your idea in the first place."

"Not like *that* it wasn't!" Rachel flung her hands in the air. "Haven't any of you been listening to anything I've said? This wasn't what I meant at *all!* This was an embarrassment!"

"You said you bet we could get away with murder," Jessie said. She slapped hot dogs onto the grill, where they hissed and sizzled.

"I said I bet we could get away with being serial killers," Rachel said. She said it again, over-enunciating each syllable. "Seer-eee-aahl kihl-lerrs. Remember? There's a difference."

"Okay, okay, jeez, don't get your panties in a bunch."

"If you even have any left, after Donnie swiped them all," Darlene said.

"I can't believe you're all treating this so cavalierly," Gwen said.

"I can't believe you use words like that," Jessie said. "Cavalierly. Jeez."

"No, Gwen's got a point," Rachel said. "The same one I've been trying to get across to you people. This is serious stuff here, okay? Life-and-death kind of serious stuff."

"We get it already, Rache. Anna, pass me those tongs? I don't want to burn anybody's weenie."

Annamaria handed them to her, then went to the cooler and got a beer, and settled herself into a comfortable position on the lawn. It was long and lush, sun-warmed and tickling where it brushed against the bare skin of her legs.

They weren't far from... from the spot. *That* spot.

It looked like any ordinary patch of lawn now. The grass hadn't withered and died, or grown back white in the shape of a chalk outline. Nothing of the sort. No blight. No cursed earth. It was a place of killing ground, but no one could tell by looking at it.

Just as no one could tell by looking at the five of them.

When the hot dogs were done, they loaded up their plates. Gwen and Darlene sat at the picnic table, while Rachel took a chance on the folding chair that sometimes snapped shut without warning. Jessie sat cross-legged in the grass near Annamaria, plate balanced on one knee, beer leaning against her thigh.

"So..." Darlene said, then hesitated.

"Yeah?" asked Jessie. Eagerly. As if she'd been waiting for this moment.

Which, Annamaria supposed, she had. They all had.

"Never mind."

"No, what?" asked Rachel. Leaning forward in the chair, expression intent.

"Nothing."

"You might as well," said Gwen. Not raising her head, crumbling potato chips to fragments between her fingers.

"I was just gonna ask... oh, hell. Forget it."

Annamaria set down her hot dog. "It's okay, Darlene... go ahead."

"Nah. Forget it." Darlene plunged her plastic fork into a mound of macaroni salad and took a big bite.

No one said anything for a few minutes.

Gwen moved from crumbling chips to pinching off bits of bun and rolling them between forefinger and thumb, then dropping the tiny bread-balls onto her plate. Rachel ate her chili-cheese-onion-dog with fork and knife, somehow making it look neat enough to please Miss Manners.

Elephant in the room.

The huge-but-unspoken.

It reminded Annamaria of when she was a little girl. When the silence was so loud it might as well have been a steady roar. Loud, heavy, thick, and tangible. A pressure that surrounded and crushed.

Her family had been like that for a long time. Existing like submariners, inside a fragile hull that only needed the smallest breach to cause a devastating collapse. Like mountaineers making their precarious way along a ledge, while tons of snow hung poised above them, ready to thunder down in avalanching white death at the slightest vibration.

One wrong move could be the trigger that would set things off. A slip of the tongue, an accidental mention of Serafina's name, and there would be howling grief, miserable rage, another piteous alcoholic plunge, another retreat into obsessive prayer.

Sometimes, though, someone had to speak. Someone had to step up, be strong, stand firm and face facts. To name, address and confront that elephant in the room.

It was too big not to say.

But Annamaria couldn't do it.

She could form the words in her mind. She could imagine how they would sound, uttered aloud in her voice.

Eight little words.

She just couldn't get her mouth to say them.

One of the others would have to.

They all knew it. She could see it in their eyes.

Then, finally, Jessie spoke up.

"When are we going to do it again?"

CHAPTER FIVE

It was never the same bar.

It was *always* the same bar. Even when it was never the same bar, it was always the same bar.

Gordon Kerr's whole life was a series of airports, airplanes, rental cars, hotel rooms, convention centers, restaurants, and bars.

Just like this one.

He had thought—long ago when much younger, more foolish and idealistic—that being a motivational speaker would make for an exciting, lucrative, rewarding career.

He'd been right on the 'lucrative' part.

The rest?

Not so much.

Oh, he made money. He made *good* money. Generous salary, generous bennies, generous expense account. Nothing to complain about as far as that aspect went.

Exciting, though? And rewarding? The routine might be shaken up every now and then by a cocktail party or some inane team-building wilderness excursion. He wasn't often assigned those gigs, which usually went to the younger go-getter types who could actually survive a hike in the mountains or descend through the forest on a zipline without wetting their pants. Past forty and paunchy didn't qualify Gordon as much of a younger go-getter.

And so, he got the seminars. Thinking Outside the Box.

Managing Conflicts in the Workplace. Changes in Today's Corporate Society. Addressing Harassment and Discrimination. Effective Interpersonal Strategies.

All around the country.

He was a pro when it came to travel, used to living out of suitcases and hotel rooms. He subsisted primarily on airline snacks, minibars, room service, and complimentary continental breakfasts.

And happy hour appetizers, served at places like this. The restaurant bar section was small without being claustrophobic, subdued without being gloomy, intimate without being crowded, solitary without being desolate. No dance floor, no stage for a live band, no gigantic TV broadcasting baseball or auto racing. Dark wood, dark leather, dark fabric, dark carpet, dark paint. Glass bottles on glass shelves in front of a glass mirror, cut glass votive candleholders on etched glass tabletops.

Gordon slid into a booth. There was a menu placard in a dark wire stand, and he inspected it, though he already knew what he'd find: wings, nachos, potato skins, onion rings, mozzarella sticks.

Always, always, always the same.

A waitress came over to take his order. That was when things stopped being entirely the same.

She was a stunner: brunette, beautiful, with a smile—even a perfunctory, polite waitress-smile—to knock the socks off.

His secret weakness was sultry, smoldering brunettes. The Monica Belluccis of the world, the Mila Kunises, the Salma Hayeks left him instantly weak in the knees and fluttery in the stomach, not to mention effects between those two locales.

Martini, extra olive. Stuffed potato skins, heavy on the sour cream and chives.

Half his age, of course. Way out of his league, of course. He had the wife, the kids, the house, all the luxuries he worked so hard to pay for but was rarely home to enjoy.

Still, a man could look. Married, not dead, as the saying went.

His wife was a Minnesota blonde who'd been Miss Camembert one year at the county cheese fair, but had packed on thirty pounds per kid since. If she knew what went through his mind on some of these trips... It wasn't always a waitress; it might be a businesswoman he met at one of his seminars, or a flight attendant, or a complete stranger he passed in the hotel lobby, but...

But, nothing. All that was only his mind. Temptation might be one thing; acting on it was another. He didn't want to become some joke or caricature, Midlife Crisis Man, lusting after young women. What next? Hair implants and buying a speedboat? The waitress

brought him his drink, promised him his food would be along in a minute, and headed for another table. He watched her as she went.

Nice legs. The skirt wasn't short enough to be trashy, but it wasn't long enough to be prudish either. Heels, high enough to be alluring, low enough to be a sensible choice for someone on her feet all day.

Maybe if he talked with her, made eye contact...

Who was he kidding?

The fantasy was there, but so was cold reality.

She came back with the plate of potato skins, arranged around a dish of sour cream sprinkled with chopped green chives. He caught a flash of cleavage as she set the plate down, as well as a glimpse of what might have been the lacy trim of her bra.

He thanked her, and she smiled again, and she left again.

That second smile had seemed more genuine. Bordering on warm.

Maybe he *could*...

Gordon downed half his martini at a gulp. *Dream on, Gord,* he told himself. *Dream on.*

The waiting was the worst part.

Weeks of waiting. Waiting and doing nothing.

Waiting to see if some environmentalist, bird-watcher or botanical class nature walk would make a nasty discovery in the wetland. Waiting to find out if some neighbor had seen five girls wearing garbage bag smocks and shower caps, trundling a yard-waste container back and forth.

Waiting through the calls and drop-by visits from Mrs. Hubert. She wasn't so much worried about Donnie's absence as she was annoyed by his refusal to turn up.

"The ungrateful bastard," she told Annamaria. "I give him a job and a roof over his head even though he's not even any relation of mine, just the nephew of that worthless piece of shit I married. And this is the thanks I get."

"Did you talk to the police?" Annamaria asked. "Or the hospitals?"

"What's the use? I filed one of those missing-persons things, but they said there's nothing much they can do. It isn't like he's a kid that ran away from home. Donnie's an adult. Legally, anyway. No law against him up and taking off if he wants." The police did eventually drop by the house, but the overall impression they gave was one of low priority, disinterest, and going through the motions. They took a cursory glance into Donnie's apartment, asked a couple routine questions–When had anybody last seen him? Was it true he'd mentioned heading for Mexico?–and that was that.

After three weeks with still no word, Mrs. Hubert decided that she'd had enough. She said she was going to pack up or throw out all his crap.

"He thinks he can stroll back in here like nothing happened, he's shit outta luck," she announced. "I wouldn't let my own husband treat me this way, I sure as hell won't let his no-good little prick of a nephew."

That was when Rachel made her move.

The five of them, she told Mrs. Hubert, would be glad to clean out the apartment above the garage. Make repairs, paint, do whatever needed doing. Then they could use it.

"Use it for what?" Mrs. Hubert asked. "I did think about maybe renting it out, but new paint or no new paint, it'd still be a dump, and nobody but Donnie is *that* desperate."

"For whatever," Rachel said. "Storage, studying… Jessie could keep her exercise equipment out there, turn it into a home gym. Or Annamaria could use it for a music studio. That kind of thing."

"And you'd each kick in a few extra bucks?"

"Five each? That's twenty-five dollars a month."

"I can do math." Her beady eyes went crafty. "Ten each."

"Thirty a month," Rachel said, "and we'll take over the yard work and other chores Donnie used to do."

The sun hadn't even gone down yet, but the Friday night cruisers were already out. They lined the curb in front of Julio's and filled the parking lot between the bingo parlor and the bowling alley, where the food-trucks set up. The prize hot-rods rolled up and down the street in a slow, steady, magnificent parade of custom paint jobs and competing stereo systems.

Someday, Rico would have a ride finer than any of those.

He would.

Guaranteed. Guaran-fucking-teed.

It'd be gloss black. With a serpent painted on the hood, a fiery-green serpent with wicked curved fangs. The rims would be gold spinners. The engine would roar like a wild animal. When Rico cranked the bass, the windshield would thump like a heartbeat.

Someday.

He weaved his way through the people congregating in groups on the sidewalks, in the alleys, and in doorways.

Guys with guys, smoking, strutting, telling dirty jokes, laughing too loud, occasionally socking each other in the shoulder or upper arm. Leather jackets, or tee shirts with the sleeves torn away. Baggy jeans. Gang colors in bandannas tied around bicep, thigh, head, neck. Tattoos.

Girls with girls, tossing their hair and swinging their hips, fixing their lipstick, laughing too loud, and pretending to ignore the guys while really scoping them out from the corners of their eyes. Short-shorts or short skirts, tight low-riders with wide belts. Skimpy tops. Big hair. Make-up. Tribal armband tats, tramp stamps.

Guys with girls, arms around each other, hands cupping a tit here, an ass cheek there, some pairs tongue-kissing, some up against the wall, dry-humping, or even doing it in the alleyway shadows.

All of them ignoring him.

Nobody said hi.

Nobody called him Rico even though it was stitched in script on the patch of his coveralls.

It was the fucking coveralls.

He hated the fucking coveralls. Turd-brown and grease-stained. 'Rico' on the front. 'Lucky Seven' on the back, above a logo of two white dice with black dots, showing a two and a five. Below the dice, more lettering read 'Gas, Parts, Services.'

At least he wasn't wearing the cap.

He refused to wear the fucking cap.

The coveralls were bad enough.

But Mr. Zelnitz, who owned the Lucky Seven, insisted. The only reason he let Rico get away with not wearing the cap was because Rico agreed to work the late shift.

So, he worked the late shift. Seven at night to five in the morning. Shitty hours for shittier wages.

At least Mr. Zelnitz humored him and called him Rico. That was better than he got from any of these whores and bastards on the street. Better than he got from his own family.

His mother gave him no end of grief, told him that he was breaking her heart and offending his father's memory. She'd wail on and on about how there was nothing wrong with the name Henry, his father had been named Henry, his grandfather had been named Henry, it was tradition, all the way back to the Garden of Eden, by the way she made it sound. Was he, her son, her only son, going to be the one to break the chain?

Try to tell her that Henry was a stupid name, a dork's name, a loser's name, and it was like spitting in her face. She wouldn't hear it. She wouldn't understand. No one on the street was going to respect a Henry. It had no cred.

Rico, now, Rico was a good name. Tough and sharp and smart.

It almost fit, too. Henry in Spanish was Enrique, and Rico was short for Enrique. So, Henry-Enrique-Rico, there it was, made sense to him.

Not to his mother. Not to his stepfather, who would just snort and rustle his magazine and grumble about how there were enough wetbacks in the country already without some white boy going and pretending to *be* one.

His stepbrothers thought it was funny as hell. They called him Henrietta, and Reeeee-cola like the cough drops in those old commercials, and laughed their asses off.

Someday, he'd show them all. He would have his gloss-black ride with the fiery green serpent painted on the hood. He'd get rid of these stupid fucking coveralls and be stylin'. People on the street would look at him with respect.

Not ignore him, the way they did now. As if he wasn't even there. Invisible, not worth noticing. Hell, the only person who did seem to notice him was some El Tubbo at the Fry-Daddy truck, and that kind of notice, he didn't need.

Looking at him, yeah right, a sneering kind of look, like she wanted him to saunter on over so even *she* could shoot him down.

He averted his eyes quick, though not so quick it was obvious he was averting them. Last thing he needed was anybody deciding to crack wise. "Hey, man, she your *giiiiirlfriend?*" they'd jeer, busting a gut while their own girlfriends tittered meanly.

Some day.

Some goddamn day.

When he had his wheels. When he had money. When he could go into a club, and the tough guys would back down, and the babes would be all over him.

Yeah, a babe on each arm. Hot and classy, the real deal. Not these skanks with their hard eyes and used bodies. Serious top-shelf babes.

He'd be Rico then, Rico forever. No more of that Henry shit. Just Rico.

Or did it need a little more? A kicker?

He touched his hip, not to check his wallet but to check his lucky piece. One he'd picked up at a pawnshop—he'd told his mother he needed money for overdue library books, and she'd believed him.

It rode there, hard and slim and confident: a switchblade, its long, silvery-steel fang hidden inside a fake-ivory handle with a snake painted on it. A sinuous, green, totally badass and evil snake. A viper.

Yeah.

That's what he would have on the hood of his car. That's what people would call him.

Rico the Viper. Hell, yeah.

Mrs. Hubert gave her blessing for the five of them to do whatever they wanted with anything in Donnie's above-garage apartment. "Keep it, donate it to the Goodwill, burn it, I don't give a damn. He shows up asking, he can come talk to me."

The *keep* option was roundly rejected on every single item. The *donate* went a bit better, though some of the furniture and clothes were in such bad shape even the thrift store rejected those offerings. The porn, of course, they automatically consigned to the *burn* pile.

That left the apartment itself. Even bare of furnishings it was grungy, and it stank.

Jessie ripped up the mottled carpeting and the decaying pad beneath, revealing warped floorboards of cheap planking. Gwen and Darlene scrubbed down the walls, sills, and ceiling with their good friend Oxy-Orange. Rachel tackled the kitchenette. And Annamaria, who drew the short straw, was stuck cleaning Donnie's bathroom.

"Why here?" Darlene asked Rachel. "You made all those speeches about how we gotta distance ourselves, not leave any evidence, then you do this about-face and want to have the crime scene right here?"

"You have to weigh the risks, right?" Rachel was taking a much-needed break after shifting aside the fridge and unleashing a scuttling horde of roaches, which she'd then chased down and stomped. "Proximity, okay, that's a risk... but having control over the setting is important, too. Access. It'd be suspicious if we were always coming and going from some place we didn't have any business being."

"And, doing it here," Annamaria said, emerging from the bathroom holding at arm's length a shower curtain so mildewed it might have been a protected wetland in its own right, "we can keep an eye on everything. We'll know if someone starts snooping around."

It took several days of hard labor, fit in around their normal schedules of classes, labs and work shifts, but at last they had the apartment above the garage scoured clean of the lingering Donnie-funk.

Then came the fun part.

All day on the corner and what did he have to show for it?

Seventeen bucks, seventy-five cents. Most of that in change, a lot of quarters, some dimes and nickels, a couple of crumpled bills.

And a dozen vouchers. Fucking damn *vouchers*.

Mel really wanted to know whose brilliant idea the program had been. He wanted to know how much it cost to print and distribute. How much had gone into the ad campaigns, for that matter. Posters, ads in the paper, radio commercials, the whole nine yards.

Did anyone ask the ones it was supposed to actually be benefiting?

Nobody had asked *his* opinion, that was for sure.

Nobody had asked Floyd, or Sheila, or Caveman, or Big Joe, either.

They all felt the same way Mel did. Total waste. Waste of time, waste of money, waste of energy, waste of everything.

"And it's a fucking insult," Floyd had said. "Treating us like kids and retards, that's what they're doing. Thinking they know what's better for us."

Charitable Community Outreach.

That was what they called themselves, the do-gooders who'd gotten this going.

And son of a bitch but people had snapped them up, latched onto the idea like it was the greatest to come along in years.

Some of them, Mel suspected, honest-to-God bought into the whole scam, believed the whole damn spiel. They really thought the vouchers were better, preferable, more appreciated, than regular good old cash money.

He sifted through his day's take, air whistling in his nose, every now and then snuffling up runners of snot when they threatened to dribble over his lips. He didn't always make it. His straggly black mustache and beard were getting crusted.

Archie watched him, one ear perked, the other flopped, tail wagging. The dog—a brown and white mutt that was probably part spaniel but Mel wasn't sure because Archie had been full-grown by the time they'd thrown in their lots together—lay on his belly on a striped blanket, forepaws out, a play-rope made of twisted and knotted socks resting in front of him.

"Don't get your hopes up," Mel told the dog, then paused. "Oh, hey, wait, here ya go buddy, this one is good for a bag of kibble at Deegan's." Most were redeemable at grocery stores, fast food joints and diners around this part of town. Some could be turned in for clothes and other items. There were vouchers for bus tokens and Laundromat tokens, movie passes to the Orion, free haircuts and shaves at the barber college, dental checkups.

Would a store exchange them for cash? No way.

If someone had a voucher for a coffee and donuts but only wanted the coffee, would they give the surplus value back as change? No way on that, either.

No exchanges, no substitutions. None for smokes, or booze, or the real necessities.

The best Mel used to be able to hope for was to find someone who'd be willing to buy the damn things off him. Some kid, maybe. Until the businesses had started cracking down, no longer accepting the Charitable Community Outreach vouchers from obviously not-homeless people.

"It's discrimination," Floyd had said. "Racial profiling."

Another bum Mel didn't know had pointed out that it could hardly be racial profiling, given that Floyd was black, Mel was white, Shelia was Native American, and he, the bum Mel didn't know, was Saturnian. Floyd told him to fuck off.

"Goddammit," Mel said again.

Archie nosed the play-rope, wagged, and whined.

"Not right now, Arch."

Ten hours of sitting out there on the hard sidewalk, with his cardboard sign.

People walking past him. Walking way around him, sometimes

even crossing the street so they wouldn't have to make eye contact. Telling him to get a job, calling him a loser. Not even twenty in legitimate money to get what he *really* needed.

And they made like it was such a wonderful system.

"Told you it'd be no prob," Jessie said, adjusting her toolbelt. "Me and my brothers, we built forts in the woods all the time when we were kids. Treehouses and clubhouses, that kind of thing."

"Except, I bet," said Annamaria, "your clubhouses didn't have inch-thick sheets of foam padding over all the inside walls."

In addition to buying, borrowing and scrounging tools and materials, Jessie had taken advantage of her sports and athletics connections and scored them several dozen old vinyl-covered exercise mats. Now the mats covered the apartment's living room floor.

"It looks like a padded room in an insane asylum," Gwen said, hugging herself as she looked around.

"Yeah, all we need are straitjackets," Darlene said.

"That might be hard," Rachel said from the kitchenette, where she was doing an inventory of the cupboard contents.

They had boxes of gloves liberated by Darlene from the campus student health center, boxes of disposable hairnets that Annamaria had gotten from the restaurant, more rolls of strapping tape, more garbage bags, Oxy-Orange, bleach, other cleaning supplies, and assorted implements.

"What are we going to tell Mrs. Hubert if she asks?" Gwen wondered.

"Insulation," Rachel said.

"Even on the windows?"

"That's why I hung the shutters," Jessie said. "Can't see from outside. Nobody'll know."

"She might want to come in. It's still her property."

"She won't haul her fat ass up those stairs any more than she absolutely has to," Darlene said. "That's why she moved out of the house and into the trailer park in the first place, isn't it?"

"Still, she might," Gwen said.

"Well," Annamaria said, with a small and ironic smile, "if she does, we can say it's for acoustic soundproofing. Seen as how this is supposed to be my music studio. Might be more convincing if I could actually sing or play an instrument."

"So take a class." Jessie shrugged and hefted her nail gun. "We *are* in college."

"As long as she gets her extra thirty dollars a month," Rachel said, "she won't care what we do up here."

"Unless it's a meth lab," Darlene said. "That's what she told me. No pot, no meth, none of that shit."

"She said that?" Annamaria asked. "What'd you tell her?"

"I said sure, no pot, no meth, none of that shit."

"Good," Rachel said.

Jessie stepped back and surveyed her handiwork. The walls were covered with the foam sheets, and over those hung quilted, waterproof moving pads. The bathroom and shower stall doors had been removed. The mirrored medicine cabinet was also gone, as was the top of the toilet tank and anything else not firmly affixed in place.

A single hefty ringbolt jutted from the wall, right about waist height, above the spot where the hide-a-bed couch used to be. Another rose from the floor, at roughly the midpoint of the room. They'd made sure that those ringbolts were attached to studs and beams, not going anywhere. Rusty lengths of chain snaked from them, heaped in coils on a twin-sized mattress that was slip-covered and resting on the layer of exercise mats. At the end of each chain was a pair of cuffs.

"Yeah," Jessie said, hands on her hips, satisfied smile on her face. "Wouldn't want the landlady to get the idea we were doing anything *bad!*"

Alpacas made noises.

Ed Reilly hadn't known that until he came to work for the Gerrittsons. Had never thought about it before. Never cared. Alpacas? What the heck did he know about alpacas? Only that they were kind of like llamas, and llamas looked like the result of some crazy crossbreeding experiment between camels and sheep.

He now knew more about alpacas than most people ever *wanted* to know.

What they ate. How much they crapped. The noises they made.

Kind of a chirruping-cooing-bleat.

They were woolly. They had coltish legs and curving necks. They had big, soulful eyes. They had puff-tufts on top of their heads.

Dr. Seuss animals. Could have come right from the pages of one of those books. Them, and the Sneetches, and the Whos down in Whoville.

Cute, in their way.

Not too stinky, either. Not compared to some of the livestock he'd seen.

Leigh would have loved them. She would have loved the farm, she would have loved being out here in almost-the-country, she would have loved the Gerrittsons, and she would have loved the alpacas.

They came crowding up to him, sticking their heads over the low fences, making their chirrupy noises, nuzzling at him with warm, wet snouts.

"Morning, Clover," he said. "Morning, Sebastian. Hey there, Mocha. Hiya, Felix. Daisy, there's a good girl. Hello, Hercules."

The barn was a long, low structure, lined with pens along both sides. It smelled of hay and dry, sweetish dung. Birds nested in the rafters, adding their own chirps and coos to the general atmosphere. Motes and chaff swirled in the thin rays of morning sunshine that slanted through the cracks. Mice skittered, and a couple of farm cats stalked them, tail-tips flicking.

He mucked out the droppings, got a bale of fresh hay from the loft, broke it apart and began spreading it.

The alpacas followed him as far as their enclosures would allow, extending their necks, dopey Dr. Seuss faces crowned with those woolly poofs craned wistfully after him. When he'd finished with the hay, he relented and dug into his pockets for some chunks of apple and carrot.

"Hey now, Herc, you had some," he said, pushing the big tan-and-russet male's head away. "It's Velvet's turn."

Velvet—a demure beige female with enormous, dewy

eyes—had to be coaxed into taking the treats from his hand. Coaxed, while at the same time he fended off the eager, greedier muzzles of Hercules, Bobo and Susie-Q.

"Ed?" Muriel Gerrittson called to him from the barn doorway. "Coming in for some breakfast? I made a skillet scramble, eggs and sausage and onion and bell peppers. With home fries and orange juice."

"Sounds good, Mrs. G., but I already ate."

Muriel had her own alpaca-poof billow of snow-white hair, a discreet hearing aid, a slight dowager's hump, and gold-framed glasses on a chain around her neck. For all that, she was spry and lively in jeans and a red plaid shirt that made him think of lumberjacks. Her blue eyes sparkled at him from a rosy, wrinkled face.

"And what did you have?" she asked. "Instant coffee and one of those awful toaster pastries?"

"No, ma'am," Ed said. "Instant coffee and a cereal bar."

She gave him a scolding look, eyes still sparkling. "Just as bad. I swear, you'll get scurvy. Come in and have something proper to eat."

"Got chores to do." He held up the hose, which he was using to refill the water reservoirs.

"Yes, we work you so hard," she said, crossing to greet the alpacas. They were even happier to see her than they'd been to see Ed, some of them going up on their hind legs to hook their forelegs over the top rails. "Here's my darlings, good morning, aren't you all my darlings? Tell Ed that he'll do his chores better if he has a good breakfast first. Tell him, Queenie."

A mature female, black and white, the matriarch of the herd, arched her neck and warbled obligingly. Muriel Gerrittson laughed and ruffled the exuberant tuft atop Queenie's head.

"You know, Ed," Muriel said as she circulated the barn, hugging alpaca necks, thumping alpaca sides, getting alpaca kisses. "Walter and I were thinking, it doesn't make sense for you to drive out here every morning and home again every night, when we've got a perfectly good extra bedroom going unused."

He stopped, the bucket of food in one hand and the big scooper in the other, and blinked at her until Hercules gave an imperial bleat and closed his strong yellowish teeth on Ed's sleeve. Ed shook him off, and dumped the food in the hopper, hardly aware of what he was doing.

"Mrs. G.?"

"We're sincere," she said. "Will you think about it, at least? Promise me you'll think about it."

"I'll think about it," he said.

CHAPTER SIX

Eight little words.

From Jessie, not Rachel, but still, eight little words.

When are we going to do it again?

And now here they were.

Standing around a body.

"I think that went pretty well," Rachel said, nodding as she gave the scene a critical once-over. "Great work, everybody. Really."

A body. Boneless, limp. Trussed up with strapping tape. Gagged. Cuffed by one wrist and one ankle.

"Does that mean we're ready?" Darlene asked. "Really ready to do it?"

"Should be."

"Excellent," Jessie said. "Took long enough. You're picky, Rache. And a slave driver."

"Hey," she said, "I told you before, if we do this, we do it right. We do it my way. Careful and deliberate."

"Yeah, yeah."

"I'm serious, Jessie."

"So what else is new?"

They stared down at the body. Waxy-pale complexion, blondish hair. Dark blue jogging suit. White sneakers.

"What's his name again?" asked Annamaria.

"Andy," Rachel said.

Darlene smirked at Jessie. "I can't believe you put your mouth on that."

"I kind of had to, didn't I?"

"Did you stick your tongue down his throat?"

"Sick, Dar. Real sick."

Gwen crouched and reached out, but her trembling fingers stopped just shy of contact. "I wonder if anybody noticed he's gone yet."

"Nobody'll care," Jessie said. "It's not like ol' Andy here has a job he won't show up for, or his wife and kids will call the police if he doesn't come home."

"It'll be fine," said Rachel. "We'll take him back when we're done."

"Provided we all still want to do this," Annamaria said.

"What's that supposed to mean?" Jessie asked. "We're not chickening out now. Nobody is. Am I right?" She glanced around to the others for support.

"I'm not chickening out," Darlene said now, jaw set into a scowl. "And you're not leaving me out because I got the pukes."

"No one's being left out," Annamaria said. "We're all okay with it, aren't we?"

"Well… it *was* pretty awful last time," Gwen said. "All that blood…"

"See?" Darlene pointed at her. "If anybody's squeamish, it's the elf-princess!"

"She didn't puke, though," Jessie said. "*You* did."

"Yeah, but she fainted!"

Annamaria swept back her hair defiantly. "And *I cried*. So what?"

No one said anything. They shuffled their feet.

"Um… Annamaria?" Gwen ventured after an uncomfortable moment. "Why… um… why *did* you—?"

"It doesn't matter," Annamaria said. "Do we want to make a big deal out of what doesn't matter? We still did it, didn't we? We did what we had to do. Never mind who cried, or who threw up, or what. We did it."

"Yeah, fair enough," Jessie said. "We sure did."

Rachel joined Gwen in crouching by the body, though she was more interested in checking the fit of the cuffs. "I wasn't wild about it the first time we had to dissect something in science class. Maybe I didn't squick out like some of the girls— some of the guys, too—but it wasn't my favorite thing to do, cutting up some dead animal. You get used to it, though."

"What, like for biology lab?" Darlene cackled. "We had to do that in high school. I was partnered with this one jackass... before they brought them out, he was all big and tough and telling me that it was okay if I couldn't handle it. Then as soon as that fetal pig hit the table? All stiff and cold with its legs sticking up? Ha! You should've seen him."

"Our school never did real animals," Jessie said. "Too many people protesting, saying how cruel and inhumane it was. We had these fake frog models instead."

"We did a cat," Rachel said. She gave each cuff an experimental tug.

"Oh God please do we have to talk about dissecting cats?" Gwen put her hands over her face. "That's so mean!"

"What, so it's mean with a cat but not with a guy?" Jessie kicked Andy in the ribs. A thin wheeze of air escaped his flared nostrils.

"Well... that's kind of mean, too..."

"Only 'kind of' mean?" Darlene made air quotes.

"Technically," Rachel said, also giving each chain a tug, "I'm pretty sure killing a live person is meaner than dissecting an already-dead cat."

"The cat must've died somehow," Gwen protested.

"Sure," said Annamaria, "but it probably wasn't tortured and mutilated first."

Darlene's eyes gleamed. "Tortured and mutilated... that's gonna be wild!"

"We can't just... well... do it quick?" Gwen asked, pale.

"We *could*, but..." Rachel chewed her thumbnail thoughtfully. "I mean, any of us could walk up and shoot someone, but you hardly ever hear about serial killers using guns. Too quick. Too detached."

"Yeah, they like the up-close-and-personal methods," Jessie said.

"Stabbing, or strangulation, for instance," said Annamaria. She sounded remote, and wasn't looking at Andy anymore. Her gaze was directed at the wall, or through it to something more distant. "They like to stab and strangle. And worse. Lots worse."

"Sex stuff," Darlene said. The gleam was, if anything, more avid than ever.

"This isn't about sex, Darlene," Rachel said.

"Yeah, there's easier ways to get laid than to grab some guy and lock him up," Jessie said, seizing Andy's ankle-chain and giving it a clanking shake.

"I know it's not about sex," Darlene said, huffy.

"What... um... what *is* it about?" Gwen asked.

"The challenge," Rachel and Jessie said, even as Annamaria and Darlene said, "Revenge."

They looked at each other and laughed. Then, again, they all spoke at once.

"Battle of wits," said Rachel.

"The rush, the kick, the thrill," said Jessie.

"Understanding," said Annamaria.

"Payback," said Darlene.

They laughed some more—everyone but Gwen, who only continued to crouch there beside Andy's bound and gagged body, watching with anxious uncertainty.

Annamaria's laughter died away first. She shot stern looks at the other three, then jerked her head toward the door in a silent instruction of I'll-handle-this.

Over the weeks of cleaning and remodeling the above-garage apartment according to Rachel's instructions, they'd had plenty of time to discuss their plans.

"Okay, so," Rachel had said, one Saturday over a lunch of sandwiches and soda. "Most serial killers follow some kind of pattern with their victims, even if they aren't aware of it. An unconscious or subconscious thing."

"A certain physical type?" Annamaria asked.

"Right," Rachel said. "Like, say, maybe the killer's mother was a redhead, and so he targets redheads without even thinking about it, symbolically trying to get back at her for rejecting him or mistreating him or something."

"Sucks to be you, Gwen," Jessie said. "You're prime psycho bait."

Gwen had touched her hair, smiled nervously, and tucked it behind her ears. "Mine's not really red. Not *red*-red. Apricot maybe. Anyway, yours is reddish, too."

"Mine's brown."

"Chestnut brown, which is still reddish."

"Let's not get sidetracked," Annamaria said. "We need to figure out what we're doing. Rachel, that's your department. How do we start?"

"For one thing, it'd be a big mistake to kill someone we know."

Darlene had raised a finger. "Uh, sorry? Too late."

"Donnie doesn't count," Rachel said. "That was an accident, a mistake, a spur-of-the-moment thing. I meant for the *real* ones. The fewer connections between us and the victims, the better."

"Strangers, you mean," said Jessie. "Random people. Piece of cake. It'd be easy enough to get some guy to go off alone with one of us. Pick him up at a club, let him think he's getting lucky, and then bam!"

"Easy for you, maybe," muttered Darlene.

"So, pick him up," Rachel said, "maybe get him drunk, maybe drug him so he can't cause trouble."

"Maybe just talk him into some bondage games and tie him to the bed," Jessie said.

"What kind of person is going to let someone he just met in a bar tie him to a bed?" Gwen had asked, wide-eyed.

"A guy," the rest of them answered in *well, duh*! chorus.

"But—"

"Trust me, Guinevere," Jessie had said. "I have a dad and five brothers. I've been hanging around guys all my life. That's the way they are. Married, single, gay or straight, they're all the same. They keep porn, they jack off six times a day, and you know any guy would cheat like *that*—" she snapped her fingers, "—if he thought he could get away with it."

"Your problem is," Darlene said to Gwen, "you watch all those chick flicks and you read nothing but that love-is-magical fantasy crap, and you think that's how things really are going to turn out. Life's no happily-ever-after Cameron Mack movie. Grow up and get real already."

***

Jessie, Rachel and Darlene took her none-too-subtle hint, and left Annamaria alone with Gwen.

Well, alone with Gwen and the body… but that hardly counted, did it? Andy was just *there*, unmoving, like a sack of laundry.

Gwen stared down at him.

Annamaria looked at Gwen.

Really took the time to *look* at her.

She'd lost weight. All five of them had, because they'd been working their butts off to get everything ready. Jessie, being fittest, had lost the least. For Rachel and Annamaria, it wasn't enough to make much of a noticeable difference. Darlene, between the exercise and the vomiting, was down twelve whole pounds and not altogether displeased.

On Gwen, though, who'd been slender to start with…

There was, Annamaria knew, such a thing as being too thin. Gwen was getting to that point. Too thin, too pale. Her eyes, always big, looked huge now. Huge, haunted, grey-green ghost eyes.

Should have done something about this before now, Annamaria thought. But they'd been so busy, and all along they'd figured Gwen would get over her reservations, get with the program, develop the same kind of enthusiasm for their newfound hobby that the rest of them had.

"Gwen," she said, pitching her voice low and gentle.

Gwen didn't answer, only stayed where she was, crouched beside the body. Her gaze was fixed on Andy's slack face, the gag taped in place, the half-lidded eyes.

Annamaria took her by the shoulders, still being gentle. "Gwen, come sit with me a minute, please?"

She let herself be led, so Annamaria pulled her up and took her to the far side of the room. Not out of sight of the body and the chains, since the apartment was too small for anyplace to be out of sight of anyplace else. But as far away as they could be.

They sat cross-legged, the cushioning exercise mats beneath them, facing each other. Annamaria captured both of Gwen's slim, long-fingered hands in her own and clasped them, not tight enough to cause discomfort, but firmly enough to make sure she had Gwen's attention.

"You don't know if you can do this?" she asked. "Is that it? Is that what's the matter?"

"I... I..." Gwen shook her head, looking down, hair shimmering like silk in the glow of the overhead light fixture.

"It's okay," Annamaria said. "You can tell me."

"Doesn't this seem wrong to you?" Her voice was a timid whisper. "To do this to someone? To... to hurt someone, kill someone? We're treating it like... like it's a game or something... but it's for real."

"I know. It isn't a game. Believe me, I know that."

"Then how..?"

"Do you like being scared all the time?" Annamaria asked, giving her hands a reassuring squeeze.

Gwen glanced up. "Scared?"

"You were scared of Donnie, weren't you?"

"Not... well..." She squirmed. "Maybe a little. The pictures he took... our underwear..."

"All those things Rachel told us? About how they start off peeping, and move on to other offenses, sex crimes, violence against women? It's all true. Men are predators. They have the luxury of arrogance, and confidence, because they're *men*. They have no idea what it's like for us. Always having to be on guard."

Gwen bit her lip.

"Always having to be alert, aware," Annamaria went on. "Harassed, discriminated against, made to feel vulnerable. Scared. Maybe someone like Jessie would deny that, get all mad about it, say she's not scared of anybody, not scared of any guy... but that's her defense mechanism, isn't it? The toughness, the bravado, that's her way of trying to hide how vulnerable she feels."

She felt Gwen's trembling hands close on hers, clutch at hers, the grip of those long fingers almost painful.

"Men don't know," Annamaria said. "We're aware of the possibility, the risk, the danger. Aware of it in a way that men never have to be, unless we're talking about prisons, or hillbilly banjo movies. They never have to worry routinely about getting raped."

A soft whimper and another tightening of the grip were Gwen's only responses.

"While us? Women?" Annamaria uttered a hollow, mirthless laugh. "We have to be conscious of it all the time. *All. The. Time.* It's always there. Men don't know what it's like. They don't live with it every second of every day. They're used to being safe. Not hunted. Not victimized. Not singled out as easy prey just because they're female."

"I *hate* that," Gwen said, and silvery tears rolled over her lower lashes. "I hate not being able to go anyplace by myself. I hate not being able to walk past some guy on the street without worrying that he might follow me, or that he's... that if there's a group of them and you hear them talking or laughing that way they do... and you don't know what they're saying, if it's you they're talking about, if they're joking about what they'd want to do to you if they could, whether they're really joking or not..."

"Men don't know what it's like," Annamaria said again. "Feeling threatened, objectified, afraid. Maybe it's time they found out, don't you think? Maybe it's time they got a taste of their own medicine. Wouldn't that be nice for a change?"

A long, shuddering sigh made Gwen's whole body shake like a sapling in a gust. "Yeah," she said at last. "Yeah, it kind of would, wouldn't it?"

"I guess we don't *have* to stick with a specific victim type," Rachel had said, the night after they'd finished nail-gunning the foam panels to the walls. The five of them had been back in their own living room by then, the television on but muted, tuned to some Travel Channel show about national parks. "But we should have some ground rules before we get started. For one thing, I'm kind of getting the idea that we want to go after men, right?"

"Right," said Darlene.

"Damn straight," said Jessie.

"See, that could be a problem," Rachel said. "Statistically—"

Jessie had groaned elaborately. "Don't give me 'statistically,'

Rache! Guys get beaten up and mugged all the time. They get in fights with each other, they kill each other."

"Can I finish? Thank you. Okay, true, men are violent toward other men all the time. Men are violent toward women. Men are violent, period. Thing is, we're talking serial killers here."

"Didn't Dahmer choose male victims?" Annamaria had asked. "He was gay, wasn't he?"

"Yeah, and women are violent sometimes too," Darlene had said.

"Battered husbands," Jessie had said, and laughed. "We had these neighbors, and the wife was this raging, abusive bitch. Her husband would be out washing his car with a major black eye, and say he walked into a door. How cliché can you get?"

"What happened to him?" Gwen had asked, her gaze reluctantly torn from the silent splendor of Yosemite's waterfalls on the muted television. "Did he report it to the police?"

"Hell, no! You kidding? They would have called him a wimp."

"What about those moms who drown or poison their kids?" Darlene had asked.

"Or the black widow," Annamaria had said. "Marry him, murder him, inherit, repeat."

Rachel had given up. "All right, all right. I'm just saying, it's important that we know we're all on the same page here. Serial killers usually have patterns. We need to keep that in mind."

"Like going after hookers," Jessie had said. "Easy targets, out there at night, getting into cars or going to sleazy motel rooms with strange men. When they disappear, who's going to notice? Who's going to report it?"

"They aren't all hookers!" Annamaria had been half-reclining on the burnt-orange shag carpet in front of the television, propped up on her elbows with her legs outstretched. But as she'd said that, she'd sat up, with an edge to her voice like an unexpected paper cut. "Not all of them, so don't say that!"

"Jeez, Anna, chill out," Jessie had said, blinking. "Dar didn't say they were *all* hookers, anyway. There's also the runaways and the hitchhikers and the druggies—"

Annamaria, who had not chilled out, had glared at Jessie. "So, they're disposable? Trash? Is that what you mean? They deserve what happens to them? Maybe you think they were asking for it by being out there where some creep could get them? Maybe they were careless and stupid?"

"No, I—"

"You don't know anything about it!"

"Oh, like you do?" Jessie had retorted.

"As a matter of fact—"

"Hey!" Rachel had turned toward them, looking annoyed. "Can we just focus on who we're gonna kill, please?"

"Annamaria?" Gwen asked, after wiping her eyes and blowing her nose on a scrap of paper towel. She leaned out of the kitchenette and saw Annamaria, over by the body.

Over by *Andy*. Poor, helpless Andy.

Annamaria stood over him, with her hands behind her back, like someone scrutinizing a museum piece.

Only this was hardly a work of art, was it?

Not even modern art, which to Gwen's mind was usually stark, industrial, abstract, and lacking any sort of beauty or soul. She liked–call her crazy–art that actually looked like something.

If this scene was in a gallery, or staged as a performance piece, what would it be saying? Bleakness and captivity.

A body on a mattress, in this room with the padded walls, the covered and shuttered windows, the doorless doorways. The only light came from the overhead fixtures: low-wattage bulbs under frosted glass. Andy on the mattress. One wrist and one ankle cuffed, chained to the ringbolts in wall and floor. Strapping tape holding a wad of cloth to serve as a gag.

"Annamaria?" Gwen repeated, louder.

"Huh?" She jumped a little, started, and turned with a sheepish smile. "Sorry, Gwen… I was miles away, I guess."

"Can I ask you something?"

"Sure, anything."

"Why are you going along with this? Earlier, you said revenge, and you said understanding. What did you mean?" She sidled closer as she spoke, until they were both standing beside the mattress, looking down at poor helpless Andy in his blue track suit and white sneakers.

Most of a minute passed. The soundproofing qualities of the foam panels were so good that Gwen could barely hear Annamaria's breathing.

"You know my car?" Annamaria said.

"Yes..?" said Gwen, carefully, not sure if this was a trick question.

It would have been hard not to know Annamaria's car. Only three out of the five of them *had* cars. Darlene drove her parents' old Cadillac—a big boat of a car that had started off white but was the color of newsprint now. Rachel, like Gwen, stuck mostly to the bus. Jessie had her Mustang, which had passed down through her family, each brother using it for a while, fixing it up, and customizing it, before passing it on to the next. And Annamaria had her tiny blue hatchback.

"It was a birthday present from your parents, right?" Gwen added. "A sweet sixteen?"

Annamaria nodded. "Practical. Reliable. Fuel efficient. They had to give me one, because they'd given one to my sister for *her* sweet sixteen. But do you know what they gave her?"

"The same kind?" Gwen guessed. "Or the same general value if not exactly the same kind. That'd be fair."

"You really are an only child, aren't you?"

"Yes, but what does that—?"

"They got Serafina a Porsche."

"Wait, what?"

"They gave her a Porsche," Annamaria said. "Silver and black. Had it delivered during her party. Fifty of her high school friends, a band, a caterer, a pile of presents almost as tall as a kindergartener. I can say that because I was in kindergarten, and the present pile came up to here on me." She held her hand at chin level. "There was only one from Mom and Dad, this little box, a velvet box, like you'd use for a piece of jewelry. When she opened it, there were the keys, and everyone ran around front and there it was."

Gwen frowned. "But…"

"Serafina was always their favorite. I know how that sounds, when someone goes around whining that Mommy or

Daddy likes Brother or Sister best, because maybe Mommy and Daddy let Brother stay up an hour later, or Sister go to a sleepover. This wasn't like that at all."

"Okay," Gwen said.

An only child she might have been, but she'd had friends and schoolmates with siblings, and she'd witnessed the kind of thing Annamaria was talking about. Younger kids in the family protesting when the older ones got more freedom, allowance, privileges. Older kids protesting that the younger ones got away with behaviors that their parents had never tolerated from *them*.

"I don't blame them," Annamaria said. "I don't hold it against them… well, not very much. But I don't blame them. Everybody loved Serafina. She was the pretty one, the smart one, the talented one—"

"Pretty?" Gwen echoed, boggling at Annamaria. "If she… but you… how… I mean… you're…"

"No, not really, not me," she said, brushing it off with a dismissiveness that left Gwen floored. "Nothing like Serafina. She was a good student, too, got straight As. Went to church. Did volunteer work. And her voice, my God, she could sing like an angel, people said so all the time. Perfect Serafina. My parents adored her. Everyone did."

"Weren't you jealous?"

"I know it might sound like I was, but that wasn't it at all, not ever. You might think someone like that would have been a spoiled brat, a complete bitch. Not Serafina. She was always kind, selfless, giving. I idolized her."

"What happened?" Gwen asked, visions of the disastrous fall of the perfect angel whirling in her imagination. Teen pregnancy, drug use or overdose, drunk driving in that black and silver Porsche… what kind of a destructive, spiraling crash had brought Serafina back to earth with the rest of them?

"She was the twenty-fifth," Annamaria said. At least, that was what Gwen heard, though it didn't make a whole lot of sense.

"The… the twenty-fifth?"

"He did thirty before they found him. That they know of, anyway. That he admitted to. She was number twenty-five."

"Oh, my God!" Gwen staggered back a step, putting her

hand over her mouth. "But if she… if your sister… if a serial killer… then how..?"

"That's why I'm going along with this. I want to understand. I *need* to understand how someone could do those things to another person. I have to know what it's like. I have to see for myself. That's why, Gwen. That's why."

Once the preliminary work had been done, once the above-garage apartment had been fully outfitted, they'd been ready to give it a test run.

Not with a real victim, though. Not for the test run.

For that, they'd used Andy.

Resusci-Andy, as he was known in the First-Aid/CPR courses.

He was a full body, man-sized dummy in a blue track suit, his feet molded and painted to look like white sneakers. His skin was the unnatural shade of pink that had been called 'flesh' before crayon manufacturers decided it was both inaccurate and politically incorrect. His hair was blondish, Ken-doll waves and ridges. He had a rubbery nose that could be pinched to seal the airway, a hard-lipped mouth that could be blown into so that the fake lungs inside his fake chest would inflate, and a ribcage that would bend and give under the application of compressions.

Andy was an older model, not one of the fancy newer ones that included electronic pulses and other sensors. He had an entire family on the shelves in the Health and Sciences Department storeroom. His wife, Resusci-Annie. The kids, one toddler-sized and one infant-sized. There was even Resusci-Rover, the family dog. And Andy's half-brother, the 'half' almost literally… a head and torso model instead of a whole-body dummy.

The other ones would have been easier to work with, all of them smaller and lighter. But for their test run, they'd wanted to do it right. They'd needed to practice hefting, handling, moving. They'd needed to know how awkward a body would be to carry, how inconspicuous it'd look, how well they could cram him in the trunk or backseat of a car, or lug him up the steps.

Andy was about the closest they'd been able to get.

Jessie knew Andy very well. She worked summers as a lifeguard, and was required to be CPR-certified. "Every year, we have to go through the same stupid shit again," she'd said. "Watch the film, then take turns blowing the dummies. At least now they also let us play with the zapper-things."

"Defibrillators," Rachel had said.

"Whatever. I also checked the schedule, and the next CPR class isn't for a few weeks, so as long as we don't get caught, we can sneak him out and sneak him back before anybody notices."

So, they'd borrowed him.

Dress rehearsal for the real thing.

CHAPTER SEVEN

Steve blinked, squinted, couldn't see anything but darkness.

His head hurt. Throbbed, really.

His mouth felt stuffed with a dry sponge.

What the hell..?

Jesus, he didn't think he'd been drinking *that* much.

A couple beers, nothing out of the ordinary.

"Get his legs, you guys."

Steve tried to speak, and couldn't.

There *was* a dry sponge stuffed in his mouth. Or *something* stuffed in there, anyway. He pushed at it with his tongue. Maybe not a sponge. Maybe a… what..? A washcloth? A rag?

Made no sense. He tried to spit it out.

Couldn't do that, either.

And his face felt funny. The skin tight. Pulled, even. As if…

Tape?

That was crazy.

Why would he have a strip of tape over his mouth?

To hold in the gag, obviously.

But why a gag in his mouth?

Where was he, anyway?

Who had said that about his legs?

A voice. A female voice? Close. Close, but oddly muffled.

He blinked again but still couldn't see anything but that dark blur.

Hands were on him. Hooked under his arms, grabbing him by the calves, and crooks of his knees. A lot of hands.

What the *hell..?*

The other, more distant sounds he could hear were also oddly muffled. Rushing-sighing noises like wind in trees. A low chorus of croaking–frogs. The eerie, warbling call of some bird.

His head really hurt. Steady pulsing throbs, aching like a rotten tooth.

Two beers, maybe three, that was all.

Nothing to cause a hangover like this.

He could feel cool air on his arms, but none on his face. His face was stifling, sweaty. The air he sucked in through his nose was humid and stale.

Had he been in an accident?

Why couldn't he see?

And what was with the gag?

"On three," said a different voice. Also female. "One… two… *three.*"

The hands lifted. He heard exhalations and grunts. He felt himself go up in an unsteady, heaving lurch, a swaying stagger, and a cry of protest gurgled from his throat. His arms jerked in a reflexive effort to help balance, and only then did he realize that they were held in front of him. Bound at the wrists. Tied, or taped, or cinched together with those zip-tie-plasti-cuff things the police used.

What the *fucking* hell..?

Had he been arrested?

Steve fought to clear his head, but didn't have much luck. He was dizzy, sore, half-suffocated, confused. Nothing made any sense.

They steadied him, and he felt his weight suspended in the grasp of what had to be four or five people. They shuffled in a slow, careful, moving-heavy-furniture kind of way.

His wrists were tied. So, he realized, were his ankles. He had a gag jammed in his mouth and sealed with tape… he had what he suddenly figured out must be a bag or a pillowcase over his head.

He couldn't move his limbs. Could only move by thrashing

with his entire body. But if he did that, the people who were carrying him might drop him.

"Not much farther," yet a third voice said. Again, female.

And familiar?

Where was he?

Where had he been before this?

The trunk of a car? He dimly recalled a sense of being closed in, and the loose cloth covering his face had a faint smell of rubber, oil, musty carpet, and exhaust fumes.

He'd been in the trunk of a fucking *car*?

Whose car?

Not his own. He drove a Jag, which devoured the highway in sleek purring gulps, but did not have a lot of trunk space.

"Slow down, damn it," a fourth voice said. "We're going backwards here, you want us to trip and fall?"

Yes! Steve thought. *Trip and fall! Whoever the hell you are, trip and fall, and I hope you break your necks, because whatever this is, it isn't funny!*

Some kind of a joke? A prank?

Hazing? Surprise party?

None of his friends were the kind to play jokes or pranks, his fraternity hazing days were several years in the past, and his birthday wasn't until January.

What, then? What the hell was going on?

He'd gone out, he remembered that. Gone out for a few beers and to shoot a couple games of pool, listen to some music, scope out the ladies, possibly even try his luck, if he spotted one who interested him.

"So far, so good," said the voice who'd done the count-off to three. "Now the stairs. Here, brace him on me."

The hands supporting the top half of his body shifted around. Steve had a moment of alarm, sure that he was going to crash headfirst onto the ground. Then he felt someone's shoulders take his weight.

Wasn't funny, whatever it was.

Had stopped being funny a long time ago. If it had ever been funny in the first place.

For a moment, Steve considered slamming his head around

hard to the right, bashing his skull into the skull of the one who had just hoisted his upper back onto her shoulders. She'd drop him, but he was starting to get pissed. Too pissed to care about hitting the ground.

"Are you sure?" asked the voice that had seemed familiar. Had a husky-smoky-throaty quality to it that would have done great on one of those phone-sex chat lines.

Not that he called those numbers. Not for those kinds of prices.

Was he recognizing it from the club?

It had been crowded, be remembered that, too. Crowded, loud, lively. All the pool tables full, with groups waiting around. Packed dance floor. Classic rock mixed with modern. And girls. Plenty of girls.

"You bet," the count-off one replied. As if through gritted teeth, but confident.

They all sounded young.

And that husky, phone-sex voice…

Yeah, from the club!

The brunette.

It was coming back to him now, the aching fog in his head beginning to disperse.

His feet and legs tipped up, and he had that surge of alarm again. The gag prevented his protesting shout from being more than a gurgle.

Stairs.

Jesus Christ, they were carrying him up a flight of stairs!

He could hear their footsteps clunking on wood as the ones holding his legs made their precarious way upward. Backing up the steps? While the strong one bore the brunt of his weight and the husky-voiced one helped support his upper body?

She was the brunette, he was certain of that now. The one who'd caught his eye. Tall and gorgeous. Smooth, golden-mocha skin. Lots of dark hair. Porn-star lips. Great legs and even better tits.

Steve concentrated on her voice, partly in hopes of making some connection that would let him figure out what in the fuck was going on here, and partly in an attempt to keep his mind off the fact that he was being toted feet-first up a staircase the way a desk or dresser might be maneuvered up to the second floor of a house.

"Ow!"

"What?"

"Smacked my ankle. It's nothing."

The brunette. Snug black skirt, not mini-short, but with a slit up the side most of the way to the hip. Sleeveless top, shiny, clingy.

A prime piece of ass, that one.

She'd been one of a trio perched on tall barstools at a high, round table between the bar and the dancefloor. Women did that, running in herds or packs, making it tougher to single them out.

The little blonde with her had been casual-cute in jeans and a fuzzy-soft sweater, sleeves pushed to the elbows, the v-neck showing off some pretty good cleavage. Kind of good-girl-next-door for Steve's tastes, but he wouldn't have kicked her out of bed.

The third had been, of course, the requisite ugly fat friend. Hunched bad-posture on her barstool, overflowing the seat-edge all the way around, face set in a sullen scowl. Oinking her way through a bowl of chips. Directing venomous glares at any guy who made a move on her friends.

Steve had run into that tactic a million times and he was convinced it was deliberate. They did it on purpose to weed out the ones not willing to put forth the effort. A guy had to run the ugly-fat-friend gauntlet to get close to the real goodies. He had to have a wingman to distract them, or a buddy who would be willing to throw himself on the grenade, take one for the team, whatever.

"Whoops!"

Gravity snatched and disorientation whirled around him.

"Oh, shit!"

"Hey, watch it!"

His heart skipped and clutched. Hot, rapid breaths puffed in and out of his nose.

"Got him?"

"Yeah, sorry… my hands slipped."

They had him steady again, and inside the hooding cloth, Steve briefly closed his eyes. He jittered with adrenaline that had nowhere to go because he couldn't fucking *move* and these clumsy bitches had damn near dropped him. He could have snapped his neck, fractured his skull.

"Okay," someone said, between labored, panting gasps. "Hang on. I'll open the door."

"Hurry up," said another, one with a soft voice he didn't think he'd heard before. "He's really heavy."

If he'd run into the travel-in-herds tactic a million times, he had never run into this one. What kind of a tactic involved taping a gag in a guy's mouth, putting a pillowcase over his head, tying him hand and foot, cramming him in the trunk of a car, and then hauling him up a flight of stairs?

What the *hell* was that all about?

Why had they... what? Kidnapped him?

Talk about absurd.

He heard a latch click and a door open, and then their shuffling procession was on the move again. Going through it. Going inside. Going from the wood of the staircase to something else, something that went sink-give beneath them and absorbed the sounds of their footsteps.

Who were they, anyway?

His... Jesus, he could hardly even bring himself to think the words... his captors, his abductors? Who were they? What did they want?

The brunette in the black skirt and clingy top was one of them. He knew it. He could tell by her voice.

Did that mean the perky-cute little blonde and the ugly fat friend were the others?

Except, there were more than two others, weren't there? At least one more, maybe two. There was the strong one who'd told them to go on three, one-two-three and then heave. She wasn't the little blonde, and he was willing to bet she wasn't the ugly fat friend, either. So who the fuck was *she*? Who else was in on this?

"Almost there," said the strong one, who had shifted her grip back to the way it had been before the staircase carry. "Just get him over to the... yeah... now let go of his legs..."

Steve's bound ankles swung down, his heels thumping onto a cushiony surface. Then they lowered him onto his butt, and onto his back, and last of all let his head fall. He was lying on what felt like a mattress.

None of his friends were the sort to play pranks, but what about his exes? He knew that a couple of them were the bitter, vengeful types. But more likely to key his car than orchestrate something as complicated and devious as this.

He tried to sit up. Not easy with his hands tied in front of him, but–

A foot on his chest, with considerable heaviness behind it, held him down. "No you don't, asshole," snarled a voice he was now sure belonged to the ugly fat friend.

"Cuffs," the brunette said.

Chains clinked and jangled.

Chains? What the *hell*..?

This was getting a little too freaky. Things had gone far enough. He said as much into the gag, but only produced some muffled grunts.

Cold metal slid around his wrist. He twitched. It click-clamped shut. He felt a second cuff encircle his ankle. A loose, linked, draggy weight led away from each.

Definitely too freaky. Definitely far enough. More than far enough.

The foot left his chest. He sensed the ones who'd knelt to cuff him rising, sensed them all moving away from him, backing away a couple of paces. Standing around the mattress? Standing around him, over him, staring down at him?

He made the loudest noises he could from behind the gag, and twisted his body in short, sharp, aggravated motions. The chains went rattle-jingle-clink. They pulled taut against the cuffs when he reached the end of their lengths, which wasn't very far. The mattress covering crinkled beneath him, felt like vinyl or plastic when his arms touched it.

This was seriously beginning to piss him off.

Everything was quiet.

Steve thrashed around some more, yanked as hard as he could on the chains and cuffs. He couldn't move very far at all. Not even far enough to get himself off the mattress. He made more noises behind the gag.

Nobody answered.

Had they gone? Had they left him here?

Was this where a bunch of his friends were creeping in, taking up their positions around the room, ready to yell "Surprise!" when the bag was whipped off of his head?

But his birthday... not until January...

Who the hell were these girls? He hadn't even spoken to them at the bar. All he'd done was a little of the old eye contact with the brunette, the flashed half-slant of a smile, the slight chin-lift nod universal signal for "How *you* doin'?" And she'd done the coy head-lower in return, the slow glance, the suggestive twining of a strand of hair around her finger.

Steve had figured he could have strolled on over right then and said hello, but he wasn't some horndog college kid desperate to score. That was probably what she was used to, and by not coming across all eager, it'd only make her more interested.

So, he'd waited and played it cool. He'd watched with amusement from the corner of his eye as a group of pretty-boys *did* make their move, three of them, the one who must have drawn the short straw looking like a man on his way to the gallows as he approached the ugly fat friend.

He remembered that... and he remembered ordering another drink... and some energetic lost-in-the-music bitch colliding with him, his beer almost ending up on the floor.

Had they confused him with somebody else? Did they have the wrong guy?

Could it be some ex on a revenge prank?

He wouldn't have expected any of them to go to such elaborate extremes as this to embarrass and humiliate him. The ones who hated his guts had declared that they never wanted to see him again, and made good on the promise.

"What now?"

They were still there, then. He kicked and bucked irritably.

"I want to see his face."

"Yeah, get that thing off."

"What about the gag?"

"Leave the gag."

"What about his clothes?"

His eyebrows shot to his hairline, not that any of them could see. His clothes? Say *what?*

"First the hood."

A hand clutched and tugged. Steve winced as his hair was pulled, then squinted again as the cloth was whisked away from his face and light seared in. He blinked several times, then took a look around.

What the *hell?!?*

His gaze darted to each of the five girls. The brunette, the blonde, and the ugly fat friend... and the energetic bitch who'd nearly spilled his beer... and a tall, willowy-looking one.

Nobody else in the room. Weird quilted sheets on the walls. Bare ceiling with a single bulb in a cheap fixture. He couldn't see much from his position on the floor.

"He isn't scared," the willowy one said.

"I told you he wouldn't be," said the brunette.

Steve grunted through the gag, trying to convey his demand that they quit fucking around, it wasn't funny, he'd had just about enough of whatever game they thought they were playing.

The one who'd collided with him was the one who'd pulled the bag from his head. She dropped it in a crumple on the floor. Not a pillowcase at all, but some kind of thick, cottony cloth. "He looks kinda pissed," she said, and laughed. Her voice and her athletic figure told him this was the one who had supported most of his weight on the trip up the stairs.

All five of them were wearing exam gloves and lunch-lady hairnets. And... weirdly... what seemed to be garbage bags pulled on like smocks, with holes for their arms to stick through.

Were they about to paint the damn room or something?

"Sure, he's pissed," the ugly fat friend said. "You slipped a roofie in his beer and then hit him on the head."

"It worked," the cute-perky blonde said.

A roofie? In his beer? In *his* beer?

He did remember feeling a little woozy after his third or fourth, a little sick to his stomach. Not much, but enough to make him rethink the idea of picking up a date for the rest of the evening. All he'd wanted was to go home and get some sleep.

"Worked like a charm," the brunette said, smiling at the blonde.

His car had been parked at the curb a block and a half down from the bar. He remembered walking to it, not reeling, but less than stone-cold sober. He remembered digging his keys from his pocket to press the remote entry fob, then dropping the ring on the sidewalk. He remembered starting to bend to pick them up.

And...

Nothing.

It would have been easy for someone to take advantage of his befuddled state and off-balance posture right then. Rush up, smack him on the back of the head, catch him on the way down, and sling him between a couple of them with his arms around their shoulders, like he had gotten stupid, shitfaced drunk and they were walking him to the car.

Except that instead of giving him a ride home, they'd dumped him in the trunk, taped and tied and gagged and hooded him, and brought him here. Wherever the fuck *here* was. An upstairs of somewhere. An upstairs room that looked like it was in the middle of a remodeling.

Still unable to make any sensible sounds, he informed them with the hottest and most furious glares he could muster that he was *not* amused. Whatever game this was, he wasn't playing. They could just cut the shit right now. Untie him, untape him, and get those damn cuffs off.

"Seriously pissed," said the ugly fat friend.

"He should be scared," the willowy one said. She said it again, this time directly to Steve. "You should be scared. Why aren't you scared?"

"Because," the strong one said, "he's a *guy*. He thinks he's got no reason to be scared. Not of a bunch of chicks."

"He probably," said the blonde, "figures that it's some kind of trick."

Steve nodded. He wasn't sure how much of his knowing smirk they could see with that wide strip of tape over his face–that was going to hurt like a bastard when it got unstuck and peeled off–but he did the knowing smirk anyway.

"Hidden camera, like on those reality shows where they

play practical jokes on people, pop a fake spider or rat at them and film them freaking out and then everybody laughs at them?" the ugly fat friend asked.

"Like that, yeah."

"But he's all Mr. Tough Guy," the strong one said, "and so you can bet your ass he wouldn't want to end up on YouTube looking like a weenie."

The willowy one stepped closer. "Is that what you think?" she asked him. "Is that really it? Is that the worst thing you can imagine? Looking like a weenie on YouTube?"

He shot her a look simmering with contempt. How dumb did they think he was? Now all five of them were tweaked because he hadn't fallen for it. As if he should have been scared? What did he have to be scared of? What were they going to do to him, give him a makeover?

"All he's worried about," said the brunette, "is humiliation. To him, that is the worst thing he can imagine. The thought that we might actually hurt him, the thought that he could be in physical danger… it'd never cross his mind."

Physical danger? Who did she think she was kidding?

Hurt him? How, by waxing his chest? Which *would* hurt like a motherfucker, but it wasn't anything he was going to be *scared* of.

"We have him," the ugly fat friend said. "He's tied up, he can't move, he can't get away, we could do anything to him that we wanted and there wouldn't be a damn thing he could do to stop us. You'd think he would, I dunno, realize that."

"You'd think," agreed the strong one.

"So, what are we waiting for?" asked the blonde. "Let's get on with it. Take off his shoes, okay?"

The willowy one leaned over him, peering down with her greenish eyes huge and quizzical. "You really don't think you have anything to be afraid of? You really don't think we could hurt you?"

Okay, *that* one was giving him the creeps. Only a little, but still.

All part of their script, he was sure. It was like Good Cop/ Bad Cop, except in this case she got the Spooky Chick role.

"We *are* going to hurt you," the brunette said, leaning over from the other side. She held up something in her gloved hand. An old pair of wire strippers, the handles encased in cracked orange rubber, the blades reddish-brown with rust.

A qualm of doubt wriggled its way into Steve's mind. He pushed it away and tried to inwardly laugh it off. They were *trying* to scare him now; that was all. It wasn't like they were really going to *use* those wire strippers on him.

"More than that," the blonde said.

She was down by his now-bare feet, holding a rectangular bin made of thick plastic. More handles, wooden or plastic or rubber-coated, some old and cracked, some new and pristine, were visible over its sides. So were more pieces of metal, some rusted, some shining. Edges and curves and points and hooks.

More qualms wriggled in, faster than Steve could push them away or laugh them off. He felt prickle-trickles of cold sweat in his armpits and along his hairline. There was a worm of anxiety in his stomach. His balls drew up tight in his crotch.

He wasn't *scared*, just… uneasy.

They were pretty good, he had to admit. Convincing. Best damn actresses he'd ever seen.

"Yeah," said the strong one. "Way more than that, dude."

The ugly fat friend selected a screwdriver from the bin. Yellow-and-black plastic handle. Long, dull-grey shaft. Phillips head. "We're gonna *kill* your ass," she told him.

Steve still wasn't *scared*, not really, but this had now gone way beyond too far. This wasn't funny at *all*. Anybody who would laugh at something like this on YouTube or one of those home video shows was sick. A practical joke was one thing. *Hostel*-style torture porn was something else!

What did they want? Did they want him to blubber into his gag, howl and cry, struggle, piss himself? No fucking way he was going to give them the satisfaction! Crazy psycho-bitches!

They weren't going to *kill* him. They weren't going to hurt him. They were just messing with his head. And when he got out of here, he was going to smack the shit out of them, girls or no girls!

"He still doesn't believe it," the willowy one said.

"He will," the blonde promised, setting down the bin.

"I'll hold his foot." The strong one grabbed him by the ankle and pressed down. With his lower legs taped together, this forced both of his feet to push into the mattress, his heels indenting.

"Mrrgh!" Steve tried to shout. Not scared, no, but mad as hell.

"Right or left?" asked the brunette.

"Right," said the blonde, taking hold of Steve's bare right foot. Her gloved hands were firm and cold.

They were all down by his feet now, the strong one and the blonde and the brunette kneeling, the ugly fat friend bent over, the willowy one crouching to tuck what he saw was a folded towel under his foot.

He searched their faces, their eyes. Looking for the hint of a grin, a sparkle of amusement, anything to say that they *were* joking, like he *knew* they had to be.

Their faces were solemn, avid, intent, clinical and thoughtful. No grins. Their eyes were not sparkling with amusement.

"Mng-grhk!" He wrenched with his legs, trying to get his feet away. Still mad as hell, but also starting to be maybe a little—

He wasn't fucking scared! He was pissed! Super-pissed, and he was going to *get* these bitches!

And he hadn't been able to budge his feet. The strong one held his legs down, the blonde had his right foot completely immobilized. Now the ugly fat friend reached in with the screwdriver, and tapped the end of his right big toe.

"This little piggy went to market," she said. She tapped the second toe. "This little piggy stayed home."

Steve tried again, heaving not just with his legs but with his whole body. He managed a grotesque jerking mockery of a sit-up, hit the end of the slack from the wrist-chain, and fell back onto the mattress.

"This little piggy had roast beef," the ugly fat friend continued, tapping his third toe, and then his fourth. "This little piggy had none."

The willowy one, having finished wedging the folded towel under his foot, now crouched with another towel in her hands. She was stark-white-pale, and trembling, but her eyes were fixed on Steve's. He shuddered at the strange emptiness he saw in them.

The other four all focused on his foot. As the ugly fat one tapped the Phillips head screwdriver against his pinkie toe, he tore his gaze away from the willowy girl and looked where they were looking.

"And this little piggy went wee-wee-wee all the way home," said the ugly fat friend. She slid the screwdriver's shaft between the fourth and fifth toes, forcing the pinkie toe to stick outward, away from its brothers.

He curled his toes, but the screwdriver was in the way. Another strangled, angry cry tried to get out and failed.

The brunette took his pinkie toe between the wire stripper's notched blades. They were open to their widest extension, but she still had to work at it, pinching the toe's flesh, seesawing the wire strippers side to side, scraping tender toe-skin, until the blades were wedged at the base of his toe. The ugly fat friend withdrew the screwdriver.

They wanted him to think they were actually going to cut it off! Just snip it like a bud off a branch or something!

Un-fucking-believable!

She hesitated and glanced at the others.

About fucking time!

Game over, they'd had their fun but they'd lost, they weren't going to get what they wanted from him–

"Here goes," the brunette said.

The wire stripper didn't go *snip*. It went *k-shunk* through meat and skinny toe-bone.

A stunning bolt of pain slammed all the way up Steve's leg and into his brain. He bucked in a convulsive lunge, back arching, butt going up off the mattress and then thudding back down. His throat felt like it would explode from the scream he couldn't get past the gag. A hot-acid flood of tears spilled from his eyes.

With all that, somehow, he still saw what happened to his pinkie toe. He saw the splurt of blood shoot up. He saw the pinkish nub, with its toenail and its wisps of hair, tumble backwards and go bouncing down the top of his right foot. He saw the raw place where it had been, welling as if someone were squeezing a wet, red sponge.

He writhed and twitched, the pain enormous and the shock even bigger. His toe! They had lopped off his fucking *toe*!

"Holy shit," one of them said.

Then all of them were talking.

"Did you see that? Did you?"

"Fuck *me*!"

"It just came right off."

"Where'd it go?"

"That was fucking insane!"

"You just… snipped, and…"

"Oh, here it is. Eew. Someone pick it up."

"*You* pick it up."

"I don't want to touch it."

"Tough. Pick it up."

"We might want to rethink the wire strippers. They're too small."

"What about those branch-clipper things?"

"Oh-god-oh-god-oh-god it's a *toe*, I'm touching a guy's toe."

His entire right foot was a howling, pulsing mass of agony. It sent rolling pain-waves up his leg. He was crying, bleeding, gushing tears, gushing blood, gushing snot, couldn't breathe, drowning in his own snot, choking, about to puke, he'd puke in his own mouth and then drown in that, too.

It didn't subside, and he didn't get used to it, but somehow he found a more manageable level and was able to open his bleary, stinging eyes to look at the crazy psycho-chicks who'd done this to him.

They stood around the bottom of the mattress, red spatters on their hands and arms, a couple of them with red spatters on their faces. The ugly fat friend still held the screwdriver, though it dangled at her side as if she'd forgotten it. The brunette had put down the wire strippers and was staring at Steve's foot. The willowy one held something in the towel, cradling it like a baby mouse, and he realized it must be his severed toe.

The strong one grinned. "Betcha he's scared *now*!"

CHAPTER EIGHT

Eight little words.

"We want you to feel right at home."

And here he was.

Ed Reilly appreciated their kindness, he honestly did. And he tried his best to show that appreciation.

They were welcoming and all, generous as could be, taking him in more like a fond relation than a hired man. They'd given him a nice room, furnished in true farmhouse comfort. His window had a view of leafy oak branches and, through those, the property next door.

Feel right at home?

He didn't know how to so much as begin explaining to the Gerrittsons the unlikelihood of it. Not without coming off sounding mean and ungrateful.

No, it wasn't the place, and it wasn't the people.

It was that, in a world without Leigh, he didn't know how he'd ever feel right at home anywhere.

How she would have loved it here! Her dream come true and then some.

"We'll buy a nice little house in the country," she'd said, the two of them cuddled under the covers in their too-small apartment's too-small bed. "A garden, a field, lots of fruit trees, maybe even some chickens. It'll be quiet, and green, and wonderful. Just you and me, Eddie, until the kids come along."

At the time, he'd chuckled and hugged her tight. Wishing and hoping, like the old song said. Why not? When you were young and in love, anything seemed possible.

Now here he was, having learned the hard way how 'anything' had its dark side, and when it came to what was possible, there could be as much bad as good.

Once unpacked, Ed could only laugh.

A sad laugh, maybe, and one not without a touch of bitterness in with the melancholy, but a laugh nonetheless.

Muriel Gerrittson kept apologizing for the room being so small, offering up her sewing room instead if he preferred, but Ed would hear no such talk. He didn't need a lot of space. Wasn't like he had much to fill it, except some clothes, and a lot of memories.

The memories, like the laugh, had their bittersweet notes.

Small as this corner farmhouse bedroom was, it was still twice the size of the place he and Leigh had moved into when they first got married. The place with the dining-room nook they'd turned into a nursery. Or rather, Leigh had... working with more than enough love and care to make up for what they'd lacked in budget. Making everything ready for that special day.

That special day... which had never come.

Wasn't for lack of trying.

Three false alarms. Five miscarriages. One stillbirth–Ethan. One preemie–Hope–who'd lasted almost a week in neonatal intensive care.

Leigh'd wanted children with all her dear, loving heart. So had Ed, but most of all, he'd wanted her to be happy. As happy as she deserved.

"It doesn't have to be a whole houseful," she'd told him. "One each, a boy and a girl would be perfect."

Even just one at all, it seemed like, was asking too much.

If it had been a matter of only his wife's physical health, Ed would have felt better about putting his foot down, telling her they needed to stop.

But the doctors had kept on insisting she was fine. They couldn't find any reason for her troubles carrying a baby to term, any explanation beyond simple bad luck.

There'd been times he thought about going behind her back, getting himself a vasectomy on the sly. If he did, though, and she *did* find out, which she would, then she'd be even more devastated.

As for other options, well, those took money they just didn't have. Adoption was expensive, and the agencies weren't lining up to give kids to people like them.

In the end, he supposed, it had turned out just as well.

What if they'd had that boy and girl, one of each, like Leigh wanted? Or even just one? If Ethan, or Hope, or both, had survived? Ed had been all set to be a father, ready to do his damnedest to be a good one, certain he could manage anything with Leigh by his side.

Being a widower *and* a single dad, on the other hand…

Would it have helped, been a comfort, knowing she'd left part of herself behind?

Would he have been able to handle it on his own, stuck in that tiny apartment, trying to make ends meet, with someone besides his own bereaved self to look after?

Or what if, even worse, the same stupid accident hadn't taken only Leigh's life, leaving him even more alone than he already was?

God, how he missed her.

Heaving a sigh, he decided there was no point moping around his new room, and ventured out to start getting himself used to the rest of the house as home as well as workplace.

The man who met Ed at the bottom of the stairs was a scrawny echo of the hale, hearty, rugged cowboy smiling from the old pictures hanging in the front hall. He had thinning grey hair, a stoop, and too-big-for-him skin that hung in tanned, leathery folds. The clunky, old-fashioned hearing aid plugged into his left ear was a far cry from the discreet, modern type his wife wore.

No ranches and rodeos for Walt Gerrittson now. No broncos, no bulls, no calf-roping, no horses. These days, it was alpacas.

But still smiling. Always smiling.

"Ed! Thought we could have us a beer," he said. "Early, I know, but what the hell, to toast your arrival."

"I'm here about every day, Mr. G."

"You know what I mean. Come on, before the little lady gets back from town. Wouldn't do to have her catch us drinking in the middle of the afternoon, would it?" He winked.

Ed followed him into the kitchen. They'd already told him to feel free to help himself to the fridge or pantry, though he knew it would be a long time before he felt comfortable enough to 'help himself' to anything.

Walter grabbed a couple of beers, handed one to Ed, and opened his own. "To our new live-in help. Now we can boss you around at all hours, how do they say, twenty-four/seven, and there's not a damn thing you can do about it."

"Suits me fine," Ed said. They tipped the cans together, and drank.

"Say, I was wondering if, next time you cut the grass, you might not mind driving the mower next door. I saw those girls out there yesterday afternoon trying to push Mrs. Hubert's noisy, dangerous old gnasher around. Miracle none of them ran over a foot."

"Sure thing, Mr. G."

"Nephew took off and left her in the lurch, I hear."

Ed, from what he'd seen of Donnie Hubert, didn't think his presence or absence was going to make a whole lot of difference. The boy had never seemed to do much in the way of actual work.

"Unpleasant woman," Walter went on after another long sip of beer. "Were we ever glad to see the tail end of her and her dog? You betcha. But that's no reason not to be neighborly to those girls, is it? They've been busting their patooties over there, clearing out and cleaning and fixing up. Least we can do is help out some now and again."

They'd done it.

They really had done it.

Rachel had to admit, she was surprised.

Not surprised that they *could*. Not technically speaking.

Technically speaking, there was no reason why they couldn't.

Surprised that they *would*, surprised that they *had*. The others. She'd been almost positive somebody would back out. They all had reasons, and if one of them went, it probably would have set off a chain reaction or domino effect. The only question had been, who might tip first?

Gwen? The most probable. She wouldn't even squash a spider, but insisted on seeing it safely released to the great outdoors. She cried over Disney cartoons and those commercials about abused animals. Gwen was weak, nice, gentle, timid. A marshmallow. Sweet, but soft.

Which, Rachel now understood, were the very qualities that made Gwen participate. A gentle, timid marshmallow wasn't about to stand up to her friends or go against the crowd.

Annamaria had also been a risk. The cross, the Bible, the statuette of whichever saint that was she kept on her dresser, the occasional church attendance... *Thou shalt not kill* and so on, right? Even before she'd told them about her sister—and *that*! Who knew? Three years they'd been roomies, and it was the first Rachel had heard! She might never have gone running at the mouth about serial killers if she'd known. If anything, it should have seemed like something to give Anna all the more reason to object. Instead, the opposite.

People were so weird. Totally predictable, except when they weren't. And when they weren't, they could take unpredictable to whole new heights.

She'd had fewer doubts about Jessie and Darlene, at least in the going-for-it department. Jessie, when push came to shove, *could* have turned out to be all show and no substance. Like a bodybuilder who looked impressive, but was unable to throw a punch or take one without crying like a baby. And, of course, Darlene... who had plenty of rage, but also the unexpected squeamishness and puking.

None of them, though, none of them had backed out. Something had carried them along. Some tide, some wave, some unstoppable juggernaut force.

They'd done it.

Made a plan, stuck to it, followed through, carried it out.

And if their victim—their first real intentional one; Donnie didn't count— had been dispatched kind of quick... well, hadn't that also been part of the plan? A lot of killers started off as novices, more theory than practice. Nobody really knew how it'd be until the actual moment arrived.

Okay, yeah, the toe thing had freaked everybody out. They might've overreacted. There might've been a little panic. Totally understandable and excusable. Here they were, needing time to think and process, while he was thrashing and flailing in his chains, making those horrible noises... was it any wonder they'd just had to make him *stop*? To do anything, whatever it took, to shut him up?

So, they had. And it was fine. A little anticlimactic, maybe, but fine. *Good*, even. Hadn't she said something about how the early kills tended to be rushed, or sloppy?

As for Rachel herself, there'd never been a doubt in her mind. Which probably made her a sociopath or something. But, so what? She didn't care.

That, she figured, pretty well answered the whole 'sociopath' question anyway.

All the preparations, all the buildup, and then the useless bastard went and croaked on them almost before they even got started.

Darlene didn't know whether to be more disgusted or disappointed.

They didn't even have a chance to get the rest of his clothes off. Shoes, socks, this little piggy, and he'd still been there thinking they were only messing around, joking, playing some kind of stupid hidden-camera prank... then the toe...

Okay, *that* part, that had been great!

Gross, but great.

The look in his eyes! Pain, yeah, but better than the pain was the realization, the rock-solid bolt of awareness, the thunderstruck belief-through-disbelief.

Priceless.

Picture of a smug shithead having to recalibrate his entire

goddamn worldview in a split second. In your *face*, patriarchal misogynist manosphere!

But then it was over, just like that. Bam. Dead, followed by the tedious cleanup and disposal. Hardly even worth the effort!

"Typical," Jessie had said with a snort. "And guys go around thinking they're so damn tough."

What a letdown!

She wished they'd at least un-gagged him. Not early enough to have to listen to a load of blustering bullshit, but, she'd wanted to hear some begging, damn it. Begging, crying, sobbing, pleading for mercy.

In the club, gearing up for it, Annamaria had been a bundle of nerves.

Serving as the bait wasn't much fun.

On the plus side, though, it did mean she got to pick.

Him, she had signaled to the others. *Thinks he's such a stud, with his smug hey-baby chin lift.*

No objections from anybody.

From there, the whole thing went like clockwork. Just as Rachel had planned. Just as they'd rehearsed.

Of course, the scene would have attracted a lot more attention if their sexes had been reversed, if it had been a group of guys 'helping' a semi-conscious girl to the car.

Which was kind of the whole point, wasn't it?

As it was, no one batted an eye, except perhaps in good-natured "guess he can't hold his liquor" amusement.

Once they'd had him taped up and stashed in the trunk, she'd relaxed. And once they'd gotten him upstairs, secured behind soundproofing and closed doors, she'd known they had won.

She expected to finally know, firsthand, what Serafina and the others must have experienced during their final, terrible moments. She wanted to witness it, *needed* to witness it, had to *understand*.

Would he, she'd wondered, hold on a long time? Maybe hoping for reprieve, or rescue, or release? Maybe just in some kind of brute, stubborn, animal instinct? Denial and disbelief right up until the very end? Clinging bit by bit to each little scrap of life, refusing to accept the truth of the inevitable?

But then they'd snipped off his toe, and suddenly it was all too much, it was shit-got-*real*, and before there was any chance for witnessing and understanding, he'd been dead.

Without any meaningful revelations or anything.

Just... *dead.*

They would have to take it slower next time.

A *lot* slower.

"How long?" asked Darlene, in a petulant whine.

"Another month at least. Maybe two to be safest."

"Aw, come on, Rachel!"

"Yeah," Jessie added. "Two months? Jesus titty-fucking Christ, we did all that work to use the place only every couple of *months?*"

Annamaria gave Jessie's choice of language a side-eyed look, but only said, "It does seem like a long time to wait."

"Fine, six weeks, then."

"Six weeks isn't so long," Gwen said, speaking up from the corner where she sat amid a confusion of textbooks and notes. "I mean, with midterms and everything—"

"Fuck midterms!" Darlene and Jessie said together.

"Hey," said Rachel, "some of us care about our grades. Besides, we can't afford too many overtly noticeable behavioral changes. We've discussed this."

Then three of them were talking at Rachel at once, while Gwen shrank behind her books.

"But the first one—"

"—such a letdown—"

"—sucked!"

"—over way too fast—"

"—didn't have a chance to really *do* anything—"

"Okay!" Rachel said, pinching the bridge of her nose. "Okay, how about three weeks?"

"*Three*—!" began Annamaria and Darlene.

"Bullshit on that," Jessie said. "The Park River Folklife Festival starts Saturday—"

"Oh, with the big craft fair?" Gwen asked, brightening.

"—crowds, concerts, beer, pot... we'll be able to snag as many guys there as we want."

"Crowds mean potential witnesses," Rachel said.

Darlene's lip curled. "What's the matter, too challenging for you?"

After only the briefest of pauses, Rachel went on. "Of course, crowds do also mean more distractions."

"That's the spirit!" Jessie pumped a fist in the air.

"And yes, with the craft fair," said Annamaria, smiling at Gwen. "Also a great farmer's market. We can get some fresh berries, maybe asparagus."

Aw yeah, when she was right, she was *right*!

Sunny spring weekend plus college town plus Folklife Festival brought them in droves. Grungy street performers: musicians, artists, jugglers, a unicyclist in the shortest cut-off jean shorts Jessie had ever seen. Microbrew snobs, PBR chuggers, potheads.

Her one concern had been that Etch and the guys might decide to show up, but this was all a bit hipster for their tastes. Just as well. She didn't need her own boyfriend cramping her style while she was on the prowl for man-meat!

"How about him?" She elbowed Dar and indicated the unicyclist.

Darlene didn't openly drool, but might as well have, and Jessie wouldn't have blamed her. Those really were some skimpy cut-offs. Everything above and below was on view, rippling muscles and mahogany skin so sweat-slicked he might have been dunked in olive oil. The way he thrust his hips back and forth to keep balance was damn near illegal.

"He's like six-four," Rachel said.

"We could take him," Jessie said.

"Up the stairs?" asked Gwen, peering doubtfully from the shade of a broad-brimmed straw hat.

"Never mind the stairs," said Annamaria. "What about getting him in the trunk?"

"Yeah, but, Rachel, *look* at him," Darlene said.

"I am. Six-four and probably two-twenty."

"Everyone is." Annamaria adjusted her sunglasses. "He's the center of attention. Even if we could get close, we'd have to fight our way through a dozen other women."

"Not if you gave him the sexy wink," Jessie said.

"Why do *I* have to—?

"Let's just pick someone else," Rachel said.

"Maybe over by the picnic tables?" suggested Darlene.

"Oh, no, no, those are mostly dads," Gwen said, sounding stricken.

Rachel nodded. "Yeah, they'd be too hard to lure away."

Gwen opened her mouth, then closed it again with a soft snap.

Jessie snickered. "Come on. There's girls playing volleyball. Where there's girls playing volleyball, there'll be guys."

Once again, when she was right, she was *right*!

In the sunshine, poles and nets marked sandy rectangles into volleyball courts. Girls mostly their age or younger squealed and laughed and bounced around. Few of them could play for shit, she observed. Only a couple had any sort of competitive spirit. The rest seemed to be there to jiggle.

And, sure enough, in the tree-shade around the edges loitered guys ranging from geeky junior-high kids to sad old fucks. Some just leered outright, but even those pretending to be reading or engrossed in their phones weren't fooling anybody.

Gwen made a face. "Eew, why do they have to do that? It's so creepy!"

"Creepers gonna creep," said Jessie, shrugging.

"And deserve whatever they get." Darlene glowered at the nearest group, who were having a lively discussion on the comparative fuckability ratings of the volleyball players.

Then one started in on the same goddamn song and dance about friendzones and chicks only dating assholes and never giving nice guys a chance, and it was as if something psychic simply went *click* in the airspace.

Jessie glanced from Darlene to Rachel, then Annamaria,

and even Gwen, and saw four versions of her own expression.

"Huh," said Rachel in a musing kind of way. "I think that's what they call self-selection."

When they brought out the shears, Mr. Freddy Friendzone's eyeballs popped out of his head.

Well, not *literally*.

That happened later.

They didn't *pop* out, either, did they? And sure not on their own.

Eyeballs, Darlene thought, were more durable than they looked. Those optic nerve things, too… who'd have guessed they were so sinewy and tough? Well, who besides Rachel? But she knew everything anyway, and the last thing any of them needed was another round of "You're so smart and we're all morons."

No, the shears were–to start, anyway–so they could cut his clothes into scraps and leave him bare-assed on the mattress cover.

He wasn't much to look at. Better than Donnie Hubert, but Donnie Hubert had been setting the bar pretty damn low. This one sported the soft kind of comfortable tummy and rounded features guys felt like they could get away with while fully expecting and demanding to date supermodels.

She still didn't get to hear any begging. By the time Rachel said they could rip the strapping tape off his face, he was past that point, reduced to wordless howls and shrieks and blubbery gibbering noises.

Still pretty awesome, though, if not entirely satisfying.

And he had cried. Cried and sobbed.

He'd even pissed himself, when the kitchen gadgets got into the game.

If he had been scared before, he'd been *petrified* by then. His dick and balls had just about retreated turtle-like into his body, as if those parts had known they were prime targets.

Which, of course, they were. Eventually.

Darlene figured she would never look at a garlic press the same way again.

Poor Mr. Friendzone.

Of course, she'd puked after; she'd puked until she thought she was going to turn herself inside-out... but, she'd also lost twelve pounds already, so bring on the bulimia!

The blood. God, so much blood.

Annamaria had known, factually, how much blood a human body contained.

Knowing was one thing.

Seeing it... seeing it was something else altogether.

Primal. Emotional. Visceral.

Everywhere.

The color of it. The consistency. The pressure and flow. The variations.

So many variations, depending on the wound. Bright, spurting arterial gushes. Sluggish maroon venous syrup. Capillaries oozing pinkish-clear.

The smell, too. The smell and the feel of it, the thick liquid heat, the tackiness and stickiness as it cooled...

Oh, so, so much blood.

Jessie signed off from Skype, missing Dad and her brothers more than ever, and looking forward to their next big family get-together, whenever it might happen to be.

A whole week of roughhousing, barbecue, farting, scratching, competitive belching, war stories, and appalled sisters-in-law. With Jessie herself right there in the thick of it. Tomboy, nothing. Screw that. She was one of them, as ballsy as any, and more than most.

Especially now.

Even if only she knew about it. Even if she couldn't tell, couldn't brag, no matter how much she might want to.

She knew. That was what mattered.

Let James talk about the insurgents over in whatever Buttfuckistan he'd last been deployed to. Let Joel go on about prison riots, and Johnny describe how it sounded when he snapped that running back's knee in the Big Game. Let Jeff share his trauma center stories. Let Dad and Jeremy talk hunting, deer blood in the snow and all that good stuff.

If she wanted, she could tell them some war stories that would blow their socks off.

How about a little premeditated, first-degree murder?

Booyah.

How about scoring a guy's back with a paring knife–another of those cheap but wicked-sharp ones, like Rachel had used on Donnie Hubert's arm–and then gripping an edge of skin with needle-nose pliers and seeing how long a strip she could peel off before it tore?

Or using those same needle-nose pliers to find out just how hard it really was to pull out someone's fingernails? Abrading his rosy little man-nipples right the fuck off his chest with a metal rasp?

Hardcore!

Definitely hardcore.

She wished she could tell them. Wished she could show them pictures, but Rachel didn't let them take any. No pictures, no video, no audio, nothing. They would have enough evidence to deal with already, without making more for the sake of souvenirs, she said.

So, no telling Dad and her brothers.

Too bad.

Gwen brushed and brushed, her hair getting smoother with each therapeutic pass.

She had the lights off and the drapes drawn. The music cycled softly on random play through Celtic strings and Gregorian chants, haunting vocals and the *Lord of the Rings* soundtracks... with tracks from the *Voices of Nature* collection thrown into the mix. By focusing on it, she could tune out any other noises in the house.

Tune them out, and make them all go away.

Brushing her hair. Brushing, brushing. Then stroking it with her palm. Long, straight, cool, silky. Crackling with faint static electricity. Sometimes there was a spark big enough to see: a quick, purple-white snap. Fairy lightning, she'd called it when she was a little girl.

The problem with watching for fairy lightning meant keeping her eyes open, and keeping her eyes open meant seeing the disappointed gazes from the walls of her room.

Daniel. Logan. Alex. Orlando.

And Cameron Mack.

Most of all, Cameron Mack.

Looking at her. Looking at her with sadness, because she was tainted. She was damaged goods. Not a decent person anymore. Not a nice girl. Not the pure and special kind of girl that he'd ever want.

She had thought—hoped—she was different. That there really might be a connection between them. A chance. Something psychic. Something destined. A link that went beyond, that set her apart from the legions of squealing fangirls. She *felt* that, felt it in her heart, felt it like a physical yearning, a lifting-soaring pull. Like flying.

Now it was ruined. Now *she* was ruined. Innocence gone. She was broken, fallen, stained. A virgin with blood on her hands.

Had *she* done those things? Those terrible, terrible things? Not just watched, not just stood by and said nothing while her friends did terrible things, but gotten right in there down and dirty herself, to revel in the gore?

Not revel. She hadn't reveled. Please, no, she hadn't reveled.

After all, *she* hadn't been the one to try and jerk anybody's eyeball out of his head with her bare hand, like it was the balky pull-cord on Mrs. Hubert's stubborn piece-of-junk lawn mower.

It wasn't like *she* had taken a hacksaw to a man's ear, sawing it off in a ragged, cartilaginous scrap that included a patch of scalp and hair, and then shown it to him. Or slit his lips with a cheese slicer. All she'd done was help hold him steady, because he sure had been thrashing around.

But she *had* been the one who'd done that thing with the little sharp manicure scissors... and the fine webbing of skin between the bases of his fingers...

And now they were already getting ready to do it again.

CHAPTER NINE

Gordon struggled toward wakefulness.

It felt like slogging through deep, thick mud. Slowing him. Clinging to him. Holding him back. Miring him. Dragging him down.

His head pounded. His face was a swollen, achy mess. He couldn't breathe through his nose... which seemed to have been replaced with a squashed tomato. The inside of his mouth was raspy and dry. He tasted a crusty, coppery slime all down the back of his throat.

Bloody nose? Oozing from his sinuses? Mouth-breathing all night as a result?

Christ, he hadn't had a bloody nose in years. The hypertension medication his doctor had put him on was supposed to take care of that.

And even when he'd had the nosebleeds, they'd never come with this much pain. It felt like he'd been punched.

He'd been swallowing the blood too. His stomach was sick from it.

A few other parts also hurt, but his head was the main misery.

Was he hung over?

He didn't remember drinking any more than his usual couple of martinis after the day's round of seminars.

Come to think of it... he didn't remember... well, anything! He didn't even know where he was.

Opening his eyes required too much effort right then, so Gordon didn't bother. He worked his parched tongue around, trying to get some saliva going. When he did, it was sour and corrosive, and didn't help the nausea any.

His eyes weren't ready to open, his ears weren't telling him much. He couldn't smell through his wreck of a nose, couldn't taste beyond that crusted blood-slime and the sour saliva.

All that left him was his sense of touch.

Padding underneath. A light blanket over the top. Nothing between the blanket and his skin. He was naked. He couldn't move.

"Smooth one, Jess," Darlene said, voice dripping sarcasm. "Why'd you have to bash him in the nose?"

"I told you, it was an accident!"

"Yeah but it means we can't use the gag. What if he yells?"

"The soundproofing works," Rachel said. "It was fine with the others, so we should be okay, right?"

"Maybe," Jessie said. She glanced at Annamaria. "Or maybe we should just do him and get it over with. He won't be much fun anyway."

"Why not?" asked Gwen.

"He's old and fat and boring. Not much of a challenge."

"He's not *that* old—" Annamaria said.

"Jesus, Anna, the guy's my *dad's* age. And he's a what, accountant?"

"Motivational speaker."

Jessie's snort said all she had to say on that subject.

"So why him?" Darlene asked. "I thought we were going for young guys, hot guys, party and club guys. Aren't we supposed to have a pattern or something?"

"We never did officially settle on one," Rachel said. "It's not, you know, a set in stone requirement."

"Opportunity," Annamaria said. "The opportunity presented itself, so I took it."

***

He'd come into the restaurant an hour before her shift ended.

Typical suit and tie. Out-of-town executive type.

He seemed vaguely familiar, though.

Or was it the look in his eyes that was familiar? The dawning glint of interest, the crawling gleam of appreciation?

She got such looks a lot. Went with the territory. A certain class of businessman seemed to view waitresses, stewardesses, and other women in the service industry as belonging to a different sort of service industry altogether.

Taking his order—martini with extra olive, potato skins—she did the usual perfunctory smile and polite chitchat. It was enough to convince her she didn't know him, but also enough to convince her he did look familiar.

He reminded her of... someone. She just couldn't immediately place the resemblance.

Over in Marcello and Bry's section, a large cougar party was noisily celebrating the finalization of one of their number's latest divorce. Which had been, by the sounds of it, a knock-down-drag-out struggle ending in a sweeping, take-him-to-the-cleaners victory for the home team. Champagne toasts had moved swiftly on to margaritas and cosmos, their mood growing progressively more raucous, their jokes raunchier, and their laughter louder.

Annamaria felt sorry for Marcello and Bry, though they seemed to be eating up the attention... or playing it in order to earn heftier tips. On the upside, at least she wasn't the only one getting ogled this shift.

She brought the businessman-type his drink, then began threading her way through the obstacle course of tables and booths, still trying to figure out who he reminded her of.

Halfway to the kitchen, the revelation hit her like a jolt from a live wire.

Stuart Greaver. The man was almost the identical image of Stuart Greaver.

Whom the media had dubbed 'Gutman' Greaver, for what he'd done to Serafina and those twenty-nine other girls.

***

Someone must have hit him.

That explained the mushy, throbbing pain in his nose.

Slugged him in the face.

Who? Why?

He couldn't remember.

Gordon wracked his brain, but he couldn't even be certain what city he was in, let alone where he was now, or what had happened to him.

Airport… hotel… conference center… bar.

Always the same.

One after another.

Except… this time…

He'd gotten in a fight?

He'd been in a few arguments before, but never a *fight*. The kinds of bars he visited, people didn't start throwing punches. The most there might be were heated words over political differences. Exchanges of insults, not blows.

His muddled head began to clear, and he remembered a crowded, noisy restaurant dominated by women his own age. Drinking, cheering, hooting women. Flirting with their waiters. Making toasts to the financial castration of yet another deserving asshole.

Whoever he was, Gordon remembered feeling bad for him. He remembered thinking his wife and her friends probably had similar parties when one of them fleeced her ex.

He remembered being glad his waitress showed him to a corner booth.

He remembered his waitress.

Brunette. Beautiful. Sultry and smoldering. A young Sophia Loren.

She'd seemed nice.

Attentive.

Friendly.

Warm smile. A soft but lingering touch on his shoulder as she delivered his second martini. Which had been very good. So good, he'd ordered a third… telling himself it was *because* they were so good, *not* because he hoped for another touch on the shoulder.

The potato skins had been okay, not great, nothing to write home about, but he devoured them anyway and assured her they were the best he'd ever had.

Now he wondered if they hadn't agreed with him. What if he had food poisoning? Was that why he felt like this?

Still didn't explain the broken nose.

Or why he was naked in a strange bed.

Or why he couldn't move. Why he was cuffed. If he *was* cuffed. Something hard and cold around his wrist, and his ankle.

Maybe it was... restraints... to keep him from hurting himself. If he was in the hospital...

Had he been in a car crash? He hadn't driven... he'd walked from the hotel. But he supposed he could have been struck by a car while walking back. He could have stumbled over a chunk of torn-up sidewalk or scaffolding while traversing an under-renovation block.

That, Gordon decided, had to be it. Some careless idiot had smacked into him while he was crossing the street, or he'd tripped and fallen. Either way, he could sue. The idiot driver, or the city.

He'd been hurt. He could have been killed. He would definitely sue somebody.

The man *wasn't* Gutman Greaver. She knew that.

It was impossible, obviously. Impossible for a lot of reasons, the biggest being that Gutman Greaver was dead. He'd died in prison while awaiting trial. Stabbed by another inmate during a riot.

Such was the official story, anyway. Annamaria had always wondered.

God knew there'd been plenty of people howling for his blood. They didn't just want him executed. They wanted him to be treated in a way that would make Guantanamo Bay look like a day spa.

"We should make torture Constitutional just for this piece of (bleep)," the father of Number Eleven had said in a televised interview.

"I hope someone cuts his throat and feeds him to the pigs," was a quote from the fiancé of Number Nineteen.

"If I had my way," the grandmother of Number Six had said, "I would kill him twice for every one of those poor dear girls."

"My mommy's dead," the five-year-old daughter of Number Twenty-Two had tearfully told Oprah. "That bad man should be killed too."

In the end, it wasn't like anybody cared about the truth. He was dead, that was what mattered.

It was closure. It was final. It wasn't months of legal wrangling and media circus and uproar over the morality of the death penalty. It wasn't the remote but terrible possibility that he might somehow be acquitted, or found not guilty by reason of insanity. The grieving survivors didn't have to worry about parole, or escape.

That was all good.

But he had died quick. A single stab, the knife angling up between his ribs to puncture his heart. He probably hadn't seen it coming, hadn't felt more than that bright, steely flash. He hadn't suffered the way his victims had. He hadn't lingered in terror and hopeless pain. He had died without any of that.

He had also died without explaining. No lengthy interviews with criminal psychiatrists. No Ann Rule, true crime, inside story version of his killings. No book or movie deals. No *answers*.

No *real* answers, anyway.

The police had all the answers they cared about. They knew the who-what-where-when. They knew the how.

They didn't care so much about the *why*.

Annamaria cared about the *why*.

He was not in the hospital.

For a while, Gordon was tempted to believe he was in a psych ward somewhere, hallucinating, raving, out of his mind.

Then he wondered if he was in Hell.

Either of those would have been better than this.

It was bad when they were gone.

It was worse when they came back.

Bad being alone. Bad having to wait and wonder. Bad having to anticipate what would come next.

Worse finding out.

Always worse.

No matter what he imagined, what he expected, what he tried to brace himself for... when they started in on him, it always turned out to be worse.

A lot, lot worse.

He felt like a small thing caught in a merciless trap. A hurt mouse. Crippled. Squeaking and twitching and scrabbling.

Helpless.

Toyed with.

Once, he wished they'd just kill him already, end it.

Then his whole mind recoiled in horror. Wishing to die? What kind of person wished to die?

The sort of person who didn't have much to live for in the first place.

He didn't think much at all for a long while after that.

And eventually, it didn't matter anymore.

"Please," he said. Sobbed, more like it. "Please, why are you doing this?"

"Tell me what it feels like," the girl said.

The waitress, the brunette, the young Sophia Loren with a voice like velvet smoke and those smoldering dark eyes.

She had... sharp things.

"It hurts," he said.

Did women have a greater ability to endure unimaginable pain? Were men not as tough as they liked to think? Did some people resist, while others gave up without a fight? Craving death, wanting it, willing it?

What had Serafina done, when it had been her turn as Greaver's victim?

Annamaria knew what had been found in that cellar. She'd read, she'd heard, she'd watched the news when her parents weren't around, she'd gleaned all the details she could in her ongoing effort to *understand*.

The cellar. The bodies. The implements. The pieces. Even before the cutting began, there must have been fear, such fear... raw, stark terror... pain and shame and humiliation.

Then came the cutting. And the burning. Torture escalating to savagery.

Had Serafina prayed for a quick death? Had she prayed for survival at all costs? Had she found her prayers answered, or been faced with the bleak knowledge that they wouldn't be?

Then—perhaps he'd gotten bored, perhaps Serafina had been beyond reaction and therefore no fun anymore—the evisceration and dismemberment.

These men so far had gotten off easy compared to what Serafina must have endured.

It wasn't the same. No, it wasn't the same at all.

**

The rest of that night came back to Gordon in hazy fits and starts.

Something hadn't agreed with him. He remembered feeling lightheaded and queasy when the brunette waitress brought him his bill, and told him that she was going off-duty but hoped he had enjoyed his meal.

The way she'd hesitated before that going-off-duty remark. As if giving him an opening to speak.

Wouldn't it just figure? All the years of temptation and fantasy vs. cold hard reality, to finally come to a moment like this, only to be getting sick? He'd only been able to mumble wanly, then left the restaurant, afraid he was going to vomit, but hoping to hold off until the privacy of his own hotel bathroom.

He remembered seeing her walking up the street ahead of him, remembered staggering and—yes, he *had* damn near tripped on a chunk of sidewalk in the renovation zone, he *should* sue the city!—and she had come back to ask him if he was okay.

He remembered trying to tell her he felt a little under the weather, and her being solicitous, offering to help, offering to drive him to his hotel. Leading him toward a parking lot, one of those downtown pay lots, no attendant, just a metal box with numbered slots where the money went in.

Something–he didn't know what, some instinct, some sense–had given him a moment's pause. A moment's wariness and suspicion. All Gordon knew was that he'd pulled his arm away from her, meaning to get out of there.

And then a fist had come flying at him out of nowhere.

The dazzling impact. The blurred glimpse, through watery eyes and parking lot darkness, of a triumphant, grinning face.

**

"Tell me," she repeated.

"I did!" Gordon knew he was whimpering and couldn't help it. "I told you... it hurts... please!"

"I know it hurts," she said. "But what does it *feel* like?"

The sharp thing this time was a needle. She'd shown it to him. Not a normal sew-on-a-button needle, but the kind that might be used on upholstery and thick, tough fabrics. For all he knew, it was the kind they used on leather, to make saddles. The eye in its rounded end was wide enough to poke a folded dollar bill through. The pointed end...

The pointed end was in his hand.

Not piercing his palm in some bizarre imitation of stigmata. She had set the sharp tip in the cradle where his index and middle fingers met, and driven it slowly down between the knuckles. An inch or so, the part with the eye in it, stuck up like the stub of a sixth digit. A skinny metal sixth digit. The rest was embedded in his hand.

If he tried to bend his fingers, the needle-spike in him moved. He tried to keep his hand perfectly still and couldn't. It shook. Damaged tendons made his fingers jitter and twitch. The blood that dripped from their ends–she had begun by systematically jabbing the needle a half-inch deep into each–sprinkled over his pale, quivering torso like abstract art.

"I want to know about the pain," she said.

"Hey, um, Anna? This is kind of... uh... fucked up."

That voice belonged to one of the other girls, the one who had punched him in the face, broken his nose.

"Tell me," the brunette said, ignoring the other one.

"It's… everything," Gordon said. Trying to find the words.

"Your hand?"

"Hurts so much. So, so much!"

She pinched the end of the needle and drew it halfway out. Gordon threw back his head and screamed at the horrible sliding sensation between his fingers.

"And now?" she asked.

"Please!"

"Which hurts worse? Your fingertips, or this?"

"Anna, c'mon, let's just—"

"Shut up, Jessie, I need to know!"

"My hand, please, it's my hand, my whole hand, it hurts!"

"Interesting," said another voice. "He's so concerned about his hand, he's not paying any attention to his leg. But then, the hand does have more nerve endings, and Annamaria's making sure he knows what she's doing, so that makes him perceive it as more painful."

His… his leg?

Gordon tried to raise his head. His neck creaked. He'd felt a minor itching irritation on his shin and calf, dismissed it as the blanket having a scratchy weave, and forgot all about it once the brunette started using the needle.

The blanket, which he'd thought they had folded to his waist, was bunched across his hips and groin. His legs–white, flabby, hairy–were bare. A petite blonde and a homely girl with dishwater hair had his right foot up on an inverted milk crate, and…

He couldn't make sense of it. Not with the pain in his hand consuming the entire world.

His lower leg was covered with colored dots. Blue, white, yellow, green, red, silver. Round dots, like they had pasted circular stickers on him, or colored him with markers. They went in rows and clusters, formed patterns here and there.

What..?

As he watched, the larger girl held up something tiny, showed it to him. A thumbtack. A regular, office-supply-store thumbtack. Short pin, round blue head. She set the tip against the meaty side of his calf and—

A garbled scream exploded from him. The girl pushed the thumbtack. He felt the skin stretch, then pop and yield to the point. He felt it jab in.

He felt all of the thumbtacks.

Every.

Single.

One.

They studded his leg like hobnails on boot soles, like the brass rivets on a leather armchair. Thirty or more thumbtacks driven into him from knee to ankle.

"And, there, see?" said the blonde. "That distracted him from his hand. I guess my grandfather was right."

"Your grandfather?" asked the fifth girl, the one who perched on another milk crate by the foot of the mattress, holding a clear plastic box of thumbtacks.

There were, Gordon saw, still a lot of thumbtacks left in the box. It was a good-sized box.

He shuddered, and it felt as if each of those thirty thumbtacks was acupunctured directly into a nerve.

"When I was little—"

"News for you, Rache, you still *are* little."

Ignoring this, the blonde said, "If we had a Band-Aid that needed to come off, or a splinter, or something, our grandfather had this way of taking care of it so it wouldn't hurt. That was what he said, anyway. He would take the corner of the Band-Aid or get the splinter with the tweezers, and then just before he pulled, he'd use his other hand to smack you."

"Oh, nice, like that's going to make it not hurt?" said the larger girl.

Gordon's fingers reflexively curled, his hands trying to clench into fists. The needle gouged sideways through his flesh. He howled.

"No, really, that was what he said. Say you had a Band-Aid on your arm, right? He'd grab it, and slap your leg, and yank the Band-Aid off, and the idea is you'd be so shocked by them both hurting at the same time, you wouldn't know which one to cry about, so you wouldn't cry about either."

"No offense," the one who'd punched him said. "But your grandpap sounds like kind of a dick."

"It does make sense, though." The brunette leaned over Gordon, studying his face, his eyes. She lifted his arm so he could see it.

The skin on the back of his left hand was tented up, pale and straining at the needle's point, about to tear. A silvery pinprick showed through, then beaded with blood. He tried to relax his hand, but that only made the upthrust needle tilt back down, creasing the skin, forcing its tip the rest of the way through.

"See?" the brunette said. Smiling. A lovely smile. "Now he's focused on *this* again."

She pushed the blunted end of the big needle back in, forcing it until two inches of red-smeared silver emerged from the back of his hand. Then she grasped it in thumb and forefinger and swiftly pulled it the rest of the way through, like she'd done a looping stitch.

Gordon shrieked, thinking of seamstresses, thinking of those yogis who did magic tricks, except there was no blood when the yogis did it, and they claimed it didn't hurt. His hand was nothing but agony and in that instant he would have chopped it off at the wrist if only it'd mean an end to the pain.

He wouldn't tell her... maybe *couldn't* tell her. Maybe the reason he didn't explain was because there weren't words. It was too big for words.

Annamaria bent over his face, gazing into his eyes, trying to search them and see behind them for the true depths of what he was feeling.

It was funny how he didn't look like Gutman Greaver now. Not much, anyway. They were of the same basic type—Rachel might've said that they fit the same profile—of well-educated, middle-aged white male, with the unfit build that came from a sedentary job and prosperous lifestyle.

Every photograph she'd seen of Greaver showed eyes like

reflective disks of polished agate. His expressions were stage sets—good ones, but still stage sets. It was all façade, all painted plywood and foam rubber and hollow plaster of Paris.

Such an ordinary face, such a harmless-looking, ordinary man. That was what had let him get close enough to Serafina and the others, luring them, lulling them, tricking them. But later… when each of them was alone with him… had he shown his true self? Had his expression changed? Had it revealed his cruelty, his hunger?

Or had those girls and women stared up into that same expressionless, emotionless stage set, those same polished-agate eyes?

What would have been worse?

She couldn't decide.

To suffer as they had suffered, while the man who did it was viciously enjoying the savage things he did? Knowing that their torment added to his pleasure?

Or to suffer as they had suffered, while the man who did it might as well have been flipping through an outdated magazine in a dentist office waiting room?

Was it about *him*? Were they keenly aware of him the whole time? Or did that awareness fade as their agonies grew? Did they turn inward until the rest of the world stopped mattering?

"Tell me," she said, as she ran a box-cutter blade down center of this man's chest, where it slit through skin and a soft layer of fat to grate against his breastbone. A long, red line opened up, the edges pulling apart, dark blood spilling. "Is it intense? Encompassing? Transcendent?"

He whimpered by way of reply. It was all he could seem to do. No stage set mask on him, oh no. His features were alive and vivid, contorting with each new injury. His eyes, ringed with dark swellings above his shattered nose, swam with tears.

Had Serafina cried?

That was a stupid thing to wonder. Of course Serafina had cried. Serafina had cried over sad movies, cried when she saw a dead possum by the side of the road, cried when she got a paper cut.

Serafina had cried. And she had screamed. She had begged. She had mewled like an animal. The whole idea of Serafina enduring in saintly, stoic, prayerful silence… that was pure invention. It was what their parents told themselves to keep from going crazy.

"Do you feel more alive?" she asked. "Is it more precious to you right now? Life? Or is it worthless? Do you feel closer to God? That He's abandoned you? That He doesn't exist at all?"

"You gonna talk him to death or what?" Darlene asked, sounding annoyed. She and Rachel had finished the other leg, and the box Gwen held was out of pushpins.

"Yeah, can we just get on with this already?" Jessie had made a couple token cuts, but in general was sitting this one out… she maintained that it was no challenge, a pudgy old fart like this.

Annamaria peered into his eyes again.

Pain. Suffering. Raw physical agony and despair.

And something else.

Something more.

He wasn't going to tell her… maybe wasn't *able* to tell her… but she could see it. She could see it in his eyes.

Fine.

She'd get her answers some other way.

CHAPTER TEN

Rachel folded the newspaper and set it aside, wanting to clip the articles but knowing it would be a mistake to do so.

Or... would it?

Keeping a scrapbook or a wall full of newspaper clippings was an obvious giveaway, the kind of thing that always turned out to be a mistake for overconfident killers in the movies. It was evidence, proof. Practically a signed confession.

In the movies.

Classic to the point of being cliché. That big pivotal scene in which the detective goes into the killer's hideout... finds the book or wall... the scene without sound, or with dramatic music, or with a hushed voiceover of previous dialogue that now, in context, makes clear what the detective should have known all along. A slow pan across the wall, or shots alternating back and forth between close-ups of the detective's face, with eyes showing the growing horror of realization, and the scrapbook's turning pages. The headlines and clippings. Photos of the victims. Lists with names circled in red or crossed out with heavy black pen-strokes.

In the movies.

In real life?

She didn't think it worked that way. And besides, even in the movies, when things got *that* far, it didn't matter much anymore, did it? By the time the police went searching the killer's house, they already suspected... or already knew.

So, there was no real harm in keeping a scrapbook, was there? As long as she didn't go flaunting it around.

The bodies had been found just as intended. The police claimed to be 'investigating several leads' even now. The story was all over the news, and the talk of campus. Rumor had it that the last places the vics had been seen were out clubbing and bar-hopping, and the working theory was that they'd left with girls, though none of the interviewees could agree on what said girls might have looked like or who they'd been.

"That investigating-several-leads thing is bullshit," Jessie said, when Gwen mentioned it in a worried tone. "My brother is a prison guard, he works with cops. That's what they always say to make it look like they're doing something, when really they don't have a clue."

"What if they *do* have a clue?" Darlene asked.

"We didn't leave them any," Annamaria pointed out. "Rachel saw to that. Right, Rachel?"

"As much as I could. But I think we should wait before the next one."

"Why?" Darlene asked. Whiny. Like someone had denied her a candy bar.

"Serial killers usually do," Rachel explained.

She spoke absently. Not really thinking about it… thinking about the police… thinking about how the focus of the investigation had already shifted away from the dead men to these theoretical girls they'd been with. The girls, investigators surmised, were still missing, yet to be reported, or not important enough to anybody else to be missed at all.

The men were only incidental in their view, killed and dumped to get them out of the way, because, naturally, the *girls* were the *real* targets. The girls were the ones being held somewhere, being tortured and raped. The girls' bodies would show up eventually. The dead men weren't, in their view, the main event.

Because of course, serial killers hardly *ever* targeted men!

One more reason why she knew they were going to get away with this.

"Say what, Rache?" Jessie asked.

"The need takes time to build up, become overpowering," she said. "If we do a bunch at once, that's spree killing, not serial killing."

"Don't they speed up?" asked Annamaria. "The need comes faster, so the intervals between killings get shorter?"

"Yes, but—"

"I want to go again," Darlene said, chin jutting, eyes stubborn. She was still throwing up, but last time it hadn't been until nearly at the end.

When, to be fair, things *had* gotten pretty extreme. They'd *all* looked a little green… except for Annamaria, anyway.

"Yeah, screw waiting," Jessie agreed. "It's like a day at Disneyland, you stand in line for two hours and then get to go on a six-minute ride?"

"That's because we did it too fast," Annamaria said. "We didn't spend enough time on it. We didn't do enough."

"We killed them," Gwen said. "We cut them up and dumped their bodies."

"We didn't torture them enough first, though."

Jessie looked askance at Annamaria. "You totally gutted that old guy. No shit, Anna. You were elbows-deep."

"Yeah," said Darlene. "You hardly let anybody else have a turn."

It had been interesting, though. The innards were more than blood. There was stomach acid to think about, and bile, and gases, and bacteria. Intestines were packed with feces—it was what they were for!—but it was still a shock to cut into a guy's belly and have that come gushing out.

Not that Annamaria had seemed to care. She'd gone right in. Swapped the box-cutter for a big butcher knife, and sliced. Rachel had been impressed by the surgical neatness of her technique and the rock-steady calm of her hands.

She'd been less impressed when Annamaria tossed the bloodied butcher knife aside, plunged her hands into the hot, slippery bulge of exposed organs, and gone rooting around to see what she could find. Hadn't even used a pair of tongs, though there had been tongs in the bin.

"I'm sorry," Annamaria said. "I got carried away. Next time, I promise. Assuming there *is* a next time."

"What's *that* supposed to mean?" asked Rachel.

"Yeah, what do you think we are, quitters?" asked Jessie.

"We're not done yet?" asked Gwen.

"Fuck no, why would we want to stop now?" said Darlene.

"But it *does* something to us," Gwen said in a small voice.

"Yes," said Annamaria. "It does."

"And ain't it fucking *great*?" Jessie grinned a feverish, wildcat grin. "I bet none of you ever felt this good before in your whole damn lives, am I right? It's a killer rush. Better than sex!"

Darlene's mouth twisted as if she'd just sunk her teeth into a lemon, but she managed to refrain from saying anything. Rachel frowned, quizzical—she'd never had sex either, and she generally felt about the same as ever. But she also said nothing.

Gwen looked around at them, her big eyes pleading. "None of us would ever do this on our own. We just wouldn't. But when we're together like this... it's... it's like we push each other into doing things we could never normally do."

"That's the best part, we're a team!" Jessie pumped a fist in the air. "Go, Team Awesome!"

Annamaria waved her to shut up. "You're talking about mob psychology, Gwen?"

"I don't know... maybe... but it's also like we're... different when we do this... we're other people. We're all some other-person who's bigger than the five of us put together, and it's that other-person who can do these things."

"Gestalt," said Rachel. "I took Psych 101, and I didn't do very well, but—"

"Which means she got an A-minus," Darlene said.

"Hey, for her, that's practically flunking."

"—but I remember that word," Rachel finished, wrinkling her nose at Jessie and Darlene. "It means that the sum is greater than the parts, or something."

"Exactly." Annamaria looked at Gwen. "Is that it?"

"I... I guess so. But it's also like... it's like when we're together this way, we're... sort of... crazy."

"Crazy people do crazy, random things," Rachel said. "They're irrational. We are being totally rational here, okay? That's why we do all the planning and stuff."

"No, I…" Gwen hissed out a frustrated breath. "In mythology—"

"Oh, crap," said Darlene, squeezing her temples. "Here it comes, fairy tale time."

Gwen pushed on, trying to ignore her. "—there were these women, maenads they were called, and they would drink a lot of wine and go after men, and then… well… tear them apart with their bare hands, and dance in the blood and guts."

"So you're saying we need us some wine," said Jessie, grinning again. "Can do."

"We aren't on some kind of rampage here, Gwen," Rachel said. "You're making it sound like we're wild animals."

"No, that isn't…"

"Well then, what's your point?" Darlene made no effort to hide her impatience.

"It…" Gwen gulped. "It's not very nice."

"We know that," said Rachel in a *well, duh!* tone.

"Yeah, no shit, Sherlock. If it was nice, it wouldn't be such a kick!"

"You don't want to *quit*, do you?" asked Darlene.

"Of course she doesn't," said Annamaria. "It's been a rough few weeks, that's all. We're tired, we're stressed out."

"You got that right," Jessie said.

"Let's give it a rest for a few days," Annamaria continued. "I promise, we'll all feel lots better soon. You'll see. Then, next time, we won't have any troubles at all."

**

Phoenix Pages, the biggest and best used bookstore in the county, was run by a warlock.

Well, not really.

He just seemed that way to Gwen.

The whole place simultaneously delighted her and gave her the creeps. Three stories of narrow rooms and weird little nooks and crannies, all crowded with a mazelike warren of shelves that extended floor to ceiling, but leaned toward each other at the tops.

The floors creaked, the stairs to the basement were loose, the windows were papered over with old posters for poetry readings and plays, and the only lighting came from wan, sputtering bulbs in bare metal sockets. She always felt like the contents were about to avalanche out and bury her alive in yellowed pages and musty binding.

Or that she might, at any moment, find some unexpected passage she'd never noticed before, and it would lead her into a secret section of spellbooks, or a portal to another world, like Hogwarts or Middle-Earth or Narnia. Which of course she didn't believe could ever actually happen...

Oh, but if it could, it'd be someplace like this!

They also sold paperbacks five for a dollar, and had a good trade-in-for-store-credit rate.

And, of course, the proprietor was a warlock. Maybe a gnome.

He was a tiny, wizened, hunched figure, with piebald pigmentation and milky, jack-o'-lantern eyes. Tufts of cobweb-colored hair fringed his balding pate and poked out of his ears and nose. Most of the time, he'd sit on a high stool behind a counter, with stacks of books like a fortification rising up around him.

Most of the time. Not always.

He could move with spiderlike speed and uncanny stealth. Never mind the creaky floors or loose stairs. One moment, he'd be perched on his stool. The next, he'd be right *there* in the stacks, craning his cocked head on his bent neck to peer up, asking in his reedy voice if he could help her find anything.

The bookstore cat was almost as weird. It was also piebald, half its face pure white but the other half a mottling of grey and black. The eye on the pure white side was vivid blue. The eye on the mottled side was the same jack-o'-lantern orange as its master's. When it sprawled on the floor between shelves, as it usually did, it took up the entire aisle. It had an insolent meow, as if it knew it was speaking perfectly clearly, only, she was too Muggle to understand.

Today, there were only a few other people in the store. She saw a bearded man in the military history section, a young mother sorting through a crate of picture books while her toddler whined about wanting ice cream, and a regal, grey-haired lady inspecting the volumes locked in a dusty, glass-fronted case.

Gwen made her way down the wobbly stairs to the basement level, ducking her head under a beam. This was where the genre fiction was shelved, with curling and discolored index cards identifying each category.

Creaks came from overhead, someone walking, more dust sifting down. The cat screeched and a child wailed and a young mother scolded to not pull the kitty's tail, kitty didn't like that.

She saw a chubby, housewife-looking woman in the Romance aisle, and a scrawny bespectacled boy in Horror. The scrawny kid had an armload of paperbacks, their covers mostly black with fangs and glowing eyes, blood-drippy red lettering or slashy silver lettering spelling out their titles. The lady in Romance had a stack of paperbacks with flowing violet or gold script and art of shirtless men embracing swooning maidens.

Both of them had similar, intent, furtive expressions while they skimmed pages, as if hoping to find the dirty parts.

The Sci-Fi/Fantasy section was the largest, taking up four aisles. As soon as she was safely in there, surrounded by names she recognized and cover art with lots of dragons, castles, and unicorns, she was able to push everything else to the back of her mind and just browse.

It felt... nice. Normal.

It felt almost like she was the old Gwen again.

Not this new Gwen. Not this stranger, this killer, this monster.

She wouldn't think about that.

She would work very hard not to think about that.

The Ten Commandments were displayed in granite and bronze, on a huge plaque set into a round, concrete dais.

Ringed by a fence, which was ringed by a flowerbed, which was ringed by a walkway, which was ringed by a swatch of lawn.

The church was very big on rings.

That struck Annamaria as odd. Rings seemed pagan somehow. Ancient. Un-Christian. Rings were for pillars of rough-hewn stone, or white marble Roman ruins.

She mused on that as she approached the plaque, then pushed it to the back of her mind as she read the words that she knew by heart. One line of the Ten stood out more than the others, as if it had been printed in a larger font. It hadn't, of course. The emphasis was only in her head.

Thou shalt not kill.

She had killed.

Killing was a sin.

Therefore she had sinned.

Sinners went to Hell.

Those sent to Hell were damned.

Therefore, she was damned.

Or would be.

Shouldn't she *feel* damned, then?

Shouldn't she *feel* the burden of her sin pressing down on her, heavy as the granite and bronze monument, heavy as a car? Heavy as the weight of the world and God's disfavor?

She hadn't burst into flames the moment she set foot on the church's property. The bells had not clanged out in ominous warning. The sky hadn't gone dark. No jagged bolts of lightning had streaked from the sky to incinerate her on the spot. The soaring, stained-glass windows had not shattered. The stone steps hadn't cracked and blackened when she stepped on them. The door handles hadn't tarnished at her touch.

The nuns who'd passed her, not in archaic, voluminous habits, but neat grey outfits with demure white wimples, had smiled at her. Not recoiled, clutching at their crucifixes and rosaries. A priest had greeted her pleasantly, his voice a soothing murmur in the echoing, vaulted cathedral. He had noted the cross on its chain around her neck and given her an approving nod.

Annamaria wasn't sure how she felt about that.

The church—a stately architectural relic from the city's early days—lingered amid the glass-and-steel edifices of downtown like a ghost. It was popular with wedding parties and moviemakers alike. Even when no services were being held, tourists prowled the grounds, taking pictures, buying postcards.

She'd sat for an hour in a straight-backed pew of gleaming polished wood, hands folded, head bowed, listening to the organist rehearse. No one had shunned her. God had not smote her down.

What did that mean?

She *had* sinned.

She was a murderer.

Didn't God care?

Then again, this was the same God who'd let Serafina die. Who'd let Gutman Greaver do terrible things to her, make her suffer, make her scream, make her bleed. This was the same God who'd let Serafina's beautiful face be sliced and burned until it was barely recognizable.

God had allowed those things to happen. Not only to Serafina, but to twenty-nine others. Wives, daughters, sisters, mothers. Innocent girls and women. Taken, savaged, mutilated and killed. Left dumped like bags of garbage, split-open and leaking.

She knew what most people thought about the victims of serial killers... even her own friends used to think those things... hookers who'd go with anyone for the promise of a few bucks, or hitchhikers willing to climb into a strange car on a dark night, or strippers, or slutty dressers... that they asked for it, that they deserved it somehow. Like what so many people tended to think of rape victims, only with an added element of stupidity.

It wasn't that way. Not always. Not even most times. Hardly ever.

Serafina, for instance. Serafina... kind, intelligent, devout, modest and sweet. She hadn't been anyplace she shouldn't have been, hadn't done anything even remotely risky. Yet it hadn't stopped what happened to her. It hadn't stopped God from letting Gutman Greaver slaughter her, leaving something so gruesome the best morticians in the state couldn't do anything but recommend closed casket.

How could any loving deity allow that?

How could any loving deity stand by and do nothing as the five of them did what *they* had done?

Unless there was no God at all.

Annamaria waited, standing on holy ground, staring at the Ten Commandments graven in bronze. She remained un-burst-into-flames, un-struck-by-lightning.

No divine wrath.

If her mother or father knew what she was thinking,

Annamaria would have gotten some parental wrath instead. Parental wrath right across the face.

Her mother had been a dedicated churchgoer even before Serafina's death. Mass at least once a week, study and prayer groups, charitable functions, social events. After, it became her main–*only*–source of comfort and support. Mass daily, hours of silent vigil, Serafina's room preserved as a shrine, weekly visits to the cemetery.

"It's God's will," her mother would have said. While rocking back and forth, clutching the family Bible, more than likely. "God works in mysterious ways and it is not for us to question. God had a reason for calling Serafina home so soon."

That reason, which Louise Voltaire never stated outright– pride, vanity, and presumption forbid!– but clearly understood nevertheless, was that her elder daughter had been too good for the mortal world. Too perfect. God had wanted her back in Heaven among the angels. Serafina was a martyr. A saint.

Throughout Annamaria's childhood, her father had deferred to his wife when it came to religious matters. He'd go to church whenever Louise pointed out that he hadn't been in a while, but would have just as soon spent his Sundays watching television. With a beer or two... or six, or ten.

Water-into-wine may have been a miracle, but there was nothing miraculous about the beer-into-bourbon transformation following Serafina's funeral. Felix Voltaire's attendance at church stopped abruptly, but not from lack of belief. He believed, all right.

"God wanted to punish me," he'd once said. Slurred, really. While little Annamaria eavesdropped from the hall. "He wanted to punish me for not going to church enough, and for drinking too much. So He took Sera. He took Sera! Punishment outweighed the crime! So now I'll never set foot in a church again and I'll drink every damn day until the score's settled! I'll show Him!"

A selfish, jealous deity who put wonderful people like Serafina on earth only to snatch them away from those who loved them? A petty, spiteful deity whose response to a man's alcoholism was to kill that man's innocent daughter?

Were either of those any better than an indifferent deity

who didn't care about human suffering and atrocities? A weak deity who couldn't prevent them?

Were *any* of those better than no God at all?

She remained un-struck-down for blasphemy, but another possibility occurred to her.

Suppose there *was* a God who did not just *let* these things happen, but encouraged them? Suppose it was what God wanted?

The blood and the pain and the death. Destruction and sacrifice.

What God wanted.

Yes.

Professor Scritchfield stepped out of the classroom for a minute, and as soon as she was gone, the gaggle of dumb bunnies sitting behind Darlene started in right where they had left off.

Haircare and makeup and clothes.

And boyfriends. And ex-boyfriends. And would-be boyfriends.

On and on.

They just would not shut up, and it made Darlene want to shriek.

Or whirl on them.

Grab the loudest mouthy-bitch dumb bunny by the neck, throttle her until her eyes bugged out and her yapping voice turned into a gurgle. Rip her hair-cared hair out by the roots. Scalp her with one good hard yank and then smack her five or six times with the warm, wet, ragged patch of skin.

Very tempting.

She'd never do it, though.

Even if she only said something... even if she did no more than turn and shoot them a would-you-knock-it-off-already look, they wouldn't stop.

They might laugh. They would definitely give her the sort of condescending smiles reserved for situations like this, when some fat cow dared stick her ugly nose in while the pretty people were talking.

On and on and fucking *on*.

It was like they didn't even know where they were.

Or what fucking decade they were in.

Darlene tried to read, couldn't concentrate with the jabbering about how this one's boyfriend was threatening to break up with her if she didn't lose ten pounds and the other one's parents had absolutely forbidden her to get a tattoo but she was going to anyway because it was her body and guys thought tattoos were hot.

Hello, this was the Womens' Studies building! This was where people majored in what Jessie liked to call men-are-shit-ology. The damn *course* was about standards of attractiveness, and how women had been inconveniencing, injuring and even endangering themselves throughout history, across cultures and around the world to cater to artificial, male ideals!

Corsets and pantyhose and high heels. Foot-binding. Lip plates. Those stacks of neck rings. Ancient Mayans dangling beads from headbands so their infant daughters would grow up cutely cross-eyed, and ancient Egyptians strapping planks to their babies' heads to flatten them into an appealing shape. Boob jobs and plastic surgery. Lead-based face powder and belladonna drops in the eyes to make the pupils all large and sexy. Botox parties.

Did they *know* how ironic that whole "guys think tattoos are hot!" thing was? Given what class this was and everything? Did they? Huh?

Dumb bunnies. What were they doing here in the first place? Were they hoping to get some beauty tips or what?

Too bad Scritchfield didn't walk in right then and hear them arguing whether the one should go for a butterfly or a flower, and whether it should be tramp-stamp, ankle, hip or bikini line. She'd go off on them, which was always entertaining to watch, as long as it was someone else under fire.

"This is not," Scritchfield had told them on the first day, "college like it used to be, back in the days when the only reason a girl would even *go* to college was to get her MRS degree."

Which she'd then had to explain, because half the class hadn't understood the reference.

"MRS?" she'd said, hooking her glasses down her nose to

peer at them over the rims. She was a small, feisty firecracker of a woman with a lot of frizzy auburn hair and a three-latte-a-day habit. "Emm-Arr-Ess, as in Mrs.? To land a man, find a guy, catch a husband. Why else would a girl need to be at a university? It wasn't for an education. It wasn't so she could have a career. It was a good place for her to meet plenty of future doctors, lawyers and bankers."

At this, the dumb bunnies had laughed. One said something about how she'd never want to marry a *lawyer*, eew, yuck, she was going to marry a soccer player like David Beckham or somebody. Another said that technology–"computers and stuff," as she put it–was where the real money-making careers were these days.

On the day of the "MRS degree" talk, Professor Scritchfield had torn into them like a chainsaw. Three had fled the classroom in tears, dropped the course and never returned.

Yeah, Darlene figured Scritchfield was all right.

Etch's navy blue corduroy bedspread was gonna give her major face-lines if she didn't roll over. Not to mention tit-lines. But Jessie was just too comfortable to give a damn.

She sprawled, sweat cooling on her skin, and made a low, contented, purring noise.

"You're welcome," Etch said, still breathing heavy. He was beside her, flat on his back, one arm outflung and the other folded over his eyes. He was also sweaty, which made him look oiled. "Whew."

"Wear you out?"

"No chance."

"So you're ready to go again."

"Gimme a minute, babe."

"Thought you weren't worn out."

"Are *you* ready to go again?"

Jessie repeated the purring noise.

He raised his elbow and turned his head enough to look at her. She grinned at him as well as she could with her right cheek mashed into the bedspread, and waggled her ass. The mattress shook. The springs squeaked. The headboard thumped the wall.

From the other side of the wall, someone thumped back with a fist and yelled, "Jeez, get a room!"

"We've *got* a room!" Etch called back. He shifted his weight in a vigorous bounce that squeaked the springs and hit the headboard against the wall again.

"Fuck you, Etchler!"

"Yeah you wish, homo!"

"Up yours!"

"Like I said, you wish!" He bounced the bed some more.

"Sure, you got energy for *him*," Jessie said with mock jealousy.

Etch rolled onto his side and ran a hand up the back of her thigh. "All for you and you know it. Every inch."

She shifted her arm so she could angle a glance in the direction of his groin. He still had the condom on, the effect sort of a glistening-sticky pale balloon drooping half-deflated against his leg. "Right now that's not saying a lot."

"Seemed like enough five minutes ago." He slid his hand over, between and up.

"Mmm, yeah," Jessie groaned, parting her thighs and tilting her hips to give his probing fingers better access.

"You like that?" Etch asked, louder than necessary and toward the wall, still groping.

"Oh, God, yes!" cried Jessie, also louder than necessary.

"You want it?"

"Yes!"

The guy in the next room hammered some more. "I'm trying to study here, damn it!"

"Trying to study?" Jessie said. "In a frat house? What does he think this is, college?"

"Fuckin' weirdo, I know." Etch stripped off the used condom and flung it in the general direction of a pile of laundry.

"Got those inches back?"

"Just about, babe." He grabbed a fresh one from the box under the bed.

"Up against the wall?" she asked.

"You know it."

Moments later, they were in position, Etch kneeling on the bed so that he faced the headboard, Jessie astride him with her back to Etch's posters of soapy sluts washing sports cars. He shouted, "Yeah!" as he thrust. Jessie moaned at the top of her lungs. Then they were fucking fast and hard. The springs squalled and creaked. The headboard whacked the wall in a series of quickening claps.

"You're an asshole, Etchler!" the guy next door hollered above the din.

Another voice from somewhere down the hall chanted, "Go, Etch, go! Go, Etch, go!"

Others took up the chant, and by the time they were done, it sounded like most of the frat house was in the hall outside Etch's room, cheering and applauding.

Guys were such jerks. Such stupid cavemen. They really were.

CHAPTER ELEVEN

Rico pretended to tinker with the car on the lift, listening to his boss and the fat prick who ran the bail bonds joint down the street. The two of them were outside the Lucky Seven's garage bay, having a smoke below the big, red and white NO SMOKING sign.

They were talking about those bodies.

Like nobody had ever ended up dead in this part of town before.

Shit, around here, it happened every day.

Accidents, not so much accidents, fights, random drive-bys, overdoses. Nothing out of the ordinary.

But even Rico had to admit, these latest ones were something of a sensation. Had people speculating like crazy: gang execution, cult sacrifice, a serial killer who went after dudes instead of chicks, a serial killer who went after chicks but also knifed the dudes who got in his way, aliens, a feral dog pack—

"Satanists," the fat prick from the bail bonds joint now said, sounding knowledgeable, nodding, dragging on his smoke like he was some kind of learned professor puffing a pipe.

"I heard they were mob hits," said Mr. Zelnitz, Rico's boss.

All those stories only agreed on two points. The guys were dead as shit, and the guys had been carved up like chicken dinners.

Rico, who was on nodding night-shift acquaintance with the retard who worked the eleven-to-six at the Shop-N-Go, had gotten what he figured was one of the closest-to-truth versions from him.

The retard's name was Lamont. His street name was L. Mo if you asked him, Elmo if you asked anybody else. The only reasons the Shop-N-Go manager trusted him on his own all night were because he was a gigantic black dude nobody would fuck with, and he was too stupid to rob the register.

Elmo told Rico that the hard-ass Russian chick who worked mornings had been behind the counter when some kids came in. They lifted a few candy bars and skin mags, then one of them had done the old finger-in-the-jacket-pocket routine, claiming he had a gun and he'd shoot her if she didn't hand over everything in the register.

"She knew he were faking," Elmo had told Rico. "So she grab him, she giving him hell, shaking him around. The other ones, they all took off, hollering they was gonna call the cops, tell their folks, you know. Then this one she had, he punch her in the titties."

"In the titties?" Rico snickered.

"Yeah, well, she din' like that. She starts really whaling on him, but he get away and run for it. By now, you know, she seriously P.O.d, so she go after him. Not supposed to do that. Not supposed to leave the store when you the only one, leave it unlocked. But she went anyway."

"She catch the kid?" It would not have surprised Rico if the kid had turned out to be one of his stepbrothers, or one of their crowd. Bunch of assholes.

"Kid take off running," Elmo said. "Around the store, over that fence–ain' much of a fence, falling down–and out across that empty lot. Trinka, she so mad she keeps chasing him, halfway across before she stops. Yells after him not to come back no more, he banned from the Shop-N-Go for life, him and all his friends. Then, as she turning around to go back, she sees it."

"The body."

"Yeah. She say she never seen nothing like it. Naked and all cut up. At first, she couln' even tell it was a guy." Elmo glanced at the bacon-egg-biscuit sandwich he'd been eating, as if his appetite had gone on vacation, setting it down with one bite taken out of it. "She say when she get a closer look, she sees yeah it's a guy all right, only they done cut him up so bad, there ain' nothing left." He bobbed his chin in the direction of his lap. "You know, down there."

That had made Rico press his thighs together, made him want to cross his legs and put a protective hand over Rico Jr. and the Twins.

He'd listened as Elmo told him how Trinka had rushed back to the store, called the police, called the manager, held it together calm and cool the whole time, then lost it completely when the body was moved, the peeled arm that had been draped over its face shifted, and the sunlight glistened on the red-black holes where the eyes had been.

"She start screaming," Elmo had said. "Pulling on her hair, scratching on her face. They hadda take her away in the amb'lance and give her a shot. She come back to work the next day, though. She won' talk about it. And she get real mad if you ask her."

"If she won't talk about it, how do you know what happened, then?"

"Manager told me."

"Oh. Did he see the body?"

Elmo shook his big bald head. "Not much. They had it covered up pretty good. He just seen this arm hanging out, fingers all wrecked, nails pulled, shit like that. He say it look like a bear got him."

Hell of a thing, and all anybody could talk about. Cops going around questioning people. Reporters going around doing the same thing. TV news crews out by the vacant lot, which was strung with sawhorses and police tape while the CSI guys crawled around doing their CSI guy routine.

"Could've been a wolfman," the fat prick bondsman said now, lighting up a fresh cig. Blue-grey smoke drifted listlessly away on the still, sweltering night air.

"A what?" asked Mr. Zelnitz. He rolled his pop can across his brow.

"Sure. Full moon the other night."

"You believe in werewolves?"

The fat prick flushed. "Doesn't have to be a *real* wolfman.

Some crazy who *thinks* he's a wolfman. Runs around on all fours, howling, eating raw meat. I'm not saying he'd really turn *into* a wolf."

"Good, because I'd have to call the Happy Wagon to take you to the Funny Farm."

The phone in Mr. Zelnitz's office rang, audible throughout the garage bay and across the tarmac by the pumps thanks to a hookup to the loudspeaker system. They kept it turned high enough to be heard over the noises of engines, radios and tools… which meant that when things were relatively quiet around the Lucky Seven, it was a shattering jangle-drill of noise that made Rico jump.

Mr. Zelnitz clapped the fat prick on the shoulder. They said their goodbyes as they dropped and step-crushed their smokes, then the fat prick headed off while Zelnitz went into the office. A few minutes later, he came into the garage, rolling his eyes.

"The wife," he said. "Youngest has the dribbling squirts again and she needs me to stop and pick up a bottle of Pepto. Guess I'd better get a move on. I'm late anyway. See you tomorrow, Rico."

"Later, boss," Rico said.

"Werewolves," Mr. Zelnitz muttered as he walked toward his car. "What a moron. Werewolves, my foot."

Then he was gone, and Rico had the place to himself. He turned on the radio, switched to a decent station, tried to finesse a free pop out of the machine the way he'd seen some of the tough guys do, failed, fished around for change, and came up with enough to feed into the coin slot.

The Lucky Seven never did a whole hell of a lot of business. Sometimes Rico wondered how Mr. Zelnitz kept afloat. Then he decided he didn't give a flying fuck.

On a night like this, a rainy squall having given way to a steamy, stagnant heat, Rico didn't even have the usual activity out on the street to entertain him. The regular crowds had abandoned their corner and sidewalk hangouts and gone indoors. They'd be at the movies or the mall or the skating rink or the bowling alley, anyplace they might find a working air conditioner. They'd be sprawled in front of their fans.

Anywhere but out on the street. Just too damn hot and sticky. Even the food trucks had moved on.

Meanwhile, he was here.

He unzipped his coveralls to the waist and shrugged out of the top half, letting it flop around his hips. The thin tee-shirt he wore underneath was sweat-plastered to his chest and back.

An old guy stopped for gas. Ten bucks' worth. He griped about the prices, griped at Rico how he remembered when ten bucks would fill up the tank with money to spare, and drove off.

Half an hour later, a frazzled-looking lady parked by the pumps, got out with a butterball of a kid, asked where the bathroom was, then called Rico a dickface when he told her that they didn't have one.

Then it was dead for a while. The dark street simmered. Rico puttered and tinkered but it was too hot to do any real work, even as midnight approached. The thermometer mounted on the side wall hadn't fallen more than two degrees since sunset.

At twelve-thirty, a single lowrider rolled past, sound system thudding. The passenger window went down and someone with a folded bandanna tied around his head squinted out at Rico. For a moment he went on red alert in case the guy was going to take a shot at him, and his hand did the surreptitious slide toward a tire iron he kept handy just in case. But the lowrider moved on, cruising slowly up to the corner, turning, going out of sight.

He wasn't hungry–too hot even to *be* hungry, unless it was for something like watermelon or ice cream or a tall, frosty mug of beer–but he made himself eat the lunch he'd slapped together anyway. PB&J, the bread limp, the jelly having seeped into it. Bag of chips, ranch flavor, which he hated, but it was all that had been left in the cupboard, because his rat-bastard stepbrothers always went for the good kinds first. A snack cake, half-squashed and oozing cream filling.

And coffee. Lots of coffee. Black, with a dumptruck's worth of sugar. Mr. Zelnitz had a coffeepot in the office. The stuff it made was awful, tasted like used oil and battery acid, but Rico drank it by the gallon because it was free and it kept him awake.

A homeless guy with a dog wandered by. Rico had seen him

before, sometimes keeping company with the witchy lady who used to hang around the Lucky Seven. They'd tried to panhandle, but quickly found out that people who'd just watched their gas tank eat most of their weekly budget weren't exactly overflowing with charity.

Must suck, but hey, he—Rico–had to work for a living. Nobody was distributing coupon books to give *him* free food or movie tickets. He felt worse for the dog, and might've offered some of his sandwich crust, if he hadn't been afraid of setting off a shouting rage-fest of crazy.

Then it was dead again. Rico, the food coma starting to settle in, made himself comfortable in the cracked vinyl office chair. He rocked it back, put his feet on a stack of crates, and let his eyes drift closed. Not sleeping on the job, just relaxing.

Daydreaming a little. Daydreaming of when he'd be out of this shitty place. When he'd be *somebody*. Rico the Viper. A babe on each arm and a tricked-out ride and a don't-fuck-with-me look in his eye that would command respect from everyone.

"Hey, hello? Hello? You open?"

His eyelids flew up and, in startled reaction, he damn near went over backwards, chair and all. A grunt of surprise burst from him. Then he was sitting up, blinking–he almost *had* been asleep after all, oops–and saw a couple of girls standing on the tarmac just inside the garage bay door.

Rico blinked again just to make sure he *was* awake. "Hi?"

"Hi," the one who'd spoken before said, and grinned. She had short, wild-spiky hair and a tan, and she was in great shape. Wearing formfitting bike shorts with a reflective stripe up each side. A light windbreaker hung unzipped over one of those jog-bras. "So, you open?"

"Yeah," he said, pushing his arms into the coverall sleeves again, zipping it halfway. "Yeah, sorry, sure am."

"Oh, thank god!" She turned to the other girl. "See? We're in luck."

The other girl was tall, thin, pale, pretty, and nervous-looking. She managed a quick half-smile, then went back to staring around all wide-eyed, fiddling with her hair.

"Well," said Rico, getting out of the chair, "this *is* the Lucky Seven."

"Must be our *lucky* day," the spiky-haired one said, her grin broadening.

His, too.

"What can I do for you?" he asked.

"Something's wrong with our car. Maybe you can help us…" She stepped closer, looked him over, read the name embroidered on his coveralls. "…Rico?"

"It won't start," said the other one. She had a kind of breathy, whispery voice.

"Broke down a couple of blocks from here," the first one said. She gave him a conspiratorial look, indicating her friend. "Kind of a scary place to be stranded at two in the morning. We were starting to think we wouldn't find anybody."

No wonder she looked nervous. A girl like that in a part of town like this? Wandering the streets at night? When she practically had 'victim' written all over her?

"Then this really must be your lucky day," he said. "What's wrong with the car?"

"Like she said, it won't start. Normally, I'm real good with cars—"

Rico tried not to smirk. What that meant, he knew, was that she might be able to check the oil, and maybe even tell the difference between a sparkplug and a carburetor.

"—but this time… I don't know… I'm out of ideas."

"We hoped," the nervous one said, "that maybe there'd be someone here who could come and take a look."

He hissed between his teeth. "Just me here, and I'm not really supposed to leave…"

"Dammit," the first one said, smacking her hip with frustration. "There's no one else? A night manager, a janitor, somebody?"

"Just me," he said again.

"Well, shit."

"I told you we should have called—" the nervous one began.

"Who? It's the middle of the night. We could call for a tow truck but that's gonna cost a fucking fortune!"

"Really, I can come take a look," Rico said, before the argument erupted. "No problem."

"We can't let you get in trouble," the first girl said.

"What the boss doesn't know won't hurt him. Let me grab

some tools and stuff, then lock up real quick. A couple blocks from here, you said? Where at?"

"We'll show you," she said. "Our friend stayed with the car—it's hers—and she might freak out if some strange guy showed up without us."

Rico felt his eyebrows arch before he could stop them. This was sounding better and better. His good deed for the day, and maybe with a nice payoff. Three college girls? The one, she was already giving him the eye.

He threw together a few tools and a flashlight, closed the bay doors, hung the clock-shaped 'Back At:' sign from its suction cup on the top inside pane of the glass office door, and locked it.

"I'm Jackie," the spiky-haired girl said, falling in beside him as they headed up the street.

"I'm Rico," he said.

"So I noticed. Cool name."

"Thanks!"

"Must be a pain in the ass working by yourself all night."

"It's not so bad. You get used to it."

"Hey, can I carry the flashlight?"

"It's kind of heavy."

"I can handle it."

"Okay." He handed it over.

"You weren't kidding." She hefted it, swung it experimentally. "Jeez. I bet you could crack somebody's head open with this thing."

"Yeah, I bet you could," Rico said.

The other one, the nervous and quiet one, trailed a few paces behind them. The night was still hot, and in the coveralls he was sweating like a pig, but he didn't care too much about that. Jackie, still at his side, had removed her windbreaker and slung it over one shoulder. With her other hand, she occasionally pinched the front of her jog-bra, pulled it out from her chest, and released. It snapped back, sending a puff of air up each time.

Their car could have broken down on them in a worse spot, but only if that spot was on the train tracks. It sat skewed crooked at the curb, in the middle of a dark stretch of block between a furniture outlet warehouse and a boarded-up row of shops scheduled for demolition.

Those shops had been, scheduled for demolition for something like five years now, while the plans and names on the 'Proposed Land Use' sign had changed a dozen or more times. Only one of the streetlights had a working bulb, shining feebly over graffiti, toppled trash cans, the stripped husk of a Toyota, and a jumble of discarded furniture packaging.

"That one there?" he asked. "The old Caddy?"

"That's the one," Jackie said.

It was old, all right. A long boat of a car, a gas-guzzler for sure, in dire need of a paint job and detailing. The current color was hard to tell under that one bulb's feeble glow, but to Rico it looked like some kind of murky mustard. It sat with its hood propped open but nobody anywhere near the engine compartment.

As they neared, the driver's door unlocked–he heard the clunk of the lock from thirty feet away–and opened. Someone got out. She was chunky and sloppy, with a mean look in her piggy eyes. A mean look that only got meaner when she aimed it at him, as if she had some sort of personal beef.

"This is Rico," Jackie told her. "He's here to help us."

"Sure am," he said, trying to ignore El Tubbo's death glare. "What's the trouble?"

"We were just driving along," she said. "And then it made a weird noise, and then it died."

"Try the ignition." He went to the Caddy's nose. "Jackie, how about that flashlight?"

"You got it," she said.

Then: WHAM and a huge, flat, concussive roar. Like a grenade going off behind his head.

He was down. On the street. Asphalt under him, digging, pebbly. The jab of what might've been bits of broken glass. What the fuck, man?

Voices reached him in hazy psychedelic warps and swirls.

"Shit, he's coming around already?"

"Didn't hit him hard enough?"

"I hit him plenty hard. He just must have a thick fucking skull."

Rico groaned. His eyes couldn't focus. They seemed to have a bunch of miniature explosions dancing around where the world should have been. Was this what they meant about seeing stars?

"What do we do? Jessie, what do we do?"

"Where's that flashlight? Wish I'd brought my bowling pin. Easier to hold onto."

"You're gonna hit him again?"

"Got any better ideas?"

Another grenade detonated in his head and it all went dark.

The next thing he noticed, besides it all still being dark, was a rumbling sound.

He had a panicked instant in which he was sure he'd fallen asleep—not just dozed, but slept the whole night away, got none of the rest of his work done, left everything unlocked and up for grabs, and the rumbling was an engine, Mr. Zelnitz arriving to find the office trashed, the register looted...

No.

This wasn't the Lucky Seven.

This wasn't even his room, the room his mother liked to call a 'daylight basement,' as if it wasn't a paneled cellar with two slivers of window that were blocked by bushes so that no daylight got in at all. The rumbling he heard wasn't the washer and dryer in the utility room, divided from his by a flimsy plywood wall.

Closer the first time. The rumbling *was* an engine.

It just wasn't Mr. Zelnitz's car.

Rico opened his eyes and saw nothing.

His head hurt like a motherfucker. There seemed to be vivid jagged-spike waves shooting through it, and each jolt or bump turned them into bolts of lightning.

She'd hit him. Jackie, or whatever her name was.

Hit him!

Brained him with his own damn flashlight!

Righteous outrage boiled up in him. Here he'd been, trying to do a good deed, trying to be helpful, a good Samerican or whatever the hell it was called, breaking the rules and risking his job to do a favor for a couple of stranded girls, and they thank him by bashing him on the head?

His vision had adjusted, but there wasn't much for it to adjust to. Blackness. Narrow seams of light that came and went, waxed and waned.

When they drove under a streetlight, he realized.

Drove.

In the Caddy. That extravagant, gas-guzzling rumble of an engine belonged to the Cadillac. And now he knew where he was. The reason he could see seams of waxing-waning light above him was because he was in the trunk.

He was in the trunk, and the Caddy was on the move. They'd gotten it started after all.

If it had even been broken down in the first place.

A setup? The whole thing?

Why?

So they could knock him on the head and—

His muddled thoughts began to clear, and all of a sudden the realization that he was tied up cut through the remainder of the fog like a blast of cold water. Both arms were bent painfully behind his back and secured at the wrists. His legs were folded at the knees, bound at the ankles.

No... not tied... *taped*. Tight loops of tape at wrists and ankles. A *lot* of tape. Winding around and around in some kind of twisted figure eight.

He was gagged, too. Something that felt and tasted like his own back-pocket grease rag was jammed in his mouth, held there with more tape.

It *was* a setup. The whole thing. It had all been planned.

Someone had it in for him.

A face flashed through his memory, the guy with the folded bandanna, the guy in the passenger seat of the lowrider that had cruised by a little after midnight.

Oh, fuck, he'd crossed a gang somehow.

He'd crossed a gang, pissed off the wrong people, and they were going to make him pay. They'd organized all of this. The girls to lead him down that dark street, get him to let his guard down so they could take him by surprise.

What had he done?

Rico wracked his memory, trying to think of whose bad side he could have ended up on, and what he might have done. He hadn't been in any fights. Hadn't been screwing around with anybody's woman. Didn't owe money. Hadn't insulted anybody that he was aware of.

A mistake? A misunderstanding? They had the wrong guy. They had to have the wrong guy!

He couldn't rotate his hands more than a fraction of an inch each way, and trying to do so made him feel like the tape wasn't only pulling the hairs out of his skin, it was pulling the skin right off his bones. He wrenched at his arms anyway. The tape-ripping pain almost took his mind off those jagged lightning-spikes shooting through his head. All for nothing, because his wrists were as stuck as ever.

Maybe it was Mr. Zelnitz who'd pissed off one of the gangs. It was possible. Sure. Likely, even. Some of them ran protection rackets, and Mr. Zelnitz was the proud, stubborn type who'd never agree to pay up. So they'd decided to make an example of him... only there'd been a mistake... and these girls thought *he* was the one they were after.

How could he explain that with a rag jammed in his mouth?

Well, when they got him wherever they were taking him, and delivered him to whoever they were delivering him to, then it'd get cleared up. The gangers would take one look and see that no way was he Mr. Zelnitz. They'd...

They'd have to let him go, wouldn't they?

Or would they decide he'd seen too much? That he was expendable?

Would they use him as an example for Mr. Zelnitz? A kind of *look what will happen to you if you fuck with us, old man* example?

Rico suddenly needed to piss. Really bad. Piss like one of those geysers they had at Yellowstone, which he'd seen once on vacation a long time ago, before his dad died. The urge to piss was a hot pressure, wanting to erupt.

He was not going to piss his pants. How would *that* look when they pulled him out of the trunk in front of a bunch of gangers? Rico the Viper, with a dark wet patch soaking the crotch of his coveralls. He could kiss any hope of street cred goodbye at that point.

In an effort to think about something else, *anything* else, anything at all besides how urgently he suddenly needed to piss and how much he didn't want to shame himself by doing it, he tried to concentrate on escape.

His knife!

His lucky piece, his switchblade, the one with the emerald-green serpent painted on the fake-ivory handle!

With bound wrists nestled at the small of his back, he groped for the rear pocket of his coveralls. The angle was awkward, painful. Felt like he might dislocate his shoulder.

But if he could reach... if he could get it... fish it out of the pocket, pop the blade set into the handle... he might be able to slice through the tape and free his hands. Probably he'd nick himself a couple of times in the process, but he didn't care. First his hands. Then his legs.

Then, if he could find a catch or jimmy the latch, he could open the trunk lid and scramble out the next time they stopped. Hell, even if it slowed. He didn't mind taking a spill. Some road-rash would be better than having the shit beat out of him by gangers.

If he couldn't open the trunk, he could be ready when someone else opened it. Coiled there, all sinuous strength and vicious speed. Like a viper. He'd strike fast and sharp with his one steel fang at whoever was unlucky enough to be standing there.

All he had to do was reach...

The pocket lay slack against his butt.

No knife.

Panic flared, and Rico did his best to quash it.

Okay, no knife. It had fallen out when he hit the pavement. Or they'd found it on him and taken it before dumping him in this stuffy oven of a trunk.

He rolled and hitched his body around as much as his taped limbs and the confined space would allow. It seemed like there was nothing else in the trunk with him. No tool kit, no snow chains, no can of that Fix-A-Flat stuff, no accumulated debris that piled up in everybody's car over time.

Empty except for Rico. Scuffed old carpeting underneath. Bare metal all around, with tangles of wires–

Wires!

If he could reach the wires that went to the taillights and

turn signals, he could yank them, and then maybe they'd get pulled over. If that happened, he could kick and thump until the cop insisted on taking a look.

As he maneuvered, the car slowed and turned and accelerated. Its movements made Rico's task more difficult, but finally he had contorted himself so that he could grip a fistful of the tangled wires.

He paused for a split second, wondering if he was about to electrocute himself, then gave a mental to-hell-with-it shrug and yanked. There was a quick yellow spark as wires snapped loose, but he wasn't electrocuted.

Too much to hope that a patrol car was behind them this very minute?

No whoop of a siren. No blue and red flashers.

Damn.

He worked his way over to the other set of wires, banging his forehead, breaking the skin. Blood dribbled into his eye. Sweat dribbled into the cut, stinging. He whammed his knee. A rough edge of metal scraped along his arm, drawing more blood.

Immediately, Rico twisted and tried to find that metal edge again. He was able to bring his tape-bound wrists up against it, and shifted his shoulders up-down-back-forth-up-down-up-down, sawing at the thick tape.

Some of it gave. Not cleanly. Partially. Pulling apart in stretchy, widening increments. His breath snorted in and out of his nostrils.

More tape gave. Unraveling in sticky taffy-loops. Connected now only by a spiderweb of gummy strings. He strained so hard he saw starbursts, and then the tape broke and his arms were free.

The Caddy slowed again, turned, went over a bump, slowed further, stopped.

Rico, still with straggling tape-bracelets on each wrist, attacked the strip holding the gag in his mouth. Keeping his fingernails clipped brutally short had seemed like a good idea when he was working around grease and grime all day, but he regretted it now as he clawed at the edges.

Doors opened and chunked closed. He heard low voices.

He got a corner, squeezed his eyes shut in a wince, and tore the tape off his face. Felt like he took about six layers of skin with it. His tongue pushed at the oily rag, forcing it out.

A key slid into the trunk lock as he touched the tape around his ankles.

CHAPTER TWELVE

The gas station one, Gwen thought, at least looked scared right from the start.

The first and second ones–not counting Donnie–had looked like they thought it was a trick or joke, and then looked mad, and only scared when they understood what really was going to happen. The third one had been confused, and then kind of accepting and sad, which was somehow even worse.

This one, though, this one was scared. Terrified, even. Almost in a panic.

Darlene opened the lid and there he was, staring up at them in the thin, yellowish glow of the back porch light. Eyes wide and wild. Face gleaming with sweat, and blood from a gash on his forehead. Cheeks and chin red and raw-looking where he'd ripped the tape off. Mouth open to yell.

"Fuck!" Jessie cried. "He's loose!"

The guy in the grubby coveralls hurled himself out of the trunk, straight at Jessie. It was a clumsy move, but he slammed into her and they both went down hard on the grass beyond the driveway. She drove her fist into his stomach and his yell turned into a pained, "Whoof!"

Annamaria and Rachel had been in the house, and hurried out when they heard Darlene drive up. But now Annamaria only stood there, stunned into immobility as Rico and Jessie struggled on the lawn.

He punched Jessie in the mouth. Splitting her lip. Making blood burst from it.

Jessie hiked her knee at his groin, connected with his hipbone.

"Do something!" Darlene said to no one in particular.

Gwen felt as immobile as Annamaria. The abruptness of it, the violence of it. He was scared, all right. Scared, and fighting for his life.

"Grab him, for fuck's sake!" grunted Jessie, spitting blood. She brought her bent arm around and the leading edge below her elbow met Rico's chin. By the look and sound of the impact, it was hard to say who was hurt more.

Rachel swore, wheeled, and ran for the kitchen door. Darlene made an ineffectual swipe at Rico's sleeve and missed. Annamaria still seemed paralyzed.

"You got the wrong guy!" he wheezed, still winded. "Lemme go!" He glanced a blow off Jessie's cheekbone, dazing her.

"Jessie!" Gwen yelped.

"Unh," Jessie said.

Rico threw himself off her and tried to scrabble away, snatching tufts of grass to pull himself along, pistoning with his legs. Gwen got him by the coveralls.

"Darlene, help!"

Darlene swiped again, this time not missing. They both had handfuls of the baggy cloth. Rico thrashed and wriggled, and the zipper, which had only been halfway up, unzipped or broke and came open the rest of the way, with a sound like a loud, metallic fart. Gwen and Darlene held on, but they only had grips on the coveralls, and Rico was shooting out of them the way a banana in a cartoon shot out of its peel when someone squeezed it.

He slipped the sleeves, and the coveralls slid-bunched-crumpled down his body, down his legs.

And there they snagged, caught on his still-taped ankles.

Ed Reilly woke groggy, at first not even sure where he was.

The Gerrittsons' house.

That's right.

He was staying with the Gerrittsons now. Had been for a few weeks, and while it was safe and homey and welcoming, it could still feel unfamiliar. Especially when it caught him by surprise, struck him sudden out of a deep, dreaming sleep.

Something had disturbed him. Some noise?

He rubbed his face, yawned, blinked.

Listened.

Annamaria knew she should be moving, should be acting.

Shouldn't she have felt full of inspiration, exaltation, and divine purpose?

Instead, she felt like a statue. Rooted in place. Stunned.

The pump jockey flopped around like a landed fish, coveralls entangling him from the knees down. Gwen and Darlene were the fishermen, holding on, trying to reel him in. Above the knees, all he had on was a plain white undershirt and briefs.

"Fucking *ow*," Jessie said.

"Wait, hey, wait," he said, still sounding out of breath from when Jessie had punched him in the stomach, blood dribbling from his cut forehead. Evidently having realized he was stuck, he rolled onto his back to raise both hands, palms out. "Listen, okay? Whoever they sent you to get, it's not me."

"Whoever *who* sent *who* to get?" Gwen asked, frowning.

"The gangers, whatever, I don't wanna know. I won't talk. I won't say anything. Just lemme go and we'll call it good, okay?"

"The hell are you talking about?" Darlene sounded irritated, but she *always* sounded irritated, so that wasn't anything new.

"I don't know who put you up to this and I don't care, all right? Just, listen, you've got the wrong guy."

"You think someone else is behind this?" Annamaria finally found her voice. "Some gang?"

"I don't wanna know. But you gotta tell them there's been a mistake."

"Ah," Gwen said. "So *that's* why he's scared. He thinks we're going to hand him over to someone else."

"Figures," Darlene said, sounding more irritated than ever.

Jessie probed at her bloody lip and the bruise already flowering on her cheekbone, then shook her head at him. "Buddy, are *you* in for a surprise."

The old farmhouse didn't have air conditioning. That didn't bother Ed. He'd never had it anyway, considered it a luxury.

A fan on a tall stand was in the corner of his room, humming and whooshing as it swiveled back and forth, stirring a tepid sort of breeze.

Was that what had wakened him?

He didn't think so. The hum and whoosh were soft, low, almost sub... sub... sub-whatever that word was for something just below the level where a person would be aware of it.

Were Walter or Muriel Gerrittson up and moving around?

He listened.

Twin snoring sounds from their room at the end of the hall. His the classic sawing-logs type, hers a shrill whine, like a drill bit striking a pine knot.

But that wasn't it either. Snoring didn't bother him any more than the lack of air conditioning.

Something in the house?

Ed sat up and listened more intently, cocking his ear toward the open window where neither leaves nor gingham curtains stirred, because there was no wind out there at all. No wind, just the flat stillness of the hot night air.

Rachel came back on the run, mind going a mile a minute. She took in the scene–bad, but could've been worse–and raced over to Annamaria with a white plastic bottle in one hand and a washcloth in the other.

"Help them," she said, jerking her chin toward Darlene and Gwen. Annamaria started as if shaken from a trance and finally moved.

"Son of a bitch," Jessie said. She seemed to be testing all

her teeth with her tongue, satisfying herself that none had been knocked out of their sockets.

"I got him," Darlene said, bundling the slack of the coveralls around her arms and bracing herself like the anchor in a tug-of-war. "He's not going anywhere."

"Hey, wait, come on! I told you, you got the wrong guy! It's not me! It wasn't me!"

"Hold him," Rachel said, unspinning the cap. It whirled off and bounced into the grass, and she made a mental note of the spot so she'd be sure to retrieve it after. She turned her head aside to avoid getting a whiff.

Annamaria neared him and he took a swing at her. Jessie bounced to her feet, kicked him in the sternum, and knocked him flat.

"Quick, Anna," she said, setting her foot on his chest to pin him to the ground.

"Gwen, get his other side." Annamaria seized him by the right shoulder and upper arm.

He tried to twist away. "Lemme go!"

Gwen steeled herself. Her expression reminded Rachel of watching her grandmother reach into a turkey to pull out the packet of giblets. Then she grabbed his left shoulder.

Darlene heaved his legs up, making it harder for him to get leverage to kick and thrash. "Squirmy fucker," she said.

Rachel covered the bottle's opening with the washcloth, then tipped it. She felt liquid soak through, shockingly cool in the hot night. Then she bent down and clapped the cloth over the lower half of the guy's face.

Maybe it stung, especially where his skin was reddened from the tape. Maybe he was preparing to holler. Either way, he sucked in a huge gasping breath as the washcloth covered his nose and mouth.

It worked pretty good. He keeled right over. She was pleasantly impressed by the effectiveness.

The others looked more amazed than impressed. They held their positions another few seconds, glancing at each other, then glancing at Rachel.

"What was that?" Annamaria asked.

"Eew, it smells," said Gwen, fanning in front of her nose.

"Chloroform," Rachel told them, holding out the bottle.

"Chloroform?" echoed Darlene. "Are you shitting me?"

"No, really."

"Chloroform," said Jessie. "That's kinda old-school, there, Rache, isn't it?"

"Very retro," Annamaria agreed.

"Well, it worked," Rachel said, feeling a little defensive.

"Yeah, but still," said Jessie. "It's like when my aunt went in to change her antidepressants, and they said they wanted to try something different and she thought they meant some new, radical drug, and instead they gave her Prozac. Prozac! Who still takes Prozac?"

"If it works," Rachel said, still feeling defensive, "then what's the big deal?"

"Sometimes the classics are classics for a reason," Gwen said, shrugging.

"What, if it ain't broke, don't fix it?" asked Darlene.

"Never mind that," Annamaria said. "Let's move him before he comes around."

Whatever he'd heard that roused him, it hadn't been from inside the house. It hadn't disturbed the Gerrittsons, either. They snored on, peaceful, from their room at the end of the hall.

Then again, anything short of a bomb blast wouldn't cause either of those two to so much as turn over in their sleep. They removed their hearing aids at night.

"So if you ever have to wake us, and you call our names and we don't answer," Muriel had said, smiling, those merry blue eyes twinkling, "please don't think we're dead."

"At least give us a shake first, see if we're cold and stiff," Walter added.

Ed wasn't wild about that scenario, but he figured those two would probably outlive him and everyone he knew, so he didn't let it worry him.

The sounds from outside, though, did worry him.

Like shouts.

Like a scuffle.

Probably nothing. He still wasn't quite used to being out here in the country at night. The noises were different. Animal noises. Owls. The rustling leaves.

He stayed sitting up anyway.

What if it wasn't nothing? What if there was trouble out in the barn? The Gerrittsons said there weren't dangerous predators in the area, but stories cropped up on the news every now and then of a coyote or a bear or a cougar driven down out of the hills. If something like that was skulking around, menacing the alpacas…

Hadn't sounded like alpaca calls… or like what Ed imagined a bear, coyote or cougar might sound like.

Had sounded more like voices. Human voices.

From next door?

Kind of late for those girls to be having a party, and on a school night no less.

But then, college was as much about wild parties and all-night drinking binges as it was about studying, wasn't it?

Couldn't hear any music.

An argument?

Trouble over there?

A boyfriend, maybe a bad break-up?

Ed didn't want to be nosy, but he didn't want to be one of those look-the-other-way-ers either.

Especially not with the stories in the news lately.

Got cocky.

Dammit.

Got cocky and she had nobody to blame but herself.

Man up and own up.

One of Dad's mottoes. Drummed into her and her brothers' heads from the time they were old enough to talk. If you fuck up, man up and own up.

This was her fault. She'd have a split lip and most likely a black eye to show for it.

She wasn't pissed at Rico for hitting her. She was, however, plenty pissed at herself for letting him get in a position where he could. For wanting to try it her way this time, no roofies dropped into some wannabe stud at a meat market bar or lonely old midlife crisis.

Drugging them was cheating, she'd thought. Anybody could incapacitate and overpower a grown man if they got him shitfaced or wasted enough.

It was the difference between getting to the top floor of a skyscraper by taking the elevator or climbing a hundred flights of stairs.

Anybody could take the elevator. Even a toddler, even a granny, even someone in a wheelchair.

Only those who were strong and fit could make it up those stairs.

So, she'd wanted to try it without the drugs, and when Darlene suggested the night-shift pump-jockey, she figured it was the ideal setup for testing things out. A little subterfuge and then a lot of force, as opposed to the other way around.

Dammit.

Split lip, black eye, her funny bone hurt like a bastard from clonking him on the chin. She was pretty sure she'd lost his switchblade too, the one she'd found in the back pocket of his coveralls and slid into her own pocket, thinking maybe she'd use it on him later just for extra kicks. It was probably out in the yard somewhere, and she figured she'd better find it before Rachel did and had one more thing to criticize about.

Fucking *ow*.

But that wasn't the worst of it.

The worst of it was, she'd fucked up and made a fool of herself in front of her friends. Jessie's plan... but he'd recovered from two bashes on the head with that heavy flashlight, he'd freed himself most of the way from the tape while locked in Dar's trunk, and he'd caught her off-guard.

Jeez, that smarted. Lots worse than the physical injuries. Her pride was what was *really* bruised.

Adding insult to insult and injury, then Rachel of all people had been the one to save the day. Rachel and her chloroform. Jessie couldn't get the better of one patronizing dick of a greasemonkey–she hadn't forgotten his look when they'd been talking about the car… he hadn't said "little lady," but it sure as fuck had been in his tone–but Rachel was the one who put him down for the count.

She was going to enjoy making this one squeal.

Even though he could have tap-danced along the hall and down the stairs without disturbing the Gerrittsons from their no-hearing-aids slumber, Ed tiptoed. He froze each time a floorboard creaked, holding his breath in expectation.

Felt strange to be prowling their house at night. Like he was an intruder instead of a guest… or live-in help… or whatever the heck he was.

Felt strange to be wearing pajamas and a robe, for that matter. He'd been a skivvies-sleeper most of his life, an in-the-buff sleeper when he'd been with Leigh. But he didn't fancy the prospect of going for a midnight snack and having Mrs. G. walk in on him.

He made it downstairs, crossed the tidy little front room, and undid the various locks, chains and deadbolts. He'd always heard how country folk never locked up, too trusting, too neighborly. Not here. Just another reminder that this was still close to the city. Near the bus lines and everything. No sense being careless.

Ed stepped out, careful not to let the screen door bang shut behind him. Wasn't any cooler outside. He heard frogs croaking in the marsh across the street, insects buzzing in the yard, and something scuffling under the porch. Possum?

There was a light on in the house next door. Kitchen light, he thought. Enough fell onto the lawn to show him how unkempt and shaggy it was getting. He'd have to see about taking the mower over there sometime this week, like Mr. G. had suggested.

Voices carried to him faintly on the flat night air: girls' voices, he was pretty sure, though he couldn't make out the words.

They sounded agitated.

***

"Tape him up good this time," Rachel said.

Darlene glanced at Jessie to see if Jessie would take offense, and sure enough, Jessie did.

"He was taped up good before!"

"Not good enough, if he got loose."

"Hey, I cracked him over the head with his own damn flashlight… twice! I thought he was out cold!"

"That's still no reason not to make sure—"

"Dammit, Rache, he *was* taped up! How was I to know he'd turn out to be Criss-fucking-Angel?"

Then Annamaria had to step in, change the subject, and deflect them. Saint Annamaria the Peacemaker. While Saint Gwen the Virtuous stood there, anxious, chewing her own lips off, wringing her hands.

It gave Darlene another chance to scope the guy. Rico— that was his name. Decent bod. Even better than she'd thought when she'd first seen him, if no Folklife Festival unicyclist. The coveralls were hideous, unflattering and baggy. But, underneath, he was pretty nice. Excellent ass. Tight, firm buns in his jockeys.

By the glimpses she'd had as he was thrashing around, the front of those jockeys seemed to boast a fairly impressive package. She couldn't wait to see him stripped down all the way.

"I hope you didn't kill him with that stuff," Darlene said.

"Um, but aren't we going to…" Gwen made a vague, throat-slitty gesture.

"Yeah, but not right away."

"Where'd you even *get* chloroform?" Annamaria asked.

"Science department storeroom," Rachel said. She hunched over, picking at the long grass. "Where's the… ah, here." She put the cap back onto the bottle and jammed it in her pocket.

Jessie taped the hell out of Rico, muttering under her breath and shooting the occasional baleful look at Rachel. Then they all hoisted him. He was total deadweight. Loose and boneless.

Warm, though.

From here, as they lifted him face-up, Darlene had a great

view of his crotch. The package *was* impressive. Even limp, it looked big.

"Aren't you worried someone will notice you took it?" Gwen asked.

"Have you *seen* the science department storeroom? Some of that stuff hasn't been touched since 1950."

Once again, Jessie took the heaviest part of the load. Had to show up the rest of them. Never mind that her face was busted to shit. She just had to be the damn Amazon.

They lugged him up the flight of steps, managing not to drop him or twist any ankles. Easier this time. Practice makes perfect.

"Not bad," Darlene said when they'd flopped him onto the mattress, untangled the coveralls and removed them, along with his socks and his shoes. "He's kinda cute."

Rachel looked at him—mask of blood, eyes rolled up, mouth hanging open—and then looked at Darlene with eyebrows raised.

"Before Jessie beat the shit out of him, he was," she said, defensive.

Annamaria hooked the cuffs onto one wrist and one ankle, then sat back on her heels and scooped a lock of hair behind her ear. "If you like that type, I guess."

"I'm thinking Dar likes that type," Jessie said, with a big old smirk and then a wince as the big old smirk stretched her split lip. "Ow."

"Fuck you, Jessie."

"Why not fuck him instead?"

Nobody said anything, and Darlene was sure that in the silence, the rest of them could hear her pulse suddenly go *wham-wham-wham*. She looked at his package again, caught herself, wrenched her gaze away before any of the others could see her looking, and had momentary trouble breathing.

"I don't think that's very funny," Gwen said at last.

"Rape never is," said Annamaria. "Neither is murder."

"Yeah, we're not in this for the laughs," Jessie said.

"A lot of serial killings do have a sexual component," Rachel said. "I'm just not sure how it'd work... logistically speaking, I mean. He's kind of unconscious. I'm no expert, okay, but isn't unconsciousness kind of not conducive to an erection?"

"Not to mention fearing for his life?" Gwen added.

"Yeah, right," Darlene said, her voice thick. "Like he could get it up."

"He's a guy," Jessie said. "They can get hard-ons in their sleep."

"But it'd still be rape, wouldn't it?" asked Gwen.

"Not if he liked it."

"Well, that's not necessarily true," Rachel said, adopting her fussy-lecturer tone. "Physical arousal and even orgasm sometimes occur during rape cases. It's part of the body's defense mechanism. Lubrication. To reduce damage, you know, down there."

"Seduction without consent?" asked Annamaria. "Still rape, I think."

"And isn't it bad enough already, what we're going to do to him?" Gwen chewed her lip. "It just seems so… so wrong."

"More wrong than crushing his nuts in a garlic press?" Jessie asked. "I'm just saying… he's ours now. He's totally in our power. We can do whatever we want with him. To him. Whatever."

There was another silence. Darlene was sure she must be beet-red, and sweating worse than ever. Moments ago she'd barely been able to breathe, and now she was breathing too heavily. In her ears it sounded like an obscene phone call, puffing and panting. She only hoped no one else noticed.

"It wouldn't necessarily have to involve *that* part of him," Annamaria said. "If, for instance, he were to be… violated… some other way."

"Roll him over and peg him in the ass, you mean?" Jessie grinned. "We got a strap-on in the cupboard? That could be a hoot! I guess if we don't have a strap-on, there's always a beer bottle, or my trusty bowling pin! See how he likes getting *that* up the—"

"What's it to you anyway?" Darlene blurted. She could feel the dregs of her control slipping away, and there wasn't a damn thing she could do about it. Everything was just spewing up and boiling over. "You've *got* a boyfriend! You can get laid whenever you want!"

"This isn't about getting laid!"

"Easy for *you* to—!" She slapped a hand over her mouth. They were all staring at her. Rachel, Annamaria, Jessie and Gwen.

All staring at her. With a range of expressions–astonishment, pity, scorn, unease.

"Um… Darlene…" Gwen said. "I've never, um—"

"Oh, shut up! Shut up! It's different! It's different and you know it, and not just because you're saving yourself for Prince Charming or Harry Potter or whoever! That doesn't count!"

"Hey, I haven't either, okay?" said Rachel.

"So what? You could if you wanted. *Any* of you could if you wanted!"

"Shit, Dar, if you want dibs just say you want dibs," Jessie said, sweeping her arm over Rico's prone body. "Go for it. Be my guest. Fuck his brains out."

"Yeah, right!" Darlene said. "Like he would."

"He doesn't have much say in the matter," Annamaria pointed out.

"Uh-huh, and he'd still laugh his ass off! How pathetic is that, huh? How fucking pathetic is that? A guy on Death Row for twenty years about to go to the electric chair wouldn't be *that* desperate!"

She was shaking, she couldn't stop the shaking even though she knew it made her flab wobble and she hated it, hated it, she knew she must be all blotchy and any minute she'd exhale and blow a big green snot bubble or something, and they just stood there *staring* at her. All with dropped jaws and wide eyes now.

"You don't know!" she screamed at them. "None of you! You don't know, you never have, you never will!"

Sounded like the college girls were having one wowser of a shouting match.

Ed stopped at the bottom of the driveway, which skirted the overgrown front yard and swung around to a breezeway and a ramshackle garage. He saw three cars: an ordinary subcompact Toyota, a vintage Mustang that looked lovingly restored, and a beat-to-shit boat of a Cadillac probably older than Ed himself. The trunk gaped wide open.

The raised voices weren't coming from the house at all.

They were coming from the garage. Or, more accurately, from the apartment above the garage, where the door was ajar and dim light showed through.

He'd seen the girls carrying tools and materials in and out of there, had heard how the Hubert woman had given them permission to fix up the place since that no-good nephew of hers had taken off for greener pastures. They were using it as a home gym or a recording studio or somesuch.

Sure didn't sound like they were rehearsing or doing aerobics right now.

He saw a glint in the tromped-down shaggy grass, off to the side of the gaping open mouth of the Caddy's trunk, and walked around to it. The pale handle and chrome fittings of a switchblade glimmered up at him.

Ed picked it up, turned it over. It had a snake painted on the imitation ivory handle. Looked like the sort of thing a teenage boy would carry around as a way of showing off how tough he was.

Wouldn't do to have someone find it by accident. Some little kid, maybe. Or someone who just wasn't watching their step and triggered its go button and got cut. He'd feel terrible if that happened because he'd gone and left it.

Ed slipped the switchblade into his robe pocket, thinking to return it in person at a more civilized hour. Maybe when he drove the mower over and offered to do their lawns. That'd be best. That'd be neighborly. He would shut the trunk for them, though, so no critters decided to crawl in there and make a nest.

The sole of his slipper came down on something that was both crackly and sticky, and made a kind of peeling-ripping noise when he picked up his foot.

A wad of tape–strapping, not scotch or duct or electrical–dangled off the bottom of his slipper.

He plucked it off and flicked it into the trunk, then eased the lid shut so that it didn't make a huge noise. Funny how everything was louder at two in the morning.

Then he went on home to try and get some more sleep.

CHAPTER THIRTEEN

"What are you looking for?" Annamaria asked, seeing Jessie scanning the ground.

The day was clear and warm, not so stifling. Enough of a breeze had come up to give the illusion of cooling the air. Brilliant sapphire sky, the sun a clear white-gold, and any leftover bloodstains didn't show against the rich green grass.

Annamaria felt good. Clean. Her hair curled damp against her bare back, and the hem of her sundress fluttered around her thighs. She hadn't slept–none of them had, and they'd been a sluggish, bleary-eyed bunch at breakfast–but apart from that… yes, she felt good.

Her hand only hurt a little… a down-deep kind of sting… but even that was somehow good. Not clean, maybe, but cleansing.

The pain…

It wasn't what she'd expected.

"Lost the damn knife," Jessie said.

"What knife?"

"Aw, Rico had this switchblade in his pocket. Cheesy thing, had a snake painted on it. I found it on him when we were tying him up, and then I lost it."

"Where?"

"Jeez, Anna, if I knew *where*, it wouldn't be *lost*."

"But you're sure you had it?"

"I'm sure. I had it, then he came popping out of the trunk

like some half-assed jack-in-the-box, and I thought for sure I must've dropped it while we were rolling around. But now it's nowhere. I've been looking ever since I got back and I can't find the damn thing."

"One of the others must have picked it up before they left. Rachel? She's the one with the eye for detail."

"Maybe, only she didn't know about it." Jessie heaved a disgruntled sigh and raked her fingers through her hair, making it stand even more on end than normal. Her lip was puffed, crusted with a scab. The black eye had flowered into a real beaut. "I've been over every fucking inch of the yard, and nada."

"It's not in Darlene's car?"

"Nope. I looked before she went to work. I even checked the trunk in case she threw it in there. Nada again."

"Oh, well, so it's gone." Annamaria opened the driver's side door of her own little car and slung her books and purse across to the passenger seat. She did this one-handed and a trifle clumsily, her left swathed in gauze. "We have plenty more knives."

People were bound to ask about the bandage, but she'd tell them the same thing she'd told her friends: a box-cutter mishap.

It was close enough to the truth.

"Yeah, but I wanted *that* one." Jessie grinned, gingerly, to favor her lip. "Figure since I beaned him with his own flashlight, I could use his own switchblade too. As… whaddaya call it… poetic justice."

"Did you ask Darlene if she saw it?"

"No way." Jessie rolled her eyes. "She's still pissed at me."

"It's not you she's pissed at."

"Yeah, yeah. It's men. It's the whole fucking world. I know, I know."

Rico, Annamaria was sure, would agree. If Rico could still speak. If Rico was still sane.

The things they had done to him…

Slow and cruel.

Taking their time.

Making it last. Making him suffer.

Until all at once they'd realized it was almost dawn. They had classes to get to, work for which they couldn't be late.

"I'm tellin' ya," Jessie said, "we'd all be a lot happier if she would've just done him. Right then and there."

"With all of us in the room?" Annamaria's eyebrows arched. "This is the girl who won't even let us see her in a bathing suit."

"Like, what, we'd suddenly notice she's fat? We know. Big deal."

"To her, it is."

"Whatever, so, we could have given her some privacy. Left her in there with him, just the two of them. She could suck him into a stiffy and climb aboard."

The corners of Annamaria's mouth tipped up a bit as she slid behind the wheel. "Not much point to it now, is there?"

Jessie chuckled and stuffed her hands in her back pockets, rocking toe-heel on the soles of her sneakers. "No shit. Talk about melt-in-your-mouth. It would have come apart like pulled pork at a luau."

"That's gross."

"Hey, the boiling water wasn't *my* idea." She made a face. "Jeez, though, it was kinda nasty, wasn't it?"

"I think the smell was the worst," Annamaria said. "The... cooking smell. Simmering. Like broth. I may never make turkey soup again."

"I may never eat *any* soup again. Did you know balls could swell up that much? I sure didn't."

Annamaria checked her phone to see what time it was. "I really need to go. Parking's going to be a nightmare. Want a ride to campus?"

"I'll walk it. I don't have anything until one, except meeting Etch and the guys at lunch." She glanced next door as an engine coughed into life with a chugging roar. "I wish we had a riding mower. That old thing Mrs. H. has is a piece of shit."

Rachel wasn't so sure about this keeping-him-alive business.

It seemed awful risky.

Oh, she knew that some serial killers did it all the time. Kept their victims for days, maybe weeks. Taking care to see that they didn't die of blood loss, or infection. Treating their wounds, even.

But the ones who did that were the real pros. The ones who'd honed their skills and practiced their art and got it down to a science.

The five of them were still more or less beginners.

She sat in her usual seat, six rows up and on the left edge of the center aisle, in the wedge-shaped lecture hall. The professor's voice droned on about stuff she already knew. If not for the importance of maintaining appearances—an importance that was apparently lost on her friends—she might as well have skipped. She was tired.

Tired, tired, tired.

And this was her long day.

Classes until five, then a lab from six-thirty to eight.

Oof.

Maybe grabbing the gas guy so late hadn't been the best idea. Not on a school night.

It had seemed smart at the time... fewer witnesses and everything, no Friday or Saturday cruisers and partiers out. At first, it had all gone okay.

Then everybody decided to be all emotional and stuff.

Like Jessie getting mad about the chloroform, as if it were Rachel's fault, when Jessie was the one who hadn't knocked him out well enough, and all Rachel had done was compensate for her mistake.

Or Darlene having her big meltdown for no reason, taking it personally when it wasn't, holding a grudge against this guy and wanting to make him suffer extra for it.

Or Gwen, whom Rachel had heard through the connecting bathroom between their rooms as they'd all been hurrying to get dressed. Making strange shrill whispery sounds, maybe laughing, maybe crying, and sometimes sounding like she was talking to people who weren't there.

Or Annamaria. Annamaria and the box-cutter. Slipped, she'd said. An accident, she'd said. Right. Okay. But it had sure looked to Rachel like Annamaria did it on purpose. Which would just be crazy. And coming after the weird shit she'd been saying to the *last* guy... interrogating him... wanting to know what it *felt* like... that had been kind of bizarre.

No wonder they were all so tired.

Tired, tired, tired.

Exhausted.

Rachel had made it through her morning classes on a high-octane mix of sugar and caffeine, but the Mountain Dews she'd chugged at break didn't seem to be kicking in.

Her head drooped against a curled, upraised fist. A long sigh eased from her lips.

"Are we boring you, Miss Simons?"

Her head snapped up with a gasp.

The professor eyed her with stern disapproval. Nearby students snickered and tittered. She blushed and looked down, where she saw a scrawl of ink across the page she'd been using to pretend to take notes.

"Well?" the professor asked.

"Sorry," she said.

"Didn't get much sleep last night, I take it, Miss Simons?"

More snickers and titters. Nudges and winks. People all around her, enjoying the show. Enjoying seeing the brainy chick on the hot seat for once.

"Sorry, Professor," Rachel said again.

"In the future, I suggest you try and limit your parties to the weekends. And if that's too much for you, at least have the courtesy to cut my class so that you don't waste my, or anyone else's, valuable time."

Every single person in the Student Health Center that day was either an asshole or an idiot.

Some were both.

Didn't matter if they were doctors, nurses, or patients.

The ones who worked in the office with her were the worst of all. Annoying, incompetent, stupid pains in the butt.

Darlene wouldn't have minded seeing each of them chained up in a small room somewhere. A cell, like in a dungeon, maybe. A torture chamber. Yeah. Being stretched on the rack, or hanging from hooks, or roasting on a metal grill over a bed of coals.

They deserved it.

So did the professors. She had a paper due this afternoon that she hadn't finished, and a test tomorrow she hadn't studied for. If she tried going to them and asking for more time, they would laugh in her face. If someone else tried the same thing, someone like Gwen or Annamaria...

Yeah, the professors deserved it too. And the snarky jerks in the financial aid office, starting with the bastard who'd rejected her grant application and stuck her with this fucking work- study job.

She wondered where she could get stuff like whips and branding irons. Rachel might know. Rachel knew everything.

Then again, they'd been doing okay with the collection of tools and utensils they already had. Going out and buying a whip or a branding iron, that might be remembered. Going to the Goodwill and taking a bunch of stuff to the register— clothes, a couple pots or pans, some dishes, stuff like that— meant nobody would give two shits about whether there was a butcher knife, screwdriver or icepick in there too.

Or a cheese grater.

Or a corkscrew.

Or the sewing kit.

Or that hinged plastic-and-wire gadget Annamaria said was for slicing mushrooms and hardboiled eggs.

It worked well on other things, too... as long as they were soft, boneless things. Fleshy things. Spongy-tissue things.

She smiled.

The office supervisor remarked on how nice it was to see her looking happy for a change.

Her smile turned into a toothy grimace.

Copy. Collate. File. Copy. Collate. Staple.

A stapler could do some interesting damage.

And what about the sharp, pinchy staple remover? Hell, just a pen or a pencil could be jabbed into an eyeball, through an eardrum, up a nose. She'd already seen what thumbtacks could do. Reminded her of a Lite-Brite toy. Punching the little translucent, colored plastic pegs through the black construction paper had been almost the same sensation as punching those thumbtacks through skin and into a person's flesh.

A single desk drawer held fifteen different ways to hurt someone.

Someone like her supervisor... or that bearded gimp who misfiled all the time... or the bitch who left her empty Starbucks cups all over the damn place.

What about the paper cutter? She could slam her supervisor's hand down on that green metal grid, raise the blade with its usual protesting screech, shove the supervisor's fingers under the bar, and... *k-shunk.*

Fingers plopping onto the counter. Their severed lengths involuntarily flexing and curling. Enameled nails and gaudy rings. Four spouting jets of dark red.

Screams and panic.

Darlene smiled again.

This time, the supervisor for some reason didn't say a single word. Only looked at her, then looked away fast, like she'd seen something scary.

Darlene almost laughed out loud.

The loudest and rowdiest corner of the quad was the one where Etch and the gang hung out. The ground was level there, so they could toss a ball back and forth or horse around, or kick back on the grass scoping out the girls.

If the weather was bad enough, they might even go to class. But more often, they'd move indoors and take over the lounge in the student union, dominating the couches, the television, the pinball machines and the pool tables.

"Hey, guys," Jessie said, sauntering on up.

"Hey, Jess," some of them said.

Wrappers and containers from the campus deli littered the lawn. A few yards away, a bird was trying with a comical lack of success to get airborne with a pizza crust in its beak.

"Hey, babe," Etch said, sliding an arm around her and rubbing his palm over the seat of her shorts.

"Hey, stud," she said, bumping her hip against his.

"Jess-*ie!*" crowed Chad. "Lookin' good there!"

"Yeah, nice black eye," said Biff. "Walk into a door?"

"Fat lip, too," Chet said. "Bar fight, that's my guess. Yeah?"

"You should see the other guy," Jessie said, giving him a grin.

"So Jess, when you gonna fix me up with what's her name, your housemate, the smokin' hot one?" asked Skip.

"Anna? Don't think you're her type."

"She a lez?" Brad's eyes gleamed. "Now that *is* hot. You girls have pajama parties?"

"All the time," Jessie said. "We put on our shortie nightgowns, have pillow fights, the works."

"No fair, you never invite me," Etch said.

"You look dumb in a shortie nightgown," she replied.

"Oh, *snap*," Chet said.

"But he's got such great legs!" Biff fluttered his lashes and made kissy-lips in Etch's direction. "I bet he'd be so *cuuuuuute!*"

"Yeah, up yours!" Etch said, glowering but laughing.

"You'd like that," Biff said.

Etch flipped him off, then tucked his hand into Jessie's back pocket, cupping her butt cheek. "We still on for the lake?"

"Absolutely."

"Excellent. Chet and Biff are gonna get the beers, Skip's covering the grub, Brad's bringing Lori and a couple of her roomies, we should be good."

"Six-ish, right?"

"Yeah. Would go earlier but me and Biff gotta work. We'll take the Yuke, swing by your place on the way outta town."

"Sounds like a plan," Jessie said.

"If that Anna friend of yours wants to come along," Skip said, "it's okay by me!"

"Don't hold your breath. I told you, I don't think you're her type."

"What, she *is* a lez?" Skip's face fell, then brightened. "What about the cute little blonde one, the brainiac?"

"What about the uggo?" Chad tossed a crumpled paper cup at Skip. "Since you're getting desperate."

Skip batted it away. "No thanks, man, I'd rather do your mom."

"Chad's mom is a definite MILF," Biff said.

"I'd do her," Chad said.

"You'd do your mom?" Chet cried. "Sick, dude!"

"Fuckin' perverts, no, I meant the uggo. I'd do her."

"So *you're* desperate," Skip said.

"Pussy's pussy," he said, shrugging. "Okay, sure, I'd prefer the hot one, but…"

"You're all pigs," Jessie said. "Total sleaze. You know that, right?"

Etch squeezed her butt. "That's why you love me, babe!"

"You're still total sleaze."

Chad leaned back with his weight propped on his elbows. "Yeah, well, not much you can do about it, is there?"

"I dunno," Jessie said. "I could always kick your ass."

He snorted. "Sh'yah, right. Like you'd ever hurt anybody."

Gwen hadn't been able to pay attention in any of her classes. Not even her favorite one from her favorite instructor. She drifted through the day like someone in a daze. Feeling unreal. Feeling as if the whole world was a fragile, soap-bubble illusion.

She'd given up at lunchtime and taken an early bus rather than seek out her usual quiet bench by the fountain, in the willow-dotted, green courtyard between the Liberal Arts building and the Psychology/Sociology building.

Not that she'd had much appetite for lunch anyway. She didn't think she was going to throw up–Darlene had at breakfast, scarfing down two cereal bars and then running to Annamaria's bathroom almost as soon as the second one was gone.

It wasn't anything like that. Gwen just hadn't wanted to eat the lunch she'd packed that morning.

A woman on the bus—a filthy, skin-and-bones bag lady wearing two sweaters and a coat despite the warmth of the day— asked Gwen for change so she could get something to eat.

Gwen offered her the lunch bag.

The bag lady took it, looked in, looked up. Her dirty face wrinkled into a scowl and she demanded to know what Gwen thought she was doing.

"You said you were hungry," she said. "It's… it's egg salad, blueberry yogurt, and carrot sticks."

The bag lady called her a Nazi cunt.

The bus driver yelled at the bag lady, told her to quit with that talk or he'd put her off the bus right now.

The bag lady called *him* a Nazi cunt.

He pulled the bus over and opened the door and made her get out.

Gwen huddled on the seat, book bag on her lap, both arms clenched tight around it. The brown lunch bag sat beside her. She hadn't wanted it before, and she wanted it even less now.

"You shouldn't give them anything," a business-suited man told her. "It only encourages them."

She didn't think the bag lady had been very encouraged, but wasn't about to say so. She just offered him a meek and apologetic smile.

The bus stop nearest their house was at the intersection where their long, looping country road met a more major avenue. Traffic signals had already been put up in anticipation of the condo complex and construction of a shopping center being finished, but at the moment they remained deactivated, with their lights swaddled in plastic covers.

The projected shopping center was a razed and bulldozed patch. The condo complex was mostly foundations, pipes, beams, and a single model home to be shown off to potential buyers.

Gwen got off the bus, hefting her book bag onto her shoulder, and holding the lunch bag at the end of her arm. She still didn't want it, but she couldn't bring herself to throw it away, wasting perfectly good food she'd paid for out of her own limited budget.

It was the middle of a weekday, and the men working on the condos were currently on break, sitting in whatever shade they could find.

She could feel them looking at her. Watching her. She couldn't see them grinning or elbowing each other, couldn't hear what they might be saying about her or whether they were laughing… but she could *feel* all that, too.

Her skin tightened. A helpless flush climbed her cheeks.

This wasn't supposed to bother her so much anymore. Hadn't Annamaria said so? Hadn't her friends practically promised? It was time for men to learn how it felt to always have to be on edge, on guard. It was their turn!

Ignore them, she told herself. *Ignore them and walk on by. It's not like they're going to chase you, grab you. The most they might do is catcall and whistle.*

If she stayed on this side of the road—which was the side their house was on—she'd pass within twenty yards or so of the nearest men. Twenty yards. That was a lot. That was plenty. Sixty whole feet. A long way.

Then how come it didn't seem like very far at all?

If she crossed the road…

If she crossed the road, they would see her and know why she did it. They would know she was too intimidated to walk past.

And if she crossed the road, she'd be over on the same side as the wetland where they'd taken Donnie Hubert. Where he was hidden, dead in the brown muck at the bottom of the pond. Dead with the sandbag taped to him to weigh him down. Rotting by now. Rotting and slimy, parts of him nibbled away by fish or bugs.

Gwen sank her teeth into her lower lip and looked at both options, feeling like a cartoon character trying to choose between two equally spooky paths through the dark woods.

Live construction workers on one side, watching her.

Dead Donnie Hubert in the swamp on the other.

She could see the house up ahead, Jessie's Mustang there but Annamaria's and Darlene's cars both gone. She could see the Gerrittsons' place beyond it, their hired man toodling around the yard on his big green mower. Even from here, the scent of fresh-cut grass hung sweet in the air.

The longer she stood here, the more she'd give away how anxious she was.

She took a deep breath and set out with a purposeful stride. Head high. Chin quivering. One hand clamped on the straps of her book bag, the other holding the folded-down top of the brown paper lunch bag in a death grip.

Annamaria wouldn't be afraid of them, she thought. *Jessie wouldn't be afraid of them. Just walk. Just walk and don't look around, and if any of them try something…*

What?

Hit them with an egg salad sandwich and container of blueberry yogurt? Warn them off with carrot sticks?

Someone did whistle. Once. An insolent wolf-whistle. Gwen flinched a little and quickened her pace.

Nobody came after her. Not chasing, not following. Then she was past the future condos and passing the windbreak line of trees, and then she was at Mrs. Hubert's property.

All quiet. Even the snarling mower-motor next door had stopped.

Relief sobbed through her whole body in a series of soft, domino cascades. She brushed her hair out of her face and started up the driveway, then jerked to a halt as someone came around the side of the house.

"Afternoon," Ed Reilly said.

He spoke amiably enough, he thought, but the girl must have been lost in a daydream, because he sure startled the bejeezus out of her.

She didn't leap a full foot in the air. She didn't whirl and bolt like a deer. She didn't scream blue murder. She didn't faint dead away. But he had the idea the only reason she didn't do any of those things was because she was trying, in that first moment, to do all of them at once.

It occurred to him as he held out his hands in a placating kind of way to show her he was harmless, that she was about the same age Hope would have been, if Hope had lived more than those six pitiful days in the incubator.

The thought, out of nowhere like that, was a painful blindside.

His daughter could have been in college by now.

This girl could have been... not his daughter, because she looked nothing like him or like Leigh. But she could have been his daughter's classmate, his daughter's friend.

"Didn't mean to scare you," he said.

"I'm not scared!" she said, in a high, shrill voice.

He could just about hear her heart hammering from ten

paces away, and he saw panic brimming in her wide, greenish eyes, but Ed let that one go.

"I'm Ed. Ed Reilly. I work for your neighbors, Mr. and Mrs. Gerrittson."

She stared at him. He was reminded of the time a sudden thunderstorm had whipped up and he'd had to go bring in the alpacas. They had stared with much this same kind of blank, formless terror.

"Gerrittson," he repeated, and hooked a thumb over his shoulder. "Walter and Muriel? With the alpacas?"

Her head bobbed once. Her long white throat moved as she swallowed. Her head bobbed again. Her gaze flickered from him to the house, then past the house to the garage, up to the door at the top of the stairs. Then back to him.

"I... I'm Gwen," she said.

Ed decided against offering a handshake. "Mr. G. asked if I'd mind driving the mower over here and taking care of the lawns. I know Mrs. Hubert's nephew used to do it, but—"

He wouldn't have believed her eyes could go any bigger, but they did.

"—with him away, Mr. G. figured we could help out. Be neighborly."

"Oh," she said.

"If it's okay with you?"

"What? Oh! Um..." Again, her gaze jittered and flickered– apartment over the garage, Ed, the Mustang in the driveway, the house, Ed, the mower parked at the property line, the tall grass, Ed–and a tentative smile faltered its way onto her face. "Um... I guess... I mean... it's Mrs. Hubert's house... but... it's fine with me. I guess."

"Well, all right then," he said. "Is now a good time?"

"I... I think so."

"Then I'll get to it." He moved away from her, then remembered the switchblade in his pocket and tried to think of a good way to voice the question.

With this skittish girl? There wasn't a good way.

He could have taken anything out of his pocket right then– keys, change, tissue, lip balm–and she would have thought he was pulling a weapon on her. Let alone pulling an actual weapon.

"Gwen?"

She had been heading for the front door, and he practically read her mind—was she close enough to get in, slam it and lock it before he caught her?

Made him soul-sick and sad to think a young girl like this should have to live in such a state of perpetual fear. What was this world coming to? The news filled with maniacs and terrorists, atrocities on a daily basis.

"I found this in your yard," he said, tweezing the switchblade by the very end of the faux-ivory handle to make it as harmless-looking as possible. The blade was retracted and he was nowhere near the go-button. "Know whose it is?"

CHAPTER FOURTEEN

The lawn looked great.

Better than it had in a long time. Better than it ever had after Donnie's usual half-assed job. Freshly mowed. The edges trimmed. The sidewalk swept clean of clippings. A really nice job.

But still.

"Sweet, pan-fried baby Jesus," Jessie said, smacking herself in the forehead almost hard enough to add another bruise to her collection. "And you told him *sure*, go ahead, mow the lawn, feel free, knock yourself out. Jesus H., Guinevere. What were you thinking?"

Gwen wrung her hands. "I didn't know what else to say."

"How about *no*?" Darlene suggested. "Or at least *no, thank you.*"

"He was offering to do us a favor. It would have been rude—"

"*Fuck* rude!" Jessie pointed out back. "What if he went snooping?"

"He didn't, though."

"Come on," Annamaria said. She was sitting beside Gwen, with an arm around her. "If she had told him no, it might have made him suspicious."

"Yeah?" Darlene sniffed. "How suspicious you think he would've been if he found our buddy Rico?"

"He wouldn't have had any reason to go up there," Annamaria said.

"He went *in* the fucking *garage!*" cried Jessie.

"Only to get the push broom," Gwen said.

"He still could've noticed something! He was right under! Yeah, okay, fine, maybe Rico wasn't going to be doing a lot of yelling, but what if he'd heard somebody down there and thumped around trying to get their attention?"

"Well, we stuck the icepick—" Darlene began.

"The icepick, sure, whatever, maybe Rico can't hear a damn thing with his eardrums poked out, but the rest of it still applies!"

"That's what the exercise mats are for," Annamaria said. "Padding and to muffle any noises."

"Yeah, but—"

"Okay, look," Rachel said. She had been staying out of the argument, thinking fast-and-furious the whole time. Not pacing, but tap-drumming her feet in a rapid tattoo on the floor. "What's done is done, right? No use arguing about it or accusing people."

"But she—" Darlene and Jessie said together.

"I said I was sorry," said Gwen. Tears welled in her eyes.

"It's all right," said Annamaria, stroking her hair soothingly. "Nothing happened this time. We're clear. Aren't we, Rachel?"

"Not *clear*-clear." Rachel gnawed her thumbnail. "But not caught either. We have to be more careful. And we better finish up, take care of the mess. Just in case."

"Shouldn't we get rid of Mr. Ed?" asked Darlene.

"He could be a real problem," Jessie said. "Especially after what he told Gwen, how he's living with the old farts now, and this thing about wanting to be neighborly. He might start showing up whenever the hell he feels like it."

"We can't afford that," Darlene said.

"We also can't afford to kill someone we know, remember?" Annamaria looked at Rachel. "That's what you told us, isn't it? Nobody too close to home?"

"This from the chick who got a guy at her work," said Jessie.

"Strangers *are* best," Rachel said. "Fewer connections, less scrutiny. I think we better leave him alone. Keep an eye on him, sure, but otherwise ignore him unless he does look like he might become a problem."

They had to settle for that, at least for the time being.

After their respective dinners–Gwen had canned soup and crackers, Jessie made a BLT with extra B, Rachel ate a grilled cheese sandwich, Annamaria heated up a bowl of leftover pasta primavera, and Darlene nibbled on the heel slice from a loaf of bread–they puttered around trying to find ways to fill time. Flipping channels, surfing the internet, making half-hearted efforts at homework or housework.

Waiting.

Waiting for it to get dark, get late. Waiting for the lights next door at the Gerrittsons' to go out.

"Good thing those farm types are into that whole early to bed, early to rise thing." Jessie said when the lights over there switched off at just past nine.

They waited another half-hour.

It was a very long half-hour.

It was a half-hour that was at least six hours in duration.

"Okay," Rachel said. "But careful and quiet, remember."

"You know it." Jessie cracked her knuckles. "Oh, hey, I almost forgot… any of you find his knife? Switchblade, about yea big, ivory handle, green snake?"

"I thought you put it in your pocket," Darlene said.

"I did, but it fell out."

"You mean you *lost* it?" Rachel didn't look pleased. "When? Where?"

Gwen said nothing.

"Didn't see it in your car?" Jessie asked Darlene.

"Nuh-unh, but I didn't look for it either."

"It wasn't in the yard," Annamaria said, "so if it's not in Darlene's car, it must have fallen out back where you grabbed him."

Gwen still said nothing.

"Shit," Jessie said.

"That's not good," said Rachel. "It would have his fingerprints on it *and* Jessie's."

"Fuck-shit," Jessie said.

"Want me to go check?" Darlene asked.

"First we better finish up. A knife with fingerprints, that's maybe incriminating. A body, that's a lot more so."

The smell of cut grass hung heavy in the air. They crossed the breezeway to the attached laundry shed, casting frequent, wary looks over in the direction of the Gerrittson place. With the windows only dark squares, they couldn't tell if anybody was standing there peering out at them. All five breathed easier when the corner of the garage was in the way.

At the top of the steps, Rachel unlocked the apartment door. They hustled inside and pulled it shut. The green cut-grass scent from outside was replaced by something thick and foul: a heavy miasma of boiled meat.

Darlene gagged but held.

"Whee-eew," Jessie said, fanning her hand in front of her face as she switched on the light.

They stared at the results of their handiwork.

After the second guy, and the amazing amount of blood that had come out of him—there really was a difference between knowing the amount in liters or pints and seeing it spilled out all over the place—they'd added a kiddie wading pool to contain the runoff.

"A tub had caught all!" Gwen had said in an eerie voice upon viewing the revision, and laughed a high, lunatic's laugh that made the rest of the girls' skin crawl.

The wading pool, though, helped. Saving them a lot of tedious scrubbing and cleanup. It was blue plastic with a ripply bottom, and had designs of fishies and little sailboats around the sides. It was also maybe half an inch deep in a coagulated mess of bodily fluids and other excretions.

Rico lay on the mattress.

Dead.

No doubt about it.

Dead, bloating, already discoloring.

It had been a warm day. A warm day in a closed room.

"Damn," Rachel said.

"Oh, for fuck's sake!" Jessie cried. "The wussy fucking up and croaked on us!"

Gagging again, Darlene whirled and blundered past Annamaria into the kitchenette, where she bent over the sink and retched up sour strings of spit and bile. Her arm struck the teakettle she'd left on the counter. It hit the linoleum, bounced once, and rolled back and forth in wobbly, seesaw arcs. The last dregs of water dribbled out.

"How did he die?" Annamaria asked. She was rubbing her

thumb against the gauze-covered pad on her other hand, as if unaware that she did it.

"We killed him," Gwen said.

"Bullshit," said Jessie.

"Look at him! Look what we did to him!"

"Yeah but that shouldn't have been enough to kill him yet!"

Rachel's face twisted for a moment, allowing a flash of revulsion to show, and then she masked it and approached the wading pool with the mattress and body inside. "I don't think he bled to death. Maybe he suffocated. Maybe it was shock, you know, from the pain and stuff."

"Or maybe he just couldn't take it," Jessie said.

"But it doesn't really matter," Rachel said. "He's dead either way. Let's get him out of here. Glove up, everybody."

They gloved up and went to work. Uncuffing Rico's wrist and ankle. Wrapping the body. Bundling up the tarps. Jessie, Annamaria and Darlene hauled the body downstairs and loaded it into the Caddy's trunk. Gwen and Rachel rinsed the wading pool with the shower attachment Jessie had installed in the small bathroom, pouring the rinse-water into the toilet, flushing it, doing this again and again until the worst of the mess was washed away and only a few stains remained in the ripples of the blue pool bottom.

"This sucks," Darlene said, coming back in and starting to collect tools and utensils into a mop bucket full of hot water and bleach.

"Yeah," said Jessie, stripping the mattress cover. "I was looking forward to some fun, and now we're S.O.L.."

"We're what?" Annamaria asked, helping pick up tools.

"Shit-outta-luck," Rachel translated as she and Gwen maneuvered the wading pool back through the narrow bathroom doorway.

"I guess we need another one," Jessie said.

Annamaria handed Mrs. Hubert the rent envelope–small bills, and including their extra thirty a month for use of the apartment above the garage–and asked if she'd heard from Donnie.

"Not a damn word. Bastard's gone, and as far as I'm concerned, he can *stay* gone. Nice job on the lawn."

"The Gerrittsons' hired man did it," Annamaria said.

"That so? The one who's living there now? Did he ask for money?"

"No."

"Hmph." Her beady eyes glittered. "Just mowed the whole yard out of the kindness of his heart?"

"To be neighborly, he said."

"Well, you tell me if he starts being a problem. I never got along so great with those two–they were always bitching about my dogs, saying my dogs upset their llamas or whatever the hell they are–and I won't tolerate their handyman harassing my tenants."

"I'm sure it's nothing like that, Mrs. Hubert."

"Hmph," she said again. "This is a bad world, Annamaria. Bad things happen all the time. Even out here where it seems all peaceful and safe. Have you been watching the news?"

"Every day."

"Then you heard about these murders."

"Yes," Annamaria said, glad that Gwen and Darlene were at class, Rachel was showering, and Jessie was at a track meet.

Mrs. Hubert shook her head, making her jowls wobble. "Hell of a thing. They're saying it might be a serial killer. And what he did to them! My God! Most of the details are so horrible they won't even put them on the news, but I play poker with a cop's wife and she said her husband's been having nightmares over it."

"Nightmares!" echoed Annamaria, widening her eyes. "That bad?"

"They were tortured to death," Mrs. Hubert said. She leaned closer, dropping her voice in a confiding manner, and giving Annamaria a blast of breath that smelled like vodka and pastrami. "Mutilated. Hacked to shreds. The one that really gave her husband nightmares, had his dick just about scalded off."

"Scalded," Annamaria said. "Really?"

"Like the killer hung him over a pot of boiling water and dunked the whole works, cooked 'em like a hot dog and a couple of poached eggs."

"That's awful."

Not to mention inaccurate… they hadn't dunked him… dunked his junk, as Jessie might've said. They'd used the teakettle. Darlene had poured. A slow, precise stream—at least, as precise as was possible, the way Rico had reacted.

"You girls be extra careful," Mrs. Hubert said. "Most likely, you've got nothing to worry about. The cops figure their killer must be one of those gay-boys, since he's been going after men instead of pretty girls, like they usually do. But with a maniac like *that* on the loose…"

"We'll be careful," Annamaria said.

"Some Band-Aid you got there. What'd you do to your hand?"

"Box-cutter."

"Agh." Mrs. Hubert's face tucked into a sympathetic grimace. "Those bitches are sharp."

"Yeah," she said. Sighed, almost.

As Mrs. Hubert waddled to her car, Annamaria skimmed her fingertips across the bandage. It completely hid the healing cut. Soon there would only be a pinkish line on her dusky skin. Then a pale thread of scar. Then possibly not even that.

It would be gone, but she would always remember how it had felt. The deep, clear slice. The moment in which nothing else existed but the pain. The timeless instant of pure concentration and focus before blood welled up dark and thick. In that instant, the room had gone away. Her friends had gone away. Rico had gone away.

There had only been Annamaria, Annamaria in the center of the pain.

It's everything, the man from the restaurant–Gordon–had told her.

Everything.

Nothing else.

That, she knew, was a hint of what it had been like for Serafina.

That, but a thousand times more powerful.

With the helplessness. And the fear.

But most of all, that pure, clear, deep pain.

***

Jessie's last class Friday afternoon was canceled, the instructor out sick.

Gee, what a surprise. Funny how that happened. Nice sunny weather plus weekend just played hell with some people's constitutions, didn't it? Such a shame. What a drag. Poor-fucking-baby.

And thank-fucking-God.

She'd been tempted to cut anyway. General Ed requirements were a great big snore. Western Civ? Biggest snore of them all. Even the expert who was supposed to be edumacating their young minds was too bored-out-the-ass to show up.

Worked fine as far as Jessie was concerned. Just meant she had a few extra hours to chill before the trip to the lake.

Etch and the guys would have already stocked up on beer, a cooler full with a supplemental twelve-pack or three stashed in the back of Etch's monster Yukon SUV, which he called the Yuke. They would think that was all they needed, but Jessie knew better. She knew how this went. How it *always* went.

They'd get out to the lake and find a good spot, put up the tents, roll out the sleeping bags, inflate the inner tubes, all that good stuff. Have fun. Build a fire and cook some 'dogs. Horse around. Cannonball off the dock. Rock-climb to the top of a boulder and piss from the height, see who could make their stream arc furthest or last longest. All while drinking can after can of beer.

Eventually, one of them would say something along the lines of, "Dude, we should have brought some tequila!" The rest would chorus agreement and regret. They'd debate going into town and decide they'd better not risk it, didn't want to get pulled over by a park ranger or county cop, with beer on their breath. "Next time," they'd say. "Next time for sure."

Nice surprise for them to have next time be this time.

She swung by the liquor store and bought three generous-sized bottles of Jose Cuervo—the liquor-store guy gave her fading shiner a dubious look but kept his mouth shut, good for him, none of his business—then bopped over to the grocery store for limes and salt.

Booyah.

Annamaria was on her way out as Jessie got to the house, dressed for work, her hair clipped back.

"Thought you were off tonight," Jessie said.

"Bry called in sick. You're back early."

"Prof called in sick."

"I guess there's a lot of that going around," Anna said, with a faint smile.

"Sucks you have to work, though. Hell of a way to spend a Friday night."

"I don't mind. Tips are better."

"Maybe, but it still bites. Anybody else home?"

"Gwen's here," Anna said. "She told me was going to take a nap."

"She okay?" asked Jessie. "She's not flaking out on us, is she?"

"No... she's... she'll be all right. I think it might help if we did something nice for her."

"Nice? Like what?"

"I don't know. Have a movie party? She's always suggesting we have a movie party."

Jessie's lip, not the sore one, curled. "That'd be cool, except you know she would make us sit through a *Hobbit* marathon or some shit like that."

"It could be fun."

"I'll have to go buy more tequila, then."

Anna laughed. "Couldn't hurt. See you Sunday, Jessie. Have fun at the lake."

"Later, Anna."

The house was dim, cool and hushed. Jessie knew that Rachel would be in the science department until forever-o'clock, grading papers, tidying labs, doing a bunch of other TA scut work. Darlene's classes ran until six or seven, a solid block of men-are-shit-ology that would leave her in an even bitchier mood than usual.

She tossed some snacks in atop her other purchases–Skip was covering the grub, Etch had said, and while Skip was a good enough guy, he could be a bit of a brain-case, having once stocked up on enough Doritos and bean dip to sink an aircraft carrier but nothing else–and set it by the front door so she could grab it on the way out. Then she went up to her room, where she changed into khaki shorts and a short-sleeved blouse with the ends tied at her midriff.

As she dressed, she could just hear low music from across the hall, through Gwen's closed door. Harps, and women singing in Irish or Scottish or elvish or whatever. She loaded sweats and her swimsuit into her pack, thought for a moment, then threw in a handful of condoms. As a finishing touch, she folded and rolled her spare yoga mat into a tight cylinder and tucked it through the straps. Outdoor sex was great, but she could do without pine needles stuck to her ass, or rocks digging into her knees.

Someone knocked at the front door. Jessie went downstairs in lithe jumps, tossed her pack so that it slid to a perfect stop beside the brown paper bag, and opened the door to find Chad standing there.

"Hey, Jess."

His bike was tipped against the porch rail, secured by a loop of plastic-coated chain. His racing helmet dangled from the handlebars. He had a backpack slung over his shoulder by a single strap, sunglasses clipped at the collar of his tee shirt, and a sports bottle of water in his free hand.

"Hey, Chad," she said.

"Others not here yet, huh? Good, was sure I'd be late."

"Late?"

Chad's brows drew together. "It's today we're going to the lake, right?"

"Yeah, but not until six."

"Six?! I thought it was four! I *knew* I shoulda called, but my fucking phone died, and—"

Jessie smirked. "I heard you dropped it in the toilet."

"Yeah, okay, I dropped it in the toilet," he said in a long-suffering way. "It was in my pocket, I was taking a shit, I went to pull up my pants and splash. Happy?"

"It's a tragedy. I hope you wiped."

"So can I come in or you gonna make me stand on the porch for two hours?"

"You want to wait here?"

"Beats biking all the way back to my place."

"Sure, whatever. But keep it down, huh? One of my housemates is taking a nap."

"Yeah? Annamaria?"

"You wish," Jessie said. "She's at work."

"Damn."

"Careful, dude, or I might start thinking you showed up a couple hours early hoping to score with her."

He stepped inside, set his backpack down by hers, and stretched. The tee shirt rode up, almost to the waistband of his bike shorts, which were so tight they might have been airbrushed on. "Could you blame me?"

"Subtle, Chad. Real subtle. Anyway, wasn't it Skip who was interested in her? Does he know you're here?"

"Nah."

"Bet he'd be tweaked."

"He'd get over it."

Jessie closed the door, and watched Chad swagger into the kitchen like he owned the place. Lots of muscle, lots of shaggy hair with surfer-sunbleach highlights, a rich bronze tan, hazel eyes.

"Where's the beer?" he asked, head in the fridge. "Ah, here we go! Want one?"

"Yeah," Jessie said. "So… Chad… you didn't tell any of the guys you were coming over here?"

"Said I'd meet them. Just didn't say when." He turned from the fridge with a beer in each hand, and bumped it shut with his foot. He grinned at her. "Guess we'll have to figure out something to do until six."

She looked at the beer he was holding out, then looked at his grin. "Oh, yeah? Like what?"

The grin widened. "I dunno." Chad leaned against the counter, tipping one brown glass bottle toward her with its neck jutting at a suggestive angle. "We could fuck."

"For two hours?"

"Why not? I got stamina."

"And you don't think Etch would mind?"

"Pff," Chad said, and took a long swig. "He lets me drive the Yuke. Hell, he lets me borrow his wetsuit."

In her mind's eye, she saw herself leap, saw herself ram a knee into his jimmies with her whole weight and momentum behind it, saw herself grab the bottles from him as he doubled over.

A bottle in each hand, and she would bring them around in twin smooth, hard arcs. Pow to the temples with their thick, reinforced glass bases, and if that didn't shatter them, she would smash them on the counter and plunge the jagged shards into his throat or gut or eyes as he was on the way down.

She didn't.

She *wanted* to, but she didn't.

She smiled at him instead, and sidled closer, and reached out to dandle her fingertips over the beer bottle's cap. "Yeah, okay," she said.

Chad blinked. "Okay?"

"But, you know, my housemates… wouldn't want them to walk in on us."

"Hey, I wouldn't mind." A light had gone on in his hazel eyes, brightening with every passing second. "They could join the fun."

"They might," Jessie said. "Probably would. But we can still get started without them." She tipped her head at the kitchen door. "C'mon. I know the perfect place."

Ed followed the sound of feeble mewing to a shadowy back corner of the hayloft and found one of the barn cats giving suck to a new litter.

The orange tabby glared at him. Her motley kittens floundered over each other, blind and clumsy as they tried to latch on and nurse.

"Easy, momma-kitty," he said. "I won't bother your little ones."

She hissed, all baleful green eyes and bared fangs.

"Okay, okay." He backed away, chose other bales of alfalfa from the far end of the loft, and broke those down to fork into the pens instead.

Alfalfa for the alpacas.

He knew it didn't quite rhyme, but it fit somehow. There was a term for it. Ed just couldn't remember what that term was.

Movement out the loft's upper window caught his eye. He looked and saw one of Mrs. Hubert's tenants leading a guy up the stairs to the apartment above the garage.

"Oh, is that so?" he said, feeling half-amused and half-disapproving.

The way the girl was smiling back at the guy, coyly, over her shoulder, as she unlocked the door... the grin of anticipation on the guy's face...

Yeah, he figured that *was* so.

"Wonder what your landlady would think of that," he said.

Flying.

Falling.

Gwen jerked awake, shuddering, hitching for breath. She had to brace herself against the bed to make sure she wasn't still plummeting. It took her a few moments to believe it despite the feel of the covers and pillows.

Her bed. Her room.

The shudders subsided and her breathing evened out.

To go from the flying dream to the falling dream... just like *that*... with no warning...

She loved the flying dream, so glorious, one of her favorites. Soaring effortlessly through the air, hair and gauzy gown billowing around her. Flying through wispy clouds. Flying with birds–white swans, or a rainbow-hued flock of little songbirds.

Sometimes a man would be flying with her, ahead of her and beckoning, or beside her and holding her hand. His face was never clear—or at least she could never remember it when she woke up. He had beautiful eyes, she knew that much. Not what color. Only that they were beautiful... and when she looked into them... she felt strong and fearless and alive.

The falling dream, on the other hand, stuck her on a bridge rail, or a ledge, or a roof, or a cliff. With no idea how she'd gotten there, or why. Teetering on the precipice. Clinging for a fingerhold. Searching for safety but unable to reach it. Barricades in the way. Faceless strangers blocking her.

And then slipping. Or being pushed by those same faceless strangers. Or sometimes… worst of all… realizing that there was no hope. Giving up. Letting herself go. Letting herself fall. Surrendering.

God, she hated that dream.

They had never crossed over like that before. Never.

When she was sure–mostly–that she wasn't going to plunge to her death, Gwen sat up. She was groggy and disoriented, certain of where she was but with her sense of time all out of whack. The clock said it was almost five… but was that five in the morning or five in the afternoon? On what day?

Flying and then falling.

So horrible!

One instant gliding, buoyant, free. Laughing from the sheer joy of it all. Her hand clasped in his, and those beautiful eyes shining at her like jewels.

Then she'd been ripped from him. Yanked earthward. Gravity like a giant iron fist, with her clenched in its grasp. The crystal-clear sky gone black, storm-shot, turbulent, raked with jagged lightning and howling wind.

Gwen peered again at her clock, deciphering the glowing dot beside the numbers as indicating PM. Almost five in the afternoon, then.

She had finished with classes for the day at two, ridden the bus back here, said hello to Annamaria, eaten ramen, and then come up here with the intention of taking a nap.

For a while, though, she'd done nothing but sit on her bed, turning Rico's switchblade over and over in her hands. Admiring the sheen of its ivory handle, the sinuous emerald snake like a mystical dragon. She hadn't mentioned the knife to the others, and wasn't sure why.

Jessie would be relieved to know it wasn't lost after all… but Jessie would claim it then, say she called dibs. Rachel might not be happy to hear that the neighbors' hired man had seen something that could be a crucial piece of evidence… Rachel would say they had to get rid of it.

Either way, Gwen wouldn't have it anymore. She'd have to give it up. Let Jessie have it, or throw it away—maybe into the swamp with Donnie, where it'd never be found.

It was only a cheap switchblade. It wasn't the One Ring or anything. It wasn't her precious. Why was she feeling all Frodo-esque about it?

Finally, still undecided, she'd returned the knife to its hiding place in the inner pocket of her purse, and gone to sleep. Until the flying dream became the falling one, waking her with a jolt.

She heard a noise from downstairs. A door closing. Someone coming in? Someone leaving? It occurred to her that there had been some other sound, some strange clatter in her dream, at the moment everything went from glorious to awful. Maybe it hadn't been a dream-noise at all.

The house was quiet now. She went to the end of the hall, then down the stairs. Jessie's pack sat by the front door, along with a paper grocery sack that had a package of Trader Joe's chili-coated dried mangoes and a bag of SunChips sticking out of the top.

And a snake. Not a sinuous, emerald-green one. A segmented, yellow, mechanical-looking snake.

Gwen twitched, scalp prickling, fists closing.

Then she saw it wasn't a snake at all. It was a bike chain, the links encased in yellow plastic stuff. The lock was still locked, and the chain had been cut. Probably by bolt-cutters, which were also lying on the floor.

The bolt-cutters weren't supposed to be in the house. They belonged out in the garage with the rest of the tools.

Frowning, Gwen went to the front door, opened it, and looked out. Someone was biking away from the house. Bronzed, athletic legs pumping in tight bike shorts. Carrying a backpack and wearing a helmet.

Before she got more than that fleeting glimpse, the bicyclist swept past the windbreak stand of trees, and was out of her sight.

CHAPTER FIFTEEN

Darlene would have liked to drive on by and hope they didn't notice her, but it was no use. The huge stupid fucking thing she drove wouldn't have been unobtrusive on a crowded New York City street or Los Angeles rush hour highway.

Out here, about the only thing moving on the road?

She might as well have been steering a parade float.

The car had been a high school graduation 'gift' from her relatives. Which really meant it was left over when her grandparents got shuffled off to the nursing home before they forgot a stove burner and incinerated themselves in their sleep. Nobody else in the family had wanted the car, but no dealer would look at it without busting a gut laughing.

The Dunfeys couldn't justify junking a perfectly serviceable car and also spending a couple of grand on even a crappy "new" used one for Darlene. This was the ideal solution to both problems.

Ideal for everyone except Darlene, but who gave a shit about her opinion?

Driving by and hoping to go unnoticed was out. She slowed, though. Giving them time to finish up and leave. The last thing she needed was to pull up in that huge stupid fucking thing, have it backfire and fart and splutter its way to rest, and get out while Etch and all his friends watched.

Laughed.

Exchanged looks behind her back.

They were stowing backpacks, coolers, tents, sleeping bags and cardboard boxes of supplies in the rear of Etch's SUV: a huge, mud-spattered, dark blue beast with gear racks on top—adjustable for bikes, skis, surfboards, kayaks—and a trailer hitch like a bulbous chrome dick above a swinging pair of Truck Nutz. Currently, there was no trailer attached, though Darlene had seen them load it with jet skis, snowmobiles, or off-roaders, depending on the season.

Wasn't enough that Jessie had a hot, buff guy. She had a hot, buff guy with money… or rich parents… same diff.

Typical.

Fucking unfair, but that was what made it so typical.

Etch's buddies—who were also hot and buff, and also either had money or rich parents—joshed around, gave each other bro-fist slugs to the upper arm, and seemed to be having a fine old time.

Jessie was right there in the thick of it with the guys. In obnoxiously high spirits, slugging one in the bicep, making mock jabs at another's solar plexus, slapping Etch on the butt, catching a heavy bundle of firewood one of them tossed to her.

They had some girls with them besides Jessie: a trio of Barbie-doll blondes with big boobs and tiny outfits. The three gathered around a bright yellow sporty convertible, chatting and primping and flirting.

Darlene bet that if she revved it and swung broadside at the last minute, she could grind all three of the Barbie-bitches to liverwurst between the vehicles.

She hoped they'd get broiled alive by sunburn and eaten alive by mosquitoes. Maybe they'd squat to pee in poison ivy and wipe with a handful of the leaves. Or swallow snake eggs while drinking from a pond and gestate a squirming knot of slithery reptiles.

Or, hell, why not imagine them being killed by bears? Falling off a cliff? Butchered by crazed wilderness cannibals? Abducted and ass-probed by aliens?

Though she'd slowed the Caddy, she couldn't make the damn thing invisible, and Jessie spotted her. Waved. Exuberant. Bouncing. Teeth flashing in a busting-at-the-seams grin of excitement. The guys glanced, said some stuff back and forth, shrugged, smirked, laughed, checked the time, peered down the road, griped at each other. The Barbie-blondes posed all sexy and cute while one of them held her cell phone at arm's length to snap a group selfie.

Please God, Jessie wasn't going to invite her to go with.

That was the last thing she needed.

Resisting the urge to run anybody over, she passed the convertible and the Yuke, parked, and got out. She was close enough to overhear the guys talking.

"—wait around?"

"I say fuck him, let's roll, I wanna get there before dark."

"Anybody try giving him a... right, shit, his phone, I forgot."

"More beer for us if he doesn't show."

"Yeah, he knows where we'll be."

"Dar!" Jessie bounded up to her. "Hey!"

"Hey," Darlene said, her voice flat.

She could see the Barbie-blonde-bitches exchanging looks—the kind of looks Darlene knew all too well, the kind of looks she had hated since she was in kindergarten, lofty "I *hope* they're not bringing *her*!" looks.

Jessie grabbed her arm and towed her away from the others. "Got a surprise for you."

"Oh Christ."

"You'll like it."

"Why do I not think so?"

"Because you're too fucking negative." Jessie made sure they were out of earshot, and leaned close. "Nobody else knows about this yet. Anna's at work and Rache isn't back, and Gwen's hiding out in her room writing love letters to the Jonas Brothers or some shit. But listen... soon as we're gone, go out back, okay?"

"What did you do?"

"You'll see!"

"Jess, let's go!" Etch called.

"Be right there!" she called back. To Darlene, she added, "If someone gets pissy about it, tell them that it's my fault and I'll explain the whole thing on Sunday when I get home."

"Jess!" Etch called, more insistently, standing at the driver's door of the Yuke with his gold hair gleaming.

"Yeah! Okay!" She flashed Darlene that manic grin again. "See ya, and have fun!"

She bounded back to the Yuke, where there was a lot of good-natured pushing and shoving as they piled in, vying for shotgun and window seats, already bickering about what music they would listen to.

One guy got into the convertible with the trio of blondes, looking pretty pleased with himself. Horns honked, engines revved, windows rolled down so Etch and the guy in the convertible could holler back and forth about what route they would take, and then, finally, they drove off.

Sure hadn't invited her along, had they? Not even a token offer. Hadn't even asked if she wanted to go. Which she didn't, and if they *had* asked she would have said no, would have given them a whole list of excuses and reasons why she couldn't.

But they hadn't even tried.

Figured, didn't it? Typical. Just fucking typical.

Darlene retrieved her purse and stuff from the Caddy, trudged over to the house, and let herself in. It was blissfully quiet. Soft music from upstairs–Gwen's room–but nothing else.

Soon as we're gone, go out back, okay?

If someone gets pissy about it, tell them it's my fault.

Why did she have the feeling that things were about to really hit the fan?

Darlene heaved a breath and decided she'd better go take a look.

"Out here?" he'd said, following her up the stairs.

"Sure. Nice and private."

"Thought you were using it for a gym or something."

"Yeah, kinda."

"Hey, what ever happened to that loser geek used to live up here?"

"Took off," Jessie had said, unlocking the door. "Went to Mexico, that's what Mrs. H. thinks."

"Phew. Doesn't smell so great," he'd said as she swung it open.
"Well, the place was pretty gross."
"Smells like something *died*."

Darlene climbed the steps, unlocked the door—they kept the key on a pegboard by the kitchen phone, on a string, not with a label that said 'Torture Chamber' or anything like that… just a plain key—and opened it.

Rachel said there was no point trying to conceal the key, hide it someplace, in a magnet box on the underside of the range hood or buried behind leftovers at the back of the freezer. All that would do, she told them, was make it more inconvenient to get at if they needed it in a hurry. And, she said, if the police ever got close enough to find the key, it was over anyway.

The apartment was dark, the windows covered and not a lot of daylight making it past her. Darlene paused for a moment, blinking to adjust her eyes, and reaching for the light switch.

She heard the squishy creak and creaky squish of something moving on the exercise mats covering the floor. She heard chains clink.

The single bulb came on.

There was a naked guy on the mattress.

A naked, bronzed, buff, gorgeous guy.

Chained. Taped. Gagged. Blindfolded.

Just… there on the mattress.

Naked.

Bronzed. Buff. Gorgeous.

Darlene closed the door behind her without thinking. When the latch clicked, the guy stirred and tugged at the chains. He made muffled interrogative noises from the back of his throat.

His clothes were piled in the corner, along with the shears that had been used to cut them from his bronzed, buff, gorgeous body.

A small scrap of duct tape affixed an envelope to his chest. DAR was printed on the envelope in bold black letters.

She crossed the room, feet sinking—squish-creak, creak-squish–into the mats. The guy thrashed some as she approached, and the muffled interrogatives got louder. A few muffled demands might've been thrown in.

Naked.

And gorgeous.

And naked.

And...

She stared.

And hung.

Impossible not to stare. The only untanned part of him was where he must have worn what must have been a freakin' skimpy Speedo. Pale bands of flesh. A lush thatch of darkish hair. The thick length of his cock resting against his thigh.

Her eyes felt like they were going to drop out of her head. Her mouth had gone dry.

He shifted and squirmed. Made indignant noises behind the gag.

DAR. Her name on the envelope.

Rip.

He flinched as the tape came loose, but it wasn't like he had chest hair to worry about. His skin was smooth as flawless leather, except for a teasing, wispy line that led like a directional arrow from just below his navel to that darkish thatch.

Darlene hesitated with the envelope in her hands. She looked over her shoulder. Looked all around the apartment. Into the kitchenette, the bathroom, everywhere. Half-expecting to find an audience crouched and hiding, watching, ready to point and jeer and laugh.

Nobody.

Just her... and him... and this envelope.

When he tried to roll side to side, he didn't get far, but his cock flopped from one thigh to the other. Big. Thick. Meaty.

It was some kind of a joke. A trick.

Everything about the trip to the lake was a front.

They'd set her up. They were all in on it: Jessie, Etch, their friends. This guy. All of them, in on it. Sure, she thought they'd driven away, horns blatting, music blaring, engines revving. But they could have circled back, all quiet and sneaky. They could be waiting out there right now. Waiting for her to do something, so they could make fun of her. Poor, fat, ugly, pathetic Darlene.

She could have killed Jessie for this. Setting her up like this. When they were supposed to be friends.

And what about this guy? Had they drawn straws? Did he lose a bet?

Very funny. Ha ha, very fucking funny. Let's put him there all chained up and naked and see what she does. Then if she tries anything, won't that just be the most hilarious thing in the universe?

Jessie couldn't be *that* stupid, could she? To risk the whole enchilada so that she and Etch and the rest of them could laugh at Darlene's humiliation?

Somehow, Darlene didn't think even Jessie would go that far.

Which meant... what?

That this was real?

It *couldn't* be real.

This guy...

She recognized him now, once she tore her gaze away from his groin to study what she could see of his face. The blindfold and gag obscured a lot, but she was fairly sure this was Chad... or maybe Chet.

Was he in on it?

He had to be. Didn't he?

"This doesn't look much like a gym," he'd said. "Where's the weights? Where's the machines? What's with the... hey... whoa... what's with the chains?"

"Okay, so, it's not exactly a gym. It's more of a..." Jessie had smiled, then licked her lips. "Playroom."

"Playroom?"

"Sure. We play out here. My housemates and me. *Play,* you know?"

"Yeeeeeaaaaah? Some of this looks like bondage stuff."

"The cuffs, you mean? And the ball gag?"

"Hardcore kinky! Etch never told me about this!"

"Etch doesn't know. Nobody does. Except us. And you."

DAR, the envelope said.

She opened it. The sound of ripping paper made Chad-or-Chet squirm and vocalize some more. Whatever he was trying to express had a quality of "Okay, this was fun, but it's getting a little bizarro-world now, so game over, not sure I like this so much after all, at least let's ditch the gag and blindfold, what do you say?"

Inside the envelope was a folded sheet of notebook paper, oddly bulky, and heavier than it should have been. Darlene saw why as soon as she took it out and unfolded it. Three square foil packets–wrapped condoms–were taped in a row across the bottom of the page.

The writing was in Jessie's hasty, tilted block caps. *Nobody knows he's here*, the note said. *I took care of it. He's all yours. Do whatever you want.*

It was for real.

Something loosened inside her, and she knew she was right. Not a trick, not a joke.

For real.

He's all yours.

Do whatever you want.

Whatever she wanted. With no one else here to see. No one to watch, judge, laugh. Just the two of them, her and Chad-or-Chet. He was all hers, Jessie had said so. At her disposal. Hers to use however the hell she pleased.

Because God knew the only way she was going to ever get this close to a guy was if he was captured and tied down? Because her friends felt sorry for her and thought they could help her get laid?

She didn't need their goddamn pity!

That's what this was. Pity. Poor, fat, ugly, pathetic Darlene can't get a guy on her own, so let's get one for her. It was a fix-up to the nth degree. He hadn't even lost a bet or drawn the short straw or volunteered to take one for the team.

Memories stewed bitterly.

Her cousin Sandi visiting for the summer when they were both sixteen, her cute cousin, half the boys in town wanting to ask her out, but the Dunfeys didn't think it was very fair for Sandi to go out and have fun while Darlene stayed home, so any boy who wanted to take Sandi on a date had to beg/bribe/blackmail one of his buddies into asking Darlene, and then her parents insisted she not only accept, but go, and then Sandi and her boy would have a great time while Darlene and whatever unlucky bastard got stuck with her would have a miserable one.

Mixed P.E. sessions in middle school, when they'd been taught how to dance, all the boys on the far side of the gymnasium acting like dancing with a girl was the worst fate that could be wished upon them but all of them secretly scoping out the pretty girls, making a big show of reluctance as the coaches told them to pair off, finally doing so, the field starting to thin, and then a sudden, scrambling rush as the boys who were left all realized that one of them was going to be stuck with Darlene, which was a million times worse than being the last one chosen for team sides.

Coming to college with the half-articulated idea of starting off anew, being outgoing, making friends, going out to a club with some girls from her dorm, watching the groups of guys negotiating among themselves to see which of them would have to talk to Darlene, take one for the team.

And now this.

Like she needed to have a guy presented this way, tied up and laid out already naked, because she couldn't get one on her own!

Which she couldn't, but that was hardly the point.

Like she wanted to fuck him in the first place!

Well, she *did*, but that wasn't the point either.

No way in hell this guy, Chad-or-Chet whoever he was, would have wanted to have sex with her on his own. No way in hell.

Oh, sure, people said guys would fuck anything, guys would fuck sheep or inanimate objects if they couldn't get a woman, guys would fuck *corpses* if they were hard up enough.

Yeah, right.

How many times had she heard it over the years?

"Man, I wouldn't fuck her with someone else's dick."

And of course then there was Jessie, who probably did think she was doing Darlene a favor here, that Darlene would be grateful to her for this gift, this opportunity. Jessie wouldn't, just *couldn't* comprehend how fucking insulting it was.

But at the same time...

Well, he *was* right here.

"You telling me the five of you bring guys out here?" he'd asked.

"A few, sometimes."

"And Etch really doesn't know?"

"I told you, no, he doesn't."

"So you've been cheating on him?"

"Hold the fucking phone! You're all asking me if I wanna fuck, no big deal, Etch lets you drive the Yuke, Etch lets you borrow his wetsuit and hey, he *pisses* in that, same diff, I'm just a piece of property, he can loan me to his buddies... and *now* you're butthurt about whether I've been cheating on him?"

He'd started to bluster and protest how that was different, not the same at all, he was Etch's friend and friends shared things.

Before he could get too far, Jessie brought her foot around in a fast, sweeping kick that knocked his legs out from under him. In the same motion, she shoved him in the chest.

Chad went over backwards and landed square on the mattress, the wind partly knocked out of him, and the rest taken up with a laugh.

"Okay!" he'd said. "Etch always told us you liked it rough, let's do this thing!"

What if he knew it was her?

If he knew...

He'd be grossed out. Revolted. He wouldn't want *her* anywhere near his dick.

Darlene stood beside the mattress, Jessie's note half-crumpled in her hand, looking down at Chad-or-Chet.

Naked. Buff. Bronzed. Gorgeous.

All hers.

Sure.

A lot of good *that* did.

He mumbled and squirmed, not struggling yet, but sounding more agitated, moving more impatiently. Darlene had been motionless in the same spot for so long; maybe he had decided that whoever had come in had also left, and he was alone again.

Seemed like a waste to just kill him.

And maybe…

It wasn't like he could *see* her. He might know it was her, but as long as he couldn't *see* her…

There had been times when guys would joke that maybe it wouldn't be so bad if they could put a bag over her head. That was the same, wasn't it?

She knelt. The exercise mats creak-squished. Chad-or-Chet bucked and thrashed, yanking at the chains, very much in a "That's enough, take these damn things off me now!" manner.

She set her hand on his belly, on his sculpted, rock-hard abs.

Chad-or-Chet froze. His nostrils flared as he drew in a startled breath. He held absolutely still.

Her hand slid down a little.

He made a low sound that could have been a laugh or a "Whoa-ho-ho!" or a "Yeah *baby*!" but he continued holding absolutely still.

Her hand slid down a little further. Past his navel. She could feel the faint tickle of that line of dark hair, the directional arrow leading toward his crotch, the arrow she was following. The edge of her pinkie crossed over into the tan line zone, from bronzed to pale.

Now only *most* of him was holding absolutely still. One part stirred. One part was getting bigger. Rising and thickening, stiffening.

He was getting hard.

He was actually getting hard.

She hadn't even touched *it* yet. She feel the wiry crinkles of his pubes, but her fingers were almost there.

Then she went ahead and grasped it.

Chad-or-Chet moaned in the back of his throat. His ass flexed and his hips bucked. Darlene felt loose skin over firm flesh, veins beating against her palm, the warmth and texture, she was rubbing his dick, she had her hand curled around this huge, throbbing hard-on, and worked it up and down, ran the ball of her thumb over the rosy cockhead, thumbed the slit, felt moisture.

Did he know who she was? Did he think she was someone else? Jessie, maybe? Jessie had been the one to bring him here... strip him... tie him up... maybe he thought Jessie had left him here a while to heighten the anticipation, then come back without a word and begun touching him. Groping. Stroking. Rubbing.

Was that why he was responding? Because he thought she was Jessie?

If he knew the truth, he'd wilt instantly. Then everyone would know. Everyone would laugh. They would laugh at her forever.

But right now, even *he* didn't know. He wasn't limp. He was swollen, big and hard, straining in her fist. Humping up and down.

Darlene reeled as a dizzying heatwave rush swept through her from head to toe. She felt warm and tingly all over... warm and slippery between her legs... her breath went in ragged gulps through her teeth... she couldn't stand it! So *what* if he thought she was someone else? Who gave a shit? He could imagine she was Jessie or Miss February or Beyoncé Knowles or Scarlett Johansson for all she cared, as long as it meant she could do this—for once in her whole stupid, miserable life, *do* this!

She let go, and his cock waggled around in the air, an engorged flagpole. Chad-or-Chet made indignant bleating noises. Darlene lurched to her feet, stumbled across the room, flipped the locks and deadbolt, and jammed the wooden wedge under the door, because the last thing she needed was Gwen or Rachel walking in.

Her hands were clumsy, not wanting to work right, but she

got out of her shoes and pants and underwear. Chad-or-Chet must've heard the sounds, must've realized she was undressing, and he must've liked the idea, because his dick swelled even more, jutting straight up, inviting her to climb on.

God, she could hardly believe she was really doing this. She was about to have sex. She was about to get laid. About to fuck a gorgeous guy.

Well, or rape him, anyway… if it counted as rape, given the way he sure didn't seem to be objecting.

She tore open a foil packet, rolled on the condom. Chad-or-Chet's taut body vibrated with eager tension. His head was pressed back, his neck arched, his grip on the chains white-knuckled.

Darlene stood with one foot on either side of his hips, then crouched, then knelt so that she was half-straddling him while she reached to position his condom-sheathed shaft. Its head slid around some, prodding. The surge of sensation almost made her lose her balance.

But she just had to get it over some… down a little… right about…

There!

His cockhead nudged in. She had a moment of unbelief–it was *in*! it really was!–and then Chad-or-Chet grunted and gave a sudden hard upward thrust. Darlene hadn't meant to cry out but couldn't help it. She voiced a long, wild wail as she dropped onto him and felt that hugeness shove all the way up deep inside.

CHAPTER SIXTEEN

"It's Muppets," Rachel said.

"It's *The Dark Crystal.*"

"Those are definitely Muppets."

"Well, it *is* a Jim Henson movie."

"Ugly Muppets."

"Skeksis."

"Okay."

"We don't have to watch it," Gwen said. "I just thought since they were doing a free movie channel preview all weekend, we might as well."

"I guess, if you want." Rachel opened her laptop.

Gwen looked disappointed. "What about the movie?"

"I'm multitasking." She'd finished up her TA duties in the science department by a little after eight–geology quizzes graded, the chemistry lab cupboards organized, a physics handout copied/collated/stapled, other odds and ends–and had just enough time before her bus to grab an iced coffee and a half-price, end-of-day banana-nut muffin for dinner.

Only Gwen had been there when she got to the house. Annamaria would be at work until midnight or so. Jessie had left for her weekend at the lake with Etch and their buddies. Darlene was nowhere around. If it was anyone else, Rachel might have speculated a date, but...

"Where's Darlene?" she asked. "Her car's here."

"I don't know." Gwen had made herself a comfortable pillow-nest on the floor. "Maybe taking a nap? I had one earlier. Or maybe she went with Jessie?"

"Camping? Darlene? Are you serious?"

"Oh. Right." Gwen peeled the lid off a pudding cup and dunked a plastic spoon into butterscotch goo. "I heard her get home while Jessie and them were getting ready to go, and then she wasn't here when I came downstairs, so I guess I just figured." She hitched one slim shoulder in a shrug, and ate pudding in dainty mouse-sips.

"I suppose it's *possible* she went along," Rachel said, but with the sort of skepticism that she would have used in allowing that it was *possible* the creationists were onto something. "Hey, you got more puddings? I'll buy one off you."

"Plenty, in the fridge, and you don't have to pay me. They were on sale."

"Cool, thanks."

"One of them didn't show up," Gwen said as Rachel went into the kitchen. "One of the guys. In case he does, or calls or something, they want us to tell him they left without him and it serves him right for being late."

"Can I have one of the tapiocas?"

"You can have *all* the tapiocas, please. I got those by accident. I thought they were vanilla and didn't read the label. Yuck. Gross little lumps."

"That's the tapioca part."

"It's still like eating cold fish eggs."

"No, that's caviar."

"Also gross little lumps." Gwen shrugged again. "Anyway, I think the thing is, he showed up early and nobody was here, so he left again. I woke up and heard someone on the porch. When I looked out, I saw someone biking away. I bet that was him." She frowned and sucked on the plastic spoon. "I think, anyway. I don't know."

The movie had camel-Muppets and evil bird-Muppets and elf-Muppets. Rachel wasn't paying a whole lot of attention, except for in a scene that involved some kind of enormous, elaborate, celestial calendar mechanism. Gwen was rapt, of course, even though she'd seen it before. She was weird that way. She could read the same books or watch the same movies over and over, despite already knowing how they ended.

The news websites didn't have much more on the murders. Nothing more that was factual, anyway.

A lot of speculation, though. Some features on local concern and preparation, community awareness, self-defense classes, talk to your children, etc.

There was the usual trotting-out of the classic serial killer profile, with the addendum that in this particular case, the killer was possibly a *gay* thirtyish/fortyish, middle-class professional, average-seeming white male, given that the only known victims so far were men, though of course that could just have been because the female victims—the *real* victims—hadn't been found or reported missing yet.

Other famous cases were brought up and examined for similarities... was this a Dahmer type, a BTK, what?

She skimmed over the tear-jerky interviews with the victims' friends and relatives. Blah-blah-blah and here was a photo of Gordon Kerr's widow and kids outside of their pricey suburban home, here was a quote from Rico's boss at the gas station—Rico's real name was *Henry*? who knew?—and his mom going on about how he was "such a good boy," blah-blah-blah. Rachel didn't care about that. The whole background angle, the human interest aspect, big deal.

The investigators weren't getting anywhere fast.

Nice to know.

They had brought a couple of so-called experts on board. There was talk of a police task force.

Fine and dandy.

They had no real clue of what they were dealing with. They were nowhere close to the truth.

Rachel was glad.

But she also found it to be more of a letdown than she had anticipated.

It wasn't that she wanted them to be caught. That'd be crazy.

What, then?

She finished off the pudding cup, scraping away every

bit and licking residue off the underside of the lid, then sat chewing on the spoon. It clacked and clicked against her teeth.

The driven killers, the ones for whom it was an urge, a need, a frenzy… they got caught because they got hasty, sloppy, careless. They rushed through it, rushed from one murder to the next, the pace increasing as the need grew. It was like a drug for them. A small dose might satisfy the first time, but after a while a larger dose would be needed, or a sooner one, or both.

Maybe it'd start off cyclical and take time to build, but that interval would shorten. One a month… then every twenty days or so… every couple weeks… so on. With less planning and care each time, until the inevitable slip that would give the police what they needed.

The careful kind, the meticulous ones who did plan everything and did do it right… their downfall usually came from something else. From pride, pride at being so damn skillful that the police couldn't keep up. There was no fun in beating someone who sucked at playing the game. No victory in a battle of wits against an unarmed opponent. No challenge, no contest.

Those were the killers who wanted to have the world acknowledge their genius and superiority. They hated being unappreciated. Those were the ones who might contact the police or media themselves. They left notes, gave hints, mocked and dared and gloated and bragged. Or they'd become offended and enraged when the proper credit wasn't given to them.

It was, Rachel knew, a short step from that to being the megalomaniac villain who got the hero in a fiendish deathtrap, explained the entire scheme, and then walked out, so the hero could escape and ruin everything.

She was *not* going to let them go there.

She didn't need to have the whole world acknowledge how clever she was, how brilliant. Stuff like that was only insecurity: an inferiority complex in action.

Still, it would've been kind of nice to see some mention along those lines in the articles. A nice ego-boost quote from whoever was in command of the task force, a "Clearly, we are dealing with a criminal of exceptional intelligence and subtlety"… was that so much to wish for?

The Muppets were converging around some big chunk of glassy, purple-black rock–the Dark Crystal itself, Rachel surmised, not that it took a genius to put *that* together–when the back door creaked open, then groaned shut and latched.

Gwen had turned off all the lights for ease of viewing, so the downstairs was in deep shadow except for the glows from television and laptop screen. The house was quiet. It was almost eleven.

They both turned and stared toward the kitchen as someone appeared in the doorway. Moving slow. Limping. Maybe even hobbling.

"Darlene?" asked Gwen in a whisper.

"Oh, hell," Darlene said.

Rachel leaned over and switched on a lamp, filling the living room with yellow light. "Yow," she said as she got a better look. "What happened?"

"Omigosh," Gwen said, putting a hand to her lips. "Are you all right?"

"I'm fine!" Darlene straightened up and smiled at them.

Maybe this was to show how all right she was, though it looked to Rachel more like Darlene had been put on the rack and stretch-cranked until her spine was about to snap. Her hair was a tangled mess. Her face was flushed. She had her shoes in one hand. The rest of her clothes were rumpled and disheveled: blouse half-buttoned and maybe misbuttoned as well, pants inside out.

"You're hurt," Gwen said.

Darlene limp-hobbled to the big, ugly recliner that had come with the house, and collapsed into it. Her socks were dirty and grass-stained. "Ho-lee shit," she sighed, and let her head loll back with eyes closed. "Holy *shit*, you guys."

"Do we need to take you to the ER?" Rachel asked. "Were you in an accident or something?"

"Were you…" Gwen swallowed and bit her lip, then finished, "assaulted?"

A snorting huff of a laugh came from Darlene, though she didn't open her eyes. "You are *not* gonna believe this."

Gwen glanced at Rachel, all worried blinking, like she was

expecting Darlene to confess that she'd been abducted by aliens or dragged off into the woods and ravished by a pack of gorillas or bikers or who-knew-what.

"We thought," Rachel said, though of course she had never really thought any such thing, "that maybe you went to the lake with Jessie and them?"

"Did they ditch you?" Gwen gasped. "Leave you by the side of the road and make you walk home?"

If so, it might have explained the limp-hobble–Darlene wasn't one for walking if she could help it, let alone hiking however many miles–but it didn't explain the state of her clothes. And she would have left her shoes on.

"No," Darlene said, with an eyeroll beneath closed lids. "But, gee, thanks, I don't know which is worse, that you think I would have gone to the lake with those assholes, or that I would have let them dump me by the side of the road. Some high fucking opinion you have of me, thanks a lot."

"She's okay," Rachel said to Gwen.

"Better than okay. Better than *ever*, holy *shit*, I ache all *over*, I probably won't be able to *move* tomorrow, and it's *so* worth it, you have *no* idea."

They looked at each other, then back at Darlene. Rachel tried to come up with some guess as to what could have left her in that condition but also happy about it. Smart as she was, she could only venture one.

"Um, Darlene?" she said. "You… uh… you had, uh, sex?"

She still didn't open her eyes, didn't say anything. A lascivious smile was answer enough. It was… unnerving… that kind of a smile on Darlene's face… a face that so rarely smiled anyway, let alone lasciviously. Rachel goggled at Gwen, who was goggling back at Rachel with her jaw dropped.

"You *did*?" said Gwen in a squeak. "Just now?"

"For the last…" Darlene peeled an eye open to look at the clock. "Three and a half hours, give or take."

"Um…" Rachel said. She made a bewildered grimace at Gwen.

"Um…" Gwen agreed. The credits were rolling, they'd missed the end of the movie, but by now not even she cared about Muppets anymore.

"Wanna know who with?" Darlene asked. Definite note of boasting in her voice. "Wanna know?"

"Okay," Rachel said, though she wasn't sure she really did.

"Well, I don't know his name exactly. Chad or Chet, I think. One of those. I'm almost positive. Chad. Maybe Chet."

"Isn't that one of Etch's friends?" asked Gwen.

"I think that's *two* of Etch's friends," Rachel said.

"You were with *two* guys?" The squeak was back; Gwen sounded like she was on helium.

"One guy," Darlene said. "I'm just not sure about his name."

"So... you *did* go to the lake?"

"Nope."

"Hang on," Rachel said. "Gwen, didn't you say one of them didn't show up and they left without him?"

She nodded.

"Well, there you go, right? He showed up. He was just with Darlene." Case closed, matter settled, it still didn't make a whole lot of sense, but who was she to argue with the facts?

Darlene and one of Etch's friends... who would have guessed? Not Rachel. But then, she'd be the first to admit that she wasn't so great when it came to understanding the whole dating thing. She'd been on dates herself, of course... she'd even gone to her senior prom with the president of the chess club. Most of the time, though, she just couldn't see the appeal. It always seemed like a waste of time. Going to movies, or worse, just 'hanging out'... what was the point of that?

"Does Jessie know?" asked Gwen.

Darlene did the huff-snort-laugh again. "Was her idea, wasn't it? I don't mind saying, okay sure, I was a little pissed at first. Like I couldn't get a guy on my own if I wanted? Yeah, so maybe I couldn't, but still... well, shit, anyway... he's still alive and everything."

"Wait, what?" Rachel asked.

"What wait-what? I didn't do any of the torture stuff, the cutting and whatever. I just fucked his brains out."

***

Chad now believed he had a fairly good idea what a bull would feel like if it got caught in a milking machine.

Oh, man.

The guys were going to fucking *die* when they heard about this.

He didn't even care about missing the trip to the lake. So what if he wasn't out there drinking beer and swimming? So what if he wasn't getting to see Lori and her roommates in their bikinis? They were a bunch of teases anyway. Looking was great and all, but Chad would rather be doing.

Even if he couldn't see who he was doing.

In a way, that made it more fun.

The blindfold, the gag, the cuffs... Jessie and her friends were into some kinky, kinky shit. They had this whole padded playroom all set up and waiting for action.

Seriously kinky.

Okay, by now he was getting uncomfortable, with his arms chained above his head and not enough slack to let him turn over. He was hungry and thirsty and needed to take a piss. A shower would have been nice, too.

But he wasn't about to complain much. Small prices to pay.

Hell, though, but his junk was exhausted. Overworked, depleted, and tender. Damn. They had put him through his paces all right. Rode hard and put away wet, which was what his sister's sexy riding instructor used to say... not always about the horses, either.

He did wonder how many of them had taken a turn, and which of them was which. All he knew was that they'd never teamed up on him—yet, at least; he remained optimistic. So far, all he'd felt was one girl working him at a time.

None of them had said a word. Chad, gagged, couldn't. So the only sounds had been breathing, moans and groans, gasps and cries. He imagined the others watching in a silent circle as whichever girl's turn it was stroked and sucked him hard again and climbed on.

Yeah. Watching. Naked and waiting. Maybe fingering themselves... or each other... maybe going down on each other… girl-on-girl right there in the room around him… the thought had been enough to get him up for another go long after he should have been exhausted.

The not-knowing was hot. Incredibly hot. Pictures of Jessie and her friends flashed through his mind, or it didn't have to be limited to them, it could have been anyone, they all could have been in on it, maybe even Lori, and her roommates weren't such teases after all.

He could have been sticking it in anyone, anyone at all. Didn't have to be limited to girls he knew. They could be charging admission, renting him out. There were plenty of lady professors who always looked at him like he was covered with chocolate, or bored horny housewives, or high school seniors eager for a preview of college man man-meat.

So what if some of them might be old, or fat, or plain, or desperate? A fuck was a fuck, wasn't that what he always said? Pussy was pussy. He didn't care if one of them had been… what was her name… Debbie or Darla or something… so what? Hell, for all he knew, his own sister could have been here; he wouldn't have had any way of telling.

If Jessie *was* one of them, that meant she hadn't gone to the lake after all. Had she begged off, made some excuse? Same would apply for Lori and her roommates. Or had the entire lake thing been a set-up? Did the guys know?

Hell, were the guys *watching*?

Chad considered that, then dismissed it. He knew his friends. No way they could have stood by and let it happen. They'd be way too jealous that none of them had been chosen, plus, they'd never be able to stay quiet.

No, they'd gone to the lake, while he, Chad, had all these girls to himself. They really would fucking die when they found out.

"Oh, dude," Skip said, seized by a sudden wistful idea. "Wish we brought tequila."

"Yeah, we could do shooters!" Lori giggled and flipped her hair, a move that made her boobs try to leap out of her skimpy bikini top.

They hadn't leaped out yet, but Skip figured it was bound to happen sooner or later. Not that it made a whole lot of difference. The scraps of cloth didn't conceal much in the first place… and when she'd waded out of the lake, they'd been soaked and clinging to the puckered points of her nipples… all he hadn't been able to tell was their exact color.

Well, there was time. The night was young, they had plenty of beer, and tomorrow was a new day full of bright potential.

"Every time," Etch said in an aggrieved tone. "Every time we say we should bring serious booze, and every time we forget."

"That," said Biff, who was in the dirt at the foot of the folding camp chairs Lori's friends had set up, "is because we're already drunk when we say it and by the time we're sober, we don't remember."

The fire snapped. Flames danced and crackled. Orange winks of sparks billowed amid the rising smoke. Water lapped at the pebbled lakeshore. There were other fires dotting the far bank, a Coleman lantern's distinctive glow from a nearby campsite, and a roaring blaze from the direction of the boat launch where some huge wedding reception or family reunion was underway.

Chet cursed as he tried to detach his latest marshmallow-toasting failure from the stick, succeeding only in sliding off the blister-charred exterior and leaving a stringy wad of molten white gunk. "Could do a liquor store run," he suggested.

Jess, beside Etch on a fallen log that had been hauled to the firepit, got up and stepped over his knees. As she was straddling him, he ran both hands up her legs to the tattered hems of her cutoffs and tried to pull her down. She bopped him on the top of the head with her beer can and he let go.

"Where you goin', babe?" Etch asked.

"To get the tequila, genius."

"You okay to drive?" He glanced at the hulking shadow of the Yuke beyond their tents. "Don't want you smashing up my ride."

"I'm not gonna drive," she said.

Skip stole a casual ogle as she made her way to the fringe of the firelit circle. Jess didn't have a huge rack, but hers was a killer bod all the same. And she was fun. Almost like one of the guys. So much like one of the guys that he could tell it annoyed the crap out of Lori, Cara and Stephanie.

Etch had lucked out, the son of a bitch. Etch had major league lucked out.

All that, *and* she came back from the Yuke with tequila.

"Excellent!" Brad and Etch cheered.

"Fuck yeah," Chet said, flinging his marshmallow stick into the shimmering embers.

"Hmf!" Lori and Stephanie shared a look. Like Lori hadn't just two minutes ago been saying how great it'd be to do shooters.

Kind of a bitch, really.

But a bitch with awesome boobage... and when she did that little *hmf!* noise, she crossed her arms under them, and they bulged up and out like offerings to the melon gods.

"Tequila time!" Biff crowed, and nibbled at Cara's ankle so that she squealed and kicked.

They did it right, too. Left hand for lime wedges and salt, right hand for the tequila. Brad cranked the music. The bottles made the rounds. Before long, Lori and Steph were on their feet, girl-dancing. Cara slithered from her camp chair and used Biff's stomach like a bench, perching on him.

"Chad is gonna be sorry he missed this," Chet said. He had moved on to the science experiment portion of the evening, dribbling tequila onto a marshmallow and extending that toward the fire to see what would happen. It went *floomp* into a blue fireball, that was what happened.

"Yeah, wonder what the fuck's up with him." Etch licked salt from the thumb-hollow of Jess's hand. "Not like Chad to miss a party. I'd've thought he'd show up early."

Jess threw back a big knock of tequila, shuddering. "Maybe he did. Gwen said she saw someone biking away. He must've knocked while she was asleep and I was in the bathroom."

"His loss," Skip said. He smiled at Steph. She wore tight pink lowrider shorts with *Hello Kitty* patches on the butt cheeks, and a white camisole top that reached only halfway down her cute navel-ring tummy.

Steph, though, was smiling at Brad while Lori was looking the other way. Which had possibilities... Lori was with Brad, but if Lori got mad at Brad or Brad went off with Steph... score Lori on the rebound?

The bottle came around to Skip again, and he juggled lime and salt and tequila the same way he was trying to juggle scenarios in his head. Cara, still sitting on Biff, was trying to show Chet how to toast a decent marshmallow, seemingly oblivious to the way Biff was rubbing his hand in slow circles lower and lower on her back.

She wasn't oblivious, couldn't be, girls never were when guys tried stuff like that, but they did like to let guys *think* they were. She also seemed oblivious to the way Chet was paying less attention to her marshmallow technique and more attention to the view he was getting as she bent forward.

Lori had pulled Brad into the dancing, shaking it for him, doing some of the old bump-and-grind, which told Skip that she had picked up on some of the vibes from him and Steph even if she didn't realize it. Etch tried to haul Jess into his lap, overbalanced, and went backwards off the log with his feet in the air and her on top of him, both of them laughing.

And somewhere...

"Hey," Skip said, shaking his head through a tequila fog. "That someone's phone?"

She hadn't dared at work, and she didn't dare at home.

People would think she was crazy.

They wouldn't understand.

They didn't... couldn't... *know*.

Annamaria pulled into the turnout and parked.

Once upon a time, she never would have had this place to herself on a Friday night. Once upon a time, this had been a sort of Lover's Lane, the wide hillside curve off of Trowbridge Road, just up the hill from the bridge itself. Once upon a time, the view would have been pretty by day and prettier by night, the valley and lights.

That once-upon-a-time had been well before her time. Serafina's classmates had come up here, couples steaming up car windows. Never Serafina herself, of course. She had been much too much a good girl to go parking off Trowbridge Road.

These days, it was a patch of gravel and scuffed dirt. Weedy around the edges. Strewn with trash. The guardrail was bent and rusty. BB-pocked signs, weathered to the point of illegibility, had been nailed to tree trunks.

The view, basically, sucked.

No more river valley rolling away into a misty morning. No more sparkling nestle of city lights against the darkness of the night.

Those things could still be seen, she knew, but only for those who'd purchased one of the pricey riverside condos that had gone up along Trowbridge when Annamaria was still in elementary school.

From here, now, all she could see was the back side of those condos. Fire escapes and air conditioning units and privacy fences.

She was alone.

It was dark, quiet. Some dim radiance filtered in through her car windows, some dim noises–traffic, and what might have been a live band from the Trowbridge Tavern–reached her. But yes: dark and quiet.

Dark, quiet and alone.

She got a bag from the footwell, where it had been hidden by a spare sweater thrown casually over it. She set it in the passenger seat and began laying out its contents like a scrub nurse preparing an operating theater.

Paper towels, a whole roll. She tore off a long strip, maybe a dozen sheets, and folded them until she had a thick, rectangular pad.

A piece of leather, salvaged from an old belt she'd been meaning to throw away. It now had several tiny, deep gouges in it. Annamaria slipped it crossways into her mouth and held it between her teeth.

Several large-size Band-Aids in their papery individual wrappers.

A disposable cigarette lighter.

The box-cutter, freshly fitted with a brand-new blade.

She ran the lighter's flame along its gleaming edge until the silvery sheen darkened, then set it aside to cool as she peeled the old Band-Aid from her left hand.

The wound ran from just shy of the base of her thumb most of the way to her wrist. It sliced across the meaty part of her palm, the rise she thought fortune-tellers called the Mount of Venus.

It wasn't infected. She wasn't stupid, after all. She took great care to keep it clean. As far as the others knew, it was healing just fine, she was applying ointment, and the Band-Aid was only to cover it so that the customers whose tables she waited wouldn't be put off their appetites by the sight of a gory scar.

Annamaria set the pad of paper towels on her thigh, and rested her left hand atop the pad. She took up the box-cutter in her right.

Anticipation and yearning swept through her even before she brought the glinting blade close to her palm. Her surroundings were already fading away… it was just her, here, now. Dark, quiet and alone. Here, now, with the sharpness and the blood and the pure, intense pain.

Her cell phone warbled from the depths of her purse.

She jumped, almost slashed her fingers off in a slewing, startled motion, and dropped the box-cutter. It nicked her leg on the way down to the floormat.

"Fuck," Annamaria said under her breath. She clawed for her purse, which was still ringing, ringing. Her left hand clenched. A single bead oozed up from where she had just touched the blade's tip against the soft-scabbed skin.

Next time she would have to remember to turn off the damn phone. She didn't normally get calls at this hour, so late on a Friday night that it was technically Saturday morning, and so it hadn't even occurred to her.

Rachel.

Talking fast. Agitated.

"Rachel, slow down," Annamaria said. "Jessie did what? I thought she was going to the lake… oh, you just talked to her? But… what?"

The story came out in rapid-fire machine gun bursts. Rattatat-rattatat-ratta-tatta-tat. The only pauses were when Rachel had to gulp in another lungful of air.

"I'll be home in a few minutes," she said.

***

Chad wished they would go ahead and unchain him already. Uncomfortable was edging into painful.

A sheet or blanket might have been nice too. Now that he was no longer exerting himself, the sweat had evaporated and he was just lying here in this empty room with nothing covering him. While he wasn't exactly cold, he wasn't exactly warm either.

The most amazing thing was, he had even fallen asleep for a while. He wasn't sure when that had happened or how, but sure enough, he'd fallen asleep. That probably had something to do with why his shoulders had gone numb.

He wanted to stretch. And pee. He wanted to get rid of the gag, too. It wasn't just being hungry and thirsty. If they took off the gag, his tongue could take over until his dick was ready to rejoin the festivities. It wasn't like they had to *force* him to participate. *Hell*, no.

Maybe they'd been filming it. Maybe he'd be all over the internet. He'd be famous. Like celebrity sex videos.

His relatives wouldn't be happy, but his friends would be outrageously jealous, then. So would every other guy in the country. Or on the planet.

Jeez, but he was going to get a cramp if he couldn't lower his arms soon. His shoulders and upper back were killing him. He was aware of a tingle in his hands… like they were falling asleep. He curled and uncurled his fists to try and get the circulation going, and shifted his position as far as he could on the mattress.

He heard the door open.

About-fucking-time!

A chillier draft wafted over him. He fidgeted. He clinked the chain and grunted through the gag.

Here he was, laying naked in front of what sounded like several girls—Jessie's housemates, he was sure, though he couldn't think of their exact names right then—and while he didn't mind being their bondage sex toy, they could at least let him take ten minutes for a piss, a shower, a Red Bull and maybe a quick sandwich. After that, he would be happy to service them as long as they wanted.

Not easy to convey all that while bound and gagged. But he tried his best.

There were murmurs and frantic hissing whispers and shuffling feet. The door closed again.

"I can't believe it," one said. "I can't believe it, she really did, she honest-to-God *did*... and the rest of you went *along* with it?"

"We didn't know!" another said in a high, shrill voice.

"Yeah, it wasn't *our* idea, okay? You think *I* would have done this? After everything I kept telling you guys? Nobody we know, et cetera, et cetera, and does anyone listen?"

"It's no big deal," someone else said sullenly. "It's not any different."

"The heck it isn't! We know him! People know he was here!"

"Jessie said—"

"Jessie is an irresponsible doofus! She locks him up here and then she goes and puts on his clothes and rides his bike down the street, makes sure those construction workers see her so that if anybody asks, people will have seen him leaving... and she thinks that's going to be good enough? I mean, come on! That's the best she could do?"

"It might work," said the sullen one.

He was starting to think that this wasn't playing out as erotic as it should've been. They were hardly all over him. They hardly seemed turned on. It was all getting kind of confusing. More than a little weird. Creepy, even.

"Oh... God... what a mess," the first one said. The one Skip had kept talking about, the hot brunette? Anna-something, wasn't it?

Chad fidgeted and clinked more emphatically. Stressing that he was beyond impatient now, way beyond impatient.

"What are we going to do?" That was the high, shrill voice. Chad guessed it belonged to the tall, shy girl with the long reddish-blonde hair.

The way she said that... gah, it sent shivers up his spine.

There were some more murmurings and whisperings, and

more noises as they moved around. He heard… what? Cupboards opening and closing? Heavy thunks and metallic clanks?

Chad gave the chains a good hard pull. They held.

He heard a sudden shrieking, mechanical whine. A power-tool whine. A drill? A circular saw? An electric carving knife?

Panic flared up in him and he tried to quash it, tried to tell himself that it wasn't like he had anything to be *scared* of. Not him. Not from a bunch of girls. He just… okay, he wanted out of here, he wanted out of here right-fucking-*now*, but that didn't mean he was… *scared*.

Maybe they'd just, like, lost the keys or something. Yeah. Needed the drill to get him free of the cuffs.

"You guys know we don't have a lot of time this time," one of them said.

Time this time? What?

"You mean we have to make it quick?" asked Anna-something.

"Yeah, I think we better."

It didn't feel very quick to Chad. It didn't feel very quick at all.

CHAPTER
SEVENTEEN

"You don't have to be so pissy at me! Okay, fine, I fucked up, I'm sorry already, what do you want, a handwritten apology? I fucked up! My bad! Are we *done* yet?"

"Done? So you said sorry, so what?" Rachel shot back. "Sorry isn't good enough, Jessie! You put us into a really bad spot there, okay? Don't you understand that? Doesn't that sink in? You put us all in a really bad spot!"

"Hey, I'm not the one who killed the dude."

"You're the one who *got* him!"

"Yeah, well, Dar's the one who fucked him half to death, and Anna's the one who ran a drill bit into his heart; you can't blame it all on me!"

"You *told* me to fuck him!" Darlene's face was plum-purple with anger, embarrassment or both.

"I did not!"

"You left a note with rubbers in it and my name on the envelope taped to his chest!"

"Yeah, well… Anna's the one who ran a drill bit into his heart!"

"And what else were we supposed to do?" asked Annamaria. "We *had* to kill him. We couldn't very well untie him and let him go, not after all that!"

"You could've," Jessie said.

"Right, great, how would that have looked?" Rachel flung her hands in the air. "After he saw the place? It's supposed to be a secret, remember?"

"It's not the fucking Batcave, Rache."

"No," Annamaria said, "because Batman isn't a serial killer."

"Batman is a vigilante," Gwen said, speaking up from where she curled huddled in her nest. "I think Christian Bale's an okay Batman, but—"

"Look, never mind Batman, okay?" Rachel got all up in Jessie's face, not caring that Jessie was taller and stronger and in a lot better shape. "You could have ruined everything, Jessie. You can't just go and *do* stuff like that. The whole point is that we're in this together, right? That means we don't all go off doing whatever the heck we want. We make the decisions *together*."

"You didn't bitch at Anna when she chose Mr. Motivational Speaker on her own!"

Annamaria cleared her throat. "She did, actually… a little… because he'd been at the restaurant and people had seen him with me."

"But—"

"This was someone you knew," said Gwen. "He was your friend."

"He was a dick, all right? He asked for it." Jessie combed her fingers through her spiky hair and shook her head. "Jesus H. I don't see why this has to be such a big damn problem."

The argument had been raging full-blast since shortly after ten o'clock that morning, when the Yuke had pulled up out front and dropped Jessie off. The only sign she showed of two nights' worth of drinking and having woodsmoke wafting in her face was some redness around the eyes. Her usual tan was burnished to a rich, golden sheen. The last remnants of the split lip and black eye were almost indistinguishable.

The others didn't look half so good; even Annamaria was rougher around the edges than usual. None of the four of them had gotten any sleep Friday night, and not much sleep since, either. It showed.

"You dumped it all on us, that's one part of the big damn problem," Rachel said. "You went out to the lake to party and *we* had to deal with the leftovers."

"Hey, I was trying to do a nice thing for Dar. Is that a

crime..?" Jessie caught herself. "You know what I mean."

"I don't need your favors," Darlene said in a grumpy mutter.

"Oh?" Jessie raised her eyebrows in mock innocence. "So you *didn't* fuck him while he was chained up all naked and helpless?"

"Hey!" Rachel banged her fist on the coffee table, knocking her can of Mountain Dew to gurgle yellow-green onto the rug.

Moving a body turned out to be a lot harder without Jessie.

"We might have to… ah… do this in more than one trip," Annamaria had said after the third time they'd dropped Chad.

"Cut him up, you mean?" asked Rachel. "I don't know. We've got plenty of garbage bags, so *that's* not an issue, but once we had the limbs and head off, we'd either have to bisect his torso or we'd be left with the whole thing, the torso, I mean, and we might have trouble holding onto it, just a torso, with no handholds, nothing to grab on to."

"Except for his—"

"Darlene, don't," Annamaria said.

"Whatever. I was just trying to help."

"Couldn't we put his torso in a bag?" Gwen had asked. "They're big bags."

"Yeah, so it wouldn't be *that* bad," Rachel said. "But another thing is, we did okay with not making a mess this time. That drill thing worked really well. Stopped his heart right away and with hardly any blood. Which is good, because Jessie didn't set up the wading pool. If we did cut him into chunks—"

"He'd leak all over the place," Annamaria said.

"Remember how it was without the wading pool? All that extra cleanup?"

"Um, but couldn't we put him in it now?" suggested Gwen. "If… if we did decide we had to… well… dismember him."

Rachel smacked herself upside the head. "Duh. You're right. That was stupid of me. Okay, so, maybe we better do that. It goes against the pattern, since we didn't do it with the others, but maybe that'll be okay. They've all been a little different.

Maybe even they've gotten worse, if you look at it a certain way. With the evisceration that one time and the scalding the other time and everything."

"So you want to chop him up," Darlene said.

"Do you think it'd be too gross?"

"Nah. Well, yeah, but let's do it. Gross is good. I haven't felt like puking once yet this whole time."

"Let's do it," Annamaria had agreed. "After all, look how hard it's been just moving him across the room. Even if we can get him down the stairs and into the trunk, are we going to be able to lift him back *out* of it once we're at the dump site?"

"Another good point," Rachel said. "Okay, then. Somebody plug the saw into the extension cord."

"What do you want me to do?" Jessie flopped back on the couch with an over-dramatic, longsuffering sigh. "I made a mistake. I broke the rules. But it worked out, didn't it?"

"*If* those guys at the construction site believe they really saw Chad biking away from here," Rachel said. "*If* none of us screws up when they want to question us about when we saw him last. *If*—"

"I get it, Rache, I get it already."

"Do you really, Jessie? Or do you still think it's a game and the worst that could happen is we get disqualified?"

"I know it's not a game," she said.

"We *all* know that, Rachel," Annamaria said. "We're all very aware how serious this is."

"Yeah," said Darlene.

"Maybe... um... maybe we should think about... not doing it anymore," Gwen said. "We could treat this like a warning sign or wake-up call or something and... and... um..." She saw the way they were all looking at her, and her voice trailed off.

"So," Jessie said after a pause. "What do you want me to do, Rache? What do you want from me? How can I make this better? I said I was sorry, but obviously that's not enough."

"It's not just me," Rachel said, giving her head a quick shake. "You did this to all of us."

"Fine, so what do the *rest* of you want? I already apologized. Do I need to get down on the floor and kiss your asses? What's it gonna take, huh?"

"Hey, wait, I never said I was mad at her," said Darlene.

"That's because you've got some culpability here too," Rachel said.

"Some who-what-now?"

"She means it's partly your fault," Annamaria said.

"Oh, so now *I* have to apologize? What was I gonna do? Jessie told me to go look, I went and looked. He was already there! It was already too late!"

"Sure, Dar, throw it all back on me, thanks a heap. I thought you were on my side."

"There aren't 'sides'—" Rachel began, making air-quotes.

"Bullshit there aren't, you're all pissed at *me*," said Jessie.

"Well, you did screw up," Annamaria said.

"Yes, Anna, I know that, you know that, we all know that, why don't we all go blog about it so the whole world knows about that? I said I was *sorry*! What more do you *want*?"

"Sincerity?"

"Oh, fuck you, Anna."

"Now, see, that sounded sincere," Darlene said.

"Fuck you, too, Dar."

"Look, *Jessica*—"

"Don't call me that; I hate it when people call me that."

"You didn't have a pile of garbage bags full of body parts sitting in the trunk of your car, *Jessica*. You didn't get busted by the cops while you were trying to dump the bags, *Jessica*—"

"Wait, what?" Rachel cut in.

Annamaria narrowed her eyes at Darlene. "So much for keeping that our little secret, hmm?"

The eastern sky on Saturday morning had been pastel pink by the time Darlene and Annamaria finished loading the Caddy with chunks-of-Chad.

"This is bad," Darlene said. "We took too long. It's late.

Someone's gonna see us. Maybe we better do something else."

"We don't have a lot of options."

"Can't we just bury him in the backyard? Over by all the dead dogs?"

"Too risky," Annamaria said.

"What about—"

"Come on, Darlene. Let's just go."

"Shit," she muttered as she slammed the trunk and trudged around to the driver's side door. "What if we waited until dark?"

Annamaria got in on the passenger side, no longer having to position her feet around drifts of empty cups, crumpled papers and junk-food wrappers. At Rachel's insistence, since they'd begun using the Cadillac for these errands, Darlene kept it scrupulously clean.

"Leave those bags in your trunk all day?" Annamaria asked as she buckled her seatbelt. "Maybe if it was wintertime..."

"Urp," Darlene said. She'd thrown up twice during the dismemberment, and this would've made three if she had eaten anything in the last couple of hours.

They drove with extra-special attentiveness to speed limits and traffic signs so that no early-morning patrol cars would have a reason to pull them over—not that they saw any early-morning patrol cars, but that wasn't the point.

Just as the Caddy had never been so clean, it had never undergone such diligent routine maintenance. Jessie crawled all over it making sure the taillights and turn signals worked, the inspection sticker was up to date, all that good stuff. It wasn't going to up and dead-battery on them, or have the radiator overheat, or anything.

"So this is where she said she ditched his bike and backpack?" Annamaria asked as they came to a boarded-up roadside produce stand that had been out of business since long before any of them had moved into the area.

"Yeah, behind one of those sheds," Darlene said, jerking her chin at a row of decrepit-looking lean-tos overrun by weeds and flanked by rusty relics that had once been farm equipment.

"Kind of near the marsh where we left Donnie."

"You wanna go someplace else?"

"I guess not. It'll have to do."

Darlene pulled onto a rough half-moon patch of cracked asphalt, which had been the produce stand's parking lot back when the road had been a major county thoroughfare, before the freeway, before modern civilized times. She three-point-turned to park nose-out with the trunk angled at the gap between the long wooden produce stand and the sheds.

She got out, crinkling her face at the morning breeze and birdcalls, squinting suspiciously at the horizon that had gone from pastel pink to a rosy gold. "Hard to believe this *isn't* the middle of nowhere. Feels like the middle of nowhere."

"But it isn't," Annamaria said. "Which is why we should hurry. Someone could drive by any minute."

"We'd hear them coming."

"Still not much help if we're standing there with bags full of dead person."

"Oh… yeah."

They began the tedious process of lugging and dumping.

"I think this one has his head in it," Annamaria said.

"This one's a leg." Darlene did the grimacing, thick, trying-not-to-puke swallow.

There was a downslope to a gully—mostly dry now, but with a few muddy patches that declared it might try to be a creek during the wetter parts of the year. A lot of other debris choked the gully already, most of it in the form of busted-up crates from the produce stand.

The bag with Chad's head, when Annamaria bowled it down the slope, struck a rock, bounced once, and landed with a gooshy smack in one of those crates.

"Probably you get bonus points for that," Darlene said, still looking greenish, but managing a grisly chuckle.

"Do I win a stuffed animal?"

"Right now it's your choice of the cheap bead necklace or the temporary tattoo. You gotta trade up your prizes if you want a stuffed animal."

"I'll take the necklace."

Back and forth. Trunk to bushes. The two bags containing torso pieces were the most troublesome. Not only were they bulky and heavy, there was considerable oozing slippage to deal with. And even through double-bagging, those parts stank.

"We've got one fucking gross hobby, you know?" Darlene said as they headed for the car again.

Annamaria hissed a sudden harsh intake of breath. She was a few paces ahead, but stopped short, and Darlene almost walked into her.

"What?" Then Darlene saw what Annamaria had seen, and also stopped short.

A bike—not a motorcycle or a mountain bike but a fleet ten-speed—was doing a slow coast toward the Cadillac. Its rider was seven or eight years older than them, and fit, in the way bike cops had to be. He wore the general bike cop uniform, complete with racing-style helmet, a neon-colored vest, and plenty of reflective strips.

"Morning," he called, in a voice that was half-jovial, half-knowing.

"Oh, God," Annamaria said, barely above a whisper.

"Mind telling me what you ladies are doing?" the bike cop continued. He braked his bike and stood astraddle it, removing his sunglasses.

"Nothing," Darlene said.

She sounded guilty as hell, and they both *looked* guilty as hell.

"Mmm-hmm," said the bike cop. "Nothing. Not a little illegal trash dumping on a nice Saturday morning?"

"Officer… I…" Annamaria's gaze flitted from the cop to the open trunk–which still held three or four lumpy garbage bags of Chad's various components–to Darlene. She mouthed an urgent word: "Gloves!"

"Maybe you had yourselves a party last night," the bike cop said. He slung his leg over, dismounting the bike and leaving it canted onto its kickstand. "Maybe some underage drinking going on. And you thought you'd bring your empties out here so you wouldn't get in trouble. Am I close?"

Darlene crammed her hands in the pockets of her cargo pants, shuffled her feet, hung her head, and did her best to look as guilty as humanly possible while trying to finger-peel and roll the gloves off.

Annamaria stripped hers off one-two, quick as a flash, like someone at a county fair cornhusking competition, doing it so fast in fact that she snagged the edge of the Band-Aid on her left palm and shucked that along with the glove.

"That what's in those bags?" he asked, sauntering over.

They stared at him, and neither said a thing.

"Well? Beer cans? Liquor bottles?"

"No," Darlene said, the word just jumping out. "No, honest!"

"How about I take a look, then?"

"That's really not necessary, Officer." Annamaria tried to use her deep, dark eyes to their best advantage, but the bike cop was unmoved.

"Got some I.D., Miss?"

He was five feet from the gaping maw of the trunk. If he'd noticed the butcher-shop smell in the air, he wasn't letting on. From his expression, he might have been amused at Annamaria's attempt with the deep-dark-eyes routine, but still was not about to go easy on them.

"In my purse," Annamaria said, striving for the sort of meek, humble timidity that would have been better suited to Gwen. She made a half-hearted gesture toward the passenger side.

"That's a nasty cut you've got on your hand," he said, following her as she leaned in the car door. "How'd it happen? Broken glass?"

"No." She straightened up, spun, and slashed in a motion so fluid and pantherlike it could have been a dance move. Bright sunshine glittered on a sharp steel edge.

The bike cop staggered backward, making a choked, gurgling noise. Blood foamed and bubbled at his throat.

"Box-cutter," Annamaria told him as he crumpled to the cracked asphalt.

"You killed a policeman." Rachel shook her head and blinked a bunch of times. "You killed a *policeman*?"

"Jeez, Rache, and you've been yelling at *me*," said Jessie.

"We had to," Annamaria said. "If we hadn't, we'd all be in jail by now."

"Were you going to tell us?" Gwen asked. She had come up from her curled huddle and sat bolt upright, arms wrapped around her knees so she could hug them to her chest.

"Well... it doesn't really count, does it?" said Darlene.

"Doesn't *count*?" Jessie asked. "What the hell does that mean, doesn't count?"

"We didn't..." Darlene faltered, fumbled, looked around for help, and finally said, "We didn't serial-killer-kill-him kill him. We just killed-him killed him."

"Oh, fuck *me*!" Jessie slithered from the couch and yoga-bent into a human pretzel with her head in her hands.

"I mean we didn't bring him here, chain him up, torture him and all that stuff," Darlene said. "Annamaria slashed and it was over, boom, like that."

"Boom-like-that?" Rachel glanced at Annamaria.

"Pretty much," she said. "He bled, he died, and it was over. I don't think he even realized what was happening. I don't think there was time. He didn't feel any pain. He wasn't afraid. He seemed... more surprised than anything else. Then he went blank and was gone."

"Yeah," Darlene said.

"But a policeman?" Gwen pulled at a long strand of her hair, twisting it and twisting it until the roots tugged part of her scalp outward in a little skin-tent by her temple. "Won't that get attention?"

"Cops really hate it when you kill cops," Jessie said. "They take it *way* personal."

"Okay, wait, everyone, wait," Rachel said. Her lips moved as if she was silently counting fast or running through a mental checklist. "Did he radio in?"

Annamaria and Darlene shared a shrug. "He was on a bike, not in a patrol car," Annamaria said at last. "If he'd had a radio, a handheld or something, we would have heard him doing it... I'd think."

"Probably," Jessie said, "hopefully, not. All he thought you were doing was dumping trash, right?"

"That's all we *were* doing," Darlene said.

"And it is another of those ways where it being us will factor in our favor," Rachel said. The others looked at her. She gave a mild eyeroll, and her voice took on its familiar, explanatory-lecture tone. "If it had been guys out there, do you really believe a policeman would have gone over to check things out without letting Dispatch or some fellow officer know? Guys plus unlawful behavior equals suspicious and maybe dangerous, right? Drugs or something. With girls, not so much."

"So we're in the clear because he was a sexist jerk?" Jessie asked.

"That depends." Rachel motioned for Annamaria and Darlene to continue. "What did you do next? After?"

"After you slit the policeman's throat," Gwen said, then flinched as they all glared. "Sorry."

"We didn't leave him lying there in plain sight, if that's what you're wondering," Darlene said. "We dragged him around and hid the body behind the fruit stand, on the other side from the gully where we threw the, you know, pieces."

"And we also hid his bike," Annamaria said. "In the bushes. Covered up so it can't be seen from the road."

"There was some blood in the parking lot," Darlene added, "but we took some dry dirt and kind of scuffed it around. Unless you got right down there and looked, you'd think it was just an old oil stain."

"Awesome," Jessie said. "So far as they know, he just went poof and disappeared."

"They *will* find him," Rachel said. "I mean, this is a *cop*, right? When a cop goes missing, they care a lot more than when it's just some normal person. Like Jessie was saying, they take it personally. They would have started looking as soon as he didn't show up wherever he was supposed to show up next. They would have retraced his last known routes."

"What if they already have?" asked Gwen.

"If we're really-super-duper lucky," Rachel said, "they'll be thinking that he interrupted a drug deal, the dealers panicked, killed him, hid the body. But we can't count on being really-super-duper lucky. If we're only regular-lucky, they'll find Chad—"

"How is that lucky?" Darlene asked.

"They'll be searching all over the area, right? They might have dogs or something. They'd have to be the world's dumbest police to not notice a pile of body parts within a hundred yards of their dead officer. They *will* find those remains. Count on it. What they'll figure then is that the one policeman arrived and discovered Chad's killer in the act of disposing of the remains, see?"

"Fucking brilliant, Holmes," Jessie said. "Dunno *why* they'd get that idea. Oh, yeah... because it's what happened!"

Darlene nodded. "I'm still not seeing how that's lucky."

"If we're *not* lucky," Rachel said, scowling with impatience, "then someone else, some witness, will have seen your car in the vicinity and be able to describe it to the police. Did anybody go by? Other cars? Other bikers? Joggers? Kids? Somebody walking their dog?"

"Nobody," Annamaria said. "It was too early in the day."

"What about nearby houses? Could anyone see that place from their porch?"

"No," Jessie said. "There's nothing around. That's why I ditched Chad's bike and pack there in the first place."

"What about driving there or back? Did you pass anybody?"

"Not on that road," Darlene said. "Annamaria's right. It was pretty dead out there."

"Dead," Jessie said. "Yeah, no shit."

"Should we go and... I don't know... check?" Gwen asked. "Maybe move them someplace else?"

"Oh jeez no," Rachel said. "We don't go back. No returning to the scene of the crime."

"We *live* at the scene of the crime," Annamaria said.

"The other crime." Rachel tapped her fingers in a quick frantic drumming, her lips doing the silent-moving again. "Okay so... I'm pretty sure that's all we can do... it was looking bad there for a minute, but nice save. We just have to be extra-cautious. Lay low, right?"

"Right," Jessie said, sounding despondent as a kid being disciplined about digging in the neighbor lady's flowerbeds after getting a brand new shovel and pail.

"And no more killing, right? Least of all, police."

"It wasn't planned," Annamaria said. "Even if he hadn't looked in the bags, he would have remembered us when someone did find the—"

"I know all that," Rachel said. "I know you did what had to be done. I'm just saying, not again, okay?"

"Of course."

"Gwen? Darlene?"

Gwen nodded, and after a moment, sulkily, so did Darlene.

"Does this mean we're good, then?" Gwen asked.

"I think so," Rachel said. "As good as we can be. We got the apartment cleaned up, so that's where we are right now. Unless there are some other problems I haven't heard about?"

"No," said Annamaria, rubbing fitfully at the new Band-Aid on her palm.

"Nuh-unh," Darlene said.

Gwen, lips pressed tight and eyes averted, shook her head.

"Um, well…" said Jessie, her grin sheepish. "There is maybe kinda one more thing…"

CHAPTER EIGHTEEN

"What do you *mean*, you killed someone *else*?"

Eight little words, but Darlene yelled them awfully loud.

"Shit, Dar!" Jessie recoiled and cast a quick look around and up.

Wouldn't have surprised her if the old house, a rickety piece of shit held together more by layers of wallpaper paste than anything else, gave way and collapsed. Like an avalanche, triggered by the volume. Down it would go, plywood and wallboard and nasty shag carpeting, crushing them or burying them alive in the wreckage.

It didn't. Which meant she still had to face the music.

"When?" Annamaria asked.

"At the lake. But look, I didn't plan it any more than you planned to do the cop. It just happened, that's all."

"If you're joking, Jessie—" Rachel said.

"No joke."

Gwen, hunched down like the last baby bird left in the nest, stared at her. "You didn't... not Etch... did you?"

"My *boyfriend*? Kill my own boyfriend? Jeez, Guinevere! What kind of psycho do you think I am? Anyway, he drove me home, didn't he? Dropped me off, remember? That's when you all started yelling at me, practically as soon as I got through the door."

"Well then who—" Darlene began.

"And it's *your* fault anyway," Jessie said, pointing at Rachel.

"*My* fault? I wasn't on your stupid camping trip. I was here, taking care of the mess *you* left for us!"

"Yeah but you had to call and bitch me out about it in the middle of the night!"

"You bet I called," Rachel said. "Darlene comes in with her clothes on inside-out, looking like she got stampeded by bulls, and she tells us what you left for her out in the apartment, you *bet* I called to find out what the heck you thought you were doing!"

"Which was exactly the problem! We're there having a fine time drinking tequila, doing shooters, sitting around the fire… then my phone rings–I should have turned the fucker off, okay, my bad–and I go to answer it and you're there screaming at me loud enough they could probably hear you in Canada, so then everybody else wants to know what bug crawled up *your* butt."

"You… *told?*" Annamaria's voice dropped to a thunderous hush. Her expression made Jessie, who wasn't even a churchgoer, think about forbidding statues of saints who really punished the shit out of people. "You broke our pact?"

"I didn't *tell!* Fuck! I wasn't *that* drunk; give me some credit, huh?"

"We keep *giving* you credit, Jessie," Rachel said, "and you keep doing these stupid things!"

"Well if *you* hadn't called me up—"

"Please!" Gwen cried. "Please, can we not do this? Can we not fight? Can't we go back to normal?"

"If you didn't tell," said Annamaria, still in that thunderous hush, "then what *did* you do?"

"Hey," Skip said. "That somebody's phone?"

"Sounds like mine." Jessie, sprawled atop Etch where they had both tumbled backwards off the log as he'd been trying to pull her into his lap, made to get up.

"Babe," Etch said in a complaining tone, wrapping his arms around her. He had no need to get up, had already gotten up in the main way that mattered, a hot hard lump pressing into the small of her back.

"Only take a minute, stud."

"Yeah well it'd only take *him* a minute, that's what I hear," Biff said.

"If that," Chet chimed in. "Thirty seconds, more like!"

The two of them high-fived while Etch did a loud, wry laugh and told them they were just assholes, and *jealous* assholes, to boot. Jessie disentangled herself from him and dug her phone out of the side pocket of her pack. The display told her it was the home number, and she flipped it open and held it to her ear, grinning, expecting to hear Dar's expressive and effusive thanks for the greatest night of her life.

Instead, she got Rache.

A severely pissed Rache.

She seemed intent on tearing Jessie a new one, and Jessie couldn't very well stand there and defend herself with everybody right there listening.

"Rache, look, I can't really talk about this now—"

"Which one's Rache?" Skip asked Brad.

"Looks like a cartoon character. Little blonde with the…" Brad curved his hands out from his chest.

Lori hit him. "Pig."

"Yours are better," he told her.

"It was not! Quit calling me that!" Jessie hurried away from the campfire. "I was totally careful!"

"You in trouble, babe?" Etch boosted himself onto the log again and snagged the tequila bottle from Cara.

Who, Jessie noticed even as she retreated toward the woods, made heavy eye contact with him and trailed her fingers over the bottle's neck… that slut… like she didn't already have Biff and Chet's full attention… but Rachel was still talking in her ear, demanding answers, wanting to know how-you-could-be-so-stupid.

"Nobody saw," she said, almost hissing the words. "I told you, I was careful, nobody knows, I took care of it!"

"Everything okay, Jess?" Skip had tottered to his feet and was peering after her, blinking like he wasn't sure which of the half-dozen Jessies he was seeing was the real one.

"Fine, fine," she said, waving. "BRB, okay?" Then she

couldn't believe she had actually said it aloud. What next? LOL?

Cara, giggling, was holding a lime wedge in each hand so Chet and Etch could both do shots, while Biff made mock-threatening gestures to sprinkle the salt down her top. Lori, unmollified by Brad's opinion regarding her and Rachel's tits, had huffily turned away… so behind her back, Brad was sharing a twinkling smile with Steph, and mouthed something at her about how *hers* measured up…

"Listen to me for a minute! Would you for fuck's sake shut up and listen?" Jessie had gotten beyond the edge of the firelit circle, into the rustling, woodsy shadows.

She was aware, now that she was up and moving, of the swimmy buzz in her head—a *good* swimmy buzz, but it still meant she had to watch where she was going. Even by daylight and cold sober, she'd be walking on deadwood, loose rocks, fallen pinecones and drifts of dry brown pine needles, roots and gopher holes. At night, with a buzz? One wrong move and she'd go ass over teakettle, maybe with a sprained ankle to show for it.

Incredibly, Rache *did* for fuck's sake shut up and listen. Jessie didn't expect it would last long, so she explained how Chad had shown up early, but of course he hadn't told anybody else he was going to show up early, thanks to his having some ulterior motives.

"Jess?" Skip's voice floated to her through the darkness.

"I said I'm fine, it's cool, be cool, fo shizzle, dawg!" she hollered in the direction of the fire. It always busted Skip up, like when Etch and Brad would hitch their pants low, put on askew ball caps, and do their White Boy Rap routine.

True to form, off in the dark, Skip snort-guffawed. "Okay then."

Rache, meanwhile, had been maintaining an intense silence. Weird how that worked over the phone. It wasn't like Jessie could read her face or her body language. There wasn't any way to know whether or not Rache was even still on the line. They could have been disconnected. It could have been dead air. But it wasn't. It was intense silence.

Jessie continued with her explanation, laying it out all nice and logical, because that was the sort of shit that appealed to Rache. Proving that she hadn't just done some crazy, impulsive thing, but that she'd given it actual thought.

"Then, once I had the cuffs on him and the gag and everything, I got all his stuff together. The clothes he was wearing, his pack, his bike–I had to cut through the fucking chain because I didn't know the combination, but I got rid of it separately, so they won't ever be able to figure out it was cut."

"What did you do with it?"

"The chain?"

"All of it!"

"Oh." She grinned. "You're gonna love this. This was brilliance to the extreme if I do say so myself!"

Then she told all about her little subterfuge, wearing Chad's things and riding Chad's bike, making sure that she rode near enough for the construction workers at the condo site to see her, but not so close that they could see she wasn't a dude.

Rache seemed less than blown away with awe and amazement. Rache wanted to know why Jessie had done it in the first place.

"Well... he kind of irritated me... acting like, because he's one of my boyfriend's buddies they can pass me around, share me like a pizza, everyone gets a piece... fucking jerk! You *bet* I was ready to kill his ass. But also it was for Dar, you know? All the stuff she says about how she never gets laid, and it was obvious she wanted to with Rico, but she wasn't going to with the rest of us there, so I thought I'd leave her one all to herself so she could do whatever she wanted before the main event. I thought she'd enjoy it. I give her a lot of shit sometimes so this was kind of like my way of making up for it."

Silence again, more speechless than intense this time. And Jessie supposed that, viewed a certain way, it *was* pretty bizarre.

"Jess? Don't get lost out there!"

"Skip, jeez!" she shouted in the direction of his distant voice. "What am I, your mommy, you can't stand to have me out of your sight for two minutes? What the hell? What *is* your problem?"

"We're out of tequila!"

"In the Yuke! Should be a bag with two more bottles!"

"Score!" he hooted. "Excellent!"

"Rache? Still there?"

"Still here," Rache said. "But... um..."

"So did Dar go for it?" Jessie asked. Her grin was back. "She fuck him? Did you guys kill him yet or are you gonna save him a while, give the rest of you a turn?"

"I don't *want* a turn!"

"Go on, Rache, he's an asshole, but he's hot. There's more condoms in my room if you need them, top dresser drawer, a whole box."

"Ugh, no thanks."

"What about Guinevere, then? Or is she still wanting to be Little Miss Virgin Princess waiting for her true love?"

"Jessie, this isn't funny! We can't *keep* him here."

"So kill him then, no big. It'll be same as the others. Listen, Rache, I need to charge this fucking thing, the battery's almost dead. Just... do whatever, okay? Keep him, kill him, whatever. See you Sunday!"

"But—"

She real-quick hit a couple buttons on the keypad with her thumb, making the phone beep, so that it would sound on the other end like the battery really was giving off its warning signal. Then she snapped it shut.

Some people. Shit-on-toast. Some people worried way too damn much. Rache was neurotic that way, always had been. If she thought she missed one single question on a test, she would fucking obsess about it until she found out for sure. This was worse. She had already been overestimating the hell out of the cops, and now she was underestimating the hell out of Jessie.

Stupid? Irresponsible?

Damn it!

Jessie wedged her phone into her pocket and leaned against a tree with her head back, so she could look up at the stars visible through the branches. There was a bright speck she figured must be a planet, though damned if she knew which one.

"You try and do something nice for someone," she said.

From a clump of bushes off to her left came three quick muffled explosions of air— sneezes—a person who had been desperately trying *not* to sneeze finally being unable to hold it in any longer.

"Skip?" Jessie asked, though it hadn't sounded like Skip; she'd heard Skip sneeze: he was physically incapable of not sneezing in a single colossal *wa-choo!* that would rattle windows and just about knock him on his ass.

She took a quiet step in that direction. Then another. And another.

On her third quiet step, someone burst from the bushes and made a scrambling, clumsy run for it. Her vision had adjusted as well as it could to the dark, which was well enough for her to see that it wasn't Skip, or Etch, or any of the guys she'd come to the lake with. Not any of the girls, either.

He snagged his foot and fell with a wheezy cry. "Oof!" The layer of pine needles was springy enough to make his landing otherwise soundless.

Some old man. *Really* old. His hair was so fine and white it almost glowed in the dark. He wore old-man clothes: a light-colored polo shirt, plaid golf pants hiked to roughly his armpits, a white belt, striped deck shoes.

Jessie stared for a moment. Her mind felt like a sports car on ice. Pedal to the metal and the engine racing, wheels spinning at a furious pace, going nowhere.

The old man flailed over onto his back and raised his shriveled, twig-bunch hands. "I didn't hear anything!" he said, his voice cracked and feeble.

Didn't hear anything.

Bull-fucking-*shit*.

That meant he'd heard *everything*.

"Swear to God... not a thing... just minding my own business..."

Everything.

The tires on her mental sports car suddenly found traction, and it was zero to eighty in four-point-two seconds, baby. Her body was nearly as fast to respond.

The branch she grabbed was more of a club than a stick. It had heft. It bulged at one end into a knob that was gnarled and knotted and hard. The narrower end fit her hand every bit as well as her lucky, creep-whacking bowling pin.

***

"You used a stick?" Darlene asked.

Jessie nodded. "Didn't take much. Damn, but getting old must suck. His bones... nothing to them... I've had piñatas that could take more hits. You could hear it when his ribs went. Like snapping celery stalks."

"Good God," Annamaria said, crossing herself without giving it conscious thought. "An old man? A harmless old man?"

"Harmless my ass," Jessie said. "Don't you get it? He *heard* me. He heard me talking all about Chad and Rico and everything. I used their names. I used some of *your* names. He knew too much. It was just like with Anna and the cop. I didn't have any choice. I had to do it."

"But you don't know for sure he heard," Gwen said. "He told you he didn't."

"Come on, he was lying," Darlene said. "He wouldn't have made such a big deal about not hearing anything if he really hadn't heard anything."

"You're positive you killed him?" Annamaria asked.

It was movies she was thinking of, countless movies where someone was struck on the head and left for dead, and perhaps they'd be in a coma, perhaps they'd have amnesia, but perhaps they would recover and be able to deliver damning testimony.

"He's dead, all right? Jeez. I bashed his head in. Even someone as—" Here, Jessie shot Rachel a sour look, "—as stupid and irresponsible as me isn't going to fuck up that bad."

Rachel barely noticed. "And what happens when they find him and want to question everyone who was camping out there that night?"

"What if they do? I made it look like an accident. There's—"

"An accidental head-bashed-in?" asked Darlene.

"How can you beat someone to death and have it look like an accident?" Gwen added.

"Let her finish," Rachel said.

"Thank you, Rache. See, there's all these little streams and rocky creeks that flow into the lake. Some have wooden footbridges and some have rope bridges, but some only have logs or stepping-stones to get across. We were near enough to one of those, one with the stepping stones. They're wet, they're mossy, they're slicker than snot. I took his head and banged it against a boulder, even used the bottom of his shoe to scrape some of the moss. It'll look like he was trying to cross but slipped and fell."

"So far, so good, then," Rachel said. "What did you do next?"

"What do you mean? I rinsed off my hands and went back before they finished off all my tequila."

"What about the stick? You didn't leave it in the woods, did you?"

"Yeah, Rache, I really am that dumb. Puh-leeze. I took it back to camp with me."

"You what?" gasped Gwen. "You kept the murder weapon?"

"I wasn't gonna leave it there."

"It would have been caked with DNA samples," Rachel said. "Hair and blood and stuff. Maybe not fingerprints, not on tree bark, but transfer of epithelials... skin cells from your hands..."

"I thought of all that," Jessie said. "Which is why I brought the fucking stick back to camp with me. Camp, you know, where we had this big roaring camp*fire*?"

"Ah." Rachel sat back. Lines of concern smoothed from her brow.

"So maybe I'm not as stupid as you seem to think." Her pugnacious expression dared Rachel to argue, spoiling for a fight.

"What else happened?" Rachel asked, with a marked lack of apology, and also a marked lack of rising to the bait. "That was late Friday night, so what happened after you burned the stick?"

Jessie scrubbed a hand up the side of her face. "I think I might've made out some with Skip, though I don't really remember. Etch was really wasted and... yeah... I think I did make out with Skip a little... Cara and Chet went off someplace... Lori and Brad got into this huge fight, so she spent the night in her car... Brad ended up in a tent with Steph... shit, I don't know. We were all pretty drunk. Could be the tequila wasn't such a great idea after all. Maybe we should have stuck with beer."

"I *meant*," said Rachel, "what happened with the old man?"

"Oh. That. Yeah. A ranger came by in the morning, was

making the rounds talking to everyone. Said the old guy was from over in the RV section, wife said he liked to go for walks at night when he couldn't sleep, but he hadn't come back and she was starting to get worried that he was lost or hurt himself or something. So the ranger asked us if we'd just keep an eye open. When he still hadn't showed up by lunchtime, people were talking about doing a search party, but before it really got organized, someone found him."

"And?" Annamaria said.

"And what? He was dead. They figured," Jessie said, her voice taking on a righteous triumphant note, "that he had been trying to cross the creek when he slipped on the moss and fell and smashed his head against a rock."

She finished with a *so, there!* look at Rachel.

"Then what?" asked Gwen.

"Then it was the usual shit with the rangers calling in the coroner or whoever the hell, and they took our names—"

"They took your names?" echoed Darlene. "That's bad, isn't it?"

"Trust me, it was just them going through the motions. Nobody was treating it like anything but an accident. No reason not to. He had his wallet and stuff, the wife even said he was on some medication that made him dizzy. Case-fucking-closed, okay?"

Annamaria glanced at Rachel, who shrugged. Darlene also seemed satisfied. Gwen had withdrawn, gazing off into space.

"Okay," Rachel said. "That it? Anything else?"

The question hung in the air, and it reminded Annamaria of that moment in a wedding ceremony when the priest inquired as to whether or not anyone had any just cause why this man and this woman and so on. As a child she'd always held her breath for what seemed an eternity right then, expectant with a sort of dreadful anticipation. What if someone *did* speak up? What then?

No one ever had, not in any of the weddings she'd ever been to. Even if they had legitimate objections, they'd always kept them to themselves.

And no one spoke up now.

***

The old man from the campground turned out to be a retired dentist. He and his wife had been doing the semi-nomadic RV thing for the past few years, using their camper to shuttle between their adult community condo in Flagstaff, visits to their children and grandkids all over the country, and various vacation destinations along the way.

It was in the local paper, two days after they found the body. *Campground Tragedy Claims Grandfather's Life*. With a scattering of linked articles about outdoor safety, park rules and guidelines, and general helpful tips.

Rachel added the clippings to her scrapbook.

Stupid?

Irresponsible?

Well, what the heck, it wasn't like Jessie had a monopoly on those.

And besides, as she'd decided–rationalized?–earlier, like with the key, if any investigators got to the point of actually finding the scrapbook, it would already be far too late.

Her room did have a loose floorboard under the bed, and the dusty space beneath would have been plenty large enough to hold the scrapbook. Heck, when she'd discovered the compartment, it had still contained a shoebox that some previous tenant had left there upon moving out. A shoebox full of badly-written lesbian smut disguised as love letters, judging by what little she'd read before tossing it all in the trash.

She could have put her scrapbook there, sure. Or she could save herself the trouble of having to rearrange furniture or wriggle under the bed every time she wanted it, and just stick it on the shelves with the rest of her binders.

The bike cop's body was discovered almost forty-eight hours to the minute from when Annamaria had whipped that box-cutter across his throat.

Officer Neil Morris, divorced single dad, had been last seen Saturday morning by the neighbor who babysat his young son. Given that he'd recently been involved in a major drug bust, the police were quick to suspect foul play.

Forty-eight hours after his death… forty-five or so hours after *Hey has Neil shown up yet?* had moved through *He better have a damn good excuse* and into the realm of *Do you think something happened to him?*… Officer Ramona Ardell had pulled over into the parking lot of that abandoned produce stand.

She, being not only Morris' colleague but also his sister-in-law, had been retracing the likeliest routes between the babysitter's house where he'd dropped off his son and the station at which he'd never arrived.

Reading the articles, Rachel supposed that someone of a more fanciful and romantic frame of mind than her–someone like Gwen, for instance–would make much of the relationship between Officers Morris and Ardell. Something turbulent, full of emotional baggage, conflict and unrequited passion.

That, Rachel thought, was bad.

Not just a cop. Not even just a more dedicated, driven, and obsessed than usual cop.

A cop for whom it was personal. Maybe romantic, maybe just familial… maybe she'd promised her little nephew that Auntie Ramona would do everything she could to find out who'd done this to his daddy, and make them pay.

Yeah, that was bad. That was *very* bad.

Dawn on Monday had been almost as pretty as dawn on Saturday, the sky pink-gold-azure, edged in lacy wisps of cloud.

Right when Rachel had been popping bolt upright in bed with the horrible realization that she had a paper due that day–a paper she'd meant to spend the weekend on, a paper of which she hadn't written a single word thanks to Jessie and Darlene and Chad and dealing with everyone else's screw-ups–Officer Ardell would have been stepping out of her car to stretch her legs and clear her head with some fresh air.

"That was when," she'd told the cameras and reporters, "I smelled something… and I knew what it was."

Before nine o'clock, the scene had been swarming with activity.

Rachel, who'd turned on the television for background noise, found the news by mistake. She ended up glued to the tube awaiting each new development.

Paper? Forget the paper. The first time in her academic

career she failed to turn an assignment in on time, but that was just too bad. She'd cut the class, say she was sick, hand it in tomorrow.

Later, while the police were doing a wider sweep of the perimeter, a rookie cop thought it was weird that the smell of decomposition was so much stronger over this way... and... he followed his nose... right to the lumpy, neatly-bagged discovery of his newbie career.

Chad, meanwhile, hadn't even been reported missing. Everyone who'd gone to the lake thought he had missed the trip and stayed home; everyone who had stayed at the frat house thought he had gone to the lake.

It was only when they all compared notes that they realized something might be wrong, and by then, the pieces—so to speak—were already being put together.

CHAPTER NINETEEN

The warlock knew something.

Gwen could tell. It was all right there in the way that he watched her, his weird jack-o'-lantern eyes following her every move. Like he could almost see into the secret chambers of her soul.

She ducked her head so that her hair fell around her face like curtains, and hurried for the stairs. No one pointed at her and shouted accusations. No one yelled, "There, her, it's her, that girl, that one, stop her, she's a murderer!"

The news still said that the police were following up on many promising leads. That they believed they were close to breaking the case.

Rachel said it wasn't true. Jessie said it was total bullshit. Annamaria and Darlene agreed with them. And they all agreed, all five, that they really needed to back off.

"Okay, look, you guys, things seriously got out of control." Rachel had said. "We're not spree killers, remember?"

"Serial killers, there's a difference," Jessie and Darlene had said, in unison, with the flat, bored tone of kids reciting their multiplication tables.

"You're saying, no more?" As she asked it, Annamaria traced her Band-Aid with one sculpted fingernail. She wouldn't look at Rachel, wouldn't look at any of them, seemed mesmerized as she ran her nail along it, over and over.

"No more," Rachel had said. "We have to see what happens.

The police officer… that cranked up the heat. We have to be extra careful now."

Following up on many promising leads. Close to breaking the case.

A detective *had* come to the house to ask about Chad, and Jessie put on an award-winning performance while Gwen stuck to murmurs and looking shell-shocked by the news—it was easy for her, hardly an act at all. And even *she* had been able to tell that the questions were perfunctory at best.

Whenever they heard any talk of the murders—it was commonly accepted that yes, there was a serial killer operating in town—it was still in terms of, "I hope they catch him/the guy/that crazy son of a bitch soon."

Him. The guy. That crazy son of a bitch.

They were comparing 'him' to Jeffrey Dahmer. They had brought in an expert, a profiler, to consult. The results were just what Rachel predicted: suspect likely a white male in his thirties or forties, middle- to upper-class, professional. Gay, maybe closeted, maybe even married, with a family, and this darker side was his repressed homosexuality trying to fight back.

Jessie had gone to Chad's funeral. She hadn't wanted to, but it would look strange if she didn't. He had been one of her friends, part of her crowd. So, she'd gone. It was followed by the frat house's idea of a wake. Which, according to Jessie, was pretty much the same as the frat house's idea of any other sort of party. A kegger, only with black crepe paper decorations.

All of them saw their schoolwork suffer, but they were hardly alone. Them and half the campus. Buddy-system programs were organized, so no one had to walk anywhere alone after dark. The Student Union offered self-defense courses.

When no more bodies turned up, speculation shifted. Had the killer moved on? Fled after the close call with the bike cop? Killed himself in remorse or fear of being caught? Been arrested on some other charge?

No one knew.

No one had a guess.

Except maybe the warlock.

But if he did know, he said nothing. He only watched

Gwen–she couldn't see him doing it, but she could feel him–as she scuttled down to the basement, where the fiction books were kept.

This was the only place—here in this dusty-musty enclosure, surrounded by binding and paper and old glue—that Gwen felt almost all right again. When she was at home, even in her own room with the door shut, she was conscious of the others, the shared secret hanging over them, the locked apartment above the garage.

They hadn't killed anybody else.

It was like a pressure, building.

It was like a strong scent, pervasive.

It was… a hunger, a craving, a need, an urge.

More powerful when they were together. Two of them at a time, that wasn't so bad… three was distracting… four was uncomfortable… and when all five of them were there, it was almost unbearable.

To get away from that heavy, building pressure, she went out. A lot. Spending money she couldn't really afford. Going to movies she had already seen. Coming here to the bookstore though she still hadn't read the last batch of paperbacks she'd purchased.

It was her escape. Now more than ever. Her only way to cling to any remnant of the Gwen she used to be.

That poor, lost Gwen. The girl who knew she was shy and thought herself gentle, kind. The girl who used to be innocent and who had never before in her life hurt another person.

She reached the end of a book-lined row and turned into the next, and found it already occupied. The man's back was to her as he scanned the spines, but he looked youngish. Her age or thereabouts. Casually dressed. Well-built. With wavy-tousled blond hair that fell to his collar.

Kind of like Cameron Mack.

Imagine if it *was*!

Of course it wasn't, and if he looked around she would see that right away; he was just someone who happened, from this angle, to bear a passing resemblance.

Didn't stop her from letting the daydream unfold, or from

seeking eager comfort in its familiar contours. The details and setting might differ, but the overall theme was always the same, as well-known and well-loved to her as her favorite pair of slippers.

Here she was, browsing among the bookshelves... and he'd come up behind her... *Excuse me,* he'd say... and she would turn... and look into those beautiful, dreamy, azure eyes... it would be him, really him, even more handsome than he was in the movies... she'd have the very book he wanted in her hands... the only copy... and she'd hold it out and say, *Here, have this one...* and he'd say, *No, I couldn't, you had it first...* and she'd say, *Really, I insist...* and he'd say, *Tell you what, you buy the book and I'll buy us Italian sodas at the coffee place across the street, and we'll sit in a booth by the window the rest of the day and take turns reading chapters out loud to each other.* And she'd say, *That would be nice, thank you.* Then he would smile that wonderful smile and say, *My name's Cameron. What's yours?*

A thrill shivered outward from her midsection, wrapping her in a sensation of dizzying breathlessness. She had to grip the edge of a shelf to steady herself. Her hands were shaking a little. But in a good way.

It was silly, she knew.

But... oh... wouldn't it be *amazing*?

To meet him like that? To just run into him, some casual encounter?

And he'd see *her*, the real her. He'd see she wasn't another of those throngs of screaming fangirls who begged for his autograph and mobbed him at world premieres. He would realize right away that she was different. She was special.

Silly.

Probably there were a million girls who believed the exact same thing. All those girls who went to the Mack Pack websites, for instance. The ones who posted every day on the message boards, or drew their fan art, or wrote their gushy, saccharine, Mary Sue fanfiction... probably, every single one of them thought *she* was the different one, the special one.

When really, they didn't understand him at all. They only saw how cute or hot or sexy he was and didn't care about the rest. They didn't know the *real* Cameron Mack. They couldn't.

Not the way *she* did. Not his innermost soul.

The man behind her in the aisle coughed.

Gwen jumped.

"Sorry," he said, and coughed again. "Dusty in here."

"Uh-huh." She didn't turn around, stood stock still, fingers digging into the edge of the shelf, shoulders tightening defensively. He had a nice voice, too, almost the exact right voice. But if she turned, if she saw him, saw his face that wasn't Cameron Mack's face, it'd ruin a perfectly good daydream.

She kept her gaze fixed on the row of paperbacks, the names printed sideways on the spines. Ks and Ls in front of her eyes, more in a general grouping than in proper organized alphabetization.

He moved closer. She stared at the books.

Kurtz. Kurtz. Lackey, Laymon. Laymon? What was *that* doing there? That belonged over in the Horror section, she was sure.

"Excuse me," the blond man said.

She wanted to scream at him not to say that, that was for the daydream, he was wrecking it! If he wrecked it, she would have to come all the way back to this reality, the reality where she couldn't really be a Gwen she liked anymore.

But she didn't.

He hadn't said it the same way anyhow. He'd said it more as a 'Pardon me, coming through' kind of thing, as he made to go past. Gwen scootched closer to the shelves, almost pressing herself into them, making sure he wouldn't so much as brush against her.

It wouldn't have mattered. The daydream was wrecked. Shattered. Popped like the airy, stupid soap bubble it was. Meeting Cameron Mack in a bookstore and going out for Italian sodas and spending the day reading out loud to each other... how naïve was that?

Reality.

The reality was, she was down here in this claustrophobic basement with some strange man. As nice and polite as he sounded, he could still be a violent maniac. Why not?

He could hurt her, if he wanted.

A new daydream, a horrid waking nightmare, flashed into her

head. She saw the blond man grabbing her and shoving her face-first against the shelves, saw him groping her skirt up her legs, slobbering and panting steamy, wolfish breaths into her ear.

The knife was in her purse—Rico's switchblade with the emerald serpent on its hilt—but she saw herself grab it only to have the man laugh and swat it from her hand, skittering away uselessly on the warped floorboards.

Were any other customers still down here? Upstairs? In the store at all? If he tried anything, and she called for help, would anybody answer?

Her mind's eye saw the warlock upstairs smile an impish little smile as he moved, spider-quick and quiet, to the front door. Saw his spindly fingers twist the lock and draw down the shade with the Closed sign on it. Saw him scurry silent to the top of the stairs, the cat accompanying him, to watch with jack-o'-lantern gleams in their weird eyes.

While the man... while he tore her clothes... while he mauled her flesh... while he hit her and curled his fist in her hair and...

Oh, no, no, please, no.

She was shaking again, and not in the good way. Her knuckles were white where she clutched the edge of the shelf. Her nails carved small shallow crescents into the wood.

The man had gone by her, but he paused. "Are... are you all right?"

Gwen nodded, clenching her jaw to keep her teeth from chattering.

"You're sure?" So concerned. And sounding more like Cameron Mack all the time, what a cruel trick, what a cruel joke!

"I'm fine," she said. Squeaked, really.

The knife. In her purse. If she could get it, if she could have it ready, her thumb poised on the button that would spring out the deadly steel fang...

"Okay," he said, after another moment's dubious hesitation.

Then he kept going, out of the aisle, out of the section. Leaving her. Alone. Untouched. Unscathed.

Moments later, she heard his footsteps climbing the stairs. Heard him say something to the warlock, and the warlock's cackled reply. Then his steps crossed the creaky floor overhead. The door's hanging brass bell jingled. He was gone.

Gwen sagged against the shelves, pressing her forehead to the row of Kurtz and Lackey, eyes shut.

Any interest she'd had in browsing was gone, dashed to pieces, shattered like a wave on a rocky shore, or a bone china cup hurled to the bricks. She seized a few paperbacks at random only because she worried the warlock might think it was peculiar if she left without buying anything... he might think she was shoplifting... she *always* made at least one purchase... and blundered upstairs.

The warlock took her money and put her books into a plastic grocery store bag, his eyes seeming to twinkle at her with amused mischief the whole while. She hurried out as soon as he'd given her the bag, doing her best to act like she was late for her bus and not fleeing like a rabbit.

Doubtful she fooled him.

Doubtful she fooled *anybody*.

The best she managed was to not go running down the sidewalk. She forced herself to walk. Briskly, yes, but a walk. There was no sign of the blond man, and he hadn't been a real threat, she knew that now. He'd only been concerned. The rest was her nerves, as usual.

She understood that, but she kept slipping a hand into her purse, touching the switchblade's faux-ivory handle. Just in case.

Her plan for the evening had been to spend most of it in town, looking through the shops, maybe seeing a movie at the Orion. Doing ordinary, old-Gwen activities... and not having to deal with, or think about, anything else. To at least pretend she was back to normal.

She reached the bus stop, checked the schedule, and saw that she had just missed the most recent one. The next wasn't for almost half an hour.

Sighing, Gwen sank onto the bench in the Plexiglas-sided shelter. She opened the bag to see what she'd bought. Two epic fantasies she'd read before, one sci-fi novel she hadn't. By the cover, she guessed it was a cross-species love story about humans and telepathic cat-people aliens. Looked intriguing, and she had twenty minutes before the next bus, so she gave it a try and was soon pulled in.

"Hey, wouldn't have any change, wouldya?"

Her breath snagged in her throat like a scarf on a thorn, but she managed not to gasp or squeak. Her hands stuttered, letting the paperback flip closed and losing her place, but she managed not to drop it.

The person just outside the bus shelter was one of the homeless people she had seen before, on the streets and at the Orion. The one with the long black tangles of hair and beard. The one whose nose whistled.

He grinned at her, exposing bad teeth. "Couple quarters? For the bus?"

Gwen clutched the book and shook her head.

"Just a couple quarters," he said, wheedling. His eyes were sunken, bloodshot.

"Sorry, I don't," she said in a faint voice.

"You gotta have a couple quarters." He shuffled closer.

She could smell him, body odor and onions under a cloud of stale beer and nicotine. He wore too-large jeans belted with a length of rope, the pants tattered at the knees and cuffs, spotted with dried paint or food stains or both. A dark-orange windbreaker hung open over a tee shirt with Snoopy on it. The shirt was so old that Snoopy looked like he had leprosy, patches of him flaking off, as he did his gleeful Snoopy happy-dance.

"I… I don't," she said again.

"'Bout a cigarette? Got a cigarette?"

"I don't smoke."

"Only need a couple quarters for the bus." He shuffled closer still.

Cars went by without slowing. Pedestrians went by without looking. Gwen checked the time and saw that it was still ten minutes until the bus was due. The sky had been overcast and dreary all day, and now, as twilight began to set in, a preternatural dusk-purple haze made the world seem like some other, stranger place.

The homeless man didn't have his dog with him—the brown and white mutt she had also seen before. He held a newspaper speckled with damp coffee grounds in one hand and a beer can in a paper bag in the other. A glaze of dried snot caked his hairy upper lip. There was a cold sore festering at the corner of his mouth, and dandruff in his eyebrows.

"Trying to get downtown," he told her. "Visiting a friend."

Willing herself not to tremble, she opened the book again and stared at lines of print, without being able to make sense of a single word.

"Oh that's nice," he said. "Gonna ignore me? Pretend I'm not here?"

"Please, I just want to read my book."

"Yeah, I know how it is. You think you ignore me, I'll go away. I got every bit as much right to be here as you. I got every bit as much right to ride the bus. You don't own the bus. You don't own the bus stop or the sidewalk neither."

"Leave me alone, please," Gwen said. She had failed in the no-trembling effort; the book shook in her hands so badly that she couldn't have read it even if she'd been able to concentrate on the text.

"It's people like you," he said, his nose whistling in annoyance. "Too good for the rest of us, can't even spare a couple quarters so a guy can take the bus downtown and see his friends."

"I don't have any quarters!" She wanted it to come out brusque and cool, but she couldn't *do* brusque and cool. It came out meek, weak and feeble.

"How 'bout a dollar then? Got a dollar?"

"No."

"You gotta have a dollar."

"I... I..." Inspiration struck. "I think I have one of those voucher books here somewhere—"

He hawked and spat a green gobbet onto the sidewalk. It splatted there like a half-melted slug. "Goddamn vouchers again!"

Gwen glanced around. No bus anywhere in sight. People walking by and studiously not looking at the homeless man. No help. No hero. No knight in shining armor to intervene and rescue her. She checked the time again and couldn't believe that less than three minutes had passed since her last peek.

"There's some for bus tickets—"

"C'mon, lady, don't be stuck-up, huh?"

Seven more minutes until the bus came. Seven more minutes of this, and what if he got on the same bus? What if he sat by her and continued haranguing her? He would do it even if she gave him the money. He'd do it because then he would be vindictive because she had lied to him before. He wouldn't let up and leave her alone.

"I really can't afford—"

"Can't afford? Sure, I bet you got a place to stay, bet you got a nice house, you don't gotta sleep under the overpass."

She stood up, hugging purse and bag of books to her chest.

"What, you leavin'? Not gonna wait for your bus?"

There was another bus stop a few blocks uphill, on Trowbridge, by the tavern. If it had been much later, Gwen wouldn't have dared go anywhere near the place, which had a neon-outline naked girl in the window, a gravel lot that tended to fill up with motorcycles on weekend evenings, and a reputation for brawls and the occasional shooting. Since it was still early enough that the tavern wouldn't be open yet...

"Hey, c'mon, I'm sorry, don't be like that," the homeless man called. "I'll shut up. Promise."

Gwen kept walking.

"Guess you *are* stuck-up, then, huh?"

He was following.

"Too good to give a crap about anybody else, am I right?"

She walked faster.

He quit calling after her.

He'd given up?

A furtive look back over her shoulder proved that hopeful guess wrong... he was following her. Hanging back, not rushing to catch up. But following. His bloodshot gaze was fixed on her, his snot-crusted upper lip curled into a sneer. He was going to follow, although he knew it scared her. *Because* he knew it scared her.

The thought of ducking into one of the shops tried to surface, but most of her mind was convinced that if she did, no matter if it was a shop she went to all the time, no matter if she bought something there or not, they would tell her to get out, stop loitering. They'd scoff at her claims of harassment from the homeless man. Laugh at her. Make fun of her.

Maybe she should have gone ahead and given him a dollar?

Then he'd ask her again next time he saw her. And again. And again.

She took another glance back. He was still there, trailing behind at a distance of maybe fifteen yards. A man and woman going by the other way gave Gwen a curious look, but she didn't stop.

She passed a daycare center with shabby playground equipment in a fenced-off space, Big Wheels and dump trucks abandoned on the bed of woodchips, late-staying children inside visible in glimpses between coloring book pages and construction paper artwork taped up in the windows. That made her think of the policeman's little boy, poor thing, so young and wanting to know when Daddy would come home.

A soft, watery sob escaped her lips. She stole another quick look back.

The homeless man was still following.

She passed a branch of the post office, and a duplex shared by a massage therapist and an attorney. All closed for the day now.

He was closer.

Ten yards behind her instead of fifteen.

She passed the Trowbridge Masonic Lodge, its parking spaces empty, its doors shut. The glass-covered bulletin board beside the front doors had notices for ballroom dance lessons, a Scrabble tournament, a pancake breakfast.

"What's the matter, huh?" he called.

Eight yards back, and gaining, although Gwen had picked up her pace until she was nearly at a trot.

Gaining and grinning.

Those bad teeth, some missing, some rotted, some crooked, some yellowed.

The bridge was just ahead of her now, and across it, the tavern, and the bus stop. Gwen didn't know how it was possible that there was so little traffic… there should have been dozens of cars, delivery trucks, people on the sidewalks… but she and the homeless man were like the only two actors on a minimalist-theater stage.

If she crossed the street, doubled back?

He would still follow her. He was invested in this now. Enjoying making her scared.

She was no longer nearly-trotting when she reached the end of the bridge. It was four lanes wide with a concrete divider down the middle, and pedestrian walkways to either side. Everything about the walkways was guardrails and signs admonishing riders to walk their bikes, no skateboards/roller skates, $500 fine for defacing or throwing litter off the bridge. The warning about defacing hadn't stopped several adventuresome taggers from leaving their marks.

Below was a slope of cheap apartment buildings and self-storage facilities, junkyards and train yards, and train tracks on a raised embankment that followed the curve of the river. The view wasn't exactly scenic. It was rusted-out hulks of boxcars and automobiles, where mounds of trash rose amid jungles of ivy and blackberry vines. Even the river looked sluggish and polluted, with brown foam scum lining its banks.

Once she set out, Gwen realized that the walkway being lower than the road bed and the thick metal guardrail rising between them meant that anyone crossing the bridge on foot would barely be visible to anyone in the passing cars.

She might as well have been in a tunnel or alley. Nowhere to go but straight ahead or straight back, and she couldn't go back, because he was already there. Stepping onto the walkway behind her. Not more than five yards behind her.

Gwen panicked and broke into a run, dropping the grocery bag with the other books in it, still clutching her purse and the one book to her chest. Her hair flew back from her face. Her heart hammered like a terrified fist on a locked door.

"Hey!" the homeless man blurted.

Surprised? Startled? Angry? She couldn't tell. She ran.

He chased.

She ran faster. Oncoming car headlights whizzed by on the bridge deck, making it seem like she was going at supersonic speeds.

He still chased. "Hey! Hey, lady!"

It sounded like he was right behind her, within grabbing distance of her flying, trailing hair. Gwen tried to look over her shoulder and see how close he really was.

And tripped.

"Aah!"

She flung out her hands to break her fall, scraping the skin from both palms and both knees in quick, skidding pain. More pain snapped up her left wrist. Her purse and the paperback shot from her grasp, the purse hitting the side of the bridge deck, the paperback skittering through a gap between the outside guard rail's posts and out into empty air above the river. Gwen flopped onto her stomach, her head jerking down so that her chin hit and her teeth clacked on her tongue. The rest of her breath was knocked from her lungs.

"Damn, lady," the homeless man said, halting a few feet away.

Gwen sucked vainly for air and scrabbled on the walkway's pitted surface. Part of her brain still thought she was running, hadn't yet clued in to the fact that she'd fallen on her face.

"Are you okay? That looked like it hurt."

She could see her purse. Halfway unzipped. Some of the contents spilling out. Her hairbrush. A pen. A tube of strawberry-flavored lip balm. Sunglasses. Some loose change—a couple quarters, bright silver against the dull concrete.

"Lady?" He took another few steps.

The purse. She hooked its strap with her fingers and yanked it to her.

"Miss? Here, lemme help you up."

He reached out.

Gwen thrust her hand into the purse, touched faux-ivory. She twisted onto her back and sat up in a lunge, thumb pressing the chrome button.

The switchblade flicked out, even brighter silver in the dusk-purple gloom than the glinting quarters. The homeless man saw it and had time to look surprised before Gwen punched it into him as hard as she could. His look of surprise ballooned into astonishment. A glottal sound—"Hurk!"—erupted from his lips.

The breath she hadn't been able to catch caught up with her instead, inhaled in a sharp gasp. She stared at her hand... *her* hand, her own slender, familiar right hand... fingers wrapped tight around the emerald green serpent.

"Hhoarrch," the homeless man said. It wafted into her face, warm and humid, reeking.

She had stabbed him just below Snoopy's happy-dancing feet. A deep crimson stain spread on the tee shirt, around the spot where the blade had gone in. A single thick trickle slowly made its way along the hilt, toward her hand.

His gaze, shocked and almost... almost *offended*... found hers. Then his eyes rolled up and his knees unhinged, and he toppled forward.

Gwen squealed and tried to scramble out from under him. The movement wrenched the blade loose, and blood gushed out in a torrent. She squealed again, let the knife fall clattering to the bridge, and braced herself against his loose, descending weight.

Panic and desperation took over. She didn't know where she found the strength, but all of a sudden she had her shoulder socked into his bleeding midsection and she was pushing, lifting, heaving, muscling him up and back and away.

Away, please God, away, away from her and toward the rail, and hot wetness soaked through her blouse, oozed along her spine, over her collarbones, between her breasts, dribbling and obscene, a violation, and she shoved with all her might, up and over, up and over the side, over the rail, out into the empty air above the river just like her dropped book.

Up, over, out... and down.

Down and down.

She saw him fall, tumbling, getting smaller as he went. Then splash, into the opaque water, the sluggish current erasing the hole he'd made.

Up, over, out, down, and gone.

CHAPTER TWENTY

Ed watched the news and read the papers and had done a whole lot of thinking, but things still wouldn't quite sit right his mind.

That college boy…

Found cut to pieces in a ditch, bagged up and thrown out like so much garbage…

Whom the girls next door had all sworn they never saw that Friday afternoon.

Muriel Gerrittson had seen him, though. She'd been puttering in the garden when he biked past the house on his way to the Hubert place. Ed had also seen him, from the barn-loft window.

Seen him with one of the neighbor girls. Jessie, her name was.

They'd claimed to have not been home when the boy must've stopped by, not home, or asleep and didn't hear him knocking.

Jessie, though, Jessie had been home. And awake. Awake enough to lead the boy out to the room above the garage, for what Ed presumed was a little hanky-panky on the sly behind her boyfriend's back.

Reason enough to lie, maybe, under ordinary circumstances. Wanting to protect reputations, spare feelings, avoid adding conflict and drama to what was already stressful to the breaking point.

Still and all, under these particular circumstances, it didn't seem right.

He went over it again as he let the alpacas into the pasture for their morning exercise—stroll and graze the dewy grass. They'd been sheared recently and looked even funnier than usual, with close-cropped bodies but still those extravagant poofs of fluff atop their heads.

The love lives of those girls weren't any of Ed Reilly's business, of course. They could be having regular orgies over there and it still wouldn't be any of his business.

But that boy was dead. Not just dead, murdered.

And the way they'd found him... butchered like an animal... dumped for the flies and scavengers... what an awful way to go, what a terrible thing for his parents. For everyone: his family and friends, the college, the entire community.

Nor was he the only one. The officer cut down in the line of duty had, according to the news, got off lucky, quick and easy, compared to the other victims.

A maniac was on the loose.

Torturing people. Mutilating them.

Right here in town. Too close to home for anybody's comfort.

Whoever had done it needed to be caught, which meant facts needed to be known and truth needed to come out. Any detail, no matter how insignificant it might seem, could be just the missing piece to lead the police to the killer. The more they knew about those last few hours of the boy's life, the better.

He leaned against the pasture rail, keeping an idle eye on the property next door while watching the alpacas. Hercules was in a frisky mood, and Susie-Q was playing the tease, frolicking away whenever the big male got close. One of the smaller females rolled in the dewy grass, legs waving. Two adolescents chased each other along the fences.

The Hubert place looked same as ever. Normal. Rundown. Quiet. Which was unsurprising; middle of a school day and all.

Something about it, though...

Or, more likely, just his nerves being jumpy.

Why not? Five girls living on their own in a ramshackle,

fairly isolated old house, with a maniac on the loose? Setup for a horror movie if Ed had ever heard one. If it wasn't for the fact of the victims all being men, he might've been worried.

To hell with that; he *was* worried.

They seemed like a decent group. Nice young ladies. Industrious and hard-working; just look at the way they'd pitched in on the chores after the landlady's nephew took off. If they sometimes held backyard cookouts or burned trash at odd hours, well, what of it?

He'd hardly spoken to them, of course, aside from his brief conversation with Gwen the day he'd offered to do the mowing. The day it had struck him how his own daughter would've been about their age, if she'd lived. Gave him a strange qualm inside. A pang, almost, at how many years it'd been, since Leigh.

Maybe it was some sort of misplaced spark of paternal instinct, but the more he contemplated it, the more he felt a need to look out for those girls. Who else would? They had each other, and they did look out for each other, but they were barely more than kids. Vulnerable and innocent, for all they might think themselves worldly-wise.

The very thought of how some brutal murderer must have nabbed the college boy just after he left... been somewhere nearby, maybe within sight of where he stood this very minute...

Yeah, much too close to home. Much too close for comfort.

Someone, he thought, should have a word with them. A neighborly word, if only to make sure they remembered to lock up, be alert and mindful, take care. Maybe let them know they were welcome to seek help next door if they ran into any trouble.

"If you really think we have to," Annamaria said, the words coming with dubious reluctance. She stopped at a light, at one of the hellish and confusing intersections around campus, and glanced over to try and gauge Rachel's sincerity.

"Don't you?" Rachel looked sincere, all right. "I mean, we all know things got out of hand. *Way* out of hand."

"I suppose."

Speaking of hands, the cut on hers had faded to a thin scar, a pale thread against her skin. She'd had to leave it alone. People had begun to notice, to remark, to suggest that maybe she should see a doctor if her accidental injury was taking this long to heal. She couldn't keep reopening it, slicing along that same line indefinitely.

That was fine, though.

She'd found other outlets. Other options. More discreet. More private.

No one else had to know what she did when she was alone in her room. With the needles. And the razor blades. No one would see those marks. No one would ever have to know.

Not unless she got on far more intimate terms with someone than she had been in a long time, which wasn't likely. It couldn't compare, could it? Not to the sharpness of the steel, the sweetness, the pure clarity.

The needle's point indenting... pressure to pain... and then the piercing, the penetration, sinking into tender, defenseless flesh. The razor's edge, that clean, cold, electrifying slice.

No, sex couldn't compare to that. Nothing else could. Nothing in the world.

Rachel had still been talking. Chattering away in her familiar fashion. Except now she had fallen silent, eyebrows raised at Annamaria. Waiting. Expectant.

"Sorry, what?" Annamaria asked.

The light had changed. Someone behind her honked: a loud, irate blast. When she flicked her gaze to the rear-view, she saw a guy in a van shooting her the finger. He roared his engine like he was threatening to roll right over her little car.

"I said, especially now they're saying they've got a suspect, it's even more important. Keep the attention on that, right? Heck, if I'd been *smart*, I would have planned it all along, framing someone, setting someone up to take the fall."

Annamaria smiled. She was aware of discomfort, the steel's sweet reminder, and wondered if any wounds had opened.

Rachel slouched in the passenger seat and gnawed her ragged thumbnail. "Good thing Gwen called us that night. Can you imagine if she'd gone into that bar or someplace instead? All scraped up and covered with blood? We would've had to come up with a cover story."

"She was in pretty bad shape."

An understatement, given the haggard wraith of a Gwen they'd found when they pulled up near the pay phone she'd used. They'd been able to wrap a blanket around her shoulders, get her into the car, bring her home, and calm her down with tea and reassuring talk.

And, obviously, take the knife away from her. To wash, they'd said, not wanting to give the impression it was for safekeeping.

Annamaria took one look at the switchblade and realized it was the one Jessie had been talking about, the one that had belonged to Rico. Strange to find Gwen with it, stranger still for Gwen to have not spoken up when they talked about it... but then, *she* had her own secrets, didn't she? So, why couldn't Gwen?

"But she's okay now," she went on. "We're all okay now."

"Yeah," Rachel said. "I think we are. I think we're good. I think we're in the clear."

Leaving the alpacas to their frolics, Ed headed around front and fussed for a while with a semi-assembled porch swing. Walt Gerrittson had bought it on sale in anticipation of the coming summer, then given up.

"Confounded puzzle," he'd said. "Instructions were in every language *but* English, and I have never seen so many little fiddly parts with no apparent purpose. If you can make heads or tails of it, Ed, you're a better man than this old cowboy."

That, Ed would have found doubtful in any case, porch swing or no porch swing. He could have built one from scratch, out of scrap wood and chains, in less time than it was taking to decipher the diagrams.

Less time, less effort, and far fewer of his swear words. He kept casting glances over his shoulder for fear of Muriel overhearing.

It didn't help that his mind wanted to wander. The girls, the college girls next door, on their own. After a while, he decided he'd feel better if he just got up and did something. Talk to them, if anybody was home. Leave a note, if not.

Only the Mustang was there, and he knew at least a couple of them didn't drive, so, he walked on over.

The post at the end of their driveway, with a barn-shaped mailbox mounted on it, had developed an almost diagonal lean. All the fixer-upper work they'd been doing, they must not have gotten around to it yet. Maybe he should offer to lend a hand there, too.

He went up to the door and knocked. Nobody answered. After giving it a minute, and another knock with similar results, Ed shrugged. Back to that confounded porch swing.

First, though, he figured he might as well take a look out back. If they had any good, sturdy lengths of wood lying around, he could shore up the leaning mailbox until he had time to get a proper new post put in.

He started around the house, following the breezeway to the garage with its attached laundry shed, and the apartment above.

When Gwen left of her last class of the day, she found Jessie waiting at the foot of the steps outside the Language Arts building.

"Yo, Guinevere! Smoothie run. Dar's driving, I'm buying, you in?"

"I have a lot of studying—"

"C'mon, it'll be a ride home, save time, quicker than the bus. And you get a smoothie. My treat." She grinned. "Strawberry Cream-Whip, you know you want one!"

"Well... all right."

They piled into the Caddy, Jessie even relinquishing the shotgun seat, and drove over to Baja Blend, where they were served by a grim-faced high school Goth girl whose stark black hair and heavy eyeliner did not mesh at all well with her colorful parrot-print uniform and hat.

"So, listen," said Jessie, once they'd gotten their cups and straws and strolled back to the car. "We kind of wanted to talk to you about what happened the other day."

"You mean, about the, um..."

"Yeah," said Darlene. "About the um."

"I didn't mean to," Gwen said. "I told you... he scared me. I was scared. He followed me, and I was scared."

"Hey, us, we're not mad." Jessie slurped on her smoothie, something healthy with wheat germ and protein powder; it looked like library paste, but she didn't seem to care. "Me, I think it's great. I was starting to worry that you weren't really, you know, into it."

"It really was seeming that way for a while." Darlene had opted for the marginally less healthy Tropical Swirl, though still a healthier choice than the chocolate chunk shake she used to get. She'd lost almost another ten pounds since Chad, and didn't want to gain it back.

"I..." she said. "Um..."

"Like your heart wasn't in it," Jessie said. "Like you went along with us only because it was the easiest thing to do."

"I helped," Gwen said. Her chin quivered. "I always helped, I did whatever you told me to. I know some of you thought I'd be squeamish but I never chickened out, did I? Not once!"

"But you weren't *into* it. I was ready to say we should maybe have you pick out the next one, some guy you really hated his fucking guts so you'd enjoy making him bleed. Then you went and killed a bum on the bridge, that was awesome—"

"Even if Rachel didn't think so," Darlene said. "According to her, it was crazy-risky, right out in public like—"

"Aw, shit, public?" scoffed Jessie. "Trowbridge? Nah. Me and Etch had sex there once, middle of morning rush hour—"

"You... you had... on the Trowbridge Road Bridge?" Gwen asked, eyes wide. "In broad daylight?"

"There was this bet he and Biff had... never mind. Point is, no one saw us. And no one saw you ventilate that walking shit-stain and chuck him overboard, so fuck it, forget about it."

"Do you think his dog's okay?"

"His dog?" Darlene asked. "What dog?"

"He had a dog. Not, you know, with him that day, but

before. I saw them by the movie theater sometimes. I'd feel really bad if the poor dog ended up... abandoned or in the pound or..."

"Ah, one of the other hobos is probably taking care of it," Jessie said.

Gwen fidgeted. "Probably, but..."

"Would it make you feel better if we went by the animal shelter and checked?"

"Jessie, what the hell?" interrupted Darlene. "Are you nuts? What about no more links to the victims? We go looking for his damn dog, Rachel's going to have a fit!"

"Hey, I'm not saying let's adopt it—"

"But if it is there," said Gwen, "they might put him to sleep, and it'd be my fault."

"Fuck's sake..." Darlene slouched behind the wheel. "Isn't it enough you've still got the murder weapon?"

"Hey, yeah, about that..." Jessie slanted a wry half-smile at Gwen.

She flinched. "I told you I was sorry. You can have it back if you want. I... I don't know why I kept it. I don't know why I didn't tell you before. It was just... *neat*. I liked it."

"Keep it. I don't mind. I was gonna use it on Rico, but no big. The moment has passed. I just like giving you shit."

"Just glad *you* found it, though," said Darlene. "Before anybody else did."

For a moment, the words trembled on the tip of her tongue. To tell them, to tell them about the handyman from next door. Ed, the one who mowed the lawn. But even just hearing how he'd gone into the garage to get the push broom when Rico was chained and gagged upstairs had made them speculate about doing something mean and drastic.

And he seemed okay, Ed did. He'd been nice to her. She didn't want to see him get hurt.

So, again, Gwen said nothing.

The garage was unlocked. Ed opened the door, grimacing at a sweltering blast of heat and stale, dank, musty smells.

Whatever work the girls had put in on the apartment

upstairs, they never had gotten around to doing any cleaning or organizing in here, either.

In the depths lurked a fire hazard waiting to happen: piles of broken furniture, ancient textbooks, newspapers bundled into bales, and splitting cardboard boxes crammed to bursting with magazines. He doubted anyone had parked an actual car in there for decades, if ever.

Overhead were rafters packed with lawn chairs, patio tables, something that might've been either a hammock or a volleyball net, crates festooned in cobwebs, and who knew what else. A single yellow, flyspecked bulb hung naked from a light fixture.

Closer to the door was tetanus-shot country. The push broom he'd borrowed to sweep up the grass clippings leaned against the wall in the company of rusted rakes, shovels, a post-hole digger–aha, good to know!—and other tools. Mrs. Hubert's clunky old mower crouched like a dog in a kennel. It seemed to snarl at Ed, as if blaming him for its exile, its denial of the chance to chew off some girl's foot, because he'd had to come riding to the rescue on Mr. Gerrittson's noble steed.

His nose wrinkled. In addition to dust, rust, mold, mildew, rodent droppings, and whatever else, there was another smell. Something faint but unpleasant. Something he'd noticed before, on the day he'd done the lawns. Had been stronger, then. A sour, spoiled-hamburger kind of reek.

He remembered glancing around, expecting to see a spare fridge or freezer that might have gone on the blink. That had happened once when he was a kid; they'd come back from vacation to find there'd been a power outage, the whole house stinking of curdled milk and rotten meat. His mom swore forever after that she could never get rid of it, even with bleach.

But there hadn't been a fridge or freezer in the garage then, and there weren't any now. The smell wasn't as thick as it had been, either.

Had something died in here a while ago? A possum or raccoon, maybe? Crawled under one of those pieces of junk, burrowed into the papers, and died? A bird in the rafters? A rat buried in the newspapers and magazines? Died, and decayed to bones and fur or feathers by now, with not as much left to stink?

Ed stepped out into the sunshine, and glanced at the stairs on the other side of the laundry shed. Curiosity tugged at him, wanting to see just what those girls had done up there besides hang shutters. See if they needed any pointers, any help. Seeing as how he was a handyman and all.

He started up the steps.

Ramona Ardell felt like she hadn't slept in days.

Reason for feeling that way? She *hadn't* slept in days.

Or, when she had, it'd been turbulent, troubled, unrestful sleep. The kind a person woke from thinking insomnia and sleep-deprivation psychosis were the better deal after all.

The nightmares were bad.

In a way, the non-nightmares were worse.

When she dreamed, the rest of it had only been a dream. When she dreamed, Neil was all right, alive and fine, untouched, unharmed.

Not the way she'd found him.

Dragged behind a rundown fruit stand. Dead. Covered with dry brush and brambles. Covered in bugs.

Face-up, eyes open. Skin sallow on top, yellow-grey, greasy like a cheap candle. Dark blotches of discoloration underneath where blood had sunken and settled. The dried rust-brown crust on his shirt.

The single, thin but deep, cut. Precise slice, her mind kept insisting on rhyming it, clanging the words, a hated song she couldn't get rid of.

Someone had done that to him. To Neil. A good cop. A good father. A good husband, not that her sister ever appreciated it. A good friend. A good man.

Someone had killed him.

Hardly rare, in the line of duty, in their line of work.

Like this, though...

Not because of his role in that recent big drug bust. Not even because he'd been working a dangerous case.

Just because of timing and misfortune.

Half the cops in the city trying to get anywhere on these murders, and Neil simply happened to cross the killer's path. By accident. At random.

He'd had no idea, which was what nagged at Ramona the most. Knowing Neil, he probably saw the car—a large, older model was the most they'd been able to guess from what tire impressions had been obtained—and stopped to see what was going on. Maybe stopped to offer help, thinking stranded motorist or something, and gotten his throat cut for his pains.

If he'd only radioed in!

But it must not have looked suspicious.

How could it not look suspicious?

How could Neil, a good cop, run into a serial murderer—a serial murderer dumping a trunkful of bagged body parts!— and suspect nothing out of the ordinary until it was too late? He'd been aware of the investigations. He'd sat through the same briefings and meetings, read the profiler's reports, knew as much as there was to know.

And now he was dead.

Dead, just like that.

Slashed nearly ear-to-ear by a very fine, narrow, sharp blade. A straight razor, theorized the forensics people, or a box-cutter.

Sudden. Up close.

What were they missing? What were none of them seeing?

Ramona was determined to find out.

They had converted the apartment to a home gym or art studio or something, wasn't that what he'd heard? Seemed unreal that anybody would want to paint or exercise in a dismal little room above a stuffy garage. Especially with the windows shuttered up tight.

The upstairs door looked to have been given a recent upgrade. New locks, a new knob and fixtures, hinges, deadbolt. A decent enough job. They did seem to have some idea what they were doing.

All set into the same original wood, though, and affixed to

the same decrepit frame. One good hard shake might...

"Don't do it, Eddie."

Ed froze, hand half-outstretched to the knob.

His arm slowly lowered. Gooseflesh swarmed over his body.

He turned in a series of slow, mechanical motions.

There was no one behind him on the stairs. No one in the yard below. No one in sight at all.

But he had heard the voice, heard it plain as day.

Don't do it, Eddie.

Leigh's voice. The voice of his long-dead, much-loved wife.

Ed decided he would listen.

He hurried down the steps and back over to the Gerrittson house, skin crawling, chilled despite the sun.

He'd just clambered over the fence into the pasture, the nearest alpacas chirrup-crooning their greetings and Velvet nuzzling at him in hopes of a treat, when he saw the big old boat of a Cadillac rolling down the road.

Rachel marched into the kitchen and slapped the morning paper down on the table between Gwen's cereal bowl and Annamaria's coffee cup.

"The Junk Drawer Killer," she announced.

"The *what?*" Darlene didn't cover her mouth in time to stop toast crumbs flying out.

"Junk Drawer Killer."

"That's what they're calling us? You're shitting me!" Jessie had been sitting on the counter, swinging her legs and munching granola. Now she boosted herself off to lean over Rachel's shoulder. "Gotta be a typo. Junkyard *Dog*, maybe, but..."

"Nope." Rachel tapped the headline, read it aloud. "*Police Question Person of Interest in Junk Drawer Killer Murders.*"

"Wait, what?" asked Gwen, setting down her spoon.

"Person of interest?" Annamaria added.

"Junk Drawer? How the *fuck* did they come up with such a lame-ass name?"

Rachel read on. "Forensic analysis has determined that a

number of various household tools, implements and utensils were used to torture the victims before their deaths. An unnamed source in the police department stated that they seem to be, quote, 'ordinary items that anybody might have in their kitchen junk drawer,' un-quote. This has led some investigators and reporters to refer to the murderer as the Junk Drawer Killer."

"Well, *that* bites," Darlene said, tossing the rest of her toast in the garbage. "We should have chosen our own name, a good one. Left a note or something."

"Too late now." Disgusted, Jessie flicked at the paper and stalked to the fridge. She took out a container of tomato juice with her name scrawled on the side in black marker. "Once they latch onto something like that? We're S.O.L.."

"What was that about questioning someone?" Annamaria leaned across the table to slide part of the paper toward herself. "Who is it?"

"Doesn't say," Rachel said. "Just that they brought in a 'person of interest.'" she did air-quotes.

All of them looked around at each other, as if doing a quick headcount. One, two, three, four, and me-makes-five.

"Not one of us," Gwen said.

"Thank you, Captain Obvious," said Darlene.

"Do you think it's true?" Annamaria asked, scanning the article. "Do you think they really have someone? Or are they only saying so to make the public feel like there's been some kind of progress?"

"Could be it's a fake-out." Jessie swirled the container, swish-sloshing the contents, and took a swig directly from the spout. "They've got zilch, so they run a story hoping it'll make the real killer overconfident."

"God forbid *that* should happen," Annamaria muttered in a dry undertone.

Jessie stuck out her tongue.

"Or to make the real killer mad," Rachel said. "Some of them are real egomaniacs, right? So they just *hate* it when somebody else gets credit for their work. False arrests or copycat killings, you know."

"But what if they *do* have a suspect?" Gwen asked. "What if they're blaming an innocent person for what *we* did?"

"Sucks to be that innocent person," Darlene said, with an utter absence of sincerity or concern.

"He might go to jail, though."

"Better him than us." Jessie swigged more tomato juice.

"It seems…"

"What?" Annamaria asked, turning to Gwen. "Wrong? Immoral? Sinful?"

"Well…"

Darlene snorted. "Pretty small beans compared to killing people in the first place."

"Looks like the only new development is this Junk Drawer thing," Rachel said. "They're attributing the bike cop to the J.D.K.. But no links to the old man at the lake, or to the one Gwen pushed off the bridge. Or Donnie. That's all good. I think we did it. I think we really did. We got away with it."

No one spoke for a pensive, musing moment.

Then three out of five, as one, said, "So, that means we can start up again?"

Eight little words… and for another long, pensive moment, no one answered.

ABOUT THE AUTHOR

Christine Morgan divides her writing time among many genres, from horror to historical, from superheroes to smut, anything in between and combinations thereof. She's a future crazy-cat-lady and a longtime gamer, who enjoys British television, cheesy action/disaster movies, cooking and crafts.

Her short stories have appeared in dozens of anthologies, as well as the collections *The Raven's Table* and *The Wolf's Feast* (Viking-themed horror and dark fantasy) and *Dawn of the Living-Impaired And Other Messed Up Zombie Stories* (zombies, obviously). She also shares the pages of Visceral, a collection of body horror, with Patrick C. Harrison III. More collections are due out in 2022.

Her latest novels include the deep-sea chompy *Trench Mouth,* the historical pioneer blizzard snow monstery *White Death,* the Splatterpunk Award winning *Lakehouse Infernal* (sequel upcoming!), the totally trashy *Spermjackers From Hell,* and the hard-to-categorize *Birthright.* Her novella, *The Night Silver River Run Red,* is part of Death's Head Press' Splatter Western line.